AF412852

THE MAGICIANS

THE MAGICIANS

A Novel
by
Paul Gropman

BETAR BOOKS

Fort Bragg, California

THE MAGICIANS

BETAR BOOKS
100 N Franklin St.
Fort Bragg, California 95437

Library of Congress Catalog Card Number 97-95339
ISBN 0-9662940-1-7

Printed on acid-free recycled paper with soy based ink.   20% Total Recovered Fiber 20% Post Consumer Waste  

Printed in the United States of America by Mendocino Lithographers, 100 North Franklin Street, Fort Bragg, California 95437

First Edition March 1998

02 01 00 99 98   5 4 3 2 1

In Memoriam

For Ben and Rose Hecht

Who cared

And for the six who dared

Yitshaq Ben-Ami
Arieh Ben-Eliezer
Eri Jabotinsky
Hillel Kook
Shmuel Merlin
Alex Rafaeli

This is a true story—if you are willing to overlook the fact that more than half of it is fiction. The historical figures, of course, are undisguised. The events described are as they occurred. My fictional characters had counterparts who were real people. Most of them are now gone. As composites they bear no relationship to any known persons.

They took up the cause of the disenfranchised, tortured and murdered Jews of Europe. While the respectable Jews of America were either unaware of, or ignored, what was happening to the Jews under Hitler, the men and women of the American League For A Free Palestine labored mightily to rescue whatever Jews they could get out of Europe during the war—or the pitiful remnant still alive after the war.

The men I have written about paved the way for the creation of the modern State of Israel. But what that land became is not what they had envisioned—a Hebrew Commonwealth—on both sides of the Jordan.

They were midwives to a new nation and, for their pains, were rewarded with calumny, obloquy—and death.

Theirs was the greatest disappearing act of modern times, which is why I call them the magicians. Their act was played out on the stage of the world and, when their act was done, they themselves vanished.

Los Angeles, California
December 20, 1997

Prologue

Mulvehill was the last to board, arriving at dockside just minutes before midnight. The black hull of the *Altalena* loomed above him in the darkness. A single unshaded light burned feebly at the top of the gangplank.

He paid the cab driver, shouldered his worn barracks bag and made his way to the foot of the gangplank, not noticing the couple who stood in the shadows against the wall of the shed. As he climbed the steeply sloping gangplank a leathery sailor leaned over the side of the hull and grinned down at him.

"A few more minutes and we'd have sailed without ye, me bucko."

A winch overhead whined and the gangplank Mulvehill had just climbed began to lift from the dock. Deep in the bowels of the ship he could feel the throb of the diesels.

The sailor, wearing only a soiled undershirt tucked into denim pants, looked down at a clipboard he held in his hand.

"Ye'd be Charles Mulvehill, I take it?"

Mulvehill nodded.

"Ye'll be bunking aft, in C-2. That's the next deck up." He pointed behind him.

The gangplank, now level with the deck, swung inboard. The ship slowly moved away from the pier. Up toward the bow a handful of men leaned over the rail, watching the black oily slick widening between ship and shore. Mulvehill leaned over the rail too. The couple who had been standing in the shadows now stepped forward into a cone of light thrown from a floodlight mounted on the roof of the shed.

Mulvehill recognized Stacy Sheridan, with Ben Hecht standing at her side. Hecht looked up at Mulvehill and threw a fair imitation of a military salute. Mulvehill returned the salute. The girl blew a kiss at him, then both turned and walked quickly away.

Mulvehill turned and carried his bag aft to where the sailor had said he would find cabin C-2. He climbed the ladder, found an open hatchway and stepped through. The first door on the left had C-2 stenciled on it. He walked through the door and almost tripped over three rifles, stacked in the form of a teepee, their butts on the deck and the guns joined together close to their muzzles by the stacking swivels.

By the dim light filtering in from the companion-way Mulvehill saw two bunks, one on either side of the cabin. The one closest to him was empty. A man was asleep in the other. Mulvehill looked at the sleeper and decided he was a youth of no more than twenty. The boy lay on his back, arms crossed over his chest, mouth slightly open and snoring softly. A tangle of black curly hair contrasted with his pale face. Mulvehill leaned over him and saw a spray of freckles on the youth's face. He grinned to himself. 'Irish as Paddy's pig.'

He lowered his bag onto the empty bunk and walked out again to the deck. The lights of New York now twinkled far astern. They were heading out to sea. A freshening breeze blew across the deck. It felt good after the humid heat of the city.

A shiver of excitement coursed through him. This was it. He was off on the great adventure. The ship would deliver tons of munitions, weapons, vehicles and aircraft parts to help the new State of Israel fight off the Arabs, who were sure to attack once the last British troops sailed from Palestine.

He felt, rather than heard, the presence of someone next to him. A man of about fifty was standing at his right side. The man was tall, with broad sloping shoulders and hands like hams.

The other held out a massive paw. Mulvehill took hold and shook it.

"I'm Stavsky," the other said. "Abrasha Stavsky. And I'm going home. At last."

Mulvehill yawned, to cover his inability to think of anything even remotely sensible to say. "It's been a long day for me, Mr. Stavsky. I'm going to turn in."

The other looked at him silently, nodded, turned and walked away.

Mulvehill walked back into the cabin. The empty bunk was neatly made up. He took off his shirt and trousers, folded them neatly and placed them on the foot locker that stood at the end of the berth and, dressed only in undershirt and shorts, pulled back the blanket and climbed in. He was asleep as soon as his head hit the pillow.

The sun slanted brightly into the porthole when Mulvehill awoke. They were sailing south, headed for their first landfall, Cienfuegos in Cuba, so the porthole on the ship's port side caught the early morning sun.

Mulvehill looked around. The youth from the other bunk was standing at the sink, stripped to the waist and splashing water onto his face. Mulvehill watched him until the other turned around and caught Mulvehill looking at him. He dried his hands, walked over and held his hand out. They shook hands.

"Duffy," the other said, "Charles Duffy."

Mulvehill grinned. "Mulvehill. Charles Mulvehill."

They both laughed.

Mulvehill nodded toward the three rifles. "What's this? Your personal contribution to the State of Israel's new army?"

"Sure. I got them cheap. Why not?"

He noticed the watch on Mulvehill's wrist. "What time is it?"

Mulvehill told him it was a quarter to seven.

"Good," Duffy said. "If you snap shit I'll wait for you and we can find the galley together."

Mulvehill threw the blanket back, found a towel in his barracks bag and went through an open door where he could see a shower. He was out again in minutes. Duffy was sitting on his bunk, rolling a cigarette.

Mulvehill dressed and both stepped through the door and started down the companionway, following their noses to the scent of coffee.

The galley was filled with men seated at tables. Platters filled with scrambled eggs and hash brown potatoes were rapidly being consumed.

A man in a white uniform rose from one of the tables where he had been seated next to Stavsky. He approached the two. To Duffy he said, "Morning Duffy." He turned toward Mulvehill. "And you, of course, are Charles Mulvehill. I would have recognized you even if Abrasha hadn't told me. Besides which, we've had a letter from Petey Horwitch, telling us of your coming along." To Duffy he said. "This is our war correspondent, courtesy of The Las Vegas News." He shook hands with Mulvehill. "My name is Phil Greenberg," he announced. "Second mate of the good ship *Altalena*."

Duffy turned to look at Mulvehill. "Is that for real? You're really a correspondent?"

Mulvehill shrugged. "Well, I do have a Press Card from the North American Newspaper Alliance. If that makes me a correspondent I'm a correspondent."

Duffy poked him. "More likely FBI. Is that it, Mulvehill? You're a spy for the FBI?"

"I can tell you what I am is hungry," Mulvehill said. "Let's eat." He walked forward to where a mess line had been set up. The two picked up trays and silverware, had food shoveled onto their plates, and found seats at one of the tables.

There were a few other men at the table. They nodded but did not speak.

Duffy looked around. To Mulvehill he said, "You and I must be the only two shcootsim on board. 'Cept for ship's crew, I mean."

Mulvehill looked at him. "We must be what?"

A young man on the other side of the table grinned. "Shcootsim. That's plural for shaygetz." He extended his hand across the table. "I'm Jerry Kolodny and I'm pure blooded Jew." He grinned. To Duffy he said, "Where did you come up with that word? Your accent's *tres* correct."

Duffy held out his hands in an exaggerated gesture. "Vot can I tell you?" He grinned. "My old man was a harness bull for twenty years. His beat was the lower East Side. He arbitrated so many arguments among Jewish families that he wound up speaking Yiddish as well as most of them. And better than this generation of Jewish kids, who don't know trayf from tsimmis."

The other men at the table now began to pay attention. One of them called across the table. "Hey, how come you two Micks joined this fracas? You are Micks, aren't you?"

"I am," Duffy said. "And so's my buddy here. We're the two Charles's, Mulvehill and Duffy." He pointed at Mulvehill. "Charles M." And pointed to himself. "Charles D."

The man across the table introduced himself. "I'm Mike Silverberg from Dayton, Ohio. And you're not quite right, Duffy. According to the ship's roster I think we've got about four gentile volunteers. And more will be joining us when we get to Marseille. I don't know why you guys are coming along to help us, but I can tell you I sure appreciate it."

Duffy had been shoveling food into his mouth. In between bites he began to explain, and the others at the table listened closely.

"I was with the First Armored Division in North Africa..." Mulvehill broke in just long enough to say, "No kidding. I was there with the Big Red One."

Duffy paused. "No shit?" Then he returned to his story. "My closest buddy was a guy from Altoona named Stovall. We were in the same platoon. After we took a beating at Kasserine Pass we pulled back to Tunis for a breather and to collect replacements."

He paused to drink some coffee. He looked off into the distance. When he began to talk again his voice had subsided almost to a whisper.

"Stovall and I went into town one night. He had heard about a bar where, supposedly, you could pick up some Tunisian nooky. We spent the evening drinking. Some broad came over and began draping herself around Stovall. I just didn't like the look of the place and tried to talk Stovall into heading back to camp with me. But no, he was sure he was going to wind up with some Arab pussy. I figured, what the hell. He's no kid."

His voice faltered.

"They found him the next day. His nuts had been cut off and shoved into his mouth."

He fell silent and the others said nothing. Mulvehill felt uncomfortable.

After a long silence Duffy said. "I'm here to pay them back for Stovall." He looked around at the others.

Silverberg said, "Jesus you're taking a hell of a lot of risk on yourself just for revenge."

Duffy looked sheepish. "Well, there's more to it than that. I used to tend bar at a little joint on Tenth Avenue. Heart of Hell's Kitchen. A little Jewish kid came in one day. He was carrying some cans wrapped in blue and white paper. I recognized the Jewish Star on them. He walked up to the bar, looking kind of nervous. 'Hey mister,' he said, 'we're raising money to drive the British out of Palestine so it can be a homeland for the Jewish people. Can I leave one here and maybe pick it up next week?'

"I looked at him," Duffy said. "Here's this little Jewish kid, probably scared shitless just coming to Hell's Kitchen but he walks into an Irish bar to ask us to raise money so the Jews can drive the fucking Limeys out of Palestine. I figured...that's real guts."

Duffy pushed his plate away and with one gulp finished the coffee in his mug.

"When the kid came back next week I handed him the can." He looked at the Jewish men around the table. He grinned. "You know. The pishky. The kid felt the weight of the can and looked real pleased. It was about noon and trade was light. I took him to a table in the back and sat him down. I made a hefty sandwich of ham and cheese for him and brought him a bottle of beer. I sat down across the table from him.

"Tell me about what you're doing", I asked.

"He began to tell me there was a small group of men and women in Palestine who were taking on the whole British force there. You guys must know that. It was the Irgun Zvai Leumi. I listened to his story and I thought of the IRA and the Black and Tans. I figured that was my fight."

"Let me guess the name of the kid," Mulvehill said. "Marvin Zelinsky."

Duffy looked at him in amazement. "That's right."

"You might say that's how I got here too," Mulvehill said.

The others rose. "Our thanks to both of you," Silverberg said. The others nodded in agreement. They shook hands all around and left, leaving Duffy and Mulvehill at the table.

Duffy took out a sack of Bull Durham and a packet of papers and began to fashion a cigarette for himself. "Sure you won't join me?" he asked. Mulvehill shook his head.

Duffy looked pensive. "Let's go out on deck," he said. "I want to hear how you got involved. And I need some fresh air."

On deck a group of men, stripped to the waist, were doing calisthenics. Greenberg, the second mate, approached Duffy and Mulvehill.

"We're having an orientation meeting at eleven o'clock, topside. I'll expect you guys there." They both nodded in agreement.

Mulvehill leaned his back against the rail. "So you were with First Armored in North Africa. I came across with the First Infantry Division but later was transferred to the 45th. We fought our way up the boot and, at Cassino, I caught some fragments from an '88. I listened to your story," he continued, "and, I guess, every GI who was in action in North Africa learned contempt for the Arabs. They would sell out either side to the other."

Duffy nodded.

"I told the truth down there," he motioned below decks, "but not the whole truth."

Mulvehill grinned. "Does anybody ever tell the whole truth?"

Duffy bit his lower lip.

"Zelinsky invited me to a meeting. He was with an organization called American League For A Free Palestine."

"I know," Mulvehill said.

"I met a girl there," Duffy continued. "A Jewish girl and a looker. I mean a real knockout, Mulvehill."

He threw the remains of his butt over the side. It flared briefly and was quickly extinguished as it hit the water.

"When that first meeting was over I asked her to have coffee with me," Duffy went on. "I suppose maybe she was curious about a Christian coming to a meeting of a group of Jews. There was probably nothing more than that to it, I figured.

"But I came back a week later and she came out with me again. We went to a small coffee shop down the street from the office. She seemed real interested in what I had to say. She had the most beautiful eyes I'd ever seen on a girl and when I talked she looked at me real serious with those big brown eyes. I damned near passed out."

Duffy breathed a deep sigh.

"When I walked her to the subway we stopped for a minute. I put my arms around her and kissed her. She didn't resist, Mulvehill. Sort of melted in my arms. We were totally unconscious of the people passing by.

"After a few more meetings we had a long talk. She was on summer vacation and would be going back to school when summer was over. I figured, what the hell. This can't go anywhere. I could imagine her telling her folks that she was going out with an Irish guy who was a part time bartender and whose old man was an Irish cop."

He looked across the water.

"She agreed that it probably didn't make any sense for us to keep seeing each other. I heard about the *Altalena* and I thought this was maybe the best way out."

He smiled ruefully.

"So I signed on to help in the fight."

Mulvehill said nothing. He thought about his own aborted affair with Stacy. There was no problem with religion there. Just a little matter of a husband to deal with. He looked at his watch. Men were coming up from below decks and assembling amidship.

"We might as well go," Mulvehill said. They joined the assembled group.

The orientation meeting was brief.

The ship's papers showed it had been chartered to pick up a cargo of sugar from Cienfuegos to carry to Genoa. Actually, they were now told, the ship would sail to Port de Bouc in the south of France, where the French Government had agreed to provide arms and ammunition, free, for the Irgun to bring to Israel. As far as anyone could tell this was a gift from the French whose resentment against the British dated back to 1922 when France's petition for the Palestine Mandate was turned down and, instead, the League of Nations handed it to Great Britain. The French had to settle for Syria.

Once loaded, the ship would head for Palestine, soon to be the State of Israel. There was still some question about how the Jewish Agency would take to an Irgun ship unloading arms and volunteer fighters. Maybe those arms might be used against the Ben-Gurion regime. But that was to be settled later. As far as the Irgun was concerned the arms would be divided, eighty percent to the new Israeli army, the Zahal, and twenty percent to the Irgun for the defense of Jerusalem.

When the meeting broke up Duffy shook his head. "Some kettle of fish. What did we get ourselves into?"

"Let's wait and see," Mulvehill said. "First we've got to get to France and that is one hell of a trip for a converted LST. Let's hope the captain knows how to handle this ship. Who is he anyway?"

"From what I hear," Duffy said, "he's an ex-engineer who piloted LSTs in the South Pacific during the war."

They walked back to their cabin.

Duffy sat down on his bunk and took off his shoes.

"O.K. Mulvee. So how did you get involved?"

Mulvehill leaned back against the bulkhead.

"After I caught a load of German shrapnel below Cassino I was sewed up in a field hospital and then shipped back Stateside. I wound up at Fort Hamilton in Brooklyn. One warm night in May I took the subway into Manhattan. I had a yen to put my elbows on the bar at The Brass Rail and see what adventures the night might bring.

"I was leaning on the bar," he smiled at Duffy, "when your friend Zelinsky offered me a drink..."

Book One

Naples. May 11, 1944 (A.P.) U.S. General Mark Clark's Fifth Army troops, after months of savage fighting, are said to be closing in on the German stronghold at the Abbey Monte Cassino. Polish troops are approaching from the East and it is expected the Gustav Line will soon be breached.

1.

He left the subway at Times Square and climbed the stairs to the street. Pausing for a moment to look around at the bustling scene he oriented himself as to direction and then walked north toward Forty Seventh street. The wound at the back of his left knee no longer hurt but, where the shrapnel had sliced through the tendon, the surrounding muscles were still weak and it helped to walk with a cane.

Crowds brushed past him on either side, rushing to their mysterious destinations, but Mulvehill walked along slowly, stopping to look into a store window when something caught his eye or to study a poster in front of a movie house. It was late in May, the night was balmy and he had elected to wear his light chino khaki uniform. Over the left shirt pocket he had pinned but two ribbons, the multicolored ETO* ribbon and the Purple Heart.

The distant rumbling of thunder and a quickening breeze hinted at the approach of an early season rainstorm. He slipped the band of his small overnight kit over his right wrist and grasped the ornately carved handle of his cane with his left hand and quickened his

*European Theater of Operations

steps. He had just reached the marquis of the Hotel Taft when the first few drops of rain fell on his shoulders as he reached the door of the Brass Rail Bar and Grill.

He pushed through the revolving door and into a hubbub. Waves of sound from voices of dozens of men and women crowding the bar beat against him and he stood quietly for a moment, relishing the cheerful noise. He thought he recognized one of the bartenders but was sure he would not be recognized in turn. Tens of thousands of men in uniform must have leaned against that very bar in the months he had been overseas.

As a couple left the bar he pushed forward to wedge himself into the opening that was left by their departure. He hooked the handle of his cane over the edge of the bar, lay his overnight kit on top of it and contentedly leaned his elbows on the bar. It felt good to be back.

A bartender, the one he thought he had recognized, approached.

The man smiled. "Captain. What'll it be?"

Mulvehill pushed his overnight kit toward the bartender.

"Can you find a place to park this among some empty bottles? I hope to have a few drinks before I register for a room. And I'll have a Rob Roy."

"My pleasure, captain."

At the sound of the bartender's 'captain', the man on Mulvehill's left turned to face him. From the corner of his eye Mulvehill saw that he was a civilian. The man took in the cane, the ribbons on Mulvehill's shirt. He smiled.

"Captain. That's what I'm drinking. Will you do me the honor of letting me buy you the first round?"

Mulvehill turned to look at him. The man was slight, probably no more than twenty, Mulvehill guessed, and wore thick glasses. Four-F, Mulvehill thought to himself. As he hesitated, the man spoke again. "Sir, I'd be pleased to buy you a drink." He lowered his voice. "I wish I could be in service."

Mulvehill nodded. "Sure."

The bartender reached into the well, brought out bottles of scotch and vermouth and began to mix the drink.

The man at his left nodded at Mulvehill's ribbons. "I notice the Purple Heart. It must be rough over there," the man said shyly. "North Africa?"

"Italy," Mulvehill responded. He looked at the man narrowly. Maybe a fairy, he thought to himself. Queers liked to pick on men in uniform, he had heard.

The bartender placed the drink before him. Mulvehill picked it up, sipped it. It was good, just the way he remembered it. He nodded at the stranger who had bought him the drink. "Thanks." He turned away.

He heard the man at his left clear his throat. "Excuse me," the other said. "I guess you were in action against the Germans. I follow the war in the papers every day." He stammered. "Gosh, I'd give everything to be able to get into the army. They turned me down. Four-F. On account of being nearsighted."

Mulvehill shrugged. "You ought to consider yourself lucky. It's no bed of roses."

"I'm sure," the other said, "but still, I'm a Jew, so I feel a special obligation."

Mulvehill felt uncomfortable. "It's everybody's war. I had Jews in my outfit as well as Irishmen, Scotchmen, Italians, even Germans." He turned away again.

"Well," the other said. He sighed.

Mulvehill felt a twinge of sympathy. It could be embarrassing to be a civilian in time of war. But it wasn't his problem.

The other spoke again, hesitantly. "Are the Jews in your outfit good soldiers?"

Mulvehill turned back to look at him.

"As good as anybody else. One of them was killed a week before I was hit. I guess you could say he was a good soldier." Mulvehill swished the drink around in his glass.

"Gee, I don't mean to be a pest," the other said.

Mulvehill shrugged. "That's O.K."

"I used to be ashamed to be a Jew," the other said. "You know, being skinny and wearing glasses."

'Oh shit,' Mulvehill thought to himself. He looked more closely at the other and thought he saw the faint shadows of pimples under the skin. The kid was probably no more than twenty. Maybe even younger.

"Are you old enough to be in the army if you weren't nearsighted?" he asked.

The other smiled. "Oh, sure. I'm twenty-two." He held out his hand. "My name is Marvin Zelinsky."

Mulvehill took the proffered hand. "Mulvehill," he said.

He finished his drink. "Thanks, Marvin," he said.

"Can I buy you one more?" Zelinsky asked.

"No," Mulvehill said.

"I guess you think I'm a pest," Zelinsky said.

Mulvehill looked at him. "What is it you want, kid?"

The other caught the hint.

He lowered his voice. "Oh, you think I'm a fairy."

Mulvehill looked at him. "Are you?"

"Gosh, no. It's just…"

"Just what?" Mulvehill broke in.

The other stammered and Mulvehill started to turn away when he heard her voice, throaty, but musical. From the corner of his eye he saw the girl as she came up behind Zelinsky. Mulvehill turned to look at her. She was short, maybe no more than five foot two, he guessed, had bright blond close cropped hair and was slim but full breasted.

And old, almost forgotten, song sounded in Mulvehill's head…

> *Five foot two, eyes of blue.*
> *But oh, what that five foot could do*
> *Has anybody seen my girl?*
> *Turned down hose, turned up nose…*

Mulvehill smiled slightly and the girl noticed him. She smiled and then spoke to Zelinsky.

"Gosh, I'm sorry it took so long, Marvin. The closest parking space I could find was three blocks from here. I think I've got time for one drink and then we better go. Ben needs your papers for the talk he'll be giving tonight."

By now Mulvehill had swung around and was leaning with his back against the bar. This girl, he thought, was certainly worth the price of admission.

He felt a tap on his shoulder and turned around. It was the bartender who had poured their drinks.

"I'm putting your kit under the counter," the bartender said. "We're open until two. You can pick it up at any time."

Mulvehill nodded and turned back to look at the girl. Zelinsky watched him and spoke to the girl.

"Stacy," he said, "This is Captain Mulvehill. We were just having a drink together."

Mulvehill leaned toward her and extended his hand. "Charles," he said, "will do just fine. And you are…?"

"Stacy Sheridan," she replied and took his hand. He held it for a moment and felt a tremor at its softness.

"Has Marvin told you why we're here?" she asked.

Marvin shook his head. "No, we've just had one drink together. I was telling the captain how I wished I could be in the army."

Stacy laughed and poked him gently in the ribs. "Not that again, Marv. You are fighting the war in your own way."

"Oh," Mulvehill said. "How's that? Our young friend here didn't say anything to me about fighting the war."

"Same war but a different battle," she said. Then, looking at Zelinsky, but with a sidelong glance at Mulvehill, she asked, "Isn't anyone going to buy me a drink?"

Mulvehill now turned sideways to the bar and beckoned to the bartender, who came over.

"I'm buying a drink for the lady." He turned toward the girl. "What'll it be?"

She looked at the bartender. "A rusty nail, please."

Mulvehill cocked his head at her. "That's a new one on me."

"Scotch with a dollop of Drambuie," she smiled brightly.

"Cooie," Mulvehill mimicked Aussie slang. "I like that. Scotch and scotch."

The bartender mixed the drink and Mulvehill dropped a five dollar bill on the bar.

"Now, how about the war with a different battle?" he asked. "Anything I might want to know about?"

"Zelinsky and I work for an organization called American League For A Free Palestine," she said. "We're getting ready to kick the British out once this part of the war is over."

Mulvehill wrinkled his brow. "You're getting ready to what?"

Stacy laughed. Again, in that throaty voice he found somehow seductive, she said, "I'll be happy to tell you but there are others, better equipped. Ben Hecht, for one."

"Are you talking about the man who wrote *The Front Page*?"

She nodded.

"Marvin and I are on our way over to '21'—one of Hecht's favorite watering places. Marvin has notes for a speech Ben is giving tonight." She pointed at a large envelope that lay on the bar next to Zelinsky.

"Why don't you join us?" she asked. "I think Ben might like to meet you."

Marvin chimed in. "Hey, that's a good idea."

Mulvehill shrugged. "If you think it's all right. I've never been to '21'." He smiled disarmingly.

"Good. Let's drink up and head over there." Stacy finished her drink. Mulvehill picked up his change and, as she and Zelinsky turned to go, Mulvehill gripped his cane and followed. Turning back to look at him, Stacy noticed the cane and Mulvehill's limp.

"Oh, I'm so sorry," she said. "I didn't notice. It's a four block walk."

Mulvehill shook his head. "That's all right. I can make it."

Zelinsky broke in, turning to Stacy. "He was wounded. I noticed his Purple Heart ribbon."

Stacy stepped back and took his arm. "Are you just back from overseas?" she asked.

He nodded. "A couple of days, actually."

"When were you wounded?" she asked.

"Months ago," he said. "Near Cassino. Do you know where that is?"

"Of course," she said. "We follow the war news closely."

"Where are you stationed?" Zelinsky asked.

Mulvehill turned to look at the youth.

"At Fort Hamilton in Brooklyn." He turned back and spoke to Stacy.

"I took the subway into town. I used to come here before going overseas."

They each, in turn, walked outside through the revolving door.

It had stopped raining. All three looked up at the sky. Clouds scudded by. The moon appeared, a beautiful yellow crescent.

"I don't think it will rain anymore," Stacy said, "and '21' is only a few blocks from here," she repeated. "Sure you can make it all right?"

"I'm fine," he assured her. "Let's go."

The girl took up a position between the two men. She took Mulvehill's arm. "Do you mind if I hang on?"

He grinned and shook his head. Her touch on his arm was light as a feather.

"Are you staying in the city overnight?" Zelinsky asked as they walked along, he and the girl shortening their steps to keep pace with Mulvehill's limp.

He hesitated for a moment and then decided to be candid. It would be interesting, he thought, to see how Stacy reacted.

"I brought a small overnight kit with me," he told Zelinsky. "Shaving cream, a razor, comb and brush, things like that."

"Yes," Zelinsky said, "I noticed that when you came up to the bar."

Mulvehill looked at Zelinsky pointedly. "If anything interesting developed I would take a room here at the Hotel Taft. Or I could always head back to

Fort Hamilton." He shrugged. "I left the kit with the bartender. I can always pick it up later."

Stacy looked at him. "Oho," she said. "Likewise, aha."

Zelinsky changed the subject.

"Where are you from, Captain?"

"My home," Mulvehill answered, "is in California. Thermal. A small town in the Coachella Valley. My father owns a packing plant nearby, in Indio. I'll be going back once I'm out of the Army."

"Are you going to be discharged from the army because of your wound?" Stacy wanted to know.

"I'm an infantryman," Mulvehill explained. "I was wounded in the leg. That's why I carry this cane. So I'm not going to lead an infantry company again. I don't know what G-1 has in store for me. They may assign me to some desk job or they may decide to let me out. I should know pretty soon."

"What's G-1?" Stacy asked.

"Personnel," Zelinsky broke in. "I like to read Army manuals. G-2 is Intelligence," he expounded pontifically, "G-3 is Operations and G-4 is Supply."

They walked along in silence and soon came to the entrance to '21'. Cabs were arriving and disgorging men and women in evening dress. Once inside the entrance they found a knot of people waiting behind a silken rope for available tables. Stacy stepped forward and spoke to the maitre d' in a low voice. He nodded, detached the rope from its brass socket and passed the three of them through.

2.

Zelinsky led the way to a table at which a man was seated alone. He wore a simple blue blazer over a white turtleneck sweater. Looking at him, Mulvehill estimated his age at perhaps fifty. He sat placidly, smoking a cigar.

So this was Ben Hecht, Mulvehill thought. He looked like he imagined Hecht would, medium height and compact.

Zelinsky pulled Mulvehill toward him.

"Ben," he said, "we have found a friend. His name is Charles Mulvehill. He was wounded at Cassino and is here to recuperate."

The older man half rose and stretched his arm across the table. Mulvehill shook his hand. He decided he would not mention having seen *The Front Page*. It would be too much like being Merton of the Movies.

Hecht pulled him around to his side where there was an empty chair.

"Here, my friend, sit here." He turned to a waiter who was hovering nearby. "Wally, please bring two more chairs." The waiter left and promptly returned with a couple of chairs. Stacy came around and gave

31

Hecht a small peck on the cheek. Then she and Zelinsky sat down. Hecht noticed the cane that Mulvehill was carrying.

He reached for it. "May I?" he asked.

Mulvehill yielded the cane and sat back in his chair.

Hecht studied the ornate carving that was the head of the cane. "That's a beautiful carving." He examined the head, exquisitely carved to represent an owl. The eyes were hooded and made up of imbedded reddish stones. Hecht looked at it closely.

"Rubellite," he said to Mulvehill, "isn't it?"

Mulvehill was taken by surprise. "Yes, that's right," he said, "red tourmaline."

The waiter, who had been standing by, coughed discreetly.

Hecht smiled and then looked at Mulvehill. "Have you had dinner? Yes? No? In either case have a drink." He looked at Mulvehill expectantly.

"I'll have a Rob Roy," Mulvehill said. "Straight up." He shrugged. "No sense changing horses in the middle of the stream." Zelinsky laughed. "Bring me the same."

Stacy nodded. "Me too."

The girl had made a bridge of her hands, rested her chin in them and looked at Mulvehill as he and Hecht were exchanging words over the cane.

When the waiter left to fill their orders Hecht turned back to the cane. "Interesting," he said. "Where did you get it?"

"My father sent it to me," Mulvehill explained, "so that I would have it when I got back to the States. It was his. He got it in World War I."

"Really," Hecht said. "Tell me about it."

Mulvehill drew a breath. The girl and Zelinsky looked at him expectantly. As Mulvehill was about to speak the waiter arrived with their drinks.

"Saved by the bell," Mulvehill said. He laughed.

"No, go on," Hecht urged. "I want to hear."

Mulvehill savored the drink. "Good," he said. "Everyone seems to know how to make a good Rob Roy." He grinned. "Or else I'm very easy to please."

The girl said something in a low voice but he couldn't make out the words. Zelinsky smiled.

"My dad was from Dublin," Mulvehill started his story, "but he was a medical student in Edinburgh when the war broke out. Although he was an advocate of Home Rule for Ireland he felt the Germans needed to be stopped from overrunning Europe. He immediately enlisted in the Gordon Highlanders. They were just arrived in Belgium and had begun to dig in when they ran into the advancing right flank of the German Army.

"My father's captain was a man named Malcolm Hay…"

Hecht broke in. "I don't believe it!"

Mulvehill looked at him. "You don't believe what? That my father was in the Gordon Highlanders?"

Hecht laughed. "No, no, that's not what I meant at all. I mean I know Malcolm Hay." He shrugged. "Slightly. We met in London some years ago. He's a remarkable man. And he's a friend of ours."

Mulvehill was confused. "What do you mean…'a friend of ours'?"

"Malcolm Hay," Hecht said, "is a genuine friend of the Jews. I hear he's in Palestine right now, writing a book about the persecution of the Jewish people by the Church over the past two thousand years."

Mulvehill was astonished. "Golly, I'll have to write to my dad about that. He'll sure be happy to learn that Captain Hay is alive."

He returned to his story.

"The Germans had set up a machine gun nest," Mulvehill went on. "Captain Hay was standing right next to my father. He raised himself up over the parapet for a better look. A machine gun bullet hit him in the head and he sank back into the trench. Dad looked down at him and was sure he had been killed. 'Mister Hay has copped it'," he said. "But dad was wrong. Hay recovered consciousness. At this point the word came down the line for the Company to withdraw. Dad and another soldier started to lift Captain Hay and carry him back with them. Hay protested. 'No, no, boys,' he said. 'I will only slow you down. Leave me here.' They hesitated. 'That's an order, men,' he told them. He gave my father his cane. 'Here, lad, you take this and keep it.' Dad and the other man joined the rest of the Company in the retreat." Mulvehill paused.

Hecht said, "Well, I'll be damned." He turned the cane around in his hands. "A fascinating story." He turned to Stacy and Zelinsky. "If he were here you can bet Hay would be on our side." He paused. "Just like Colonel Patterson."

"What do you mean, our side?" Mulvehill wanted to know. "And who's Colonel Patterson?"

Hecht laughed.

"I mean the organization that Stacy and Marvin and I are committed to."

"What organization is that?" Mulvehill asked.

Hecht shook his head.

"Stacy will tell you. I've got to leave in a few minutes." He turned to Zelinsky. "Marvin, you've got the papers?"

Zelinsky lifted the envelope that had been on his lap.

"In the meantime," Hecht said, turning back to Mulvehill, "please finish the story about Malcolm Hay."

Mulvehill sipped his drink.

"He was captured by the Germans who overran the Highlanders' position," Mulvehill told the three. "The Germans treated him in one of their hospitals and, later in the war, exchanged him for some German prisoners of war. But the wound caused a sort of partial paralysis."

"Yes," Hecht told the others. "He walks with a limp, like our young friend here."

They looked at each other. Stacy blew a long feather of smoke from her cigarette.

"Just to belabor an old cliché," she said, "truth is stranger than fiction."

"Anyway," Mulvehill concluded, "that's about the end of it. Dad got through the war with just a slight wound..." He hesitated and the others looked at him. "That's strange," he went on, "I never thought about it before but Dad was wounded in the leg too. Just like me." He shook his head.

Hecht rose. He reached over to shake Mulvehill's hand again. "I have to leave now," he said. "Marvin has arranged a meeting with the senior senator from New York. He's in town briefly. We're hoping to enlist him in our cause. The senator offered to bring some friends and I'm to give an impromptu speech. But I want to be sure of my facts. Marvin has brought along notes that I'll want to refer to."

Zelinsky stood up too. He looked at his watch. "We better get going, Ben. I don't know if we'll catch a cab right away."

Hecht handed the cane back to Mulvehill and quoted…'there are more things in heaven and earth, Horatio, than are dreamt of in your philosophy'.

He smiled.

"From Captain Malcolm Hay to your father some twenty five years ago, from your father to you…and to you here tonight. Amazing."

He walked around to Stacy and kissed her on the cheek. He turned back to Mulvehill. "The drinks, and dinner, if you haven't eaten yet, are on me. I hope we shall have the pleasure of seeing you again before you go back home." He turned and walked toward the entrance. Zelinsky had preceded him.

Stacy looked at Mulvehill.

"Are you hungry?"

Mulvehill waggled his fingers.

"*Comme ci, comme ça.*"

She grinned. "I am."

She beckoned to the waiter who was still standing nearby.

"Wally, bring us two menus please."

While they waited for the waiter to return she held out the cigarette pack to him. Mulvehill shook his head.

"No thanks. I'll accept a cigarette once in a while to be sociable, but the truth is, I don't really care for them."

He grinned.

"Probably the only bad habit I've failed to acquire," he said. She smiled. "Naughty, naughty. But you're lucky. My mouth feels like a motorman's glove." She crushed out the cigarette she was holding with a grimace of distaste.

Wally returned with two oversized menus. Mulvehill looked at Stacy as she studied hers. The profile was devastating. Was she married? Her ring finger was naked of adornment. A girlfriend or mistress of Ben Hecht? He hoped not and consoled himself that the pecks on her cheek administered by Hecht had not seemed ardent.

He observed the concentration with which she studied the menu. Cute, he thought. She looked up and smiled brightly. "Beef Wellington for me," she told Wally. The waiter turned.

"I think I'd like a Monte Cristo sandwich," Mulvehill told him.

"Sir," the waiter looked perplexed. "I'm afraid I don't know what that is."

Mulvehill described the sandwich, how the cheese was to be allowed to melt over the ham and then the entire sandwich dusted with confectioner's sugar.

Wally listened intently. "Very good, sir. I think I've got it down. Now we've got to be sure I can get one of our chefs to make it." He collected the menus and walked away.

Alone with Stacy, Mulvehill looked at her.

'Behold thou art fair, my love,' he thought to himself, 'Behold thou art fair.' Whatever the talk about an 'organization', he thought, being here alone with her had been worth the long subway ride into Manhattan.

The girl leaned back in her chair and folded her arms. Although cigarette smoke from nearby tables swirled around them, her eyes were wide and clear. She cocked her head and looked at him. He looked back, his eyes half closed.

"What?" she asked.

The noise of the room subsided to a hum for him.

"I was just thinking," he said.

"Oh?"

"The Song of Solomon. Do you know it?"

"Ah." She smiled, and her smile was sweet and tender. "I was raised on the Old Testament," she said. "My father is a hellfire and brimstone preacher. He still lives in Andalusia, Alabama, where I was born and raised."

He looked at her. "Your father is a preacher. You mean a rabbi?"

She laughed, the throaty laugh that beguiled him. Somehow it seemed sensual.

"You think I'm Jewish? No. Southern Baptist, or I was until I came to New York and got my head turned around."

"What do you mean by that?" Mulvehill asked.

"Oh, I've done enough reading to come to the conclusion that there was the historical Jesus…and the mythical Jesus. I don't buy a lot of the information about the mythical one."

Mulvehill looked at her. He shook his head.

"Let's get back to Ben Hecht," he suggested, "and this mysterious organization."

Stacy smiled, and waved her arm at the empty chair where Hecht had been sitting.

"When I first met him," she said, "more than a year ago, Ben was chairman of The Emergency Committee to Save the Jews of Europe," she explained, "an organization raising money to get Jews out of the Nazi hell of Europe, while there were still Jews alive to be saved. For all we know they could all have been killed by the Germans by now. The organization had originally been formed a few years ago by Robert Briscoe, Lord Mayor of Dublin; an Irish Jew, if you can imagine such a thing. He and Colonel Patterson, whom Ben referred to, started it. The colonel had been commander of the Jewish Legion in World War I.

"Briscoe went back to Ireland and a handful of Palestinian Jews who came over here as emissaries of Irgun Zvai Leumi carried on the work. As the war continued and it became less likely there would be many more Jews they could get out of Europe under the noses of the Germans, they decided to start slowly building propaganda toward the day Germany and Japan were licked and they could concentrate on getting the British out of Palestine so it can become a genuine Hebrew Commonwealth."

She placed her hands flat on the table and looked at Mulvehill defiantly. Two pink spots now burned in her cheeks.

He shook his head in bewilderment.

"What's this Irgun whatever you called it and how did you get mixed up with a bunch of Jews who want to fight Great Britain? I've never come across any Jews who were known for being tough. You said you're not Jewish."

She looked around the room. After a long minute she turned back to him.

"You said your dad was from Ireland," she said quietly.

He nodded.

"Do you remember the Easter Rebellion?" she challenged.

He shrugged. "That was 1916. I wasn't born yet."

"Neither was I," she retorted, "but I know about it. And I wasn't around for the War Between the States, and I sure know about that."

He reached across the table and put his hands on top of hers. Again he felt electricity course through him at the touch of his hands on hers.

"You're putting a lot of passion into this cause," he said. "Tell me more about it."

She pulled back her hands from under his, shook her head and laughed.

"Unh, unh. Another time." She stretched and he looked pleasurably at the lift of her breasts under the sweater.

"Here comes Wally," she said, "and I'm starved."

The waiter placed the Beef Wellington before her. She picked up her fork and knife and attacked the food with gusto. Mulvehill laughed and looked down at his plate. He grinned at Wally. "This looks perfect. Your chef is inspired."

Wally smiled politely.

"Very good sir. I hope you both enjoy your meal." He retreated.

Mulvehill looked at her. The bright spots had receded from her cheeks.

"*Bon appétit*," he said.

"Up the rebels," she replied.

He laughed and they both ate.

The meal over, Mulvehill leaned back.

"Gosh that was good. How was yours?"

"Ambrosia." She wiped her lips with the napkin and then ran her tongue around her lips. The tongue was small and pink and gave Mulvehill ideas.

'In for a dime, in for a dollar,' he thought. He looked at her levelly and asked, "Are you married?"

She laughed, a golden peal of laughter. Then she leaned toward him and put her hand on his arm. Involuntarily he shivered. She noticed. Tenderly, she asked, "If I were single would you want to make an honest woman of me?"

"Does that mean you're not?"

She laughed again, this time a tinkling silver bell.

"Yes," she said, "but don't let it bother you. I'm planning to divorce him when he gets back."

"Back from where?" he wanted to know. "Is he a soldier?"

She cocked her head. "In a manner of speaking. Is he in the army? Yes. Is he a soldier? No. He's a reporter with Stars and Stripes. In Italy, I would imagine."

Abruptly, she changed the subject and asked... "What's your middle name, Charlie?"

He looked at her. "Joseph. Why?"

She smiled. "Charles Joseph Mulvehill. I like it." Then. "The heart has reasons, Charlie." She raised her glass. "Here's to love."

'Damn her,' he thought, 'was she toying with him?'

They finished their drinks.

He looked around the crowded room. There was a sprinkling of men in uniform, mostly officers. For the most part the people there were civilians. The women were dressed smartly. Some of the men, the civilians, in evening dress. Money, he thought and found himself, somewhat bitterly, resenting the opulence, the languor and, especially, the safety of this room. He thought of the dogfaces he had left behind in the dirty mountain war, fighting their way up the Italian boot.

Wally brought coffee for both of them. Stacy reached for the pack of cigarettes she had left on the table, shook her head angrily and tossed the pack away from her, to the other side of the table. Mulvehill watched her in silence. They sipped their coffee.

She picked up his cane from where it was hooked over the edge of the table.

"Does it hurt you to walk?" she asked.

"No," he told her, "but it does slow me down. I'm hoping the Army will send me to a rehab center. But not far from here, I hope."

She laughed.

"That would be nice," she said. "Shall we take a walk? It's a beautiful evening."

She turned, caught Wally's eye and he hurried over. "The check, please, Wally."

"Yes, miz Sheridan, right here." He placed it before her. She looked at it briefly and signed her name.

They rose from the table. Her jacket was draped over the back of her chair.

Mulvehill helped her put it on.

When they emerged from the night club the sky was cloudless. No sign of the recent shower remained. He thought about her comment that it was a beautiful evening. It must have stopped raining when she had first arrived at The Brass Rail. Was she commenting on the weather? Maybe, he thought, she meant their meeting. It had certainly made the evening beautiful for him. Gosh, she was special. Somewhat mystifying. Maybe that, in addition to her good looks, was what made her special for him. That, he thought ruefully, plus the fact that she was the first civilian woman he had met since coming back to the States.

She looked up and caught the look on his face.

"What, Charlie?" she asked.

He looked at her, archly.

"The heart has reasons, Stacy," he said. And felt better.

She poked him in the ribs, gently.

Leaving '21' they headed East, toward Fifth Avenue. They walked slowly. The streets were quiet here, away from the hubbub of Times Square. Mulvehill looked at his watch. It was just past midnight. He still had time, he thought, to get his overnight kit from The Brass Rail. They walked for a few minutes in silence.

Mulvehill stopped, and the girl stopped with him.

"Tell me about your husband," he said.

She looked up at him. Her head barely came to his shoulder.

"All right," she said, and then tugged at his arm until his head was lowered to hers. "Come here, you big galoot," she ordered, and kissed him. It was a light kiss, really just a brushing caress of her lips but, again, he felt electricity course through him.

"You'd like Michael," she said. "Most men do." She hesitated. "And more than a few women. That was the basic problem. The first time I found lipstick on his handkerchief I shrugged it off. It could have been an impetuous woman. But the second time and the third time? No. Those weren't accidents."

They had come to Fifth Avenue and turned south. Mulvehill said nothing and, after a short pause, she continued.

"I really couldn't blame him. He was a sports writer for the Brooklyn Daily Eagle and knew everybody who was anybody in the world of sports." She paused and turned to look up at him. "Did you ever meet Max Baer?"

He looked at her incredulously. "Did you?"

She grinned. "The three of us had a drink one night. Baer was staying at the St. George Hotel in Brooklyn for some reason and Michael went down there to interview him. He took me along. When Baer took my hand in his, Land o' Goshen," she fell back into her native Southern drawl, "I swear his hand covered not only my hand but my arm halfway up to the elbow. I'd never seen a man's hand that big."

She thought back to the incident and chuckled. Then, turning serious, she said, "After a few squabbles about Mike's affairs with other women we just sort of drew apart." She stopped and look up at Mulvehill. "He's not really a bad guy, Charlie, and he probably ought not be married at all. Anyway, he was called up soon after we were married. I'm sure he's not in any danger and, when he gets back, I'll tell him I want a divorce."

Once again she grasped Mulvehill's arm but, this time, made no attempt to kiss him.

"Uh, are you romantically involved with Hecht?" he asked.

She stopped and turned to face him.

"My goodness, Charles Joseph Mulvehill, you certainly are nosy."

Mulvehill blushed.

She giggled. "Anyway, Charlie, I'm trayf."

His brow wrinkled. "You're what?"

She laughed. "Trayf. Not kosher. Oh, I suppose Hecht might take an interest if I showed the slightest interest in him. Then again, maybe not. He has a reputation as a womanizer. But he's dead serious about the organization. More serious," she said, "than his work in Hollywood. You know about that, don't you?"

He shook his head.

"Ben Hecht" she said, "is probably the most successful and best paid screenwriter in Hollywood. Legend has it that he makes a thousand dollars a day."

Mulvehill shook his head. "Whew."

She smiled. "Ben has said that, for him, writing a script was no more effort than playing a game of pinochle."

They turned a corner. She was leading.

"How's your leg?" she asked. "Does it hurt?"

He shook his head. "I could probably walk all right without the cane but it has become sort of a habit."

"Do you want to tell me more about the organization?" he asked. "And how did you become involved if you're not Jewish?"

She laughed. "Strangely enough it was through Marvin Zelinsky."

He looked at her.

"You don't mean…?"

She laughed again.

"No, we were both working for a publishing house on Madison Avenue. He had just read a book about Palestine and was terribly excited. He wanted to know if I knew that, in a sense, there was no such thing as a Palestinian. Palestinians, he said, were Jews. The rest of the inhabitants were roving Arabs who did not consider that they had any national aspirations aside from being Arabs. Later, when the Jews there began to make noises about founding a Hebrew Commonwealth a few of the better educated Arabs began to militate for a Palestinian homeland.

"One day," Stacy continued, "Marvin asked me if I would like to meet Ben Hecht. He was going to be talking about the destruction of the Jews of Europe to a group of writers and editors. It was just at that time that Michael had admitted he was having an affair with a girl, one of the reporters at the paper. I didn't want to go home early so I accepted Marvin's offer. That evening," she said, "changed my life."

They walked along in silence for a few minutes. She was beautiful, Mulvehill thought to himself, and had brains to boot.

He walked along in a reverie and realized that the girl had started talking again.

"I'm sorry," he said, "what were you saying?"

She looked at him.

"Hecht told the people in the audience...it wasn't really an audience...just eight or nine of us sitting in someone's living room...that until Hitler began talking about getting rid of the Jews Ben had not really thought of himself as a Jew. 'Until then,' he had said, 'I was only related to Jews. But, in reaction to Hitler, I became a Jew and began looking at the world with Jewish eyes.'"

Mulvehill said nothing.

"A few days later," she said, "I called Hecht and told him I would like to volunteer to work for his organization. I was still sore at my husband and this seemed like a good idea. It ought to take my mind off my marital problems."

"Did it?" Mulvehill asked.

She laughed. "It was incredible. I found myself going to fund raising meetings five and six nights a week." She turned to look up at Mulvehill.

"When I got to know the men who had come over from Palestine I was quite impressed. They were unlike any Jews I had ever met. And when you live in New York," she laughed, "you meet a lot of Jews."

"Unlike them, how?" Mulvehill wanted to know.

"They're not afraid, or embarrassed, to be Jews," she said, like a number of Jews she knew. "Like Marvin Zelinsky," she explained. "Until he had met the Palestinians he had been ashamed to be a Jew. Working with them gave him the courage to come alive as a Jew."

She related that the men from Palestine were unimpressed by any of the bigwigs they had attracted to their cause. They were bold, dedicated, and single-minded in pursuit of their goal. They were all members of an organization called Irgun Zvai Leumi, an underground group in Palestine surreptitiously arming themselves to drive the British out of Palestine.

"Irgun Zvai Leumi," she explained, simply means National Military Organization. "Pretty much like the Irish Republican Army. And, like the IRA, who were fighting to get the British out of Ireland," she went on, "these men had declared war on Great Britain.

The war…our war…," she said, "is just an incident for them. Their war is with England. Right now, because England is at war with Germany, they've declared a truce. But when Germany is beaten, and it will be, they'll take up arms against England again, to drive the British out of Palestine."

"Why are you so sure that Germany will be beaten?" he wanted to know.

"Don't you think so?" she asked.

"Yes, I'm pretty sure we'll beat Germany because our planes are pulverizing German industry. But, even so, we've got to put men on the Continent. In the final analysis it's still an infantryman's war. I don't think it will be over until we walk into Berlin. And then we've still got to beat the Japanese."

Suddenly, she yawned. "Oh, Charlie," she said, grasping his arm. "It's late and I'm beginning to unwind. Are you going to check into the Taft now?" she asked.

"No," he said. "I have a room in the BOQ* at Fort Hamilton, where I am stationed until they decide what to do with me. I thought I might stay in town overnight so I brought along a small overnight kit. I left it with a bartender at The Brass Rail. I think I'll just pick it up now and head back to Brooklyn."

"Do you have a car?" she wanted to know.

"No. I'll just take the subway. That's how I came up this evening."

"You will not," she said. "I have a car and I had enough ration stamps to fill it with gas. I'll drive you back."

"Oh, no," he protested, "you said you're tired and that's a long, long drive."

*Bachelor Officers Quarters.

"Okay," she said, "so you'll drive. Please Charlie. I want to do it. And I want to see you again. May I?"

He grinned. "Still recruiting?"

"Stop it, Charlie. That's not fair. I do want to see you."

He turned serious. "Thank you, Stacy. I'm flattered. I really am."

"All right then. No more arguments." She took his arm. "Here, this way. The garage is just in the next block." Her car was a 1940 Ford business coupe. She drove him back to the Brass Rail.

"You go in, Charlie, and pick up your overnight kit. I'll circle the block."

He was back outside and standing at the curb when he saw the car round the corner and pull up. She jumped out and ran around to the other side. "You drive, Charlie. I'll navigate."

She got in on the passenger side. He got in behind the wheel. She gave him directions for how to get to the Williamsburg Bridge. He had not driven more than a dozen blocks when her head fell against his shoulder. She appeared to be asleep. He kissed the top of her head. It smelled clean and he inhaled the fragrance of a light perfume she was wearing.

When he arrived at the bridge Stacy was still sleeping. Half way across she awoke, told him how to proceed to Fort Hamilton and was again asleep. She did not awake until he pulled up at the gate.

3.

The following morning Mulvehill lay on the cot in his room. He had been spinning airy fantasies about Stacy. He sighed. She was married and would, or would not, divorce her husband when he got back home. And his own plans were in abeyance until the army decided what it wanted to do with him. For all he knew, in a week or days, he could be a thousand miles or more away from New York.

He picked up a tattered pulp paper magazine that was lying on Schroeder's bunk on the other side of the room. The cover had been torn off but, idly turning the pages, he came across a story that looked interesting, *Drink We Deep*, by Arthur Leo Zagat. He was only three pages into the story when there was a knock on the door. He put the magazine down and called out.

"Come."

The door opened and a youngster with corporal's stripes entered. The boy saluted. Mulvehill sat up and returned the salute.

"Sir," the boy said, "Major Levy in the AG* office sent for you."

*Adjutant General

"Right," Mulvehill acknowledged. "I'm going to wash up. Tell him I'll be there in three minutes."

The boy saluted and left.

Mulvehill rose, stretched, walked into the bathroom and washed his face. He combed his hair and put on his shirt. He thought of Stacy. He would soon know what the army had in store for him.

He announced himself to the orderly and the sergeant opened the door to the major's office. Mulvehill walked through and saluted. Major Levy rose as Mulvehill came in and returned the salute. To the sergeant he said, "Close the door please." He nodded for Mulvehill to take the seat facing his desk. Mulvehill took off his overseas cap and tucked it under his belt. He could see his personnel file lying open on the major's desk.

The major was short, probably not more than five six, Mulvehill guessed, was corpulent and affected a pencil line moustache. His coat hung on a hanger. His shirt-sleeves were a trifle long for his arms and bunched up around his wrists.

'Why doesn't he have the shirt tailored?' Mulvehill wondered.

Major Levy sat back in his chair, pulled open his desk drawer, took out two cigars and offered one to Mulvehill. The captain decided to be diplomatic and accepted. They lit their smokes.

"Captain, the medics' report says you're finished with infantry for good," the major told him. "By the way, you're up for the Bronze Star."

"Oh goody," Mulvehill said. "I'll run down to the PX and buy me a ribbon."

They both laughed.

"It's for the Cassino action, you know," Levy said. "Must have been murder out there."

"Murder's a good word for it," Mulvehill gritted. "The German 88s were looking right down our throats. That's when I made captain, when Holloway was killed."

"I know. That's what I wanted to talk to you about. Listen," the major said, "if you stay in the army you'll be sent somewhere to shuffle papers. And since yours was a battlefield commission you'll most likely be reduced back to your permanent grade of first lieutenant."

"What do you mean 'if I stay in the army'. Do I have a choice?"

"Exactly," Levy told him. "I have the authority to issue a medical discharge. It's up to you." He leaned back, blew a smoke ring and looked at Mulvehill through the smoke. "I figure the war's only half over. We've still got to land on the shores of Europe and even after the Germans are licked, there's still the war in the Pacific."

He looked pensive. "Do you think you'd want to be walking around in civilian clothes? You're a big strapping guy. Once you stop limping people will look at you and wonder why you're not in uniform.

"Cripes," the major continued, "I wouldn't like that. Look at me," he laughed. "A Four-F looking guy if ever there was one. I kept after my old man to get me a commission so I could at least pass as a soldier even if I don't look like one."

Mulvehill was incredulous. "Your father got you a commission?"

"Sure," Levy said. "He's one of the richest men in Omaha and a big contributor to both senators and twenty congressmen. It was no trick at all."

Mulvehill shook his head.

Levy smiled. "Every wheel moves with grease. I'll bet you're thinking, 'shit, it's true what they say about the Jews, they control everything'."

Mulvehill grinned. "Well, now that you mention it." He bit down on his cigar and then took it out and laid it on the ash tray. The major seemed to invite his confidence. Mulvehill leaned forward.

"Do you know anything about an American League For A Free Palestine?" he asked.

Levy shook his head. "No."

"Well," Mulvehill pressed. "Have you ever heard of men named Peter Bergson or Ben Hecht?"

"Well," Levy said, "Ben Hecht. Of course. The highest paid screen writer in Hollywood. I met him, once. He was a buddy of David O. Selznick and they were in Omaha together when *Gone With the Wind* opened." He laughed. "My old man had the hots for Vivien Leigh." He shrugged. "But who hasn't? Anyway, she came out with them so my dad made a big fancy dinner at the hotel. He owns it," he added parenthetically.

"What do you want to know about Ben Hecht?" he asked.

Mulvehill briefly told Levy the story of his meeting with Hecht, Stacy Sheridan and Marvin Zelinsky.

"Oh, now I understand," the major said. "Jabotinsky's gang."

"Who's Jabo-what's his name?" Mulvehill wanted to know.

Levy laughed. "Probably one of the most brilliant Jews who ever lived," he said, "and one of the most feisty. My father hates his guts. He calls him a fascist. Or did," he corrected himself. "Jabotinsky died a few years ago."

"A fascist?" Mulvehill looked skeptical. "How can a Jew be a fascist?"

Levy laughed. "You planning on getting involved in a Jewish cause? You'll wind up standing on your head." He puffed on his cigar then took it out and set it down on the ash tray next to Mulvehill's stogie.

"Let me tell you something. I don't know much about these guys you met but I admire them. Of course," he grinned, "that's not anything I would say in front of my father. He'd disown me.

"The people you met are the political arm of the Irgun Zvai Leumi, a bunch of tough Jews, if you can imagine such a thing," he went on. They're sort of the equivalent of the Sinn Fein and the IRA*.

But," he added, "I don't even think of Jabotinsky's boys as Jews. They're Hebrews. That's something different."

He looked out the window. Mulvehill offered, "I thought you didn't know anything about them?"

*Irish Republican Army

"Well, it's true I don't know much," Levy replied. "But I know they were at war with the British in Palestine before Germany attacked Poland and started World War II. Then the men of the Irgun closed ranks. Most of them volunteered for service in the British army. But not all of them. There was one guy, Abraham Stern, who maintained that Britain was more of an enemy than Germany because they wouldn't let any Jewish refugees into Palestine. Stern said that it was the British, not Germany, that were keeping Jews from getting into Palestine. So he left the Irgun and started his own group, and kept up an underground war against the British in Palestine.

"The British CID* found him and murdered him. His group called themselves LEHI…those are Hebrew letters for Fighters for the Freedom of Israel…but their enemies, whether British or Jewish, called them the Stern Gang, like they were a bunch of hoodlums.

"Well, I think that's enough about politics for one day. The question before the house," Major Levy said, "is, what do you want to do? Stay in or get out?"

"When do I have to decide?" Mulvehill wanted to know.

"Oh, a week, ten days. Nobody is going to pressure you."

"Thanks, major. I've got to think about this." He grinned. "There's a girl I met, who's part of this so-called 'gang' as you referred to them."

"Really," Levy looked interested. "A Jewish girl?"

"No," Mulvehill replied, "Southern Baptist."

* Criminal Investigation Department

Levy smiled, and made a face. "Southern Baptist? Hubba hubba. I'll bet she's a looker. Well, think it over and let me know what you want to do. If you decide to get out I'll draw up the papers. If you stay, we'll have G-1 arrange an assignment for you."

Mulvehill reached forward and snuffed out his cigar in the ash tray. "Thanks for the smoke." He rose and picked up his cane. "I think I'll have an answer for you by tomorrow." He saluted. Levy returned the salute perfunctorily.

Outside the building Mulvehill started back to the BOQ. After a few steps he realized that he was swinging the cane rather than leaning on it. He stopped. 'Well, I'll be damned,' he swore to himself. He flexed his leg. It seemed there was less tightness than before.

Back in his room at the BOQ he shuffled through a small mound of papers on his table and found the matchbook where Stacy had scribbled her phone number on the inside of the cover. He walked back into the hall and found the pay phone. He dialed her number. On the fourth ring she answered, breathlessly.

"Charlie," he said.

"Oh my," she said. "I've got to catch my breath. I was almost one flight down when I heard the phone and rushed back up." Her voice slowed. "How are you, Charlie? And where are you?"

He told her. "Can I see you, Stacy?"

"Yes." She hesitated for a moment. "I'm on my way to a rehearsal. Ben Hecht's written a play, *We Shall Never Die*. The money raised will go to the Irgun. If you like, you can meet me at the rehearsal hall." She gave him an address on Eighth Avenue. "I'll be there for at least two hours so you don't have to hurry."

He looked at his watch. "It's four-thirty. I think I'll stand the retreat formation and then see if I can get a lift into town."

"Okay." Stacy hesitated for a moment and then, "Charlie. Bring your overnight kit. I don't want you to have that long ride back to Brooklyn late at night."

"Bye, Stacy. I'll see you later."

He hung up the phone and stood looking at it pensively. 'What did she mean, he wondered?' It could mean something, or nothing.

He went back to his room, emptied his pockets and undressed. It had been quite a warm day for May. He decided to shower and put on clean suntans.

Dressed again, he headed out to the parade ground. The bugler was blowing *Retreat* and the enlisted men trotted out and took the formation. This was the part of the day of garrison life that Mulvehill liked best.

Here in the States the army still performed very much like the old Regular Army. Company and Battalion Commanders took up their posts at the heads of their units. The First Sergeants called the men to attention and reported to the officers.

The commands came down the ranks. "Attention, at ease, dismissed." The men broke ranks and now there was an idleness in their manner. The day officially was at an end. Now the men had the evening ahead of them until *Tattoo* and then *Taps*.

Mulvehill watched the formation from the porch outside the headquarters building. He liked the army. Now that he had the option of getting out he had to think about it.

He headed for the gate. He had decided to leave the cane behind. He limped, but only slightly.

The MP at the gate saluted. "Evening, sir."

"Evening." Mulvehill walked up to him. "Corporal, I'm heading into the city. What are my chances for getting a lift?"

"Easy, captain. Wait here with me."

A weapons carrier pulled up. The MP asked the driver where he was headed. The soldier replied that he was driving to Penn Station to pick up a contingent of men.

"That's great," the MP told him. "I've got company for you. Right here, sir," he told Mulvehill. "You've got a ride into Midtown Manhattan."

The driver saluted. "Glad to have your company, sir."

Mulvehill climbed into the truck.

The driver shifted gears and they were off. He looked at Mulvehill's ribbons. "I see you're back from overseas, sir." He shook his head. "I've been in the army for two years now and all I do is drive this truck back and forth to the city."

"Count your blessings," Mulvehill told him.

"But gee, sir, the war is passing me by."

"It'll pass you by a lot quicker if you're in a grave in Italy, or on some island in the Pacific."

"Well, I guess you're right," the soldier agreed. "But still. Excuse me for asking, sir. But I see the Purple Heart. Is it really rough in combat?"

"Rough enough," Mulvehill agreed. "But when you're there you just do what you have to do." He broke off to look at the neighborhood they were driving through. "Nice houses," he commented. "What do they call this neighborhood?"

"Bath Beach," the driver told him. "I'm going to pick up the Belt Parkway. That will get us to the downtown tunnel. Then I'll take the West Side Highway up to Thirty Fourth Street. We'll be there in no more than half an hour."

Mulvehill continued to look out the side panel and the driver lapsed into silence.

It was still warm and the streets were filled with people idly walking. On a side street he could see some youngsters playing stick ball. Here they played on paved streets and had to move aside when an auto came down the street. Lots different from his boyhood in the Coachella Valley. There they had all the space they needed. Here the schools were fenced in. He didn't think he would like to live in this city. But, in its own way, the city was exciting.

The driver left the West Side Highway and drove east across Thirty Fourth Street. Mulvehill read off the number on Eighth Avenue from the matchbook Stacy had given him. "How far is that from here?" he asked the driver.

"Shucks, just a few blocks, sir. Let me drive you up there. I don't have to be at Penn Station until seven o'clock." He took a left turn and headed uptown. They passed the theater district and Mulvehill saw a marquis that read *The Voice of the Turtle.* John Van Druten's New Hit.

Mulvehill noted the playwright's name with a slight shock of recognition. Van Druten owned the AJC ranch in Thermal and Mulvehill's father packed carrots from the writer's ranch.

The driver noticed the same marquis that had attracted Mulvehill attention. But he had a different reaction.

"Wow," he said. "Margaret Sullavan. Gee, I'd like to see her." Mulvehill nodded. "Me too."

The driver had turned off Broadway. He drove back to Eighth Avenue and headed uptown. They both read the numbers. "That's it." Mulvehill tapped the driver's arm.

"Right, sir." He pulled over to the curb and Mulvehill got out.

"Thanks, corporal."

The driver leaned over and picked up Mulvehill's overnight kit from the floorboard. "Don't forget this, sir."

Mulvehill grinned, took it from him and flung a snappy salute. "Thanks again, corporal."

Mulvehill looked after the receding truck. He tucked the overnight bag under his arm and entered the hallway. He could hear noises that sounded like chanting from above and took the stairs two at a time. He was pleased to note that although he felt a tugging at the back of his knee where the surgeons had sewed the tendon together again there was no pain. The door at the landing stood open. The room beyond was large and crowded with people. A stage at the far end was filled with perhaps twenty or more men. Each held a sheaf of papers in his hand. Mulvehill entered the hall and took up a position against the wall where he could look around until he saw Stacy.

One of the men on the stage was reading lines and the others followed his speech with a chant repeating his words. Mulvehill listened.

"Before our eyes has appeared the strange and awesome picture," the leader intoned, *"of a folk being put to death, of a great and ancient people in whose veins have lingered for so long the earliest words and image of God, dying like a single child on a single bayonet."*

The chorus repeated his words as a chant.

"We are not here to weep for them," the leader continued, *"although our eyes are stricken with this picture and our hearts burdened by their fate.*

"We are here to honor them and to proclaim the victory of their dying.

"For in our Testament are written the words of Habakkuk, Prophet of Israel…'They shall never die.'

"They shall never die though they were slaughtered with no weapon in their hand.

"Though they fill the dark land of Europe with the smoke of their massacre, they shall never die.

"For they are part of something greater, higher and stronger than the dreams of their executioners.

"Dishonored and removed from the face of the earth, their cry of Shema Israel remains in the world.

"We are here to strengthen our hearts, to take into our veins the pride and courage of the millions of innocent people who have fallen and are still to fall before the German massacre.

"They were unarmed. But not we!

"We live in a land whose arm is stronger than the arm of the German Goliath. This land is our David.

"Almighty God, we are here to affirm that our hearts will be a monument worthy of our dead.

"We are here to affirm that the innocence of their lives and the dream of goodness in their souls are witnesses that will never be silent. They shall never die."

Mulvehill understood almost nothing of what was being proclaimed by the reader on the stage and yet he felt himself strangely moved by the lyric words. He looked around. Against one wall he saw Stacy seated on a chair. Next to her was a rather stately looking woman of about forty and, on the woman's other side, Ben Hecht.

Stacy looked up and saw him. She waved.

A man in shirtsleeves, standing before the stage, was now talking to the man who had read the lines. The actor leaned down toward him.

A number of the people were walking around, silently reading from sheets of paper, apparently memorizing lines. Mulvehill threaded his way through the crowded floor and approached Stacy. She reached up and took his hand.

"Charlie. Thanks for coming. I want you to meet Rose Keane. She's the stage manager for the play." Stacy nodded toward the woman at her left. Mulvehill nodded back. At this point, Hecht, who had been looking toward the stage, hearing Mulvehill's name, looked around and saw him.

"Captain. How nice to see you again."

Mulvehill nodded. "Nice to see you too, Mr. Hecht."

Hecht nodded, rose and walked toward the stage. He turned briefly and waved at Stacy. She nodded to him and to Rose Keane.

"See you both tomorrow."

Stacy took Mulvehill's arm. They headed for the door. Once outside the building and back on the street Mulvehill asked, "What's that all about?"

"It's a play that was written by Ben Hecht. It played to capacity crowds last winter at Madison Square Garden. And raised several hundred thousands dollars," she smiled. "More money to be put to good use by the Irgun."

Mulvehill shrugged. He looked at Stacy. She looked even better today than the night before. He didn't have much interest in her preoccupation with the cause she had allied herself with.

She took his arm and they walked down the stairs to the street.

"The actors and actresses here tonight," she inclined her head upwards toward the rehearsal hall they had just left, "are rehearsing for the road show. We expect it to play Chicago, St. Louis, Los Angeles and several other cities. We hope to raise a lot of money."

"For what?" Mulvehill wanted to know. "Is this why you invited me here, to give me a propaganda pitch?"

"Partly," she agreed, and smiled. He noticed for the first time that she had dimples in her cheeks.

"There's a coffee shop I like that's not too far from here. Can you walk all right," she asked, and then, "Where's your cane?"

He grinned. "I want to make believe I'm a complete man."

She squeezed his arm. "Let's put it to the test."

Again he was nonplussed. Was this more double entendre?

She pulled on his arm. "This way soldier."

They walked to Seventieth Street and then she led him eastward. At Amsterdam Avenue they turned and she led him to the coffee shop. The evening was balmy and the streets filled with people. Inside the coffee shop they found an unoccupied table and sat down. A waiter approached.

"Have you ever had an egg cream?" Stacy asked Mulvehill.

"What's that?" he wanted to know.

She smiled. "You'll find out. Two egg creams, Jack," she told the waiter who, it turned out, was also the owner and dishwasher. There were only about eight tables in the store.

"I've got some pretty exciting news, Charlie."

"Oh," he raised his eyebrows.

"Charlie, I haven't had a cigarette since we parted. What do you think about that?"

"Very nice," he countered. "Can I take any credit?"

"You can take it all," she replied. "I like you, Charlie and, somehow, I thought to myself, if he doesn't smoke I want to quit."

"Well, that's very flattering but why do I have this strange feeling that I'm being set up for something?"

Jack returned to the table and set down two glasses. He pushed one toward Mulvehill, who looked at it. The drink was pale chocolate in color and had a white frothy ring around the top. Two straws were stuck into the drink.

"Try it," Stacy urged.

Mulvehill sucked some of the drink up through the straws. "Pretty good," he acknowledged. "Very refreshing."

Stacy drew the drink up through her straws.

"Jewish nectar," she sighed.

"Aha," he said. "You're trying to convert me to Judaism. But it won't work," he warned her. "I'm an unregenerate pagan."

She lay her hand on his forearm and again he felt the tingle.

"Charlie. I like you and I'm going to tell you the truth. I'm sort of a hired Hessian. I am on the payroll of the American League For A Free Palestine. It's an organization that was formed, originally, by several of the men who came over here from Palestine. It's headed today by one of the brightest men I've ever met. And I want you to meet him." She laid her hand on his arm again.

"Charlie, you won't even believe he's Jewish. He looks and sounds like an Englishman. Yet his uncle is the grand rabbi of Jerusalem. His name is Peter Bergson."

"Wait a minute." He shook his head. "First of all I'm still in the Army so I don't see any possibility of taking time off to do volunteer work for your League. Second, I don't know anything about your organization and it was my impression that once we win the war the Jews of Europe, and all the other Europeans who have been taking a beating from Hitler, will be saved. And third, how is this any of my business in the first place? And fourth, what are the Jews themselves doing?"

"Well said, my friend. I will answer your questions." She finished her drink, sucking up the last of the beverage noisily. Mulvehill followed suit and laughed. "I feel like I'm a kid again. But you're right. It is good."

Stacy stood up. "I live just a few blocks from here, Charlie. Let's go up to my place. We can talk there."

He followed her, his overnight kit dangling from a wrist strap. They walked up to Seventy Third Street and crossed Broadway. She stopped in front of a five story brownstone building. Stacy stepped down from the street to a recessed door. Inside the vestibule she drew a key from her purse and unlocked the door. They climbed the steps, which had been trod by so many feet over the years that they were slightly hollowed. They had passed the third floor landing when a sudden excruciating pain traversed the area behind his kneecap and shot up his leg to the groin. He was unable to suppress a groan.

Stacy turned and saw him sink to the step. His face had turned pale. She took his arm and sat down beside him.

"Oh Charlie," she cried. "It was so thoughtless of me. I had forgotten all about your wound. Shall we go down?"

He shook his head. "No. It's all right." The pain was receding and the color returned to his face. He took a deep breath. "How much farther?"

"Just to the next landing. Do you think you can make it?"

He grinned faintly. "O.K. You go ahead. I'll follow."

She stopped before the door at the head of the steps and waited for him. He followed slowly and was gratified to find that the pain had not returned.

Stacy unlocked the door, pushed it open, and turned on the light. Her apartment was a single room, with a sink and hot plate in one corner. At the far end, facing the street, was a bay window with cushions on the ledge. He had always liked a bay window. At home that was where he sat to do his homework, most evenings, when he was in high school.

He felt the urge to urinate.

"Does this so called apartment boast a toilet?" he wanted to know.

She pointed to one of two doors near the sink.

"Right through there."

The bathroom looked feminine. Two pairs of hosiery were strung over the shower rod. Several bottles of scent were arrayed on top of a sheet of patterned paper she had spread across the toilet tank top. The wallpaper was a pattern of small red hearts punctured by arrows. He resisted an impulse to look in her medicine cabinet.

He lowered his trousers and looked at the back of his knee. The scar was purplish but there was no redness above or below. The sound of the urine splashing in the bowl embarrassed him and he hastily flushed the toilet to mask the sound. He pulled up his pants, buckled his belt and left the toilet. Stacy was lifting a coffee pot off the hot plate. She set it down on a small table and looked at him.

"Hello Charlie." She approached him.

"Hello Stacy." She stood before him and looked up into his face. Again he enjoyed the fragrance that came from her. He hesitated a moment and, because it seemed the right thing to do, he kissed her.

She kissed back, tempestuously. The tip of her tongue parted his lips and probed his mouth. She withdrew and leaned back in his arms.

"Charlie. Coffee, tea…or me?"

4.

He awoke to the sound and smell of bacon frying. The strips were sizzling and the aroma quickened his normal appetite. Stacy stood at the hot plate. She wore a loose flowered wrapper. Her hair, cut short, nevertheless looked faultlessly coiffured. She heard the movement of him in her bed and turned to look at him. She smiled.

"Hello, lover."

He stretched, luxuriously. "Hello, yourself. How did you know I was going to fall in love with you?"

"You're beautifully muscled, Charlie. But those scars on your back made me cry. You never said anything about those other wounds."

He shrugged. "The same shell that cut my leg spewed fragments of hot metal in all directions. Those German 88s are hell when they hit. Can I help?"

"You sure can. Come over here and kiss me."

He got out of bed. Nude from head to foot he was built like the Apollo Belvedere. He came toward her and kissed her obligingly.

"Oh, oh," she squealed, "I don't know if we're ever going to have breakfast."

"Oh yes we will," he countered. He went back to her bed, snatched his shorts and T-shirt from the floor and went into the bathroom. He showered quickly and was out in five minutes. He struggled into his trousers, buttoned his shirt and spread his arms. "Tra la."

Stacy had spread a tablecloth, placed two plates on opposite sides of the table, and commanded him to be seated. She poured coffee, shoveled fried eggs and bacon on both plates and set out toast in a separate plate. She sat down opposite him.

"Tra la, yourself. Let's eat."

They ate slowly. The bacon was crisp. The eggs, which she had fried sunny side up, were faultlessly made, the yellow mounds round and unbroken until he cut through with his fork. She had buttered his toast for him. The coffee was hot and strong.

After a few bites and a sip of the coffee he leaned back in his chair and sighed.

"I don't care if she ain't good looking,
if she's fair and square and'll do my cooking," he sang.

Stacy threw a piece of toast at him. He caught it in mid air. They both laughed. They finished their meal. Mulvehill wiped his mouth. "That really was good, Stacy," he assured her. He nodded toward the bed. "Now I know about two of your talents."

She came around the table, sat down on his lap and kissed him. She crooked one arm around his neck.

"I've been to Washington, Charlie. I was working with Peter Bergson on the formation of a new organization, the National Committee of Hebrew Liberation. I have a cousin who is a U. S. Congressman so I was able to open a few doors. Peter," she told Mulvehill, "is one of the most brilliant men you are ever likely to meet." Abruptly, she changed the subject. "Are you going to stay in the Army or get out?"

He drank the last of his coffee. "I think I'll get out."

He looked at her levelly. "This isn't a come on, is it?"

She leaned closer to him, looked him straight in the eye. Hers were wide and clear. In the morning light they looked violet.

"I think you know better than that," she said. "You've certainly been with enough women to tell sincere passion from faking."

He shook his head.

"That's where you're wrong, Stacy. You're only the third woman with whom I've ever gone to bed."

She looked at him. "I don't believe it. A good looking guy like you?"

"Believe it or not," he countered, "it's true. I was a virgin until I was twenty-two."

Stacy shook her head. "Incredible."

He grinned. "The first time was with my math teacher at UCLA. At that tine," he said, "I thought I would study engineering, but it turned out I had a hell of a time with geometry. My math teacher invited me to come to her house one evening. She was going to give me some private instruction." He grinned. "It was private, all right. She taught me some angles I had known nothing about."

He looked at the coffee pot on the hot plate. "Is there any coffee left?"

She got up, brought the coffee pot to the table and poured a cupful for him. "What about you?" he asked.

She shook her head, sat down opposite him, leaned her elbows on the table, made a bridge of her hands and looked at him.

"Go on," she urged. "That was the first time?"

He nodded. "And almost the last. Soon after that I was in the Army."

"O.K.," Stacy persisted. "Who was number two?"

"That was in North Africa," he said. "We had a lieutenant in our battalion who was a meteorologist. The Army called him back to London, to join the staff at SHAEF.* He had somehow met a French girl in Tunis who had become his mistress. After the battle at Kasserine Pass our outfit pulled back to the outskirts of Tunis. The lieutenant, his name was Wickstrom, and I had become buddies on the troopship coming down from England. Before he left for London he took me into Tunis to meet his girl. She didn't speak a word of English, so far as I could make out, but for Wickstrom's purpose that didn't really matter. He took out a key that he had to her apartment and, in front of her, gave it to me. *Comprenez vous?* he asked. She nodded her head. Wickstrom turned to me. 'She only fucks for her friends,' he said to me, 'and doesn't have an enemy in the world.' Wickstrom laughed, shook my hand and took off.

"Does my language shock you?" Mulvehill asked.

Stacy shook her head. "I've heard worse."

* Supreme Headquarters Allied Expeditionary Forces

Mulvehill smiled. "We went to her apartment. Her husband was a captain in the French Navy. I learned that from looking at pictures in her apartment."

"Before or after?" Stacy interrupted.

Mulvehill shrugged. "Well, you asked, so I'm telling you. The truth is I've always been rather shy."

Stacy kissed him. "You're sweet."

He rose from the table, walked to the bay window and looked out into the street. For a minute he stood there looking at the people hurrying up and down. He turned back to her.

"How did you get involved with these guys," he asked, "and why?"

She crossed her legs.

"Two years ago I was a freshman at the University of Alabama," she said, "at Tuscaloosa. I was just another Southern girl with bobby sox and a Southern drawl. My father's hellfire and brimstone preaching had begun to wear thin for me. I'm not stupid, Charlie, and I had come across enough contradictions in the Bible to make me want to get away and think things through on my own.

"When Pearl Harbor was bombed I pretty soon found that college didn't seem very important. And I had already slept with four, maybe even five guys." She shrugged. "Maybe an overreaction to my father's fundamentalism. Anyway, I didn't even wait to finish my freshman year. I borrowed a hundred dollars and headed north. I had been reading Thomas Wolfe and decided if New York was good enough for him it was good enough for me."

Mulvehill sat down on the window ledge of the bay window and Stacy had risen from her chair. She crossed her arms over her chest and slowly paced back and forth, not looking at Charles. He had the feeling she was maybe wanting to get something off her chest.

"My first job in New York was cashier in a movie house in Brooklyn. That's how I met Michael. He came to the movies one night and afterwards hung around until I was through for the night. He wanted to come back to my apartment but I was sharing it with a Jewish girl. I would talk with her about the Old Testament and found it always made her nervous. She was embarrassed by the tales of violence in the Bible. Like David and Bathsheba, and Jael, who drove a tent pin through Sisera's skull. Have you noticed that so many Jews, although they sound and act brash, really feel inferior, like they are unwelcome guests?"

Mulvehill shrugged. "I haven't known any Jews, Stacy, except for the two men in my outfit. They pretty much kept to themselves."

Stacy had stopped her pacing.

"Can't you ever call me anything but Stacy?" she complained. "Like maybe, honey, or sugar, or sweetheart?"

"How about 'doll'?" he asked.

She looked at him critically, then nodded her head. "Okay. I'll buy that."

She paused and then went back to her discourse.

"That's why I like these guys from Palestine. They don't apologize to anyone for anything. They know what they stand for and they know what they believe in. You've got to admire people like that, Charlie."

Mulvehill looked up at her.

"How did you meet them?"

"Well, as I told you it was through Marvin Zelinsky. I had only worked at the movie house three or four weeks and had seen Michael every night after work when he sent me up to see a woman he knew at Vogue magazine. She offered me a job as a research assistant. I liked that," Stacy said. "I've always enjoyed looking up information. Marvin worked in the mail room so I got to know him slightly. He told me about a meeting that was being held at the apartment of one of the editors one evening. Hecht was there and had brought Peter Bergson with him.

Ben talked about the need to try to get as many Jews out of Europe as they possibly could."

Mulvehill broke in. "But if the war had already started, how could they do that?" Stacy became animated. "When one of the girls asked that question Hecht introduced Bergson. Believe it or not, Charlie," she said, "Bergson said that until as late as 1943 there were still underground Jewish groups working in Rumania and Hungary, where the Germans had not yet penetrated, so it was possible to get Jewish refugees from Germany and Poland down the Danube and to ports where they might get on ships for Palestine. That was the object of Hecht and Bergson's talk. Basically it was a pitch for money to buy or lease boats to be used for escape."

Mulvehill rose from his seat on the window ledge. He shook his head. "I guess here in America we never knew much about what was going on."

Stacy nodded. "The U. S. newspapers didn't report much about it. Maybe it was really official policy not to report it. It would make it look as though it was a Jewish war." She shook hear head angrily. "And the Jews in America, most of them, were too timid to speak up.

"Ben Hecht was the only Jew of any consequence to write about it. And for his pains," she smiled, "the influential Jews of America said he was exaggerating. Actually," she went on, "they said much more than that. Even tried to get him arrested."

Mulvehill laughed. "I'm not sure I'd want to get mixed up in anything that's so controversial."

Stacy walked over to him, circled his waist with her arms and looked up into his face.

"It could be fun, a couple of *goyim* like you and I working with a daring bunch of Palestinian Jews."

He looked down at her. "Goyim? Is that what they call us?"

She reached up and kissed him.

"After Peter had finished his speech that night they passed the hat. Literally. My editor had a broad brimmed hat from Lily Dache." She grinned. "I dropped in a dollar. As the meeting broke up I joined a small knot of girls who were asking Bergson questions. That was the idea. Actually," she shrugged, "they were flirting. Bergson is a rather good looking man. But dead serious. He is passionate about his mission, not about girls."

"What exactly is his mission?" Mulvehill asked.

"To raise money. Some of it goes to buy broken down tramp steamers to get as many refugees out of Europe as they can. Some of it, I think," she pursed her lips, "is to squirrel away funds to buy weapons to fight the British in Palestine after the war is over."

Mulvehill shook his head. "I don't know, Doll. It sounds pretty confusing to me."

She sat down and put on her shoes. "Shall we take a walk? It looks like a lovely day. How's the leg?"

He stood up on his toes, then did a deep knee bend. "Feels pretty good."

She kissed him. "Can I talk you into doing the dishes while I put on some makeup?"

"You can talk me into anything." He hugged her. "Almost anything."

She blew him a kiss. "The soap's under the sink." She went into the bathroom and closed the door.

"A fine thing," he called after her. "A captain in the U.S. Army doing KP."

He washed the dishes and cups, dried them and set them out on the counter top next to the sink. Suddenly he grinned. He had made love to three women and all three had been either married, separated or divorced. He looked at the closed bathroom door. This one, he thought, was really special.

She came out. She had drawn a blue silk scarf around her neck that was a pleasing contrast to her white blouse and blue skirt.

She opened the door and made a mock bow. "Après vous, monsieur." She locked the door behind her and took his hand. They descended the stairs. Out on the street they looked up. The sky was cloudless. A fresh breeze blew in from the river. He looked down at her. "Which way?"

"The Hudson's just a couple of blocks from here," she told him. "Okay?"

He nodded. "Okay."

They walked along. Stacy noticed that he still walked with a slight limp, throwing his bad leg out in front of him.

They came to the river. A tug boat chugged by, hauling two barges in its wake. Stacy motioned to a bench. They sat down.

"Charlie. Let me talk. I'm not going to try to talk you into anything." She took his hand in hers. "Just listen. Okay?"

He nodded.

"Peter calls himself Bergson, the name he took when he came to the United States. His real name is Hillel Kook."

"I'm not surprised," Mulvehill grinned. "If I had a name like that I'd change it too."

Stacy smiled indulgently.

"But because his uncle is a noted rabbi in Palestine," she went on patiently, "he didn't want to embarrass the family so he adopted a pseudonym."

She paused, looked across the Hudson to the Palisades cliffs on the far side.

"His closest companion here," she went on after a slight pause, "is a man named Sam Merlin. Merlin is a man without family or kin. His family was blasted by the Germans in Bessarabia. Multiply Sam's story by a few million," she said, "and you get the picture of what has been happening to the Jews of Europe."

Mulvehill reached down and picked up a twig from the ground. He twirled it idly in his fingers. "What would you want me to do?"

She put one hand on his neck.

"I had said before," she reminded him, "that I felt that Jews are a sort of nervous people. No matter how successful they become they seem, deep down, to feel insecure." She laughed. "Ben Hecht who, as you might suppose, has a way with words, calls it 'living in the scabbards of their enemies'."

He smiled. "Yes, I would say that's a rather provocative phrase."

"Have you ever been to Thirty Seventh Street and Seventh Avenue?" she wanted to know.

Mulvehill shook his head.

"That's the heart of the garment district. The industry is dominated by Jews. I've been down there a few times on fashion photo shoots. When you eat lunch in any restaurant in the area the hubbub is deafening. Men are shouting to each other across the room. And yet you can sense an undercurrent of uneasiness. They know what has been happening to the Jews of Europe. Maybe they're afraid it could happen here."

He looked at her. "You're not serious?"

She looked back at him. "Have you read Sinclair Lewis' book *It Can't Happen Here?*"

"I not only haven't read it, I never heard of it. My goodness, Doll, you certainly are serious."

She smiled. "You're the one who should be serious. You were right in the thick of it. What do you think this war is all about?"

His brow furrowed. "You don't mean it's about the Jews?"

"In a way, yes. Look, Charlie." She took his hands. "I have to go downtown to Wall Street. I've got a meeting with an investment banker who may make a major contribution to the Committee. Why don't you go over to the Library on Fifth Avenue. You'll be able to get a back issue of *Reader's Digest*. Look up the February 1943 edition. There's an article there by Ben Hecht. It's called 'Remember Us'. Read it."

She reached in her purse. "Here's the key to the apartment. I'll be back by six." Suddenly she grinned. "You think you can handle those steps again?"

"I think so." He looked at her. "What have you got in mind?"

She hugged him. "How about making goggena shnetzena hetzena petzena pee?"

He laughed. "You really are becoming Jewish hanging around with those guys. First you give up a perfectly good Southern accent. Then you start talking Yiddish."

"There are worse things that could happen to a girl."

She poked him in the ribs.

"Anyway, that's not Yiddish, silly. It's a play on Eddie Cantor's song 'Making Whoopee'."

They kissed. They walked slowly back up the slope and down Seventy Second Street to the subway entrance at Broadway. He waited until she had gone through the turnstile and then headed for the bus stop. He took the Broadway bus down to Forty Second Street and then transferred to the Crosstown bus. At Fifth Avenue he dismounted and stood looking at the stone lions in front of the Library.

He mounted the steps. A librarian directed him to the room where periodicals are kept. In a few minutes a young woman came out and handed him the *Reader's Digest* he had asked for. He found an unoccupied table in a far corner, sat down and began reading.

As the telling of the draconian measures enacted by the Germans against the Jews unfolded he drew in his breath sharply. Stacy was flirtatious, even, from what she had said, sexually promiscuous before she had married Sheridan but, he felt sure, underneath it she was a highly principled young woman. No wonder she had eagerly joined the Palestinian Jews in their campaign to try to save the European Jews who had not yet been murdered by the Germans.

The article by Hecht related that the information he was reporting had been obtained by eyewitnesses who had escaped the holocaust and, in part, from underground sources who had smuggled the information out to Switzerland.

He read of the execution of the Jewish population in Munich and of the extermination camp of Treblinka.

The article told of freight cars into which hapless Jews had been jammed so tightly they could not lie down. The cars were lined with quicklime. By the time the cars arrived at their destination the victims had become corpses partially consumed by the lime. The bodies were dumped into trenches that had been dug for the purpose. It reported that, in Silesia, some twenty thousand Jews had been herded into an open field and held there at gunpoint while Luftwaffe pilots strafed the field using the Jews as practice targets.

Mulvehill raised his head from the article and looked around. The reading room was filled with dozens of people, reading or taking notes. At one table he saw a bearded old man reading. The man wore the small black skullcap affected by religious Jews. He looked around, studying faces. He thought he could identify a dozen or more who were, he felt sure, Jews.

The room was quiet. From the street he could hear the hum of cars and buses driving by. He tried to imagine the events he was reading about happening here in America.

He continued to read. In Cologne a number of Jews were forced into a neighborhood synagogue. When the synagogue was full the doors were closed. Nazis in uniform poured gasoline around the foundation and, with torches, set the building on fire. When some Jews, screaming, jumped through the windows they were fired upon by rifles and machine guns. Hecht had written that a German officer, Colonel Wolfe, had been promoted to General for his enterprising slaughter of Jews in the Warsaw ghetto. Some he marched naked to the incinerator. Others, having the temerity to venture out into the street, were summarily shot to death. Mulvehill read of rabbis being hung, of Jewish women being raped and then tortured, of German soldiers forcing old Jews to rub excrement over their heads and faces while they prayed.

He put down the magazine. He suddenly remembered a photograph he had seen, perhaps it was in the Los Angeles Times. Two German soldiers were holding a bearded Jew's arms pinioned while a third was cutting off his beard. Half a dozen other soldiers were in the picture, watching the scene and grinning. He remembered that. But this!

What kind of men were they who could perform such butchery on a weak and defenseless people?

He stood up and returned the magazine to the librarian with the article only half read. He did not think he had to read any more. He suddenly understood the ferocity of the two Jewish men in his platoon, before he had been commissioned a captain and given a Company to command. They had volunteered to serve as point and first scout and, if that were not enough, they were ready to go out on any dangerous assignment.

He left the library and walked swiftly north on Fifth Avenue. He felt like having a cigarette but, because he was not a habitual smoker, he did not carry a pack on him. At Forty Sixth street he turned off the Avenue. Approaching Sixth Avenue he found a small bar. A lone drinker sat at one end. Mulvehill took a seat at the other end. He ordered a shot of Scotch.

He was aware that he felt like crying. He thought about the article he had been reading. He suddenly understood the dedication of the Jews who had come from Palestine. What he could not understand was why no one else had written about this. Could it actually be phony propaganda? He thought about that and decided that the editors of the *Reader's Digest* were not fools. Surely they had a research department to check the facts for authenticity before they would publish such an inflammatory article.

He ordered a second drink. Finishing that he went back out on the street and started walking swiftly but, after a few steps, he slowed down. The wound began to throb. Still, he walked on. He came to Broadway and turned north. Stopping from time to time it took him the better part of an hour to reach Seventy-Third street. He used the key Stacy had given him to enter the apartment. The climb up four stories tired him. The bathroom had a good sized tub. He ran the water as hot as he could take, undressed and eased himself in. The heat soon gave relief to the throb in the wound. He slowly massaged his leg. He had almost dozed off when he heard a key in the lock. The door closed and Stacy came into the bathroom. She saw the drawn look on his face.

"You've been to the library."

He nodded. She sank to the floor on her knees, took his head in her hands and began to shower kisses on him.

"Now you know," she said.

He nodded and kissed her. "I want to meet Mr. Bergson," he said.

5.

They arrived at the cluttered offices of American League For A Free Palestine on a side street near Fifth Avenue. Stacy led Mulvehill past rows of battered desks to a small office. Two men were engaged in conversation with a third man who sat behind a desk as worn as those in the outer office. Most of the desks had been occupied by young women. There were only a few men in civilian clothes. Mulvehill recognized Marvin Zelinsky bent over a desk in a corner.

As Stacy appeared in the open doorway the man behind the desk saw her and smiled. The two men facing him turned. All three smiled. Mulvehill let a fleeting smile pass across his face. Who wouldn't smile, he thought, seeing Stacy?

The two men left the office, making room for Stacy and Mulvehill to enter. The seated man rose and Mulvehill noted that he was of medium height. He reached across the desk and extended his hand to Mulvehill. They shook hands.

Mulvehill realized that what Stacy had told him was true. Bergson had sandy colored hair and a blond moustache. Dressed in a British uniform he could easily have passed as an Englishman. He waved them to two chairs facing his desk. Stacy and Mulvehill sat down. Bergson pulled his chair forward to be closer to them.

"Captain Mulvehill, Stacy said you may be interested in the work we are doing. We are appreciative of any help anyone is willing to provide our organization." The smile had left his face to be replaced by a look of intense seriousness.

"As long as you are in the U. S. Army the only help we can accept would be a donation." A slight smile passed across his features and he was serious again.

"Stacy is quite impressed with you, Captain. And let me say, in all sincerity, my companions are as impressed as I am." He reached for a cigarette pack on his desk and held it out to Mulvehill, who shook his head.

Bergson lit a cigarette.

"You understand we are an organization principally of Jews. Stacy joined us," he said, "because she felt that helping Jews is a matter of simple justice, as it would be to help anyone in need or in danger."

"Stacy said you are the leader of a group of six Jews from Palestine," Mulvehill said in response, "who are here to raise money to drive the British out of Palestine."

Bergson nodded his head.

"True, it didn't start out that way but that is our purpose today." He blew a feather of smoke over their heads. "Three years ago we tried to interest Americans in helping to support a movement to raise a Jewish Army in the Middle East. General Montgomery's forces had been beaten back by Field Marshal Rommel's Afrika Korps almost to the gates of El Alamein. We failed."

He stubbed out his cigarette.

"We then raised money to buy tramp steamers to sail refugee Jews from ports on the Danube to Palestine. We were a little more successful with that program.

"Two of our number are now serving in the U.S. Army."

He leaned forward.

"For us, in the work we are doing here, there are no furloughs. We came here on a mission of the greatest importance. Every move, every thought on our part is dedicated to the accomplishment of our mission."

He looked quickly at Stacy.

"Stacy says you will be accepting a discharge from the Army. You will, of course, want to visit your family?" He looked questioningly at Mulvehill, who nodded.

"And Stacy says you live in California. True?"

Mulvehill nodded again.

"In that event," Bergson continued, "let me say that we have two stalwart women out there helping us in our cause; Ethel Longstreet and Frankie Spitz. If you think you may then want to help us, Stacy can give you their phone number. We maintain a small office in Los Angeles." He changed the subject.

"How did you feel about fighting Germans, may I ask?" Bergson said.

Mulvehill looked down at his nails. He thought for a moment and then looked up at the man on the other side of the desk.

"I've killed Germans in North Africa and in Italy," he finally said, "but I never gave it any thought beyond the fact that they were the enemy."

"And now?" Bergson asked.

"I read an article that Ben Hecht wrote," he said.

Bergson said, "Ah."

"I've got a different view of Germans, now," Mulvehill frowned. "I find it hard to believe that human beings can be that cruel."

He bit his lip.

"I suppose if I had been sent to the South Pacific," Mulvehill continued, "I would have been killing Japs without much more knowledge beyond the fact that they had bombed Pearl Harbor."

Bergson smiled.

"I think that Americans are not a very political people," he said.

Stacy laughed.

"You're too kind to us, Peter."

"Well," Mulvehill said, "we don't live as close to other countries as Europeans do, so we don't tend to get emotionally involved with other people's problems. Hitler and Hirohito were just two guys with funny moustaches until the bombs fell on Pearl Harbor."

"But doesn't your religion impose certain standards?" Bergson asked.

"If you're talking about Christianity," Mulvehill laughed, "that leaves me out. Stacy's a Christian, anyway her father's a Baptist preacher. But I'm not. Christian, I mean." He shook his head. "At least I don't go to church. My father is a free thinker and my mother, God bless her, tends to go along with what dad does. The people who work for us, of course, are all Catholic. That's what Spain brought to Mexico. Mother often goes to Mass on Sunday with Consuelo, our foreman's wife." He grinned. "I've always thought she did that just to tease dad."

The telephone rang. Bergson picked it up, listened, and then placed it back on its base. He stood up.

"I must go now, but I enjoyed talking with you. Have you met Marvin Zelinsky?"

Mulvehill nodded.

"Marvin can give you some pamphlets if you want to know more about our work," Bergson said. "He's sort of our librarian."

Mulvehill said nothing. The two of them shook hands and Bergson left.

Stacy reached across to Mulvehill. "I think I could stand a drink. There's a nice little place down the street. What do you say?"

"I say, capital, or as our German prisoners used to say when something went right for them like eating their first American meal…*prima.*"

They rose.

"I don't think I want to read any pamphlets, Doll."

She grinned and took him by the hand.

"O.K."

They took the elevator down to the street. A hot May sun beat down on them. The bar she led him to was dimly lit and cool. Stacy took him by the hand and led him to a booth in the corner. They sat down.

The waitress approached.

"Hi, Stacy. The usual?"

Mulvehill looked at her. "What have I got on my hands, a lush?"

"Certainly not," Stacy pouted, "it's just that Melanie has an exceptionally good memory."

"Melanie," he laughed, "is not the only one with a good memory."

He looked up at the waitress.

"I'll have a sweet Rob Roy. And bring the lady…the usual."

After the drinks were served Stacy sipped her daiquiri. Her eyes looked impish.

"How old are you, Charlie?"

Mulvehill plucked at his chin. "Let's see. This is the end of May. Golly, I've got a birthday coming up. I'll be twenty-five on June sixth."

Stacy poked him. "What? You're just a baby."

"Oh yeah," he countered. "And how old are you, Madam?"

"Twenty," she told him.

"My God," he rejoined. "Jail bait. If you're just twenty now, how old were you when you got married?"

"Nineteen."

She fished around in her purse and brought out a crumpled pack of cigarettes.

"See," she said, "I haven't smoked in two days."

Mulvehill looked thoughtful.

"We did a lot of night patrolling when it was as much as your life was worth to try to light a cigarette," he said quietly. "I finally discovered that the less I smoked the less I wanted to."

Stacy tossed the package of cigarettes into the ash tray.

"I'm quitting too. My, aren't we virtuous."

She put her hand on top of Mulvehill's.

"What did you think of Bergson, Charlie?"

"He's awfully serious."

"Peter Bergson," Stacy said, "is a very unusual man. He's a highly political man with the instincts of a high-powered American public relations man. He knows how to motivate people and it makes no difference to him how important they are. The only thing that's important to him is his cause."

"And his cause," Mulvehill broke in, "is to drive the British out of Palestine?"

Stacy shook her head.

"No, that's just a means to an end. The end is a Hebrew Commonwealth, on both sides of the Jordan. That's the only way, Peter is convinced, that Jews can ever feel free and independent."

Mulvehill sipped his drink. She was cute enough to be a chorus girl, he thought, and was involved in an extremely difficult, if not dubious, enterprise.

"Peter and the others who came here from Palestine," she said, "are all sort of protégés, or disciples, of a man they call Zeev Jabotinsky."

"I've heard that name before," Mulvehill remembered.

Stacy sucked on the straw in her daiquiri and then pushed the glass away. She dabbed at her mouth with a paper napkin and then leaned back against the leather cushion of the booth. Her eyes took on a dreamy look.

"Jabotinsky," she said, "whose first name is Vladimir, but whose friends call him Zeev is, or was, a modern Old Testament Prophet."

She leaned forward and her eyes opened wide.

"Golly, imagine that, Charlie, knowing a real live Prophet."

Mulvehill finished his drink.

"Did you know him?" he asked.

She shook her head.

"No," she said, "but Peter and his friends did. Jabotinsky died just a few years ago. He anticipated the coming slaughter of the Jews. As early as 1937 he spoke before the members of the Peel Commission in the House of Lords. He warned of what was coming. He compared it to a sort of social earthquake and said that millions of Jews must be urged to leave their homes in Europe and be allowed to enter Palestine. He was ignored."

Mulvehill nodded.

"You've really made a study of this," he said, "haven't you?"

She reached out for his hand.

"It's history, Charlie. I love history. And best of all this is part of history that most people know nothing about.

"Way back in 1931 a man named Berl Locker, of Poale Zion, a Socialist group, spoke before the World

Zionist Congress in Geneva. He compared Vladimir Jabotinsky to the Hitlerites in Germany. And just think," she brought her head close to Mulvehill's, "this was nearly two years before Hitler was named Reichschancellor.

"It was reported here in the New York Times. You can go back to the library and read the whole article." She looked at him triumphantly.

Mulvehill was puzzled. "What would make a Jew call another Jew a Hitlerite? What did Jabotinsky do to arouse such resentment and anger?"

Stacy shook her head. "Peter says that Jew fighting Jew is an old pastime. It is, perhaps, he thinks, the only way a Jew can express his anger and frustration. If he starts shouting at Christians he will most likely get his face punched. Or worse."

Mulvehill shook his head wearily.

"I think I need another drink. How about you?"

Stacy shook her head.

"One is my limit, Charlie. I need to keep my head clear for more important things."

"Like what?" Mulvehill said, leering at her like Groucho Marx.

She laughed and beckoned the waitress.

Melanie approached and tendered a bill. Mulvehill paid.

"Can you afford that, Charlie?" Stacy asked. "How much does a captain get paid?"

He grinned. "I'm flush. The Army gave me a hefty paycheck, dating back to the day I was wounded."

They walked out of the bar into the bright late afternoon sun.

"Should we take a walk?" Mulvehill suggested.

Stacy hooked her arm in his and looked up at him.

"Let's pass on the walk. Why don't we take a cab back to my place?"

He smiled down at her. Goggona hetzena?"

She scratched his palm with her little finger. "Well you got the right idea, Charlie," she laughed, "but you got the words wrong. "It's goggena shnetzena."

He walked out into the street and waved his hand. A cab pulled up immediately.

She got in and he followed. "You've got the Midas touch, Charlie." She snuggled against him. "You wanted to know what I had said at '21' that first night when you said maybe you were easy to please. All I said was 'try me'. Marvin heard. That's why he smiled."

"Poor Marvin Zelinsky," Mulvehill said. "I told him I thought he was a queer."

"Oh, no," Stacy smiled. "He's got a girl friend, Iris Katz. You'll probably meet her one day. Peter called Marvin our librarian. Marvin may file the documents but Iris has them all in her head. She's a walking repository of the history of the Irgun."

Stacy smiled again and her dimples showed.

"Iris is what the Jewish boys call 'zoftig'."

"What's that?" Mulvehill wanted to know.

Stacy laughed. "Va-va-voom." She made big curves in the air to illustrate a large bosom.

The cab arrived at the building where Stacy lived. They got out and slowly climbed the four flights to her room. The evening was still warm from the heat of the day. Stacy locked the door. "I'm sweaty," she said. "No," Mulvehill corrected her. "Horses sweat. Men perspire. Women glow."

They undressed and went into the shower.

They dried and got into bed. Later, he awoke. The radium dial on his watch told him it was two thirty. The street outside was quiet. In the distance he could hear a car horn blow, a squeal of brakes, the rattling of an ash can.

He turned to look at Stacy. The coverlet was down below her waist. In the dim light cast through the curtains by a street lamp outside the window he looked at the slender loveliness of her body. He kissed her breast. She stirred and murmured something.

Quietly, Mulvehill got out of bed and dressed. He leaned over and kissed her and she awoke. "What is it, Charlie?" she asked drowsily.

"I'm going back to the Post," he whispered.

"Why, Charlie?"

"It's been a long day, sweet. I think the long ride back to Fort Hamilton will be good for me." He kissed her again.

"Okay," she said and was again asleep.

6.

It was late in the morning when Mulvehill was awakened by Captain Stowe, the roommate who had replaced Schroeder, bounding into the room. "It's on, Mulvehill," he boomed. "Hundred and First Airborne has jumped behind the German lines. U. S. First Army has gone ashore at Normandy. It's D-Day."

Mulvehill reached over and turned on his bedside radio. The announcer was heard through static caused by the long wavelength from a ship in the English Channel. "I've just returned to this ship offshore of the landing site at Omaha Beach," the voice squawked. "Elements of Fifth Corps are fighting against fierce German opposition on the beach between St. Laurent and Grandcamp Rocks. Casualties are heavy." The radio switched to another announcer.

"Here, on the beach near Cherbourg," the announcer reported, "mountains of stores are piling up as ship after ship quickly unloads. This beachhead position was quickly consolidated and forward troops of Seventh Army are fighting their way toward the little town of Carentan. We have learned that farther east, near Bayeaux and Caen, British Second Army is moving swiftly inland…"

Mulvehill jumped out of bed. At last. This was it. If combined British and American units could connect inland they might forge a striking force and make their way to Paris. He rubbed his leg. God, if he could have been there. At least these troops would not have to put up with the freezing rain and sleet of the Italian winter. He gathered up his clothes and a towel and headed for the washroom.

He was shaved and dressed in time for lunch. The excitement on the Post was palpable. Every radio was turned on at top volume.

At the officers mess Mulvehill ran into Major Levy. The shorter man sat down at the table with Mulvehill. "How about that, Captain? Its finally on. The invasion we've been waiting for."

Mulvehill nodded but ate silently. He might as well make up his mind now. The Army really had no practical use for him. Stacy had left word she would be in Washington with Bergson for a few days. They were looking for a headquarters building from which they could operate the recently formed Hebrew Committee of National Liberation. She would be back in New York tomorrow. He was not at all clear what assistance he could give the group that Stacy had thrown in with, or if he even wanted to.

He turned to Levy.

"Major, if I want to get out, how long will it take?"

Levy was eating creamed beef on toast. He waved a fork at Mulvehill. "I don't know why the men don't like 'shit on a shingle'. I love it." He laughed. "If that's what you want captain, I'll have the papers drawn up tomorrow. Hey, tell you what." He turned thoughtful. "Suppose I arrange for your discharge on the West Coast. I'll have travel orders cut so that you can have fifteen days to get back there. You can pick up your discharge papers at Fort MacArthur in San Pedro. O.K.?"

Mulvehill thought about it. "O.K."

Those arrangements would be good. He could stop off and see his older sister, Jean, who was an ensign in the WAVES* and stationed at Navy Pier in Chicago. He could spend some time with her between trains in Chicago and then with his folks and younger brother and sister when he got back to California. He thought about Stacy. He knew he would miss her. But it would only be for a few weeks and then he would return to New York.

There were several letters waiting for him when he returned from lunch. One of the men from his unit in Italy had written to say that the fighting had been fierce and casualties were heavy. The second Jewish man in his unit, Corporal Greenglass, had been killed by sniper fire as they attempted to capture a small hill town called San Pietro.

There was a short letter from Lt. Wickstrom, the meteorologist who had been sent to London from Tunis. Now, Mulvehill realized, the reason for calling Wickstrom to London was to track the weather for the cross-channel invasion of France. And they had called the weather correctly to the day.

* Women Accepted for Voluntary Emergency Service

Lastly there was a note from Marvin Zelinsky. He wrote that Stacy had called the office to say she would be in Washington a few days longer than she thought and would he call Captain Mulvehill and tell him? In a footnote Zelinsky asked whether Mulvehill might have dinner with him and his girl friend?

Mulvehill thought that one over.

Well, why not, he finally concluded. The kid had been embarrassed that Mulvehill had thought he might be homosexual and wanted to show him that he had a girl friend. Mulvehill found a dog-eared Manhattan phone book in the lounge, looked up American League For A Free Palestine and dialed the number.

He asked for Zelinsky and the youngster quickly came on the line. Mulvehill told Zelinsky he was accepting the offer for dinner but would have to get back to him about the time because orders were being arranged for him to leave for California and he did not yet know when he would be leaving.

"Gee," Zelinsky said, "Stacy will sure be sorry if you have to leave before she gets back."

"Well, let's cross that bridge when we get to it," Mulvehill said.

After lunch he sauntered over to Major Levy's office.

"Sometimes the Army can move quickly," Levy told Mulvehill. "We can get you on a train out tomorrow. Is that O.K.?"

"What time?" Mulvehill wanted to know.

The major called in the duty sergeant. "Look up the schedule for the Twentieth Century Limited to

Chicago for tomorrow evening. We want to have a Pullman berth reserved for the captain."

The sergeant saluted and left.

"I've got a date in Manhattan tomorrow afternoon," Levy said. "I'll be happy to give you a lift in the staff car."

"What time?" Mulvehill asked.

"Well, I'm meeting a lady for cocktails at four. Is that O.K.?" Levy asked.

"I'm sure it will be." Mulvehill said. "Suppose I meet you here at three?"

"No, let me send the corporal up for your bag," Levy replied. "He'll bring you back here and we'll leave together."

Mulvehill shrugged. "O.K."

He waited until the duty sergeant returned with the news that Mulvehill was booked on the Twentieth Century Limited to leave for Chicago at eight. He went back to the BOQ and called Zelinsky again.

"Our dinner will have to be early," Mulvehill said, hoping maybe the whole thing could be called off. "I'm leaving tomorrow and have to be at Grand Central by 7:30 if I'm to catch my train for Chicago. That means," he told Zelinsky, "we'll have to meet for dinner no later than 5:30."

"Oh, that's fine," Zelinsky quickly replied. "My girl and I can walk over from the office. We get off at 5:00."

"Good," Mulvehill said, "then it's all set. Where do we meet?"

"Ruby Liu's, just off Times Square," the youth replied. "Do you know where it is?"

"No," Mulvehill said, but if Zelinsky would give him the address he was sure he could find it.

"It's on the north side of 46th Street, just off Times Square. Do you eat Chinese?" he added.

"People, no. The food, yes," Mulvehill replied drily.

"Ha, ha," Zelinsky chuckled. "That's funny."

*　*　*

Major Levy's date, to Mulvehill's surprise, turned out to be a tall, willowy, looker with a fantastic figure and ashen blonde hair. A valet had driven off with the major's staff car and Mulvehill had followed him into the bar, on a side street in the Fifties, just off Madison Avenue.

The three of them had one drink and then Mulvehill excused himself. He had studied the girl as they sipped their drinks and, Mulvehill had concluded, she was taken with Levy's rank. Otherwise they seemed to have nothing in common.

"I can walk over to the Chinese restaurant from here," Mulvehill said as he rose from the booth where they had been sitting. "The walk will be good for me and I'll be there in plenty of time for my dinner meeting."

The blonde smiled and Levy held his hand out. "Good luck, captain. Maybe we'll meet one day in California."

They parted.

It was not quite five when Mulvehill left the bar. He walked leisurely over to Fifth Avenue and then down to 46th Street. Although he arrived early Zelinsky and his girl friend were already there, seated demurely on spindly chairs in the combination lobby and cashier's booth.

Zelinsky jumped to his feet as Mulvehill entered. The adulation that the youth showed Mulvehill fairly oozed from him. He pumped Mulvehill's hand vigorously.

His girl friend was as Stacy had described her. She seemed to be all curves, from her round face and hair that was a mass of round brunette ringlets to her generous bosom and well padded rump. She rose at Zelinsky's prompting and shook hands with Mulvehill.

"It's really nice to meet you," she said. She smiled and deep dimples formed in her cheeks. Her skin had that creamy look that makes many fat girls look even younger than they are. Her eyes were bright and merry and Mulvehill warmed to her.

The restaurant's owner or maitre d' came out and beckoned for them to follow. He found a booth for them in a corner towards the rear. The ceiling was gilt and adorned with coiled dragons. The walls were brocaded tapestry.

A waiter arrived and handed them menus. His face was an inscrutable mask out of the T'ang dynasty but his voice, when he asked for their orders, was strictly New York.

"Do you like soup?" Zelinsky asked Mulvehill. "Their egg drop soup is delicious." Mulvehill nodded agreeably. "If you serve moo shoo pork," he told the waiter, "I like that."

"Absolutely," the waiter replied.

Zelinsky ordered the moo goo gai pan for himself and Iris Katz.

The waiter poured hot tea for them into tiny china cups and left to have their orders filled.

Iris lifted her cup and drank from it. She set it down and wiped her lips.

"Do you think it strange," she asked, "that Marvin and I, and Stacy Sheridan, whom you've met, should be working for a foreign group while we are at war?"

He shrugged. "The fact is, Iris, I haven't thought about it at all. I met Marvin in a bar. He introduced me to Stacy Sheridan and Ben Hecht. Stacy has told me why she is working for the organization and I respect her dedication."

"Ben Hecht is brilliant," Iris said, "and that's why I'm involved."

"Me too," Zelinsky broke in. "You know, I was ashamed to be a Jew until I read a book Hecht had written. It changed me overnight."

Mulvehill listened politely.

"You know, captain, it's strange but many of our strongest supporters aren't Jews at all," Iris said. "Ben Hecht's co-chairman is Senator Guy Gillette of Iowa. Some others who believe in our cause are Senator

Claude Pepper, the actor Burgess Meredith, assistant secretary of the Navy Adlai Stevenson, Hazel Scott, Frank Sinatra…"

"Any Jews at all?" Mulvehill smiled.

The soup arrived and ended their discussion.

Mulvehill tasted it.

"Very good," he said.

When the soup was removed Mulvehill leaned back and looked at his watch.

"We're going to get a cab to take you to the station," Zelinsky said.

"Captain," Iris said, "Stacy told me she hopes you may want to help us in our work. Is there any possibility of that?"

Mulvehill looked at her. She was the first Jewish girl he had ever had even a nodding acquaintance with.

"I don't know, Iris. Stacy says that the basic purpose of your organization is to raise money to help an underground group in Palestine drive the British out." He paused to gather his thoughts.

"As an American of Irish ancestry I'm not wild about the British. But just think," Mulvehill said slowly. "Great Britain was really the only country fighting Hitler until his split with Stalin. I think I was moved, along with most Americans, when we heard Churchill's famous speech about 'blood, sweat and tears'."

"Yes," Zelinsky broke in excitedly, "but that was the same Churchill who divided tiny Palestine into two countries and gave the larger slice to Abdullah, a

Hashemite prince from Saudi Arabia. They called the larger portion Transjordania."

The waiter's arrival with the food again interrupted the conversation and Mulvehill busied himself folding the leaves of the moo shoo pork and pouring the plum dressing over it. He gave himself over to the food but noticed that Iris merely seemed to be picking at her food abstractedly. How could she have become fat, he wondered, if she generally ate so sparingly?

She watched him eat and, when he finished, she spoke.

"Captain…"

Mulvehill waved his hand. "My name is Charles. Let's not be formal, Iris."

"I think I can honestly share your admiration for British valor," Iris said. "But there is more than one side to any story. May I tell you ours?"

Mulvehill spread his hands. "Of course."

She clasped her hands and leaned forward. Her bosom spread over the table and Mulvehill could not help but think that she must be a handful for little Marvin Zelinsky. He tried to concentrate on what she was saying.

"During World War I the British wanted to win the Jews of the world to their side. At the same time a Jewish chemist in London, named Chaim Weizmann, developed synthetic acetone, an important ingredient in the manufacture of smokeless gunpowder. In appreciation," Iris related, "Lord Arthur Balfour, then working in the Foreign Office, wrote a letter to Lord Rothschild in which he stated…'His Majesty's

Government views with favor the establishment of a Jewish homeland in Palestine'…" Iris stopped and smiled ruefully.

"Leave it to the British," she said, "to word a statement so it could be interpreted in more than one way. To the Jews in Palestine it meant that Britain was committed to converting Palestine into a Jewish homeland…all of it."

She sighed, and Mulvehill marveled that her face, which was designed by nature to be jolly, could turn so lugubrious.

"To the Arabs," she continued, "it meant that the British would maybe set up a small portion of the land, maybe a canton, that would be Jewish. We think," she went on, "that privately the British reassured the Arabs not to worry that, at most, they would establish a sort of British-Jewish suburb." She sighed again. "Like maybe give Tel Aviv to the Jews and they'll be happy."

She pushed her fork around the food and lay it down beside the plate. Zelinsky looked at her with adoration in his eyes.

"A lot of the Jews in Palestine," she said, "especially those like David Ben-Gurion, Moshe Shertok and Golda Meyerson, who had cushy jobs in the Jewish Agency, were content with the arrangement. They did not want to upset the British." A note of bitterness crept into her voice.

"But there was one Jew who did not share that view," she said. "A man named Vladimir Jabotinsky." Her eyes lit up. "Did you ever hear of him?"

Mulvehill smiled. "Recently. But tell me more about him."

Zelinsky picked up the story.

"Vladimir Jabotinsky was a Russian Jew who was well versed in many languages. He came to England shortly before World War I and promptly fell in love with everything British. When the war broke out," Zelinsky said, "Jabotinsky pleaded for the Jews to support England in its struggle with Germany. He asked the British government to let him form a Jewish Legion to fight on England's side."

Iris laughed.

"The British," she smiled, "almost agreed. They let him recruit Jews in England to serve as muleteers. The unit was actually called the Assyrian Jewish Refugee Mule Corps. Jabotinsky preferred to call it the Zion Mule Corps. But whatever its name it was a contingent of Jews who were shipped to the Dardanelles to carry ammunition up to the lines at the Gallipoli campaign… and carry the dead and wounded down on the backs of their mules."

Iris finally picked up some moo goo gai pan on her fork and chewed on it.

"Jabotinsky was always an admirer of the British," she finally said. "He marveled at their colonizing ability that enabled them to create such a worldwide empire that it was said 'The sun never sets on the British Empire.'"

Marvin tried his hand at a joke. "I thought the reason the sun never sets on the British Empire was because God would not trust an Englishman in the dark."

Iris reached over and squeezed Marvin's hand. Mulvehill smiled.

"Twenty years later," she said, "Jabotinsky still believed in British fairness, but he was becoming discouraged. In 1937 he appeared before the Royal Commission that had been assigned to submit a report to His Majesty's Government on conditions in Palestine.

"Jabotinsky spelled out what the influential 'establishment' Jews of the world wanted. His words were mild. He did not excoriate the establishment Jews of the World Zionist organization. Jabotinsky was speaking for all the Jews, not just those who saw Palestine as a sort of a British-Jewish suburb. He referred to the phenomenon called Zionism as seen by its mainstream proponents as 'a model community, a stage setting of Hebrew culture or a second edition of the Bible. All these wonderful toys of velvet and silver,' Jabotinsky implored, 'are nothing compared with that tangible momentum of irresistible distress and need by which we are propelled and borne.'"

Mulvehill picked up his teacup.

"He certainly had a way with the English language," he smiled, "and you've got quite a memory."

She looked at him and her eyes were luminous. Mulvehill had never before encountered any people so fervent about their beliefs. He thought it was quite admirable and, although he was not yet convinced that he wanted to become involved, he was beginning to think that these people represented a refreshing point of view.

"Jabotinsky," Iris continued, "until his death in 1940, wanted a Jewish state in Palestine now. Not in some distant day."

"But isn't that what all Jews want?" Mulvehill asked.

"Maybe, but that is not the issue," Iris said. "The British, and Mr. Roosevelt too, don't want a bunch of impoverished refugee Jews descending on Palestine. It would make the Arabs unhappy. And they don't want to make the Arabs unhappy. Don't ask me why." She shook her head dolefully, but the brightness never left her eyes.

"And there is another reason," she continued. "Almost all American Jews venerate Mr. Roosevelt. They consider him a great friend of the Jews."

"Don't you?" Mulvehill wanted to know.

Marvin leaned across the table. "I have yet to go into a Jewish home that doesn't have a picture of Mr. Roosevelt hanging on the wall. So if Mr. Roosevelt doesn't think now is the time to try to help the Jews escape Hitler's henchmen, all the influential Jews of America are willing to wait. Unfortunately, every day they wait another 70,000 Jews are fed into the German incinerators. Jabotinsky saw that coming. He talked about it and warned against it. So the Jewish establishment considered him a nuisance. There's more to it than that but, for now, captain, that should be enough." He reached for the teapot.

Mulvehill pushed his plate away. He looked at his watch.

He smiled at Marvin and his girl friend.

"I thank you for an interesting history lesson," he said, "but I think I had better head for Grand Central.

"California here I come," he grinned.

Iris stood up. Marvin rose and stood beside her. Mulvehill thought of a tug boat nosing up against an ocean liner. Iris looked at him seriously.

"It would be a great advantage if you should decide to work with us. Maybe once you get to California you will remember us and think about it." Suddenly she smiled and it was like sunshine breaking through the clouds.

"Can we get you a lift to the station?" Marvin asked.

Mulvehill shook his head.

"I'll be all right. My bag is already checked in," he said. "I enjoyed meeting you both." He extended his hand and each shook it in turn. He turned briskly and walked away. Once out on the sidewalk a cab pulled up almost as soon as he raised his hand.

From the cab he looked out at the bustle on the street abstractedly. He thought of a movie he had seen at the Post Theater one evening. The story was about England at war. It was called *This Above All* and featured Tyrone Power. The British certainly were valiant, he knew. A handful stood against the might of Germany at Dunkirk. Churchill's words about the British Air Force echoed in his ears. 'Never in the history of human conflict have so few done so much for so many.'

And yet, this same brave nation had stood in the way of letting refugee Jews escape from the horrors of the Nazi regime to Palestine when there had still been time. He was still thinking about the riddle when the cab pulled up in front of Grand Central. He paid the driver and walked to the luggage locker where he had stowed his bag when Levy had brought him there on their way to the lounge for the major to meet his date.

Suddenly he felt cheered to be leaving New York. First he would meet his sister in Chicago and then, in just a few days, he would be back in California with his family. He braced himself with his cane in one hand and walked briskly toward the ramp down to the platform where he would board the Twentieth Century Limited.

7.

Chicago was hot that June day when Mulvehill arrived to meet with his sister Jean. He had started to walk from La Salle Street station but, as rivulets of perspiration began to trickle under his arms, he changed his mind and flagged a cab. He didn't want to meet Jean drenched in sweat. She was three years older than he and he had always respected her almost as much as he loved her.

She was pacing in the lobby as he entered and looked chic in her white Navy uniform, her long legs scissoring as she walked. She turned, saw him, and strode toward him, resisting the impulse to run toward her kid brother. They embraced.

"Oh, Charlie, Charlie, you look just wonderful. And so handsome in your khakis, Captain Mulvehill." She stood back a pace and saluted. They both laughed and then hugged again. People in the lobby looked on, smiled, and assumed they were young lovers. Arm in arm they walked into the dining room.

They both ordered salads. "Too hot for meat, don't you think, Charlie?"

He ate sparingly, wiped his mouth, and leaned back in his chair. Jean took a metal cigarette case from her purse, opened it and held it toward him.

He shook his head. "I've quit Jean. I think I got over it in the hospital. I'm hoping I can get back to long walks and, maybe, even be able to run again. I want to be able to do that without getting winded."

"Good for you, Charlie. I still like a smoke, especially after a meal." She laughed. "Remember that poster that used to be on the side of dad's packing shed?"

"You mean the one that showed the girl looking at the man who was smoking and said… 'blow some my way'? What was that? Chesterfield? Lucky Strike? Sweet Caporal?" Mulvehill joked.

Jean reached around the table and poked him in the ribs.

"Sweet Caporal, indeed," she snorted. "Who are you kidding? That was before your time."

They both laughed. "Gee, it's good to be with you again," Mulvehill said. "God, you're so beautiful, Jean. I'll bet you drive the swabbies crazy. And they can't even ask you for a date, you an officer and they lowly boots. Are you dating anyone?"

She nodded. "Uh huh. And I asked him to meet us here at 1:30." She looked at her wristwatch. "He should be here anytime. He's a lieutenant commander. But, better yet," she smiled at him over a wisp of smoke, "he's an orthopedic surgeon. I'd like to hear what he has to say about your leg. Maybe he can help you."

He grinned. "My, my, aren't you the calculating floozy."

She looked past him. "Here he comes now."

Mulvehill turned and followed her gaze. The man who approached was tall, maybe six foot three. He was burly, nearly bursting out of his uniform, had a ruddy complexion and a broad smile. Mulvehill rose.

"Bill," Jean said to the man, "this is my brother Charles." The two men shook hands. To Charles she said. "Officially, Charlie, it's Lieutenant Commander William Hale. He had an office here in Chicago before the war."

Hale pulled out a chair but, before plumping himself into it, he leaned over and kissed Jean. Mulvehill looked, watched his sister clutch the officer's arm as she returned his kiss, and decided that this was more than a casual date.

Jean picked up her menu and looked at it. She turned to Hale. "Bill, you're just in time for dessert." To Mulvehill she said, "Bill loves cherry pie."

Mulvehill looked at them both. "Really, that's my favorite too."

Jean threw the menu at him. "It is not, you dope. You know that your favorite was always mom's lemon meringue."

Mulvehill looked pained. "Really, I must have forgotten." The three of them laughed.

"Charlie," Jean said, "I told Bill about your wound. I'd like him to examine you."

Commander Hale shook his head. "Not really necessary."

To Mulvehill he said, "According to what your sister told me it's more than five months since they sewed you up in Italy. Right?"

"More like six months," Mulvehill responded. "Jean says you're an orthopedic surgeon."

"Best in Chicago," Hale grinned. "Except for my partner, Sam Hardy. He's ten years older than I and besides, someone had to stay with the practice while I'm in the Navy." He laughed. "We were a pretty well known team at the hospitals." He grinned. "Who could forget Hale and Hardy?"

He laughed. "Actually, it was Sam Horowitz when he was in medical school. Then he fell in love with Victoria Hardy. He decided he liked her name better than his so when they were married he just took her name." He hunched his shoulders and held out his hands, mimicking his partner. "'So where is it written that a woman has to take her husband's name? Why can't a man take his wife's name? Ha?'"

They laughed. Jean said, "He's got a point." She looked quizzically at her companion. He looked at her. They both grinned.

Mulvehill looked at him. "Your partner is a Jew?"

The Commander looked at him curiously. "Yeah, why?"

Mulvehill shook his head. "It's the damnedest thing," he said. "I don't think I've known three Jews all my life. Now, all of a sudden, I'm up to here with them." The waitress came with coffee and their pies. After she had left, Mulvehill launched into the story of his meeting with Ben Hecht, Iris Katz and Marvin Zelinsky of the American League For A Free Palestine.

Hale looked at him. "Interesting. I wonder if my partner knows anything about this. How long will you be in Chicago?"

"Not long enough to see anyone," Mulvehill told him. "I'm taking the Santa Fe Chief at six."

Jean's friend looked at him. "O.K. By the way, Charles, would you be good enough to get up and walk across the room and back."

Mulvehill rose and walked to the door and back. Hale observed him closely. When he returned and sat down, the surgeon looked at him judiciously.

"There was no sway from side to side. The limp is slight but straight forward and back. Your battlefield surgeon did a good job of sewing the tendon back together."

Jean put her hand on Hale's arm. "Bill, what would be your prognosis?"

"Professionally, I would have to say that the limp will always be there. The tendon was inevitably foreshortened by being sutured. On the other hand," Hale shrugged, "old Mother Nature is always making liars of us doctors." He leaned towards Mulvehill. "Son, it's not a bad limp. Do a lot of walking and do some stretching exercises. And hope for the best. Who knows?" He looked at his watch. "Uh, oh. Duty calls." He rose from the table. Jean took his hand and pulled him toward her. They kissed. He straightened up, put on his cap and shook hands with Mulvehill. "Nice meeting you, Charles. Have a good trip home." To Jean he said, "Tonight?" She nodded. He walked swiftly away.

Mulvehill looked at his sister. "Serious?"

She hugged herself. "I think so. What do you think?"

Mulvehill took her hands in his. "I think he's O.K. But I'd say trust your female instinct."

She laughed. "I'm wondering what it would be like to live in Chicago permanently. Charlie, you have no idea how cold it gets here in the winter."

"If it's any worse than Italy," he replied, "I'll take California."

"Gee, it'll be nice for you to be home again. You have no idea how mother worried about you. She felt badly about your being wounded but secretly, I think, she was relieved that you would be shipped home." She rose from the table. "I've really got to get back too."

He stood up and put his arms around her. "Golly, Jean, it was good to see you, even for a little while. Do you get any furloughs?"

"Oh, my, yes," she assured him. "Actually I got to go home for a week last Christmas."

He kissed her. "I'll stay here long enough to have another cup of coffee. Then I'll just wander around Chicago. It's my first time here."

"O.K.," she said. "Let me get the bill, Charlie."

He shook his head. "Uh, uh. My treat."

She kissed him again, turned and left. He watched her walk out the door noticing, meanwhile, the admiring glances of half a dozen men in the room. He smiled to himself, found himself thinking of Stacy and realized that although he had given her his home address she had failed to give him hers. He shrugged. Well, he could always write to Marvin Zelinsky and get it that way.

He drank his coffee slowly, relaxing and looking around the room. Although overhead fans circulated the air the heat of the day was beginning to penetrate. He might as well take a walk. He watched for the waitress and, when he caught her eye, beckoned. She sauntered over.

"Bring me the bill, please."

She curtsied, turned and walked away. He watched her retreating figure. Not bad, he thought, and grinned.

When she handed him the check he gave her a ten dollar bill. She returned with the change on a plate. He looked at it idly. "That's O.K.," he said.

She smiled broadly. "Why thank you sir."

He rose. "I'd like to see the Chicago River. Which way is that?"

She gave him the directions, and lowered her eyelids. "I'm off at eight," she said in a low voice.

"That's nice," he said, "but I'll be on a train on the way to California by then."

"Ooh," she said. "Lucky you." She picked up the plate and walked away.

He followed her directions and, in a few minutes, arrived at Michigan Avenue. He turned and walked toward the river. The sturdy drawbridge impressed him. He leaned over the parapet, looking down into the swirling water below. He was feeling pleasantly relaxed when he felt a tap on his shoulder. He straightened up and looked around. The man who had tapped him on the shoulder was of medium height, slightly balding and had a pencil line moustache. Then it dawned on him.

"Ben Hecht," he said, "what a nice surprise."

The other held out his hand. "Captain Mulvehill, if I remember correctly."

Mulvehill shook his hand. "I'm flattered."

Hecht shrugged. "What are you doing here in Chicago?"

Mulvehill told him. Hecht nodded. "Of course. Marvin told me you were going home to California to be discharged from the army." He turned and leaned with his back against the parapet. "What train are you taking? And when?"

When Mulvehill told him he exclaimed, "That's great. I'm taking the Chief also. Maybe we'll have a chance to talk." He fanned himself with a newspaper he was carrying. "Chicago summers haven't gotten any cooler," he laughed.

"Have you spent much time in Chicago?" Mulvehill wanted to know.

Hecht laughed. "Only the best years of my life. God, what a city. I was a newspaper reporter here." He chortled. "Sandburg called it the city of the big shoulders."

"Who is Sandburg?" Mulvehill asked.

Hecht looked at him crookedly. "Who is Sandburg? Only America's best poet."

Mulvehill looked sheepish. "Oh, you mean Carl Sandburg."

Hecht laughed and changed the subject. "Are you planning to eat dinner before you board…or on the train?"

"I don't know. I really haven't thought about it."

"Meet me at King's Restaurant at five-thirty. We'll have a drink," the older man said, "and then we can go to the station together. Do you know where it is?" Mulvehill was unsure whether Hecht was asking about the station or the restaurant. He admitted that he had never been to Chicago before.

Hecht looked at him bemused. "Ah, youth." He took a pad from his pocket, jotted down an address and gave it to Mulvehill. "Chicago. I knew this city inside out. As a reporter," he confided, "I got to know it all: saloons, mansions, alleys, courtrooms, depots, factories, hotels, police cells, the lake front." He looked at Mulvehill crookedly. "I'm on my way to see some old haunts. Then we'll meet at the restaurant." He walked across the bridge, turned a corner and was out of sight.

Mulvehill walked along Michigan Avenue until, at a corner, he saw an elevated train structure to the left. He walked in that direction. Now the streets were crowded with people, about a quarter of them sailors and soldiers. There was an electric quality to this city, he decided, as throbbing with life as New York but, somehow, friendlier. His leg began to ache. He found a restaurant that had large plate glass windows looking out on the street. Inside it turned out to be a cafeteria. Just right for his purpose, he thought. He bought a cup of coffee, found a seat near a window and sat down, looking out idly at the passing crowds.

Suddenly, he shook himself. He was startled to find that he had dozed off. He finished his coffee, left the restaurant, and found his way back to Michigan Avenue. At one corner he came to a large hotel, the Stevens, and saw that it had been taken over by the USO. A hostess approached him. "Would you like me to direct you to the Officers Club, sir?"

He shook his head. "No, if you don't mind, I just want to rest." He took a seat in a large leather club chair. In a moment he slept again. When he awoke and looked at his watch he saw that it was ten past five. He went to the rest room, washed his face and felt refreshed. He asked for directions to King's Restaurant and arrived there just at five thirty. He looked around. Hecht had not yet arrived. He went to the bar, decided that he had enough of Rob Roys, and ordered a martini, straight up.

He had savored the first sip when Hecht arrived and sat down on the next stool.

"What are you drinking?" Hecht asked.

Mulvehill told him. When the bartender arrived Hecht pointed at Mulvehill's drink. "The same."

He swung around on his stool to survey the room.

"God," Hecht mourned, "I used to know everyone in this room. And they all knew me. Now I look around at a roomful of strangers." Fitting his action to the words, he looked around. A tall, thin, stooped man with a thatch of hair white as snow approached. He stopped in front of Hecht.

"Can I be mistaken," he said in a quavering voice, "or is this Ben Hecht?"

Hecht peered at the stranger. His eyes widened. "Is it possible? Dick Finnegan?" The stranger smiled, forlornly. "How are you, Ben?"

Hecht got down from the stool. He embraced the stranger. "Finnegan. By God. Dick Finnegan." Mulvehill sipped his drink and watched the two men embrace. The older one detached himself. "My wife is waiting," he said. "She drove into town to pick me up. We live out in Aurora." He shook hands with Hecht. "I see you've become a successful screen writer. I dare say it pays better than your old job on the *Journal*." He smiled. "It was good seeing you, Ben." He walked away.

Mulvehill looked at Hecht. The other's eyes were moist. He took a handkerchief from his pocket and blew his nose. He shook his head morosely.

"That was Richard Finnegan. Assistant city editor of the old *Chicago Journal*." He shook his head. "How long ago was that?"

He shook his head again. "Finnegan had been a handsome young man with a head of hair black as coal," Hecht mused. "Now he must be in his seventies." He turned back to his drink. "It can be very painful to look back on one's lost youth. Some day you'll discover that. Do you mind if we head for the station now? I'll call a cab."

Mulvehill shrugged. "As you wish." He finished his drink and reached for his wallet. Hecht put his hand on Mulvehill's wrist. "No, no. This was once my town. I'm buying." He paid the bartender and they left. Arrived at the station Mulvehill said, "I've got to get my bag. I left it in a locker."

Hecht nodded. "Why don't we meet in the dining car? Let's go there when the first bell rings."

Mulvehill nodded. "Sure." He retrieved his bag from the rental locker and started down the platform looking for the number of the Pullman car that would match the number on his ticket. A red cap approached and Mulvehill yielded his bag, showed the red cap his ticket and followed him aboard the train. "This will be your berth, sir," the porter told him. "The lower. I'll just put your bag on the rack for now." He swung it aloft. Mulvehill reached into his pocket and found two quarters, which he handed to the red cap. The other nodded, thanked him, and left to find another passenger to serve.

Mulvehill looked around. The car was filling with passengers. Because this was a Pullman car most of the other passengers were civilians. Here and there he saw an officer from either the army, navy or marine corps. He settled into his seat and looked out the window. He was still in uniform but beginning to feel like a civilian. The travel order filed away in his bag was his last link to the military. In a few days now he would be a civilian in fact. He could take off his uniform for good. A late arriving passenger, a portly man in his middle years, took the seat opposite him. Mulvehill nodded. The other nodded back, loosened his tie and opened a magazine.

Outside he could hear the conductor call… 'Board'. A door clanged shut and the train lurched into motion. A few screeches as couplings grated against each other and then the train steadied and settled into a smooth run.

Mulvehill looked out the window as the train picked up speed. He was actually on the way home. He closed his eyes and listened to the clacking of the wheels against the rail connections. Yes, he could hear it plainly. Ca - li - for - nya; Cal - i - for - nya; Cali-fornya; CalifornyaCalifornyaCalifornya...

He sighed and began to visualize his homecoming. It had been more than a year since his last furlough before going overseas. Then the convoy to Northern Ireland, training there, and the long sea voyage to Algeria. The first terrible combat with heavy casualties at Faid Pass in North Africa, the invasion of Sicily, the landing at Salerno and the slow fighting north until the action below Cassino where he had been hit.

Now, for him, it was all over. He dozed again. He awoke to hear the dining car steward coming down the aisle, his little wooden hammer striking the musical chime and the steward's chant...'First call for dinner...'

He stretched, pulled his tie tight and stepped across the outstretched legs of the man in the seat across from his. He weaved his way down the aisle and through two cars until he arrived at the dining car. Hecht was already seated. He had put on a pair of half spectacles and was studying the menu as Mulvehill arrived. A waiter approached as Mulvehill took his seat opposite Hecht. The waiter smiled and handed Mulvehill the menu. The Negro had large white teeth and a few gold caps. "Evenin', suh. We have some fine pot roast for dinner."

"Really," Mulvehill said. "That sounds very good. I'd like mine with lots of mashed potatoes and heavy on the gravy."

The dining car waiter laughed, a hearty, booming laugh. "Yes, suh, captain." He turned to leave but Hecht detained him. The writer tapped Mulvehill's menu. "They've got cream of celery soup. I really like cream of celery soup. How about you.?"

Mulvehill laughed. "Why not?"

The waiter took both men's menus, laughed happily and left.

Hecht stretched. "Back to California. Haven't been back there in more than seven months. I never go back, as many times as I've been there, without remembering the first time." He shook his head at the memory.

"My friend Herman Mankiewicz had moved out to Hollywood. That was in 1925. I, in the meantime, was running out of money in New York when Manky sent me a telegram. He had wangled me a job at Paramount Studios." Hecht smiled benignly at the memory. He may have forgotten Mulvehill's presence. He gazed absently out the window.

He shook his head and looked at Mulvehill again. He smiled.

"Hollywood. What a town that was. It never slept. It had the look of an airplane propeller; skimpy and powerful." He smiled at Mulvehill, thinking back to a happier, more innocent time.

He looked at Mulvehill intently. "You can fall in love with a city on sight. I fell in love with Hollywood the first night I spent in it. You're from Southern

California so you know Hollywood. How do you feel about it?"

Mulvehill shook his head. "My home is a hundred and twenty miles from Hollywood. I spent one year at UCLA," he told Hecht, "and never got down to Hollywood and Vine. I suppose it sounds terribly provincial of me but Hollywood never held any attraction for me."

"Not at all," Hecht replied. "I remember what you told me about your father. A man like that would have a fine son like you. How many are there in your family?"

"We're six all told," Mulvehill said. "My oldest sister is in the WAVES. In Chicago. I had the pleasure of having lunch with her today. I have a younger brother who is sixteen and a sister who is just fourteen."

Hecht interrupted him. "How old are you, Charles?"

"Twenty-five," Mulvehill said. A thought struck him. "You know Stacy Sheridan, Mr. Hecht, because she was with you when I met her. She said she's twenty. Is that true?"

Hecht smiled. "So far as I know."

"Do you know her husband?" Mulvehill asked.

"Slightly," Hecht shrugged.

"How well do you know her?" Mulvehill asked.

Hecht looked at him. "Why do you want to know?" he grinned.

Mulvehill looked at the older man searchingly. "Did you know she planned to divorce her husband when he comes home?"

"I know she said that, Charles, but I wouldn't bet on it." Hecht looked across the table at his companion for a long moment. Then he said, "Stacy Sheridan is a very moral young woman."

The waiter interrupted their conversation by arriving with a steaming tureen of soup. He ladled portions into each of the men's plates. Hecht sniffed the aroma rising from his plate with a look of blissful anticipation. He lifted his spoon.

"*Bon appétit*, Charles."

8.

The club car was more than half full when Hecht and Mulvehill entered from the dining car. Hecht saw two chairs at the far end, near each other. "Here, Charles," he said. The older man walked swiftly forward, waiting for Mulvehill to catch up. "You're walking without your cane. The limp is not bad. What did you do with your cane?"

"I shipped it on ahead," Mulvehill replied. "And I wrote my dad the story about Malcolm Hay. I wonder if he has been able to locate him in Palestine. I don't know how the mails are operating during the war."

Hecht nodded. "You'll be home day after tomorrow and then you will know." He settled himself in the chair and waited for Mulvehill to be seated.

They faced each other and smiled. Mulvehill patted his stomach. "That meal was too good and too much." He stretched his long legs out before him. "are you going to Hollywood in connection with the League work?"

Hecht laughed. "In a manner of speaking. I'm going to Hollywood to write a screenplay. My work for the League," he smiled ruefully, "is not for pay. But

131

once this screenplay is done I'll have enough money to last me for the next six months."

Mulvehill's eyes widened. "Does writing for the movies pay that well?"

Hecht laughed. "It does if you have a good agent. Mine is the best. Leland Hayward."

"Do you know what story you will be working on?" Mulvehill asked.

Hecht shrugged. "It's called *Spellbound*. The story of a female psychiatrist, played by Ingrid Bergman, who falls in love with her patient." He laughed. "Typical Hollywood trash." He looked at Mulvehill. "When you said that Hollywood did not hold any attraction for you…you inadvertently admitted that you have good sense. And good taste." He withdrew a slender cigar from a metal case and proffered it to Mulvehill. The latter shook his head.

Hecht pulled away the cellophane, crumpled it and tossed it in a nearby ash tray. He lit the cigar and let a streamer of smoke filter through his lips.

"Hollywood," Hecht said, "is one of the bad habits of our generation. It is an industry that has lamed the American mind. And yet," he paused and waved his cigar like a wand, "it is Hollywood I can thank, possibly, for getting me finally involved in a cause that is singularly and totally Jewish.

"Hollywood, you see, Charles…is a town, an industry, an empire of toymaking invented by Jews, dominated by Jews and made to flourish by Jews…and a few embattled Irishmen." He smiled. "Oddly enough, although I know Jews aplenty in Hollywood my intimates there are mostly Gentiles; John Dekker, John Barrymore, Thomas Mitchell, Gene Fowler. Much as it was when I was a newspaper reporter."

He drew slowly on his cigar, savoring the smoke, his eyes half closed. It seemed to Mulvehill as though Hecht were, perhaps, speaking to himself.

"Many Jews…timid Jews, nervous Jews, over-sensitive Jews, are fearful of Jews becoming too prominent. They are afraid that Jewish prominence will bring on more anti-Semitism. I think this is nonsense of the most pathetic sort." His eyes opened and he looked intently at Mulvehill.

"In 1941 I had finished writing a movie, *Comrade X*, and had gone back to New York to clear my head of the fog that Hollywood seems to instill."

A train rushing by in the opposite direction drew their attention by its clamor. When the train had passed they looked out the window. Streaks of pink in the sky heralded the approach of night. Westward their train sped, chasing the setting sun.

Hecht looked at the glowing tip of his cigar.

"Surrounded by Jews in New York, my mishpoche…"

"What was that?" Mulvehill wanted to know.

"Relatives," Hecht explained. "All Jews are related you know." He smiled. "Anyway, being back in New York I suddenly became aware of Hitler's ambition to rid the world of Jews.

"The German mass murder of Jews brought my Jewishness to the surface. I had in the past, perhaps foolishly, fancied myself as having been only related to

Jews. Living in New York again and reading, in Jewish periodicals, of the murder of the Jews I suddenly became a Jew and began to look on the world with Jewish eyes." Hecht's eyes, as he said this, seemed to turn inward.

"I felt no grief or vicarious pain," Hecht said softly. "I felt only a violence to the German killers. I saw the Germans as murderers with red hands. Their fat necks and round, boneless faces became the visages of beasts. Their descent from humanity was as vivid in my eyes as if they had grown four legs and a snout.

"This was almost a year before Pearl Harbor, Charles," he reminded Mulvehill, "and we were not yet in the war. And even if we were," he sighed, "I was too old to enlist in the battle for Europe."

"But we were attacked by Japan," Mulvehill reminded him.

"True," Hecht smiled, "but at that time my attention was focused entirely on Hitler's murder of the Jews. I was too old for the army, but not too old for anger. I went through the days holding my anger like a hot stove in my arms. There seemed nothing to do with it but carry it and suffer its heat."

A door opened. People entered the car. It became full. Waiters brought drinks to the passengers. Hecht looked at them unseeingly.

"The anger I was feeling," he looked at Mulvehill, "led me to join an organization for the first time in my life. The organization was called 'Fight For Freedom'. It was headed by a handsome and eloquent fellow named Herbert Agar and was dedicated to bringing the

U.S. into the war against the Germans. My work in the organization consisted of writing war propaganda speeches and a pageant called *Fun To Be Free*, which my friend Charles MacArthur helped me write and which was staged by Billy Rose in Madison Square Garden."

Hecht continued to tell of his activities at that time and Mulvehill listened. Now, he thought, if Hecht talked long enough he would reveal what his 'Committee' hoped to have Mulvehill do for them. The white jacketed waiter approached them. "Drinks, gentlemen?"

Mulvehill looked at Hecht. "Mr. Hecht?"

"Ben," Hecht said. He shook his head. "No."

"I'll have a Rob Roy," Mulvehill said.

Hecht smiled, "Ah, yes. I remember. The night at '21'." He continued the story of his activities in New York.

"I wrote and staged shows for the Red Cross. I busied myself with War Bond Drives. I was aware," he said, "that I was doing all these things as a Jew. My new activity in behalf of democracy was inspired chiefly by my Jewish anger. In my earlier years I had not been a partisan of democracy. Its sins had seemed, to me, to be more prominent than its virtues. But now that it was the potential enemy of the German police state I became its uncarping disciple."

Hecht smiled.

"Thus," he said, "in addition to becoming a Jew that year I also became an American…and remained one."

The waiter arrived with Mulvehill's drink. Mulvehill reached into his pocket and laid a bill on the waiter's tray. The man started to reach in his pocket for change. Mulvehill shook his head. The waiter smiled and turned away. Mulvehill raised his glass to Hecht in unspoken salute. The older man nodded.

"I dreamed night and day of a German collapse," he said, "but I wanted something more than their defeat as a nation. I yearned for their ostracism from the human family. How could the Germans, by then already methodically launched on torturing and murdering millions of harmless Jews, ever be allowed to sit in the conclaves of men again? I knew, even then, that they would be allowed, that their crime against the Jews would be overlooked as if it had been an unfortunate bit of war strategy and not a befoulment of the human spirit.

"And another bitter thought was in my head. How could the Jews whose butchery was going on before an indifferent world ever be a people of dignity again?"

He drew on his cigar. Mulvehill sipped from his drink. He was silent. The thoughts Hecht was expressing made him feel uncomfortable. He himself had not known about the persecution and murder of the Jews until he had read Hecht's article in *Reader's Digest*. And now that he knew he felt embarrassed before Hecht's righteous anger. And he felt grateful that, at school, at play, or in the army, he had always been repelled by the coarse jokes and crude remarks about Jews he had heard.

"I knew," Hecht went on, "that the Germans would be beaten in battle if the U.S. joined against them, and I was certain their miserable megalomania would be knocked out of them—for another few decades. But I felt there would be no victory for Jews in this. As I walked the street a million Jewish men, women and children had been butchered, and millions more will be killed before this war is over. Yet there has been no voice of importance, Jewish or non-Jewish, protesting this foulest of history's crimes.

"A people to whom I belonged, Charles, who had produced my mother, father and all the relatives I had loved, was being turned into an exterminator's quarry, and there was no outcry against the deed. No statesmen or journalists spoke out. Art was also silent."

He looked at Mulvehill intently. "Was the Jew so despised that he could be murdered en masse without protest from onlookers, or was humanity so despicable that it could witness the German crime without moral wince?"

Hearing the outrage in Hecht's voice Mulvehill rolled the glass between his hands. Both men were silent for a long minute. Half way down the car two men and a woman, glasses in their hands, began singing songs from the movie *Meet Me in St. Louis*.

Hecht leaned forward. He put a hand on Mulvehill's knee. "I am telling you of my deepest feelings, Charles, because although I am a Jew I was unknowing and inactive myself through six long years while Hitler built up his army. I am, perhaps, overreacting now from a feeling of guilt, or shame, or remorse. But I want you to know how I became involved with those young men from Palestine. If you are going to work for us, and I hope you will, because it is clear to me that you are representative of all that is best in American youth, you will understand the true nature of the task before you."

Mulvehill sipped his drink. "I'm listening."

"All right," Hecht continued, "at that time, in 1941, the unassimilated Jews, the Yiddish Jews, were expressing their horror in the Jewish newspapers. In the synagogues the Jews were weeping and praying. In thousands of homes where Yiddish was spoken the German murderers and their deeds were cursed. But these were the locked-away Jews who had only the useless ear of other Jews, and possibly," Hecht smiled grimly, "of God."

He angrily flicked ash from his cigar.

"The Americanized Jews who ran newspapers and movie studios," Hecht ground out, "who wrote plays and novels, who were high in government and powerful in the financial, industrial and even social life of the nation were silent."

He sighed.

"Talking of these things at home in Nyack one evening, I received an unexpected gift from my wife. Rose had been conferring with Ralph Ingersoll, the editor of P.M., a feisty New York afternoon newspaper. Ingersoll agreed to take me on as a newspaper columnist, at seventy-five dollars a week. A little less than the thousand dollars a day I commanded in Hollywood," he grinned.

"I was grateful to have a forum larger than my dinner table and I went to work at once. I wrote of New York as I had once written of Chicago in that city's *Daily News*. But now only part of me was a newspaperman. I was as much Jew as reporter and I wrote often of Jews. My column reported the incredible silence of New York's Jews in this time of massacre."

Hecht rolled his cigar between thumb and forefinger. He tapped some gray ash into the stand at the side of his chair.

"I continued the column while writing movie scripts in Hollywood," he went on. "There, the movie chieftains, nearly all of whom were Jews, protested that I was on the wrong tack with my Jewish articles. They told me that Ambassador Joseph Kennedy, lately returned from beleaguered London, had spoken to fifty of Hollywood's leading Jewish movie makers in a secret meeting in one of their homes.

"He had told them sternly that they must not protest as Jews, and that they must keep their Jewish rage against the Germans out of print. Any Jewish outcries, Kennedy explained, would impede victory over the Germans. It would make the world feel that a 'Jewish war' was going on.

"As a result of Kennedy's cry for silence," Hecht went on, "all of Hollywood's top Jews went around with their grief hidden like a Jewish fox under their Gentile vests. In New York the influential Jews I met had also espoused the Kennedy hide-your-Jewish-head psychology.

"I argued," Hecht said, "that a moral outcry against the massacre, regardless of who raised it, would fill the Germans with doubts and fears. It would make them realize they were acting outside the human family. Such a single avaunt from the King of Denmark kept the Germans from murdering the Jews of that land."

"How was that?" Mulvehill wanted to know.

"When the Germans occupied Denmark," Hecht said, "they announced that they were going to 'clean' Denmark of Jews. The King of Denmark, with the German heel on his neck, could not hope to fight off the German army that had occupied his land. But he had moral courage. The Danes, he told the German occupiers, would never stand for this crime against humanity.

"As the Danish Jews had been ordered by the Germans to wear the yellow armband with the Star of David on it," Hecht explained, "King Christian put the yellow armband on his own sleeve. And asked that every loyal Dane do the same. They did. And the Jews of Denmark were thus protected from the Germans until, to ensure their safety, they were smuggled out one night, and across the sea to neutral Sweden."

"Quite a courageous act," Mulvehill said. He finished his drink and set it down.

"Yes," Hecht agreed. "So I argued with my timid Jewish friends that the sound of moral outrage over the extinction of the Jews would restore human stature to the name Jew. In the silence," Hecht said, "this stature was vanishing. We Jews in America were fast becoming the relatives of a garbage pile of Jewish dead. There would be no respect for the living Jews when there was no regret for a dead one.

"I sat down and wrote out my thoughts in a column under the heading *My Tribe Is Called Israel*. I pointed out that I was writing of Jews because that part of me which is Jewish was under a violent and apelike attack. And I wrote that my way of defending myself was to answer as a Jew. My angry critics…and there was a horde of them…were saying that they were proud to be Americans and of wearing carnations and that they were sick and tired of efforts such as mine to increase the Jew consciousness of the world."

He laughed.

"I ridiculed them. In my column I wrote…'Good Jews with carnations, it is not I who is bringing Jew consciousness back into the world. It is back on all the radios of the world,' I explained, 'and that they could not escape it by hiding behind carnations.' A few days after that column was published I got a letter signed by a man named Peter Bergson, of whom I had never heard. He asked to meet with me. Somehow," Hecht said, "there was a mysterious ferment in that letter that caused me to agree.

"We met in '21'," Hecht pointed out the window toward the vanishing East, "at the very same table where I first met you, Charles. Bergson had brought with him a tall, sunburned man in a sort of naval uniform. His name was Jeremiah Helpren. He had recently created a Hebrew Navy for the non-existing Hebrew Republic of Palestine," Hecht grinned. "The navy had consisted of a lone training ship that had run aground in the Mediterranean a few months before and been put out of service. Helpren had come to the U.S. in search of some Maecenas to buy him a new navy."

Mulvehill laughed. "Quite a crew of eccentrics you collected."

Hecht nodded. "You have no idea. Just listen…"

The waiter arrived. Mulvehill ordered another drink. Hecht still declined.

"I studied Bergson," Hecht continued. "I saw what you saw; a man in his thirties, of medium height, with a small blond moustache and an English accent.

"Bergson had praised my column rather extravagantly and told me of the fine Jewish renaissance begun by a man named Vladimir Jabotinsky, of whom I had never heard. Bergson spoke the name with such pride that I asked to meet him and was told that he had died recently in New York."

"I know," Mulvehill said.

"You do?" Hecht was surprised. "How?"

Mulvehill told him of his meeting with Major Levy and Levy's reference to 'Jabotinsky's gang'.

"Ah," Hecht said. "Jabotinsky, you see, is the key to the entire situation."

"Oh," Mulvehill said, "How?"

"Jabotinsky was, without doubt, a latter day prophet," Hecht said. "Somehow he saw what was coming and he traveled from one Jewish community of Europe to another, warning the Jews to get out."

Mulvehill nodded.

"Had the Jews listened," Hecht suggested, "and started a wholesale exodus to Palestine in the Thirties, when a Jew could still get in, there might be no need now for us to try to save the remnant of Jews still left alive in Europe. They would all be safely out of the Nazi's clutches.

"But," he shrugged, "they didn't listen and I suspect Jabotinsky died of a broken heart when he saw what was happening. His idea was to have a strong independent Hebrew army in Palestine. The British and American Jews, who are frightened half to death at the idea of Jews with guns, opposed Jabotinsky. He was called a fascist, and worse.

"Bergson and the other five Palestinian Jews now in America are all disciples of Jabotinsky," Hecht went on. "When the Haganah, Palestine's alleged Jewish army, was unwilling to get tough with the British, Bergson and his friends broke with the Haganah to join the Irgun Zvai Leumi. Except for the truce between the Irgun and England until this war is over, the Irgun is determined to drive the British out of Palestine."

The waiter arrived with Mulvehill's drink. Hecht looked up. "Well, maybe one. A man as well as a woman has a right to change his mind. Ask the bartender to mix some Scotch with Drambuie."

"Very good, sir," the waiter said.

Hecht waggled his finger at Mulvehill. "Let me buy this round."

Mulvehill nodded.

The club car crowd had begun to thin out. Mulvehill looked out the window.

"There's a beautiful full moon riding high," he said. "Gee, it's going to be good to get home."

Hecht followed the other's gaze.

"After a third round of drinks at '21' that night," he picked up the thread of his story, "and not realizing that my guests had not eaten that day, Bergson started to talk about matters in Palestine. I told him that as a Jew I had no interest in Palestine and I felt that its problems confused the issue. In my mind the issue was the cowardly silence of America's influential Jews toward the massacre of Jews going on in Europe. Both men," Hecht recalled, "smiled politely at my irritation with their Palestine talk and their sudden silence on the subject impressed me as something more than good manners. They left after asking permission to call on me at my hotel. Rose was writing movies in Hollywood and I, during her absence, was living at the Algonquin."

The waiter arrived with their drinks. Hecht paid. He and Mulvehill saluted each other and drank.

Mulvehill set his glass down. He loosened his tie and leaned back.

"I've been listening to you and something is beginning to percolate around in my head," Mulvehill said. "You made a point of underscoring the timidity and cowardice of American Jews. I know nothing about that but, if you're right, having people like Stacy and me on your team makes it easier to get your story across. Jews can hardly call us anti-Semitic if we represent a group of Jews, and they're hardly likely to call us fascists as they did Jabotinsky." He looked at Hecht.

Hecht looked back, unsmiling. He moved the swizzle stick around in his glass.

"I was a reporter for a good many years in Chicago," he finally said. "I covered a number of murder stories. One is particularly instructive."

He sipped his drink and set the glass down.

"A voluptuous young woman had slain a dentist in his office," Hecht recounted. "I arrived with the police to find the shapely slayer still kneeling over the dentist's body. She held an emptied revolver in her hand and was moaning, winningly, 'Oh, I love him. Oh, I love him so.'

"This declaration," Hecht continued, "fascinated me. I spent much time with the unhappy girl in her cell discussing the ins and outs of love and hearing from her the long tale of wrongs done her by the wicked dentist. He had refused to marry her on finding out, in a hotel room," Hecht allowed himself a smile, "that she was not a virgin. This narrow-mindedness had shocked the young woman. She asked me, tearfully, how could a man scorn someone who adored him because of some foolish and forgotten accident in her past? She allowed me to read the ardent correspondence that had passed between them, and I shed a tear beside Juliet. To the day she was sentenced to imprisonment for life, I considered this young woman a romantic figure, a poor sweet creature driven to murder by the greatness of her love.

"I was astounded," Hecht went on, "three years later to read one morning that my heroine had tried to stab to death one of the guards in her prison. My editor," Hecht now grinned, "who considered me an authority on this case, due to the reams of misinformation I had already offered our readers, ordered me to rush to the scene. The young woman remembered me gratefully. She wept again for amorous wrongs done her, this time by the prison guard. The lecherous turnkey had seduced her by words of love, unmeant. She had discovered that his affections had strayed to a newcomer, in durance for having beaten her child to death. What could she do but what she had done?" she cried.

Hecht drank.

"When I left the prison," he told Mulvehill, "it occurred to me that this young woman was a murderer—and that I had been taken in by her other talents."

Hecht looked steadily at Mulvehill.

"I am not taken in by the other talents of the Germans," he said.

"Charles, the Germans are murderers. They are still busily engaged in systematic murder of the Jews. My young friends from Palestine are trying to save any Jews they can." He shook his head. "I don't know how many Jews may still be left in Europe, if any. But if any can still be saved I'll try too. We need all the help we can get. I'm hoping you'll help too."

Hecht finished his drink. "I'm going to bed," he said. "If you are interested we can talk some more in the morning."

9.

Mulvehill was awakened by the porter calling softly through the curtains of his berth.

"Cap'n, they'll be closing the dining car in twenty minutes. If'n you want breakfus' I 'spect you better hurry."

Mulvehill opened his eyes. The drinks of the night before had left him with a slight headache. He looked out through the window. The sun was high. The mountains in the distance were mauve colored. He reached for his trousers, struggled them on in the berth, grabbed his shirt and emerged from behind the curtains. The other Pullman berths had already been made up. Passengers looked at him and smiled.

He slipped his shoes on, grabbed his kit and hurried down the aisle to the washroom. He shaved quickly, tucked his shirttail into his trousers, combed his hair and was ready for breakfast. The dining car was nearly empty. Hecht was seated at the far end. A sheaf of papers lay on the table before him.

His greeting to Mulvehill was perfunctory. He lifted the papers.

"These were waiting for me in the telegrapher's office at Albuquerque. I'm going out on the observation platform for some fresh air." He dropped the papers on the table, gave a quick nod and left.

The waiter set the menu down before him. Mulvehill waved it aside.

"Can you have the chef fix me two eggs over easy? And white toast and coffee?"

The waiter smiled. "Yessuh. We have some fine Canadian bacon this morning."

Mulvehill looked up and returned the smile. "Thank you. That would be nice."

He picked up the papers that Hecht had dropped and turned them around to look at them. The first sheet seemed to be a photocopy of a telegram. He looked at the print.

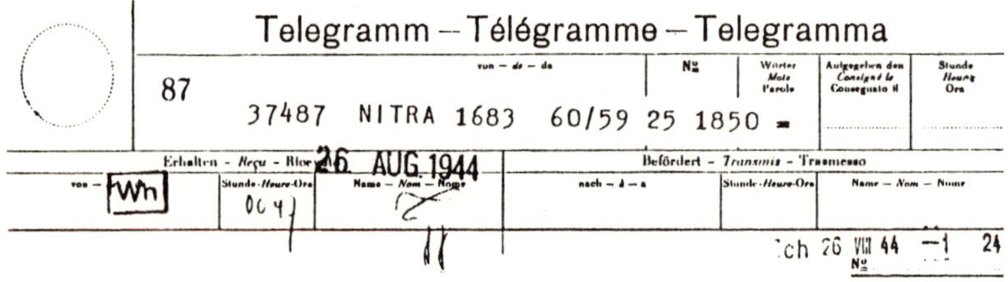

Other than he recognized the language as German it meant nothing to him. He turned the page. What followed was easier to read.

Nitra, Slovakia
June 1942

The ancient provincial town of Nitra, situated picturesquely on the spur of a mountain chain of the same name, was a citadel of faith in a double sense. On top of one of the hills surrounding the town was a thousand-year-old church that was the seat of the Catholic clergy of the city and its Episcopal See, the Theological Seminary, the library and the dormitories for the young seminarists.

But that quaint city was, at the same time, the home of an important Yeshiva of dedicated Torah learning and housed a great Jewish orthodox community. The old, venerable head of the Yeshiva, Chief Rabbi Ungar, was also the titular head of orthodox Jewry in Slovakia. His lean and ascetic appearance and the refined spiritual features of the scholar, with his white beard, was most impressive.

His was a strong personality and he was revered as a wise man. His particular domain was 'The Vatican', as this citadel of orthodoxy was humorously called. And this 'Vatican' with its expansively complex layout of buildings, set one within another, was at the same time an important bastion; a hiding place for Jews who went there into hidden bunkers in order to escape deportation. At various times there were large numbers of Jews hiding there. In moments of danger it was possible to cross from there over the border into Hungary, which was close by. For the defense group that shepherded the Jews across into Hungary the most important personality soon to emerge from the strictly orthodox milieu of 'The Vatican' was the Talmudic scholar Michael Dov Weissmandl, son-in-law of old Chief Rabbi Ungar.

With the death, from natural causes, of Chief Rabbi Ungar there was no leading personality to take over the office of the Landeskanzlei (the orthodox Central Office).

It was then that Weissmandl suddenly appeared in the capital and began to take matters into his own hands.

On meeting this man for the first time one could hardly imagine the unusual personality that was hidden beneath the exterior. He was far from handsome, his black beard was not carefully groomed, nor were his clothes neat and tidy. With his appearance, the act of moving about on the streets of the town, filled with German army troops and the notorious home-grown anti-Semitic Hlinka Guards, was by itself heroic.

Such a figure had to serve as a magnet for the brutal instincts of both German and Slovakian Jew haters—and it did. His appearance on the streets often inspired insults and even physical attacks, yet Weissmandl could not be persuaded to change his appearance or withdraw from danger.

Nothing in his appearance indicated his genuine modesty and bashfulness, his ardent soul, sharp intellect, wisdom, practical philosophy and his cheerful temperament and serenity. One would hardly guess that behind the obvious maturity of a fifty-year old lurked the heart and spirit of a very young man.

And this man, in the course of his participation in the rescue work continually going on in the capital had to enter into a circle composed of people whose outlook on life was vastly different. Still, his judicious prudence, modesty and humaneness won the hearts of all. Because of the boldness of his plans he soon came to be called 'The Partisan Rebbe'. Though he could not, because of his appearance, go to government offices and authorities he was an inexhaustible engine of energy and ideas, a 'perpetuum mobile' untiringly shuttling between meetings in the orthodox Central Office and secular groups occupied in rescue work.

He became the uncontested authority among the strictly orthodox and close collaboration with him also required dealing with other groups with which he worked. All became available to him for action whenever he beckoned—as all were dependent upon each other in situations that became steadily more desperate.

It was then the Spring of 1942. Deportation trains were rolling north from Slovakia with increasing regularity. The trains carried away parents, brothers, sisters, relatives and friends. A flourishing upright Jewish community was being transported to a fate that the people suspected was cruel and dangerous, yet the real nature of what was to come was still unknown.

Soon, messages and reports began to arrive by clandestine routes. The reports were shocking. It had been announced in advance of transportation that families would be kept together. They were told they were being sent to work camps. The messages that arrived now told a different story. After a journey lasting eight to fourteen days, upon arrival the families were separated, with men going one way and women another. Children, depending upon their ages, were sent either with the men or the women. The situation, the reports read, was indescribable.

The people were left without possessions of any kind. Not a piece of cloth, linen, watches or jewelry was left that could be bartered for bread or potatoes. What had escaped the eyes of the guards was robbed by the Nazis. The reports arriving in Nitra were read with shock and disbelief. Even though the reports came from friends and former neighbors the news was hard to believe. Something had to be done immediately.

Weissmandl and another rabbi, named Frieder, went to work. Reliable messengers, Gentiles who could travel through the countryside, had to be found. They had to be familiar with the routes into Poland and able to speak the language. The couriers selected had to establish clandestine contacts, must be able to smuggle valuables and letters across the border and bring back receipts. A vast supply of watches and other jewelry was collected and stored for future use. An active secret service was organized to maintain contact between the Jews in Slovakia and Poland.

As the work was going on, one day in November, Rabbi Weissmandl appeared in the office of the group. He was pale, his limbs trembled. The terrified group gathered there began to ply him with questions. Weissmandl simply produced a piece of crumpled paper from his pocket. A few words in a shaky hand had scrawled in pencil...'For Heaven's sake, brothers, help us. We are all about to be murdered.'

"One of our messengers has just arrived from Poland," Weissmandl sobbed. From his pockets he produced other scraps of paper. He told his companions that the messages on the scraps that had been brought to him must be brought immediately to the attention of the Chief of State or the Slovaks who were cooperating with the Germans who, he thought, could not know of the dire consequences resulting from the deportation. They must be shown to the local clergy, Weissmandl said, and a report must be dispatched to the Pope, in Rome.

Weissmandl's idea to intervene directly with the Pope was based on his assumption that Monseigneur Tiso, as President of the Slovak Republic, was also parson of his parish at Banovce, and was under the direct supervision of his superiors in the Church. If he were threatened with excommunication by Rome he would yield to the

Pope's authority. It was Tiso who had collaborated in deportation of the Jews of Slovakia. He had even agreed to pay the Germans for the cost of deportation, the sum of 5,000 Slovak Crowns per person, paid for out of the Slovak treasury.

Two letters were sent to the Pope, in Rome. One was written on stationery of the Central Office in Nitra. The second letter was a personal petition from the rabbis of Slovakia. Weissmandl composed the letter of appeal. To deliver the letters to the Pope the Central Office paid Karol Sidor, Slovakian ambassador to the Vatican, 30,000 crowns. An additional 1,000 crowns was paid to Josef Sivak, Minister of Education, to bring news back from the Vatican.

Sidor himself brought the reply from the Papal Secretariat of State, Cardinal Magliori. The letter bore the date March 14, 1942. Referring to the Jews of Slovakia, the Cardinal wrote...'The people (the Jews), some sources say approximately 80,000 while others claim 135,000, are allegedly transported to the district of Lublin, in Poland, and that mothers, husbands and children are separated from each other. The Secretariat of State hopes that these reports do not correspond to the truth, for such measures, painful for so many families, could not be executed by a State which claims to be guided by the principles of the Catholic Church. On May 8', the Brief continued, 'the Ministry of Foreign Affairs in Bratislava ordered Ambassador Sidor to inform the Holy See that the Slovak Jews will be permanently settled in the District of Lublin, and their families will remain together. Jews of the Catholic faith (sic) will, according to the assurances of the Reich, be settled elsewhere.'

Reading this dispatch, Weissmandl and his terrified companions noted that the Holy See, apparently, had no objection to the idea of Jews being deported from their ancient homeland in Slovakia to Poland, but only objected to the separation of the families after transit to Lublin.

In May, with the Slovak government busily engaged in assisting in the deportation of the final remnant of Slovakia's Jews, and knowledge of the extermination process in Poland beginning to seep out, a further communication from the Vatican was sent to the Slovak government. 'The Holy See is convinced that the Slovak government will take no steps to further deport forcibly people of the so-called Jewish race. The more painful to the Holy See', the letter continued, 'is the report that such deportations are actually taking place. This pain is increased by the reports from several sources that the Slovak government intends to carry out these deportations, regardless of women and children, and even not to exempt those who belong to the Catholic Church. The Church cannot react with indifference to decrees that will cause physical suffering and spiritual distress to so many of the faithful as a result of isolation from their Church.'

Catholic Archbishop Kmetko had his residence in Nitra. President Tiso of Slovakia had worked for several years, when he was still a simple cleric, as private secretary to the Archbishop. The late Rabbi Ungar, Weissmandl's father-in-law, had somehow been acquainted with Kmetko. Weissmandl thought that the old Prelate had no knowledge of these events and that a personal petition might produce favorable results. At the time, between Purim and Passover of 1942, Rabbi Ungar was still alive and Weissmandl prevailed upon the older man to visit with the Archbishop. This was before any knowledge of any systematic execution of the Jews had surfaced and the deportations had only just begun. It was before Weissmandl became publicly involved.

Rabbi Ungar met with the Archbishop. No evidence of any prior familiarity between the two was shown by the Archbishop. He glared at Ungar. 'This is not just a deportation of the Jews', the Archbishop stated icily. 'There you will not die of hunger and pestilence—there you will be killed—young and old, women and children, and that will be your punishment for your killing of our Saviour.'

By Autumn of 1944 the last remnant of Jews left in Slovakia, Rabbi Weissmandl among them, had been interned at the Slovakian Concentration Camp Sereth to await deportation to Poland. The rabbi decided to make an attempt to escape from the camp and to reach Bratislava, to see the Papal Nuncio. He succeeded in bribing his way out of the camp. The time seemed to him to be favorable. News had been received of the advance of Allied armies in the West and by Russian forces in the East.

Weissmandl believed the war to now be in its last stages. He had heard that warnings had been issued to the Hungarian Government by President Roosevelt and by the King of Sweden, urging that the deportation of the Jews now be halted. It was rumored that Cardinal Seredi of Hungary was also making efforts in the same direction. Perhaps now the Vatican might be persuaded to intervene. Weissmandl managed to make his way to the Nuncio's office where he told of his escape from Camp Sereth and pleaded for halting the deportation of the last 20,000 Jews still remaining in Slovakia: He told the Papal Nuncio of the intervention by Hungary's Cardinal Seredi with Regent Horthy. Seredi had threatened Horthy with excommunication if the deportations were not ended. Why could not the same result be achieved by a warning now to President Tiso of Slovakia?

"First of all," the Nuncio told Rabbi Weissmandl, "today is Sunday and on Sunday we do not deal with profane matters." The rabbi was thunderstruck. He could not believe what he was hearing. Was it possible that the Nuncio did not know about Auschwitz? "Your Eminence," Weissmandl cried, "we are all going to be slaughtered. Is the blood of thousands of innocent children a profane matter?

"I beg of you, Your Eminence," Weissmandl cried, "please take this action immediately. The Almighty will bless you for it."

The Papal Nuncio, personal representative of the Pope, stood there, his face distorted with rage, his eyes glinting with malice.

"There is no such thing as blood of innocent children," the Nuncio retorted. "All Jewish blood is guilty. You say Seredi threatened Horthy with excommunication," he ground out. "Seredi himself should be excommunicated. Who gave him the right to intervene on your behalf? And as for you I shall call the Gestapo immediately." As the Nuncio turned to the telephone Weissmandl fled, and made his way back to the camp, to his wife, his children, other members of his family and the final group of Slovakia's Jews.

The final transport was arranged, the last of the Jews, Weissmandl and his family among them, were loaded aboard the box cars. His companions urged him to try to escape from the train, make his way to the capital at Bratislava and there still try to find someone in power who might intervene and save that final remnant. They managed to force the door, Weissmandl was pushed, or jumped, from the train. No help was found in Bratislava and ultimately the rabbi was able to make his way to Switzerland. Before having been put on the train he had managed to get one last letter out to be sent to the leading Jews of Switzerland and for transmission to the Jews in the free lands.

'Brothers, children of Israel,' he wrote, 'have you all become insane? Don't you know in what hell we are living? For whom do you keep your money? Do you really want to wait until we send a special messenger to plead with you? To you all our pleas don't even seem to have the effect of a beggar standing at the door. After so much

Mulvehill put the pages down on the table, his eggs and bacon untouched. The waiter approached. "Something wrong with your breakfast, suh? Can I get you something else?"

"I lost my appetite," Mulvehill said. "Just bring me a cup of hot black coffee, if you will." He sat unseeing. When the waiter returned with the coffee Mulvehill sipped it. He sighed. Finally, he rose, and walked out to the observation platform to talk with Hecht.

The writer was standing at the railing. As Mulvehill came out the older man tossed his cigar stub onto the tracks, watching the sparks scatter.

Mulvehill stood with his back against the door, silently, until Hecht looked around. The younger man held out the sheaf of papers to Hecht.

"If there is this much hatred in the world," Mulvehill said, "do you really think you can save any Jews?"

Hecht took the papers from him. He rolled them up into a cylinder. He slapped the cylinder against his thigh.

"We have saved Jews until now," he said. "A few thousand, actually. Can we save any more? I don't know. But we'll keep trying."

They both sat down. Hecht turned in his chair to face Mulvehill. He placed a hand on the younger man's knee.

"Maybe it's unfair to try to get you to work with us. But there is a special reason why you can be of more help than any Jew we could attract to the cause."

Mulvehill smiled sadly. "Tell me what you think I can do."

Hecht tapped him on the knee, lightly. He looked thoughtful. Finally he said, "I've indicated that a large number of Jews…an overriding majority, really, are very timid, even obsequious."

Mulvehill laughed. "The few Jews I encountered in Palm Springs didn't look or sound very obsequious.

You should hear the way some of them talked to the waiters and waitresses."

Hecht smiled sourly. "I know what you mean. I see that too. But watch them when they are among Gentiles who are their peers. You'll see a different attitude."

He crossed his arms.

"Consider a dog who has been beaten habitually by his owners. You see him slink along with his tail between his legs. He might get frisky or rambunctious if he comes across another dog..."

Mulvehill laughed. "Not a very flattering picture of America's Jews."

"No, but a true one nevertheless," Hecht said, "and here is my point. Our young friends from Palestine are a different breed. They grew up where the only anti-Semitism they encountered was from Arabs and some British soldiers. That didn't faze them, although there are a large number of Jews in Palestine who bend the knee to the British Mandatory power. I'm pleased to say that Peter Bergson and his companions here do not have the Jewish ghetto mentality. They see Palestine as their country. They are proud, courageous, and steadfast in the goal..."

"I'd like to hear your version," Mulvehill interrupted.

Hecht sighed. "Well, it's a long story but I think you need to know. It will help you decide whether you want to help us." He leaned closer. "When I first met my Palestinian friends they were here with a specific objective. England was at war with Germany but

America was still technically neutral. Bergson had an idea. There were about two hundred thousand young Jews in Palestine, by their estimate, and these Jews wanted to fight against Germany. Rommel's Afrika Korps was then practically hammering at the gates to Cairo…"

"Well, what stopped them?" Mulvehill broke in. "Why didn't they just join the British Army?"

Hecht shook his head dolefully.

"I told you it was a long story. Complicated too." He sighed. "It seems that the British had what they called a 'law of parity' which means that to be even-handed to both the Arabs and the Jews in Palestine only one Jew could enlist in the British army for each Arab who enlisted. As very few Arabs were enlisting…almost no Jews could get in."

Mulvehill laughed. He slapped his knee. "Can you beat that? The British can be pretty tricky." He thought about the rabbi in Nitra. "I guess there are different forms of anti-Semitism."

"Well," Hecht went on, "you can see that my friends would want to be in a position where they might be able to twist John Bull's arm. They came to America with the idea of trying to interest some influential American Jews in supporting the idea of A Jewish Army of Palestinian and Stateless Jews." Hecht paused.

"And…?" Mulvehill prompted.

Hecht looked across the vast distances of the land the train was then passing through. He turned back to Mulvehill.

"After my first meeting with Peter Bergson," Hecht went on, "he called one day and asked if he could meet with me in my room at the Algonquin. I agreed, told him at what time he could show up, and continued with my task of the day, outlining a play I was working on. Bergson showed up at the appointed hour, with two other men and a young woman in tow.

"One of the other two men," Hecht told Mulvehill, "was Sam Merlin, a tall, dark, moody, distant-looking man with a curved pipestem clenched in his teeth…"

Mulvehill nodded. "I've met him."

"I learned later," Hecht went on, "that he was a stateless Jew, a man without family, government or passport. His home in Bessarabia had been blasted and his kin wiped out by the Germans. He had escaped being murdered and made his way to Paris to work as a journalist. There he met Jabotinsky and came to this country with him, to serve as his secretary, without understanding a word of English. By the time I met him, little more than a year later, he had acquired a fine vocabulary.

"The young woman sitting straight-backed under a large black picture hat," Hecht said, smiling at the recollection, "was a beauty from Jerusalem named Miriam Heyman. They had brought her along, I suspect," Hecht grinned, "hoping that a look at Jewish loveliness would add to my enthusiasm for the cause."

Mulvehill smiled. "I think I would have liked to see her. Your group seems to have a penchant for pretty women, if Stacy Sheridan is any example."

Hecht looked at Mulvehill. "You like Stacy?"

"Don't pass this around, Ben," Mulvehill answered. "I think I'm in love with her."

Hecht said nothing. He tapped his thigh thoughtfully with the rolled up story of the rabbi from Slovakia.

"In my room that evening," Hecht continued his story, "Bergson had told me that they wanted me to be the American leader of the great cause in which they were engaged. I had not quite understood what this cause was, beyond that it had to do with Jews and raising millions of dollars to improve their status in Palestine. Listening to him," Hecht recalled, "I felt sorry for my visitors and their cause, both. They could have selected no more unqualified and uninformed and un-Palestine-minded man in the entire land. Their choice of me made them seem naive and a little overdesperate."

Hecht paused. He looked closely at Mulvehill. The train, at that moment, shot around a curve, causing both men to sway to the side and reach for handholds to steady themselves.

"You see, Charles," Hecht leaned forward, "except for the fact that you are a Gentile and I am a Jew, I was then as much in the dark about what they were up to as you are now. Their long range objective then, as now, is to drive the British out of Palestine."

"Well I can sympathize with that," Mulvehill broke in. "I have friends back in California who are partisans for the Sinn Fein and IRA." He grinned. "Once an Irishman always an Irishman."

"All right," Hecht countered, "I am also friendly to the IRA but I wouldn't want to go around making speeches for them."

"Good Lord," Mulvehill sat back in his chair. "I hope your friends don't think I could be even remotely qualified to do that."

Hecht shrugged. "Wait until you meet those two ladies from hell in California, Ethel Longstreet and Frankie Spitz. If that is going to be their plan for you they'll write the script and train you in posture, stance, gesture and elocution."

Mulvehill laughed out loud. "I can just see myself standing in front of a Jewish audience and giving a spiel for some Jewish underground army in Palestine."

Hecht leaned forward and poked his finger into Mulvehill's chest.

"Now you've pinned the tail on the donkey," he said. "When Peter Bergson, or Sam Merlin, or Alex Hadani or one of the others do that...and every one of them has...they are called Jewish fascists...and worse. That's how alarmed most American Jews become if they think they might be accused of favoring a Jewish cause over an American one."

Mulvehill pushed his overseas cap down over one eye, leaned back, and laughed. "Boy, wouldn't that be a kick."

"Exactly," Hecht chimed in. "What would a Jewish audience call you...a fascist for favoring a Jewish homeland in Palestine for any Jew still alive who wanted to go there?"

Mulvehill grinned. "I see your point."

"Let me get back to my early adventures with these quite wonderful men," Hecht went on. "The young woman, Miriam, somehow vanished. I never saw her again.

"Their first objective," he continued, "was the one I mentioned a little while ago. If they could get Americans interested in the idea of Palestinian Jews fighting alongside the British in North Africa, but in an army under their own banner, my friends believed they would be gathering supporters for their cause after the war was won. So," Hecht said, "I agreed to join them." He shook his head and smiled.

"A cause without nickels, without cohorts, or a roof over its head, and with an army that numbered six men and…occasionally…a pretty girl." He laughed. "I found myself, nevertheless, eager to belong to it. The talk of the Palestinians had confused me somewhat. But I was pleased by their personalities. The fact that they were, possibly, Mad Hatters was less important to me than that they were Jews of gallantry and good health. They were also Jews who told neither Jewish lies nor anti-Jewish lies. Their sense of reality was as deep as their idealism. And their idealism was devoid of the communistic escape dreams that usually distinguished Jewish idealism. I found even their gloomy pronouncements invigorating, for they were made without fear.

"When I told Bergson and Merlin that I was willing to help bring an army of Stateless and Palestinian Jews into existence, Bergson nodded. 'Good,' he said quickly, 'What we must do,' he said, 'is stir up

American excitement for such a Jewish army. We will make a campaign first in the press. Then we go to Washington and get a number of senators and congressmen to make speeches in both Houses. After that we tackle the War Department. It will have to do what Congress wishes. And if the War Department acts—the British will have no choice. They must put a Jewish army into the field.'"

"Gee," Mulvehill marveled. "That sure doesn't sound like the quiet, thoughtful man I met in New York last week."

Hecht laughed.

"Bergson is a brilliant man. And he approaches major events with a sense of detachment. But he can become quite excited when thinking in terms of what he wants to accomplish. Taking on both houses of Congress seemed, to him, a wonderful idea."

"How did his plans work out?" Mulvehill asked.

Hecht looked down at his nails. He clenched and unclenched his hands.

"When Bergson first talked to me about the Jewish Army idea I thought that the British would jump at the chance to increase their army's strength in North Africa by two hundred thousand men," Hecht said at last. "I was, at first, puzzled by the odd British notion of their law of parity." He smiled. "And my Palestinian friends threw no light on the subject. At last it dawned on me."

"What dawned on you?" Mulvehill wanted to know.

"If the Irgun men were able to get a Jewish army organized under British sponsorship that would be fine while the war with Germany was going on, but what about after?"

"Well, what about after?" Mulvehill responded, "I don't get it."

Hecht smiled. "Let's say they got the Jewish army going. They would have a well-armed fighting force. A fighting force capable of fighting the Arabs. And," Hecht grinned, "maybe the British too."

Mulvehill lifted his eyebrows. "Ah."

"Ah is right," Hecht said. "That is exactly why the British were against organizing a Jewish army. It might lead to their losing Palestine to the Jews. And that's not what the British want. They prefer a docile Arab fiefdom that they control by paying off the sheiks and using fellahin as cheap labor."

Mulvehill rested his chin in his hand. "What happened?"

"Things went swimmingly at first," Hecht told him. "Congressman Andrew Somers introduced a resolution in the House calling for a Jewish army in Palestine. Senators Gillette, Thomas and Johnson approved the idea. Assistant Secretary of State Berle was also in favor. Finally Secretary of State Cordell Hull came out in behalf of a Jewish army. A bright young fellow named Adlai Stevenson, working in the Navy Department, thought it was a great idea and won over Secretary of the Navy Frank Knox."

Mulvehill broke in. "All this talk of a Jewish army but all I hear are Gentile names."

Hecht grinned. "You catch on fast. Listen.

"The first obstacle that Peter reported," Hecht continued, "was the first Jew he and his friends approached. They wrote about the idea to Supreme Court Justice Felix Frankfurter. The letter they got back read…'*It would be improper for a Supreme Court Justice to express an opinion on this issue…*'"

"Shee-it," said Mulvehill, "if you will excuse the expression."

"Shee-it, as you so eloquently express it," Hecht said, "is right. Peter thought that Frankfurter's response was rather odd. Maybe that was the way with Supreme Court judges, he thought. But he had also written to Chief Justice Harlan Stone. He didn't have long to wait. Stone's letter read…'*It's a wonderful idea. I wish your program for a Jewish army in Palestine success. Call on me whenever you are in Washington again.*'"

"I am beginning to suspect that maybe there never was a Jewish army," Mulvehill interjected.

Hecht said, "I had been in Hollywood when all this was going on. When I returned to New York my Palestinian friends told me that the idea had been killed…and by a high ranking Jewish army officer."

Mulvehill shook his head in amazement.

"I wanted to know what happened," Hecht went on. "Merlin explained. Hearing of the Jewish army idea a delegation of American Zionists, led by Rabbi Stephen Wise, had come to Washington to scotch the campaign. A Jewish congressman, Sol Bloom, had spearheaded the attack."

Hecht had wanted to know why the Zionists didn't believe in a Jewish army.

'It's not a matter of what the Zionists believe,' Merlin had told Hecht. 'They fought the project not because they are against it,' he said, 'but because they are against us. Stephen Wise will not tolerate any other Jewish organization working for Palestine and stealing honors and publicity from him.'

Mulvehill stood up. He walked to the rail and back again. He looked down at the tracks. "I'm not sure it was a good idea of yours to tell me this," he said to Hecht. "Major Levy, when I first told him of my meeting with you, said I would wind up standing on my head if I got involved with you guys."

Hecht pulled him by the hand. "Sit down, Charles."

The two men faced each other.

"During the American revolution, Charles, were all the colonists on the side of the rebels? There were warehouses in Philadelphia stocked with shoes that the owners wouldn't sell to Washington's army. More than half the American colonists were Tories. But that didn't stop a gallant Frenchman named Lafayette from coming over here to join Washington as an officer in the Colonial army." He paused, then went on. "I'm not going to try to influence you…"

The door opened and a waiter stuck his head out. "Lunch, gentlemen."

Hecht nodded. "Thank you." He turned back to Mulvehill. "One more story. Then let's go in and eat.

"I had written a pageant called *We Will Never Die*…" Hecht began.

"I heard some of it," Mulvehill said. "It's very moving."

Hecht shook his head impatiently. "Billy Rose, who was staging the pageant, had an idea. He called Governor Dewey in Albany and asked that the day of our pageant be declared an official day of mourning for the State of New York, in memory of the Jews killed by the Germans. The Governor agreed. He would issue a proclamation to the press.

"At noon the next day the Governor's secretary called up to say that Rabbi Stephen Wise had brought a delegation of twelve important Jews to Albany and obtained an audience with the Governor. At that audience," Hecht said, "the rabbi had tried to induce Dewey to cancel his 'Day of Mourning' proclamation. According to the Governor's secretary the rabbi had told Dewey that he was likely to lose most of the Jewish vote in New York City if he did not break with the *dangerous and irresponsible racketeers who are bringing terrible disgrace to our already harassed people.'* The secretary concluded that we could no longer be certain of the Governor's promised action, and hung up."

Mulvehill looked at Hecht.

"Billy Rose asked me what we should do," Hecht said. "I suggested we do nothing. It was the Governor's dilemma. I proposed we wait and see what he decides. Two days later Governor Dewey issued the proclamation declaring our pageant an official day of mourning for the State of New York, in memory of the massacred Jews of Europe.

"Our pageant," Hecht concluded, "played two performances in its one night at Madison Square Garden. Some forty thousand people squeezed in to witness it. Another twenty thousand crowded the streets outside and listened to the performances and Kurt Weill's great music piped over loud speakers."

Mulvehill punched Hecht's shoulder. "Count me in." He grinned. "I've met Bergson and I'll be proud to be one of your gang of dangerous and irresponsible racketeers."

He laughed. Both men rose and entered the dining car.

"I've got my appetite back," Mulvehill said.

10.

A little less than an hour out of Yuma the Atchison, Topeka and Santa Fe tracks make a marked turn toward the northwest from their formerly westerly route and carry the Santa Fe trains on a steady run for the next three hundred miles to their terminus in Los Angeles.

The change in direction brought the early morning sun streaming into Mulvehill's berth. He squinted, opened his eyes and looked out at the harsh terrain the train was passing. A look at his watch told him it was only just past six of that June morning. He pulled his trousers on and swung his legs out into the aisle. Good. This morning he was the first one out. All the other Pullman berth curtains were drawn. Holding his shoes in his hand he padded down the aisle to the washroom. It took him less than fifteen minutes to shave and wash.

Save for an elderly lady seated alone at one table the dining car was empty. He selected a table and sat down. The same waiter who had served him yesterday approached.

"Good mornin' suh. I do hope you feel better this morning."

"Oh, yes," Mulvehill told him, "and if there is any Canadian bacon left in the kitchen I'd like to order it again."

"Yessuh. And will it be eggs over easy?"

Mulvehill laughed. "You've got a good memory. And white toast."

The waiter made notes on a pad and left.

Mulvehill made a bridge of his hands and rested his chin on them. He knew this part of California. It wouldn't be long now before they would start passing grove after grove of orange trees. In five hours, he estimated, they would be pulling into Los Angeles. From there to Thermal was no more than three hours but he would have to find out at what hour he could get a bus that would take him down there. The thought of being back with his family after the long months of training, the troopship journeys to Northern Ireland and North Africa, the first fire fight and the slow, slogging battles up the coast of Italy were now behind him, and forever.

He could hardly visualize being a civilian again. His first thoughts were of sleeping again in his own bed in his room under the eaves of the large ranch house.

His reverie was interrupted by the arrival of the waiter. The steaming platter brought tantalizing odors to his nostrils. Everything smelled so good. He cut into the bacon. The waiter stood by watching expectantly. Mulvehill broke the eggs so that the yolk ran over the bacon. He lifted the portion on his fork and put the food into his mouth. Chewing, he put the fork down on his plate, made a circle of his thumb and forefinger and winked. The waiter smiled and went back to the kitchen.

He was half through his portion when Hecht arrived and took the chair across from him. The older man was too wise to speak of the serious matters that had carried the brunt of the conversation the past two-and-a-half days. He watched Mulvehill eat and, when the waiter arrived, Hecht gestured at Mulvehill's plate.

"I'll have the same," he told the waiter.

Mulvehill finished eating, took a draught from his coffee cup, and sat back.

"Sure beats eating out of a mess kit," he laughed.

Hecht smiled. "How long were you in the army?"

Mulvehill thought back. "Gosh, it will be just two years in a week or so. But what an eventful two years. Seems like a lifetime."

Hecht nodded. "I'll bet. How did you go in?"

Mulvehill thought back to his time at UCLA. As soon as he heard Pearl Harbor had been bombed his first impulse was to head for a recruiting station on Monday. After sleeping on it he reasoned that the war would not be over for a long time. He might just as well stay in school until June. He explained to Hecht that it was well he did so. The head of the history department advised Mulvehill to apply for Officers Candidate School. He did and was saved from the ignominy of doing KP as a lowly private.

Hecht listened. "What had you originally planned as a career before we were attacked?" he asked.

"I thought I would probably go into my dad's business," he told Hecht. I've always gotten along well with my father. I like the help we have in the packing shed. They are decent, hard working people. And I like going out and calling on growers." He grinned. "I'm sure that's what I would do now if I had not walked into The Brass Rail one night a month ago and run into Zelinsky, Sheridan and Company.

Hecht smiled but said nothing. They each finished their coffee. The older man rose.

"I'll be heading back to my compartment," he said. "I've got some writing I want to finish before we arrive in Los Angeles." He looked at his watch. "If I don't see you at the station, remember me to your folks." He smiled. "I think they have a son to be proud of."

Mulvehill accepted the compliment graciously. "Do you have any children, Ben?" he asked.

"A baby girl," Hecht answered. "She's at our home in Nyack with my wife." He turned to go, then looked back at Mulvehill. "I'll be in Los Angeles six to eight weeks. If you want to get in touch with me call Selznick International Studios. You can leave a message with David. His secretary will see that I get it." He reached out and shook the soldier's hand. "Good luck, Charles." Then he walked away.

Mulvehill paid his bill, left a handsome tip for the waiter and returned to his seat. The berth had been made up and his bag was on the overhead rack. He pulled it down, tightened the straps and put his cap on the seat beside him. He looked out the window at the soaring crest of Mt. San Jacinto. They were getting close. Another two hours, he reckoned and he would be getting off.

His fellow passenger, on the seat facing him, was holding a copy of Life Magazine.

"I'm finished with this, captain. Would you like to look at it?" He held it out to Mulvehill.

"Thank you." Mulvehill took the proffered magazine and began to idly turn the pages. He found he couldn't get interested. Thoughts of home kept intruding. He was aware of a mounting sense of excitement. He kept looking at his watch. The minutes now began to drag. He left his seat, walked to the platform between the cars and looked out at the now familiar scenery. Finally the train entered the yards and he could see the tower of the station. They swept past the arte nouveau cum Spanish building and then slowed. The brakes squealed as the last car softly banged against the retaining bumper at the end of the track. Redcaps stood near the rubber-tired baggage wagons, waiting for the passengers to alight. He went back to his seat, settled his overseas cap on his head, drew his tie tight, picked up his bag and headed back to the platform at the end of the car.

The conductor lifted the metal platform that gave access to the steps. He swung down to the cement station platform. The passengers waiting ahead of Mulvehill descended and left the train. He looked out and a shock coursed through him. A small throng awaited him; his mother, father, sister and brother and the packing shed foreman with his wife and two boys,

holding aloft wooden standards that supported a hand-lettered cloth sign:
"WELCOME HOME CAPTAIN MULVEHILL. WELL DONE. OUR HERO"

Other passengers stood patiently behind him, looking out at the welcoming committee and smiling. He descended the steps, trying to mask the limp that still slowed him down. His mother and sister rushed forward. He saw his mother's ample breasts bouncing under her cotton wash dress and looked away in embarrassment. His sister Lynn, whom the family had always called Cookie, reached him first and threw her arms around him. He hugged her briefly and then swung her aloft.

"Cookie. How big you've grown. You're quite a young lady."

She now threw her arms around his neck. He kissed her warmly and put her down. Now it was his mother's turn. She was alternately crying and laughing.

"Oh, Charles. Thank God. Thank God. You're home again. And safe."

She threw her arms around him and kissed him. He was fully a head taller and as he bent down to kiss her head he noticed a few silver strands among the honey colored hair he remembered so well. Looking across her shoulder he smiled at his father, who winked back at him but Charles thought he saw just the trace of moistness in the older man's eyes. His father held his younger son, Michael, by the hand, restraining him.

Charles hugged his mother. "It is good to be back, Mom."

She stepped away and the elder Mulvehill let go of his younger son's hand. The boy rushed forward, grabbing his older brother's hand and pumping it furiously. He looked up at his brother. "Gosh, Charles, I can't wait until I'm seventeen. I'm going to enlist in the Marine Corps. That's for me."

Mulvehill laughed, punched his brother's shoulder lightly, but said nothing.

His father approached. They shook hands. "It's good to have you back, son," he said, and there was a catch in his voice. He cleared his throat and turned away.

Now Rodriguez stepped forward to shake Charles' hand, his two sons, Enrique and Luis, respectfully following a short step behind their father. His wife, Consuelo, a further step back.

"Ay, Carlos, it is good to have you back," the old man said. "Muy bien."

"Por nada," Charles responded.

Now Consuelo stepped forward, reaching for Charles hands and kissing them. He drew the woman toward him, kissing her on both cheeks and then hugging her warmly. She was a tall woman for a Mexican, and shapely. Now she began to cry, and held his hands tightly.

"Ay, Carlos, since you went to the war your mother and I made novenas, many times, together, although she is not of our faith. And I," she cried, "each week I lit a candle before the statue of Our Lady of Guadalupe. And now you are back. I will light another candle tomorrow."

Mulvehill's father stepped forward, taking Consuelo gently by the shoulders.

"Now, now," he said, "we are all back together. Let us start for home. On the way we will stop in Pomona for lunch."

The Rodriguez boys stepped forward. Each shook Charles' hand briefly, then ran to the pick-up and jumped into the back.

The elder Mulvehill shepherded his family to the Buick. Father and son got into the front seat, his mother, sister and brother seating themselves in the back. Charles draped his arm negligently across the back of the front seat, looking back at his family fondly. His mother patted his arm. Cookie whispered to her mother, "How handsome Charles is." She leaned forward and put her hand on his shoulder.

"Charles, we have a new principal at Thermal High. Mr. Higbie. You know what? I'll bet you can't imagine. Mr. Warner, who was principal when you went there. He's a commander of a submarine. A commander of a submarine. In the Pacific. Charles, how could that skinny ole' man, why I'll bet he's maybe thirty five. How could he become a commander of a submarine? Gosh."

Charles smiled. "I don't know, Cookie. Maybe he had some skills we knew nothing about."

She tapped him on the shoulder. "And Mr. Hornsby is in the army. In Alaska. What do they do up there?"

He laughed and tousled her hair. "I'm sure I don't know, Cookie."

But she wasn't through. "And Miss Simpson, who taught civics and music, she's in the WAC.* She sent the school a picture of herself in uniform. Charles," she hesitated. "I told Mr. Higbie you were coming home. He looked up your record, how you were captain of the baseball team. He wants you to make a speech to the whole school at assembly."

Her mother rebuked her. "Lynn, dear, you really shouldn't have talked to Mr. Higbie about Charles until he was home."

"No speeches, Cookie," Mulvehill said. "That's definite." He shook his head.

His mother put her hand on his arm. She turned to Cookie. "Dear, your brother has been through a terrible ordeal. He wants to rest. I want you to respect his privacy."

Cookie was contrite. "I'm sorry mother."

Michael, behind his mother's back, made a face and stuck his tongue out at Cookie.

The day grew warmer as they drove along. All four windows were down. Mulvehill looked out at the familiar terrain. During his two years at UCLA he had driven this route dozens of times. He could trace the towns in his mind's eye. Now they were approaching Pomona, where his father would probably pull up at Stacey's Rest, known for its wonderful chicken pot pie. Then Banning. After that…Thousand Palms, Indio, and then…home.

At the restaurant he gorged himself on the pot pie and then, for dessert, Mrs. Stacey's lemon meringue

*Women's Army Corps

pie, another specialty, and one of which Mulvehill was especially fond.

The elder Mulvehill pushed himself away from the table and rose. "That was good. We've got another hundred miles to go. Let's take a bit of a stroll before we get back in the car."

Cookie and Michael ran ahead. Alberto took Consuelo by the hand. They walked sedately a few steps behind David and Eleanor Mulvehill, who walked with Charles between them. The Rodriguez boys trailed their parents.

Alberto nudged his wife. "You see, the boy has a limp just like his father. It is the work of God." He crossed himself.

The group walked silently. The day was quite warm. A thought occurred to Charles. "Dad," he said, "I sent your cane, wrapped in paper, ahead. Did it arrive okay?"

His father nodded. "And your letter. About Captain Hay. That he should be living now in Palestine. I wonder what to make of that."

"The man I met in New York said he was writing about Jews," Charles said.

His father nodded. "Ay, he was a studious man." The faint Scots burr, acquired during his time in Scotland, had never left him completely. "Even in the training camp I would often see him with a book in his hand. And minutes before the Boche attacked he was seen with a book in his hand. It was said he was writing about the Catholic Church in England."

The older man broke off and changed the subject. "How is it with the leg, Charles? Does it pain you to walk?"

Charles shook his head. "No pain now, just a bit of stiffness. I plan to drive into Los Angeles in a few days, if I can borrow the car, dad. The Veterans Administration will arrange for me to have a medical exam." He looked at his father. "I'm entitled to some disability pay."

They had reached the edge of town. The older man looked at his watch. "It's a long drive ahead of us. We'd best be getting back to the car."

Mrs. Mulvehill called ahead to her children. "Michael. Cookie. We're returning to the car. Come children."

They obediently turned around and headed back.

Beyond Riverside the road was virtually empty. The older Mulvehill increased the speed of the car to fifty. He looked in the rear view mirror. "Alberto is keeping up with us but I don't want him to push the old pick-up too hard. We've got to make these cars last through the war."

His wife sighed. "The war." She leaned forward and put her hand on her son's shoulder. "How long do you think it will last, Charles?"

Charles shrugged. "Hard to say, mom. The Germans are tough fighters. If we have to fight them all the way to Berlin I suppose it could go on for another year or more. The advantage we have is that our troops are younger, stronger, better fed and better armed." He turned to look at his mother. "And then there are the Japanese to beat. Tougher fighters, still."

His mother sighed again. "The Japanese. Charles, did you know that all the Japanese families on the West Coast have been sent away into prison camps? I think it's awful. The Sugiwaras and the Hatas and even that poor old Mr. Watanabe who had the camera store in Indio. They say that they might be spies for Japan and some of the people call them awful names." She began to cry. "They call them Nips. I think it's just awful. I know these people. They were all fine, dedicated, hardworking people. And my goodness. Some of their boys are in the U.S. Army. What a way to treat their parents."

Her husband nodded. "That's true, hon. But the government people back in Washington, they don't know these people the way we do." He shook his head. "All kinds of people get hurt in a war, Eleanor."

The day grew warmer. Charles' eyes grew heavy. He slept. In his sleep he heard the German 88s and his own 155s answering back. He saw shrapnel tear into Corporal Lane's chest. He bled to death within minutes. He was only twenty two. He heard again the one that hit him. He shuddered and awoke with a start. His mother put her hand on his shoulder. "What is it dear?"

He turned and smiled at her. "Just a bad dream, mother." He took out his handkerchief and wiped his face. He was sweating profusely. He ran his fingers over the scar behind his knee. No wonder they called it a million dollar wound. He was out of it now. Out of it forever. He let his hand swing outside the window. Even the air rushing by was hot. He wished they were home already.

His father turned and looked over at him. Mulvehill thought his father probably knew what his dream may have been like. Perhaps he, too, had such a dream after his wound. But why now? The action where he had been wounded was now seven months behind him.

As they drove through Indio Cookie pointed and called out. "Mom. There's the new Foster's Freeze. Can we stop and have one? Mom? Dad?"

Their father swung off the road and around behind the building where he could park in the shade.

"Might as well take a break. Then we'll head home."

They all got out of the car. Charles reached into his pocket. "Hey kids. I'm flush. This one's on me."

His mother smiled and put her hand on his shoulder. "My, it's good to have you back, dear."

Rodriguez, seeing them pull off the road, followed suit and parked next to them. Charles waved. "C'mon guys, it's my treat."

They lined up before the service window, each one placing his order. Michael sat down on the running board of the Buick. They others stood around, each licking the creamed confection, savoring its taste and coldness.

They all piled into the car and the pick-up and revved the engines for the short remaining run down to Thermal. Mulvehill's pulse quickened as his father turned down the dirt path to the house. On the porch, wiping her face with her apron, stood Mrs. Johnson, their housekeeper for the past dozen years, who had remained behind to prepare a huge steak dinner. Seeing Charles she ran down the steps and quickly towards him.

"Oh, Charles. How good to have you back." She embraced him. "Thank God you're safe." She began to sob.

Charles laughed and took her around. "Now, now, Mrs. Johnson. No tears, please. I think my mother cried enough for the both of you."

She wiped her tears and smiled brightly. "All right, Charles. I promise."

The Rodriguez family, who had pulled up behind them in the driveway, remained seated in the pick-up until the elder Mulvehill called out. "Alberto, Consuelo, boys, come on around to the water pump. Wash up, then we'll all go in to eat."

Seated at the head of the long table in the living room Mulvehill senior put his hands on the table. "We're all back together again. Let us offer up a prayer of thanks." They all bowed their heads, repeating together the words of The Lord's Prayer. Then they began to eat and a buzz of conversation filled the room.

After dinner all four of the Rodriguez family stepped up to thank the Mulvehills, then excused themselves and left.

Charles walked out on the porch and sat down on the railing. His father joined him, took out a pipe and pouch, slowly filled the bowl with tobacco, lit the pipe and drew on it contentedly.

"I saw the sweat stain your shirt, Charles. Was it a bad one?"

"Bad enough," he told his father. "Did you have them too?"

The elder Mulvehill shook his head. "No, maybe it was because of my medical training." He shrugged. "I don't know. Different men react in different ways. You may not have another one."

But he did.

That night the dream took a different shape. He was dancing with Stacy. They were in a room like a USO hall. Men would come up and tap him on the shoulder as they danced. He turned and saw with a shock of horror that the first one was Wieczorowski, who had been riddled by machine-gun fire at Kasserine Pass in their first engagement with the Germans. Wieczorowski vanished and others came in a procession. In quick succession they came up to him. There was Carter and then two others whose names he couldn't remember. Then Steve Perry, who had been cut down in the water at the Salerno landing.

He awoke, his heart pounding and his pajama top drenched with sweat. He left the bed, slowly padded downstairs and walked out onto the porch. The heat of the day had dissipated but it was still warm. After a few minutes on the porch he went back upstairs, took off his pajama top, washed himself and then returned to bed. He slept fitfully the rest of the night, but the dream did not return. When he awoke to a hot sun shining in through his window he picked up his wristwatch from the bedside table. It was already past nine.

He showered quickly. When he emerged from the bathroom he saw that his mother had taken his uniform from the chair where he had left it. He opened the door to his closet and studied his civilian clothes. He finally took out a pair of grey slacks and put them on. The waist fitted as well as it had two years ago when he had worn them last. From the dresser drawer he took out a blue, short-sleeved, polo shirt and drew it on over his head. It, too, fitted well. So the army hadn't had much effect on his physique.

He descended to the dining room. It was empty. He walked through the swinging door into the kitchen. Only Mrs. Johnson was there, drying a pile of dishes that were stacked on the drainboard.

He walked up and stood next to her. "Where is everyone?"

She dried her hands on her apron. "Everyone's at the packing shed. It's a work day, sleepyhead." She hugged him. "My hero. Ham and eggs?"

He grinned. "Sure." He went back into the dining room where he found the morning paper on the table. He folded it and took it back with him into the kitchen. Mrs. Johnson had set out silverware and a dish at the table in the breakfast nook near the bay window. He squeezed into the bench that was built into the wall.

The first page was filled with news of the war in the Pacific. On page three he found dispatches from the European theater. The Fifth Army had advanced far beyond Rome and was approaching Leghorn on the coast. In France Patton's Third Army was racing ahead of his oil supply.

Mrs. Johnson slid the ham and eggs down on his plate and set a tray of toast before him. He ate hungrily. He finished his coffee and went out back to the garage. His motorcycle rested on its support. It looked well cared for. He turned on the ignition and the needle flickered. He went back into the house.

"Mrs. Johnson, I'm going to drive up to the shed. Maybe I can help out."

"Your first day back? Oh, I don't think Mr. Mulvehill will stand for that, Charles. Why don't you just take it easy today?"

He shrugged. "You're probably right. Maybe I'll just wander around and look at the old places I used to haunt."

He left the house, straddled the motorcycle, turned on the ignition, stepped down hard on the pedal. The engine roared into life. He wheeled out and down the driveway. At Thermal High the doors were closed. A few boys were taking turns throwing a basketball at the hoop. He didn't recognize any of them.

At the barber shop old Bill Hoskins welcomed him effusively. He sat down in the familiar old chair and let Hoskins wrap the sheet around his neck.

"Just a trim, Mr. Hoskins," he said. The barber nodded and then began to ask about the war. Mulvehill parried the question and then closed his eyes, feigning sleep.

Afterwards he drove over to the Shell station and checked his gas tank. It was full. The attendant was someone he didn't recognize. He drove back home. Mrs. Johnson prepared a garden salad for him. He went upstairs and lay down for a nap. The dream started with frightening ferocity. This was one in which Captain Holloway, who had preceded him as company commander, had been killed by a sniper. Two of his own men spotted the sniper in a tree and shot him dead. They were battering the dead body with their rifle butts when Mulvehill came up and stopped them.

He awoke drenched in sweat. The realism of the dream was frightening. He was going to have to do something about this. Maybe he could talk it over with an army doctor in Los Angeles.

He showered, dressed and walked downstairs. The house was empty. Mrs. Johnson had probably gone shopping for dinner.

He took a long walk. When he returned he saw the Buick in the driveway. His mother and father and Michael and Lynn were back.

At dinner he said, casually, as though it were the most natural thing, "I'll be driving up to Los Angeles tomorrow for my physical at the VA. I'll be back by dinner."

They nodded.

He left early the next morning and was at the Veterans Hospital before noon. The doctor looked at the wound on his leg, nodded, and said, "Looks good."

The physician rose from his stool and was about to leave the room when Mulvehill stopped him. "I'd like to talk with you about dreams I'm having."

The doctor sat down again and listened quietly. When Mulvehill finished, the doctor, who was a major, wrote on his prescription pad and handed it to Mulvehill. "These will help you sleep more quietly. You're suffering from guilt, son. It will wear off."

"Guilt?" Mulvehill asked. "Guilt about what?"

"That you're alive and the others are dead. It's not uncommon. But the fact is," the major told him, "you did your job and you did it well. The Bronze Star citation proves that." He got up again and patted Mulvehill's shoulder. "It will wear off. Believe me. Don't fight it. Just take the pills at bedtime. You'll know when to stop."

Mulvehill rose. He thanked the doctor and left. He was back home well before dinner. There were two envelopes addressed to him leaning against the sugar bowl on the dining room table. One, in a plain white envelope, was from Peter Bergson. The other, in a light blue envelope scented with lilac, was from Stacy.

11.

Mulvehill heard Mrs. Johnson clattering dishes in the kitchen. He picked up the two envelopes and climbed the stairs to his room. He took off his shirt and went into the bathroom. He washed, combed his hair and went back to his room. He sat down on his bed, picked up the letter from Bergson and opened the envelope.

The letter was a single page. It had been typed on an old typewriter. Some of the letters typed so close to each other that they almost overlapped. A few characters were very light. The 'l' was missing.

My Dear Char es:

There is much excitement here. The news of A ied troops entering Paris eads peop e here to be ieve that the war in Europe is a most ended.

I do not think so. The Germans, a as, are redoubtab e so diers so I am afraid much severe fighting sti ies ahead.

However, Americans are so preoccupied with the war in Europe that I fear it wou d be presumptuous

With his pen Bergson had lettered in the missing
l's.

Mulvehill folded the letter carefully and tapped the
edge of the folded sheet thoughtfully against his palm.
He was sure that Bergson was right but it now changed
his plans. He had intended to meet with Ethel
Longstreet and Frankie Spitz on his next trip into Los
Angeles. It now seemed pointless. He slid the letter
back into the envelope and placed it in the drawer of
his bedside table.

He picked up the blue envelope and held it to his
nose. The scent was faint but there was no mistaking it.
That was Stacy. He felt a pleasant glow thinking of her.

Carefully he slit open the envelope and took out
three folded sheets. The letter was handwritten, in tight

scrolled letters of Palmer penmanship. He smiled and lay back on his bed, holding the pages aloft with one hand, the other hand behind his head.

> *Dear Charles,*
>
> *I have missed you frightfully but now, I am afraid, I bring you news that will trouble you as much, perhaps, as it pains me to write it.*
>
> *You know that it was my intent to divorce Michael when he returned after the war. I never worried about him as I was sure that the work he was doing as a reporter for the army newspaper Stars and Stripes was in no way hazardous. I was sure also, that as long as there were women to be found he would not hesitate to avail himself of their charms.*
>
> *Last week I received a letter from him that was remarkable in its expression of a seriousness that was out of character for the Michael I knew.*
>
> *He had followed the victorious American troops, he wrote, into Rome. Italian wine flowed freely and the Italian people seemed to welcome their release from German occupation.*
>
> *After three days of drinking, which Michael admitted to in his letter to me, he had become acquainted with a young Italian woman who claimed to have been one of the partisans of Italy who had all along opposed Mussolini's unholy alliance with Hitler.*
>
> *Some of her partisan friends had been captured by the Germans, had been tortured and then slain. Somehow, the young woman he met, whose name was Gina, had come upon a deserter from the German army. His name was Helmut Steiner and he had been an orderly to General Kesselring. Feeling certain, from*

dispatches sent to the General, and which he had surreptitiously read, that Germany was going to lose the war, he had quietly left the General's quarters as preparations were being made for the withdrawal of German troops from Rome, and had hidden himself in the back room of a local tavern.

The bartender, an anti-fascist, had brought news of the man to the partisan unit of which Gina was a member. The deserter was spirited to her house where he had been hidden until the Americans entered Rome.

Gina was the only one of her unit who spoke English. When she met Michael she had told him of the deserter and that the man had a dreadful story to tell. Michael, with his trained nose for news, wanted to meet Steiner and Gina brought Michael to her house. She served as interpreter.

The man said that a platoon of German soldiers, under orders from General Kesselring, had rounded up 335 men, women and children suspected of being Italian partisans and had marched them to the Ardeatine Caves, not far from Rome, and had there machine-gunned them all to death.

Michael wanted to know if Gina had seen the bodies. She said she had not, that the cave had been sealed. Michael persisted. This was a big story. The German agreed to lead Michael to the cave if they would get him civilian clothes and go out at night.

Michael, ever resourceful, did better than that. He obtained an army uniform for the man and a WAC uniform for Gina. The next step was to borrow a Jeep and get hold of two picks and shovels from Quartermaster Supply.

They set out at night. Arriving at the cave Michael probed the cement seal for a weak spot. He began to chip away and taking turns with the German they managed to penetrate the masonry, which had been applied in haste.

Michael entered the cave holding a flashlight. The stench of decayed flesh, he wrote, had been overpowering. He remained in the cave long enough to see the pitiful mounds of the dead. Some of the flesh of the corpses had begun to rot but he could make out corpses of children, some of whom, he felt, could be as young as five and six.

Mulvehill lay the letter down on the bed. He got up and paced back and forth in his room. The Germans, he thought, must be absolute beasts. If they would do this to Italians then the stories he had been told by Ben Hecht about the murder of Jews was all too true. What kind of people were these? He had fought the Germans as soldiers and, as soldiers, had respected them as military foes. But there was obviously a dark side to the German character that Americans had known nothing about.

He went back into the bathroom to relieve himself and to drink some water. He went back, picked up Stacy's letter again and sat down at his little table near the window.

Michael, Steiner and Gina placed crumbled masonry back in the hole they had hacked to conceal the opening and headed back for Rome. He left Steiner with Gina at her apartment and drove to the Hotel Metropole, where he hoped to find Mathews of the New York Times news bureau.

He told Mathews what he had seen at the Ardeatine Caves. The following day the two of them drove back to the cave accompanied by the Times' photographer. The story broke in the New York Times the next day but, because it had to pass the army censor, the cave first had to be visited by officers from Army G-2 and, then, the story was given to the entire news pool so that Mathews was unable to have a scoop on an exclusive basis but did, at least, rate a byline on the Times front page.

This experience, Charles, had an overpowering effect on Michael. He had many sleepless nights, he wrote me, and began having nightmares.

He wrote me a long letter of apology for his woman chasing after we were married. It must have shamed him terribly because it had to be read and passed by army censors. But, apparently, he was so moved by the experience that it changed his whole outlook on life.

Now, he wrote, he was going to ask for assignment to an infantry unit. He wanted a chance to take a crack at the Germans. And even more than that, he implored me to give him a chance to be a real husband to me if he survived the war.

How could I say no, Charles? I had been flirtatious at college and, I think, was perhaps even indiscreet enough to confess to you that I had even been promiscuous. But I am, at heart, a one-man woman. I had not hesitated to let you make love to me...I had even encouraged it...because I felt that we would not only make love to each other but that we were in love.

I apologize to you. It breaks my heart to write this letter but I believe Michael is being sincere. If he is I cannot refuse him. I am still his wife. But if I find I am wrong and he cheats on me again I promise you I will fly to your arms as quickly as transport can carry me.

Otherwise, Charles, this is goodbye.

I do love you.

Stacy

Mulvehill sat looking at the letter. He fought the urge to crumple the paper and throw it away. He got up from the bed, paced back and forth across the width of his bedroom. He picked up the letter, folded it carefully and slipped it between the pages of a book on the shelf above his bed. He looked at his watch. It was a little before five. In about half an hour the family would be back from the packing shed. He didn't want to have to sit at the table with them now.

He quickly ran down the steps and into the kitchen. Mrs. Johnson looked up from the range where she was stirring soup.

"Pea soup with ham hocks, Charles. I know you like that. Want a taste?"

He smiled at her. "Thanks. I'll pass for now. Mrs. Johnson…" He hesitated and she looked at him questioningly. He walked over and put his arm around her shoulder.

"I'm feeling restless. Tell Mom and Dad that I decided to ride my motor bike down to the Salton Sea. I always feel calm there."

She looked up at him, put the ladle back in the pot. "Are you all right, Charles?"

He smiled at her. "Of course. But it's not easy to get back into the routine of civilian life after the army. Understand?"

She took his hand. "I understand dear. I'll tell your folks."

He patted her hand, withdrew his and left the house.

In the garage he checked the tire pressure on the wheels of the motorcycle. He pushed down hard on the pedal and the motor roared to life. He mounted, gave the bike full throttle and roared out to the highway. He headed south. In less than twenty minutes he passed through the tiny town of Mecca and shortly was skirting the western shore of the Salton Sea. Formed in 1905 when the waters of the Colorado River had broken through the wall of an irrigation canal it flooded an area of more than four hundred square miles. It had become a refuge for the few people who were attracted by its loneliness. The lower part descended to a depth of nearly three hundred feet below sea level.

He passed an occasional tarpaper shack and here and there a house trailer that had pulled up close to the shore. When he came to a small knoll bordering the sea he pulled up the bike and cut the motor. The placid waters of the inland sea were empty of life. He found a lone yucca tree and sat down in the sparse shade it afforded. It was hot. He took off his shirt, pulled his knees up, folded his arms across his knees and rested his head on his forearms.

Normally not given to introspection his thoughts turned back to his brief affair with Stacy. What had he really expected of her? She had said she planned to divorce her husband when he came back from overseas. Had he, Mulvehill asked himself, thought Stacy and he would then be married? He realized that he had not thought that far ahead. He enjoyed her company and sexual intercourse with her had been exciting and fulfilling. But, he supposed, his was a healthy male sexual appetite. When the few opportunities to have sex with women had presented themselves he had been prone to take advantage of them. Yet, in the main, when he was not with women he was not bothered by any overwhelming urges.

Now he sat on the sand, thinking. He had thought, when his discharge papers came through, that he would return home, spend a week or two with the family and then head back to New York. The idea of working with the Palestinians' committee had seemed worthwhile and challenging, largely because he had no clear concept of what would be entailed.

Now, with the arrival of both Stacy's and Bergson's letters, the entire picture had changed, and abruptly. Now he had to think about what he was going to do. He knew that he could work with his father and the Rodriguez boys in the packing shed but the prospect, now that he thought about it, did not seem particularly appealing.

What then?

He knew he had better get busy with something. He was deeply pained by the knowledge that the pleasant times he had with Stacy were ended. But he was not prone to brood. He felt sure that America's armed might, which grew month by month, would ultimately overwhelm both the German and the Japanese armies. How long? Who could tell? Three months, six months, a year?

He had been a student at UCLA when the Japanese had bombed Pearl Harbor. The start of the Fall semester now lay only six weeks in the future. He was pretty sure he didn't want to live at home now. Hopefully the war would be ended before Michael was old enough to enlist in the Marine Corps.

He lifted his head and looked out across the water. He was twenty-five so, if he went back to school, he would be considerably older than most of the other students but, he felt, that need not be a problem. And life in Los Angeles would be far more diverting than life in Thermal. Or even Indio.

Yes, that was probably the best course to follow. He stood up, put his shirt back on and mounted the motorcycle. He headed north, toward Thermal and home.

Book Two

Guam. Thursday, August 9, 1945 (U.P.) The second mighty new atomic bomb to rock Japan fell on the teeming city of Nagasaki today and first reports indicated that the attack was as successful as the explosion that had devastated Hiroshima three days earlier.

12.

He was working the trading desk when the news came clacking across the Reuters wire. Gainsley, who was standing at the printer, saw it first and ripped the sheet out. He tossed it on the desk in front of Mulvehill, who read it even as he was taking an order for 200 shares of Western Travelers Life, and passed it along to Feinstein, at the trading slot immediately to his left.

Feinstein read it aloud. "Hot damn," he chortled, "now I won't have to go."

The news spread swiftly among the eight men on the trading desk and then was passed down to the retail department, where some one had already heard it by phone.

The trading desk paused for a moment at the stunning import of the news, and then went back to the frenzied activity of receiving and jotting down buy and sell orders.

Feinstein, between calls, poked Mulvehill in the ribs with a pencil.

"You know what this is going to do to the market?" he asked, and then answered his own question. "It's going to go crazy, wacky, cocksucking mad. Shit, we'll need ten more traders to handle the business."

It was Friday noon in Los Angeles, but Thursday in Guam, where the B-29 carrying the atom bomb had lifted off the runway to carry its lethal cargo to the Japanese homeland. Mulvehill figured that the war with Japan, following these two devastating blows to the home islands, was sure to be over within a week. When the market closed today, he decided, he would head home for the weekend. He wanted to be with his family at this climactic moment in history.

For the next hour he had to sit at his post, taking the orders that were coming in by phone with increasing speed and intensity. Stock market investors were buoyed by the news of the impending defeat of the hated Japanese, and now, with the defeat of Germany three months behind them and the end of the war in the Pacific imminent, investors were gleefully thinking of twelve million men and women shedding army khaki and navy blue to spend the savings of four long years buying the new clothing, automobiles, refrigerators, dishwashers and homes that would soon go into production.

At four o'clock in New York the closing market bell rang on Wall Street. In Los Angeles it was one o'clock. Mulvehill wrote his tickets for the last few orders to come in as the market closed and sat back, drained.

It had been a hectic, but exciting and rewarding summer. His classmate in English Lit, Bud Green, had an uncle who ran the trading desk for Mitchum, Jones & Templeton. If Mulvehill was willing to take the basic stockbroker exam, Bud assured him, they could both spend the summer on the trading desk at MJT and make enough money to see them each through the next year at UCLA.

He and Green had both taken the exam, which was simple and, true to Bud's prediction, they were both hired for the summer.

The work was arduous, the pace frenetic, but both acted as a stimulant for Mulvehill. After two school semesters that he found not at all demanding the change was electrifying. Going back to UCLA had seemed preferable to working the packing shed, which he felt sure would be stultifying after combat, but he knew he was only marking time. A major in English Literature was interesting but, he knew, it would not lead to any kind of future unless he decided to go forward to a teaching credential. That, too, held no charm for him. It would mean that, as he grew older, he would be dealing with students who would seem to him to be younger and younger.

The proof of that hypothesis was apparent in his classes at UCLA. The boys, all of them high school students when he was already in the army, were callow. The girls even more so. The opportunities for dates were manifold but, and he smiled at the thought, he might just as well be dating Cookie.

A few weeks before the June semester came to an end he had carried his tray of food to an empty table in the cafeteria. He was eating his meat loaf and mashed potatoes when he became aware of someone standing at his table. He looked up. The woman had blazing red hair. She was buxom, and surely not a student, too old for that.

She looked down at him quizzically. "Mulvehill?"

He looked at her. Did he know her? Had she been a teacher of his before the war? He looked at her more closely. Suddenly it came to him. The red hair had fooled him. She had died her hair, which he remembered as blonde.

"Miss Holm?" He rose from his seat.

She smiled. "Formerly. It's Mrs. Scarlatti now." She nodded at the vacant seat next to him. "May I?"

"Of course." He took his books off the seat and she sat down.

He sat down.

"Please," she said, "don't let me interrupt your lunch."

He wanted to know if she had eaten. "Yes." Could he bring her a cup of coffee? "Later. After you've finished your lunch."

As he was about to pick up his fork she placed her hand over his.

"It's Charles. Right?"

He nodded. "It's nice of you to remember."

She laughed. He remembered the throaty laugh. "Dear Charles. Do you think I would forget?"

He blushed and she laughed again.

He ate hurriedly now and, to cover his embarrassment, he said, "Does Mr. Scarlatti also teach math?"

"He did," she said. "He was at USC. We were married in 1942. A few months later he was in the army. And a few months later, dead. At Bougainville."

He looked at her mournfully. "I'm sorry."

She nodded. "It happens. It happened to a lot of good men." She took out a cigarette. "Do you mind?" He shook his head.

"Did you get involved in the war, Charles?" she wanted to know. "You couldn't possibly have been going to school all this time."

He answered between forkfuls of meat loaf. "I was in the army."

"Aha." She drew on her cigarette. "When did you get out?"

He briefly told her of his wartime service, the wound, and his return to the States.

She looked at him steadily.

"I'm a mother now, Charles. I've been on maternity leave."

He nodded. "I guess your baby is about three years old now."

She shook her head. "No. It's a little girl. Just four months old."

He was confused. "You said your husband was killed at Bougainville. But that campaign was the Fall of 1942. I don't understand."

She leaned closer. "Think, Charles."

He caught on "Oh."

She laughed. "Oh, indeed." She tapped out her cigarette. "The baby's father has a rich father. All of my expenses have been paid in full and Junior was sent back East to Princeton." She changed the subject. "My mother-in-law has forgiven me. She baby sits while I'm in school. But I'm home alone at night. I learned how to make lasagna. Do you like lasagna, Charles?"

Mulvehill was relatively innocent but he wasn't dense. His sexual experience with his one-time math teacher had been quite ecstatic. But he had been much younger then.

She swiftly wrote an address on a business card and pushed it toward him. She squeezed his hand, stood up and left, but not before saying, "Anytime after seven, Charles." Then she was gone.

He sat looking after her, then slowly continued to eat his lunch.

It was more than an hour later, during the class in European History of the Middle Ages, that he began to drowse and, drowsing, found himself reliving his previous sexual experience with Miss Holm, whom he remembered as Magda, and who was now Mrs. Scarlatti. In the course of his recollection he began to feel a crawling sensation in his loins and shook himself awake.

He now had to think, logically, about whether he ought accept her invitation. He debated the subject pro and con. He had already begun to doubt the wisdom of returning to school for the Fall semester. If he did not return to school there was little danger of any serious involvement. She had made it abundantly clear that her invitation was amorous. She was surely at least ten or more years older than he. He'd had a few dates with girls he met at school but, in every case, the interest on his part was tepid. He compared them to Stacy Sheridan and, frankly, there was no comparison. Mrs. Scarlatti seemed to be offering an opportunity for untrammeled sex. He felt her card in his pocket. He knew now he would call her. But not tonight. He didn't want to appear too eager.

He called her the following Tuesday. Was she doing anything tonight? No. Could he come over? Of course. He had her address, didn't he? Yes. Well, then, could he come over after eight? She would be through with the baby's dinner.

When he rang the bell she came to the door in a wrapper. She held out her hand and seemed genuinely pleased to see him.

"Come in, Charles. I'm just doing the dishes. Make yourself comfortable."

He followed her back to the kitchen and sat down in the breakfast nook. It looked just like the one at home, the same built-in benches, the window looking out to the garden in front of the house. But the hanging lamp overhead here was different, a modern copper shade rather than the Tiffany at home.

Magda went over to the sink and put on rubber gloves. As she washed one dish after another he watched her. The folds of the wrapper hung against her backside. The material was opaque enough that he couldn't see through but he could not make out any lines to indicate that she was wearing panties. The wrapper also lay flat against her back. He was sure now that she was wearing nothing underneath. It certainly seemed clear that she was ready for him.

He became aware that he was breathing hard. He took a deep breath. Easy, Charles, he cautioned himself. Don't behave like a horny schoolboy. And laughed silently to himself. He was a schoolboy and, sitting there and watching her, he certainly was horny. He took a deep breath.

Magda turned off the water and drew off the gloves. She turned to face him.

"Would you like to see Lisa?" she asked.

He stood up. "Sure."

He followed her into the baby's bedroom. They approached the crib. The little girl lay there, on her back, playing with a plastic ball that hung suspended over the crib. Magda picked the baby up and kissed her. She held her out to Mulvehill. "Would you like to hold her?"

Mulvehill demurred. "She looks so little I'm afraid I might hurt her."

Magda laughed. "All right." She put the little girl back in the crib and leaned over to kiss her. She covered her with a pink blanket and turned on the night light, which was a translucent clown.

Mulvehill followed Magda out of the child's bedroom, but instead of going into the living room she led him into her own room. In the half light that came through the door to the child's bedroom Magda stood near her own bed. She dropped the wrapper from her shoulders. He had been right. Underneath she was nude. In street clothes she had appeared buxom. Nude, she was voluptuous. Strange, Mulvehill thought, he couldn't remember from his previous affair with her, more than two years earlier, that he had then seen her nude. But that was silly. He must have.

She held out her arms. "Come here, Charles."

Later, he awoke. The radium dial on his wristwatch told him it was one-thirty. Beside him, Magda stirred and stretched. "Honey," she murmured, "Mother Scarlatti will be here at seven. Be sure you're gone by then."

He sat up. "I'll go now."

"All right," she murmured softly, turned over and was asleep.

At school, she passed him in the hall and, stopping for a moment, whispered, "I'm a creature of habit, Charles. Next Tuesday O.K?" He nodded, and each continued down the hall in a different direction.

It became a steady Tuesday night liaison. But the next time they awoke in the night Magda said, "I don't like to see you getting up in the middle of the night to get dressed and go home. If I set the alarm for six would that be too early? Mother Scarlatti gets here at seven."

For Mulvehill that arrangement was better. Waking up early had never been a problem for him. He was young and virile. Magda was avid. Now it became a pattern to have a quickie in the morning before he had to get dressed and leave.

With the end of the semester the pattern changed. With no school for either of them it was no longer necessary for Magda's mother-in-law to be there every morning. When she arrived unexpectedly one evening to find Charles there Magda introduced him as a math student who had come over for instruction regarding a problem. But in the summer? All three saw the excuse as preposterous, but the old woman gave no indication of what she might be thinking.

Mulvehill knew a pang of sorrow. The old woman had lost a son to the war. It should have been her son there. There was much sorrow in the world. Suddenly Mulvehill thought back to the dossier Hecht had handed him in the railway car. He wondered if the writer might be in Hollywood, but he couldn't remember the name of the producer Hecht had suggested he call if he wanted to get in touch with him. No further letters had come from either Stacy or Bergson.

When Mulvehill began to work at Mitchum, Jones & Templeton's trading desk he was through by one in the afternoon, when the market closed. He began to go to the gym at the Hollywood "Y" for a workout three times a week. But Japan's surrender was announced on a Tuesday. That was not his day for a workout. Mulvehill threaded his way through the jubilant crowds that thronged the streets. He walked through Pershing Square, which was jammed with celebrating men and women. The least he could do was have a drink in honor of the hundreds of thousands of American soldiers, sailors and marines who had not lived to see this day. He made his way to the Redwood Lounge next to the Times building. Oddly enough it was virtually empty. All the celebrating seemed to be going on outdoors. He ordered scotch with a water chaser.

He continued to drink slowly, pacing himself not to get drunk. It seemed important to him to remember the names of all the dead from his outfit. Slowly he began to recite the litany. Wieczorowski was the first. Then it was Carter...and after that...was it Stowe or Goldstein? He couldn't remember. But the one he remembered most clearly was Holloway, dying in the Italian mud as the rain kept beating at them. He ordered another drink. Shit. Goddam. He began to pound on the bar. The bartender watched him curiously but said nothing. Finally Mulvehill arose, somewhat unsteadily, and carefully scooped up the change from the bar. Then he dropped it back and said to the bartender, "Sorry, Mac." The other nodded and then asked solicitously, "You O.K?" Mulvehill nodded and walked out into the street.

He didn't want to be alone any longer. He headed for Magda's place. It was after six when he got there. Magda was standing at the window, looking out.

"Oh, Charles, it's finally over." She threw her arms around him and began to weep. "I never really got to know Frank really well. We hadn't been married very long..." she sobbed. "Now he's lying in the earth on that South Pacific island. It's not fair." She turned and pointed.

"Look."

Mother Scarlatti was lying sprawled in the easy chair. An empty bottle of wine lay sidewise on the table.

"She cried herself to sleep," Magda said. "Poor dear."

Hearing voices the old woman opened her eyes.

Mulvehill stood over her. "Can I take you home, Mrs. Scarlatti?"

The old woman nodded. "Thank you." Mulvehill helped her up and walked her out to Magda's car. He drove her home and then returned to Magda's house. The baby was sitting up on the floor. "She's precocious," Magda said. "Only five months. Bet you she walks before she's a year old." She sat the baby in her high chair, warmed some soft cereal and fed her.

When Lisa was finally asleep, they undressed and went to bed. That night their lovemaking was ferocious. They awoke later to hear Lisa crying. As Magda sat up Mulvehill pulled her back. "I'll go."

He lifted the child out of her crib and walked back and forth with her until she fell asleep. He lay her down gently and covered her with the summer blanket. The heat of the day had dissipated and it was now pleasantly cool. In the kitchen he poured a tall glass of water. He went back into the living room and turned on the reading lamp. He ran his fingers over the bindings of the books on Magda's shelves.

His finger stopped at a book with orange backing. At the top of the spine it read 'Ben Hecht'. The title was *A Guide For the Bedevilled*. He drew the book down from the shelf, sat down in the rocking chair under the reading lamp and opened the book.

When the first light of dawn came in through the windows Magda awoke. Finding him missing from her bed she sat up, pulled her wrapper around her and walked into the living room.

Mulvehill was sitting in the rocking chair, still reading.

13.

When Magda entered the room Charles closed the book, inserting his finger between the pages to mark the place where he had stopped reading. She came close and looked down at the book. "What are you reading to keep you up all night?"

He held up the book with the binding facing her so she could read the title.

"Oh that," she snorted. "Does that interest you?"

"Very much," he said, "but what is it doing on your bookshelf?"

She made a dismissal motion with her hands but Charles was insistent.

"It was a guy I dated for awhile," she said when he persisted. "Dr. Brown, in Anthropology."

"Herman Brown?" he wanted to know.

"Yes," Magda said. "Do you know him?"

He shook his head. "No, but I heard he's a good teacher."

Magda laughed. "He may be a good teacher, but a lousy learner."

"What does that mean?" Mulvehill asked.

She shook her head and took the book away from him. "Are you going in to work today?"

"Of course," Charles replied. "What time is it?"

"It's five thirty." She ran her free hand between his legs. "Lisa's fast asleep. We've got time for nooky if you're game."

"I'm not only game, but gamy." He laughed. "Are you going to tell me what Dr. Brown has got to do with Hecht's book being here?"

"In the shower," she agreed. "But first to bed. Are you coming or do I have to drag you in?" She lunged between his legs but he was quick as a cat. He lifted her up and carried her into the bedroom. She squealed with pleasure.

Afterward they showered together. While she lathered his back she told him that she had dated Dr. Brown for a few months, but it had come to nothing. He was serious, hinted at marriage, and brought her Hecht's book on anti-Semitism. She read a few pages and then, bored, set it aside. Magda had a healthy sexual appetite and the energy to indulge it. Brown was lackadaisical. After several only partially satisfying episodes she bid him goodby.

Mulvehill and Magda both turned and he lathered her back. "I need someone like you, Charles. You know how to ring my bell."

He turned her around and kissed the nipples of her breasts. He straightened up and lifted her chin with his forefinger. "God, I love being with you but where is this going to lead? I'm twenty-six Magda and you're..."

"Forty-four. Shit, I don't know, Charles. I just know that I love being with you. I just love to screw. Is that so wrong?"

He turned off the shower and they stepped out. He began to dry her with a large thirsty towel.

"Right or wrong is really academic, sweet. I like it too. But there's really more to life than sex."

She kissed him. "Not when I'm with you baby."

"All right. But I have a hunch my life is going to move in a different direction than yours."

She looked into his eyes, searchingly. Her eyes were a deep violet. "What do you mean, hon?"

They dressed and went into the kitchen. As she poured coffee for him he asked, "Have you seen *Gone With the Wind*?"

She looked at him, puzzled. "Of course. What woman hasn't? But what has that got to do with what we're talking about?"

Instead of answering he asked another question.

"What was the name of the man who produced the movie? I used to know but now I can't remember."

She shook her head in puzzlement and then answered.

"David O. Selznick. What about it?"

He drank from his coffee cup while she buttered his toast.

"I was reading Ben Hecht's book because I met him in New York. He's a Jew. Did you know that?"

She shrugged. "So what? So is Herman Brown. What has that got to do with anything?"

Mulvehill grew pensive. "Hecht and I came out to California on the train together," he said. "He and some men from Palestine he was working with wanted me to help them raise money to rescue European Jews who were trying to escape from Hitler."

She shook her head impatiently. "That was a terrible episode. I've had lots of Jewish kids in my classes. Most of them are pretty bright. Some are obnoxious. But I have a simple philosophy, sweetheart. Live and let live."

She puffed on her cigarette. "You're confusing me. Let's get back to *Gone With the Wind*. Why did you ask me about that?"

He laughed.

"When Hecht and I parted on the train when we got here he told me that if I ever wanted to get in touch with him I could call the Selznick studio. Now I want to get in touch with him but I couldn't remember Selznick's name. That's all." He stood up and kissed her. "You reminded me. I'll call Selznick later. But now," he looked down at his watch, "I've got to get to work."

She stood up and clutched him. "You're not going to walk out on me for some Jews, are you, hon?" She began to sniffle.

"I'm not going to walk out on you, Mag, but there are some things I've got to do. We'll talk about it later."

She followed him to the door and essayed a smile.

"Dammit. I don't know if I love you…or love it."

He took her hand. "How about some of both?" He kissed her.

The streets were again crowded with people celebrating the war's end. He got to the office fifteen minutes before the market opened. Three of the traders failed to show but trading was light. About ten o'clock he took a break. He went out to the reception desk and leafed through the phone book. When he got to Selznick International Studios he carried the directory over to the guest phone and dialed the number. When he told the woman at the switchboard that he wanted to leave a message for Ben Hecht she put him through to Selznick's secretary.

"Good morning. Mr. Selznick's office."

"Hi. My name is Charles Mulvehill," he said. "I'm not calling for Mr. Selznick. I just want to leave a message for Ben Hecht."

She laughed. "Hi, my name is Barbara. So you're the mysterious Mr. Mulvehill. I've had a note pinned up here for more than a year. If you called I was to be sure and get your phone number. Oh, hell," she interrupted herself, "I've got to take another call but promise you won't go away."

"I promise," he told her.

In moments she was back on the line. "Mr. Hecht is not in town but we expect him in a few days. Where can he reach you?"

He gave her the number at the trading desk and at Magda's house, where he was now practically a boarder. Even Mother Scarlatti had come to accept him as a fixture. And she was careful to knock loudly before entering the house. Mulvehill had come to believe that, as much as she grieved for her lost son, she had a genuine affection for Magda and was happy to see that the younger woman was not lonely.

Hecht's call came the following Tuesday.

"Charles, what a nice surprise. When can we get together?" Hecht asked.

"The market closes at one, our time. Anytime after that," Mulvehill told him.

"Good," Hecht said. "How about tomorrow? Can you meet me at Hernando's Hideaway in the Beverly Wilshire at two? I'll have lunch sent in."

When the trading desk closed the following day Mulvehill walked over to Wilshire and waited for the bus. He was at the hotel at ten to two. Hecht was seated in a booth. When he saw Mulvehill he stood up and walked over.

"Charles." He grasped him by the hand. "How really good to see you again. I've ordered breast of turkey sandwiches sent in from the kitchen. Is that all right?"

Mulvehill shrugged. "Sure. Why not?"

They looked at each other.

"It's a different world than the last time we talked," Hecht said. "According to what I hear from my friends," he shook his head sorrowfully, "about six million European Jews were done in by the Germans before we finally beat them. I don't know how much of a victory that is." He grimaced.

"Well," Mulvehill countered, "at least we rid the world of Naziism."

Hecht shook his head. "I'm not so sure that's a real victory. The only thing I liked about the Germans, as a matter of fact, was their Nazi government."

Mulvehill looked at the writer incredulously. He finished chewing his first bite of the sandwich.

"What?"

Hecht grinned sardonically.

"Under the Nazi regime," he said, "we were informed that men were not free to think and act honestly and all their social maneuvers were dependent on the whims of a dictatorship." Hecht grinned. "I don't understand what is wrong with that sort of government—for Germans."

Mulvehill picked up his sandwich.

"I think that calls for some explanation."

Hecht smiled.

"All right. You eat. I'm not hungry." He leaned forward. "Let me tell you why I prefer the Nazi regime—for Germans. It makes the German obvious, easy to understand, and infinitely less of a menace than when he is posing as a zither player in a Tyrolean hat. Now that we've beaten the Germans I see our war against them as similar to throwing stones at a man's hat and taking care not to hit him. Now that we have knocked his hat off he will only put another one on. I," Hecht went on, "prefer him in his true native topper. It is not a pretty hat, the Nazi bonnet, but it is a German one, and when he wears it, the German is a true German, and we are safe from his wiles."

Mulvehill put his sandwich down.

"I can understand your saying that now," he interjected. "You wouldn't have said it when the Jews were still alive—in Germany. Would you?"

Hecht smiled bitterly.

"Of course. You're right, Charles. But please indulge me while I relish my bitter ex post facto rumination.

"Looking back across the horror of the last six years, and now that there are no Jews left in Germany, I consider the Nazi government as not only suitable for Germans, but ideal from the point of view of the rest of the world as a German government."

He sighed, beckoned the waiter to bring him another cup of coffee, and continued.

"It should be left to them, now that we have defeated them, as a gift from Tantalus."

Mulvehill wiped his mouth.

"Who?"

Hecht smiled.

"Tantalus. You remember your Greek mythology. The king of Sipylus, son of Zeus and the father of Pelops and Niobe. Tantalus was admitted to Olympus by Zeus, but abused the friendship of the gods by a crime variously reported as serving the flesh of his son Pelops to the gods at a banquet; stealing the nectar and ambrosia of the gods; divulging their secrets; or denying knowledge of a golden dog stolen from the shrine of Zeus. His punishment in the underworld became proverbial. He was afflicted with an insatiable hunger and thirst, and had to stand up to his chin in a lake, the waters of which receded whenever he tried to drink of them; over his head hung clusters of fruit which eluded his grasp whenever he tried to reach them."

Mulvehill grinned. "Oh yeah. I forgot. You're pretty hard on a defeated people." Hecht smiled grimly.

"The story of Tantalus is where we get the word 'tantalize'. You think that's worse than what the Germans did to the people they conquered, brutalized and murdered? And I'm not just talking about the Jews."

Hecht drank from his coffee cup. Mulvehill ate his sandwich and thought of the peace that had come to the world following the defeat of Germany and Japan.

He was brought out of his reverie by Hecht's voice.

"Let's not punish the Germans. They should be allowed to remain Germans in the open, with a good spiked fence around them such as is used in rendering a zoo harmless. Within this Nazi zoo," he smiled, "maintained by the world for the diversion of philosophers, the Germans could then listen to Beethoven and dream of murder—and inconvenience no one. When their claws had grown too long and too sharp we could send in manicurists."

Mulvehill smiled, continued to eat and said nothing.

"Now that the war is over," Hecht said, "I offer this plan as the only one that can satisfy all sides—Germans, policemen and humanitarians.

"I prophesy," Hecht went on, "that the Germans, now that they have tasted the wonders of pure dictatorship, will never be content with less. They will pretend—but they will plot and suffer—until they can be Nazis again. The name does not matter, nor the name of their leader. The important thing is the surrender of human rights and the existence of diversion. The Nazi government provided them with both. It is a very stimulating system. The Germans," Hecht said, with what Mulvehill thought was just the trace of a pontificating manner, "are a torpid people, and need much to stimulate them into any kind of activity.

"As individuals," he continued, "there is no hope for them. They would all sit around and become cases of obesity and melancholia, and their professors—whom Nietzche called Germany's national disease—would end up strangling the thought of the world. The Germans need Naziism just as the man who, having no natural potency, needs high-powered drugs. The Fuehrer was their Spanish Fly. I see no reason to deny them the only diversions possible for them—rape, murder and lunacy—providing they are forced by the police to practice them on each other.

"Locked firmly in the middle of Europe as Nazis, with storm troopers, hangmen, concentration camps and Gestapo intact, the Germans would handle their own problem of extermination in their own way. Their massacre would not have to be on our conscience. At the same time, they could be watched and studied as criminals, and contribute much to our understanding of abnormal psychology."

Mulvehill laughed. He wiped his fingers on his napkin and looked around for the waiter. Hecht lifted a finger and the waiter materialized. Mulvehill ordered tea. The waiter hesitated. "Mr. Hecht, was there anything wrong with the sandwich?"

Hecht shook his head. "Bring me a fresh cup of coffee, please."

Mulvehill leaned back against the leather cushions of the booth.

"An interesting hypothesis," he smiled.

Hecht smiled back.

"A pleasant daydream. No more than that." He sighed. "Because such practical things never come to pass in the world."

"Now that the war is over," Mulvehill said, "what are the plans of your friends from Palestine?"

Hecht grinned. "I visited them before getting on the train in New York. They seem to be thriving. They have a real office now, with glazed glass on the door. The legend reads American League For A Free Palestine. They've got a switchboard with a girl who knows how to handle a PBX, a water cooler... everything."

"But what are their plans?" Mulvehill repeated.

"Charles, our friends are realists. They worked as hard as they could to spirit the remaining Jews out of Europe while they could," Hecht said. "They bought battered ships, which they tried to sneak past British patrol boats that guarded entry to the Holy Land. Sometimes they succeeded, sometimes they failed.

"And always," Hecht emphasized with a fist, "the British stood in the way. So now, with the war finally ended, a feisty handful of men and women in Palestine, the soldiers of the Irgun Zvai Leumi, have taken up the battle to drive the British out of Palestine and proclaim a Hebrew commonwealth."

"That's good," Mulvehill said. "It reminds me of the 1916 Easter Rebellion with the IRA fighting the Black and Tans in the streets of Dublin."

"So you see the similarity," Hecht nodded.

Mulvehill leaned back. He closed his eyes and sang softly, and not unmelodically:

> *Early on a Sunday morning*
> *High upon the gallows tree,*
> *Kevin Barry gave his young life*
> *For the cause of liberty*
> *Just a lad of eighteen summers*
> *Yet there's no one can deny*
> *That he went to death that morning*
> *Nobly held his head up high.*

Hecht smiled sympathetically. Mulvehill continued:

> *Shoot me like an Irish soldier*
> *Do not hang me like a dog*
> *For I fought for Ireland's freedom*
> *On that dark September morn'*
> *All around that little bakery*
> *Where we fought them hand to hand*
> *Shoot me like an Irish soldier*
> *For I fought to free Ireland.*

Hecht sipped his coffee. They both sat silently. Hecht leaned forward.

"All right," he said, "you've got the idea. It's the men and women of the Irgun against the might of Britain."

"What do you think I could do to help?" Mulvehill asked. "I've asked that question before, you know."

Hecht laughed. "I know. But, you know, things were in flux."

"I'm convinced that the British have behaved shabbily. Even more than shabbily," Mulvehill went on. "So if there are guys in Palestine like Bergson and Merlin and their friends who are willing to risk their necks to drive the British out of Palestine, I'm willing to do what I can over here."

Hecht changed the subject.

"What about the job you're working on here? Are you a stockbroker?"

"No," Mulvehill told him, "I work on the trading desk. In brief, I'm a wholesaler of stocks. We buy them at one price, called the bid, and we sell them at a higher price, called the asking price."

"What about school?" Hecht wanted to know.

"Well, I took the job with the understanding that once the summer was over I would go back to school. But," Mulvehill said, "it turns out I'm pretty good at this work. I could quit school and stay on. I'm sure they would keep me."

Hecht shook his head. "Not a good idea."

"Why not?" Mulvehill asked.

Hecht reached across the table and rested a hand on Mulvehill's arm. "I saw your kid brother and your little sister on the station when we arrived in Los Angeles.

Do you think you'd be setting a good example for them?"

Mulvehill looked at him wide-eyed.

"Gosh," he said, "I never even thought of that."

"And what about your mother and father?" Hecht pressed on. "How do you think they would feel if you quit college after three years? Don't you think it would be a bitter disappointment for them?"

Mulvehill nodded. "I suppose so."

"Finish school," Hecht urged. "I think you'll be better for it. Listen," he continued, "Bergson will be out here next month. Go back to school. When Peter arrives let's the three of us sit down together. And then I'd like you to meet Ethel Longstreet and Frankie Spitz. They are our Praetorian Guard out here. I bet they'll have some ideas too."

Hecht signaled for the waiter, paid the bill and rose from the table.

"I've got to get over to the studio where I'm writing a pot boiler. I'll be in town for at least six more weeks."

They left the restaurant together.

14.

Hecht had been right, Mulvehill gratefully conceded to himself, as he stood among his fellow graduates attired in the traditional black cap and gown. He looked over at the guest section and was able to make out his mother and father, Michael and Cookie. His mother looked particularly pleased. Even his sister Jean, now out of the Navy and married to Dr. Bill Hale, had come out from Chicago to see her kid brother receive his diploma.

The year had passed with astonishing speed. He was a good, although not brilliant, student and, with Magda looking over his shoulder to see that his papers were properly prepared, he had received consistently good grades. Magda, as a teacher, knew how lessons could best be prepared to achieve passing grades.

The speeches over and the ceremony at an end the graduating students, after moving the ceremonial tassel from left to right, boisterously flung their caps into the air.

He joined his family. Michael, who had been disappointed that the war had ended before he could get into it, was mollified with an appointment to West

Point, arranged by his father with the help of their congressman.

Magda, too, showed up for the ceremony and Mulvehill introduced her as his math teacher and grade adviser. She, for the most part, behaved with decorum but managed to surreptitiously reach behind him and pinch his butt.

She had accepted the idea that he would have to go down to the family home for a few days following graduation but would get back up as soon as he could. The family drove down to Thermal the same afternoon and dinner that evening was adorned with a festive cake in honor of the graduate, and eaten under hanging balloons and bunting.

Consuelo helped Mrs. Johnson serve and the rest of the Rodriguez family were guests at the dinner. The meal over, Rodriguez and the boys left. Consuelo stayed on to help with the dishes. Now the family sat around relaxed. Mulvehill senior asked the inevitable question about what Charles now had planned for the future.

"I can go back to work as a trader at Mitchum Jones and Templeton," he informed his folks, "but I'm not sure that's what I want to do. I've had a letter recently from Ben Hecht. He's going to be out here in a few weeks and has suggested that there would be a job for me with his American League For A Free Palestine."

"Well, that's a very fine cause," his father nodded judiciously, "But it's not quite a career, is it?"

Charles laughed. "Hardly." He furrowed his brow. "You know that a degree of Bachelor of Arts in English Literature is hardly an entree to a career in business."

"Charles," his mother put her hand on his arm, "have you considered coming in to the family business? Michael is going to make a career of the Army and your father will want to retire in a few years."

"Makes sense, Mom," he assured her, "but let's at least wait until I meet with Hecht and hear what he has to say."

He was hardly likely to admit that Magda, whom they really knew nothing about, had become a habit. He was not about to give up her embraces.

Jean came downstairs. Her bag was packed and she was ready to head back to Chicago and a pleasant life as the wife of a highly successful orthopedic surgeon.

"Who's going to give me a lift into Indio?" she asked. "If I catch the 8:15 Greyhound bus to Los Angeles I can make the Santa Fe Chief later this evening."

Michael took her bag from her. "If dad lets me drive the station wagon," he volunteered, "I'll be happy to take you to the station in Indio."

Their father rose. "You can drive, Michael, but we're all going."

"Yahoo." Michael gave a fair imitation of the rebel yell. He bounded down the stairs of the porch and headed for the garage where the station wagon was parked. The family followed.

"Consuelo, I would have given you a ride home," Mrs. Mulvehill called into the kitchen. "But I don't know when we'll be back. Why don't you call Alberto and tell him to pick you up when you're through helping Mrs. Johnson with the dishes."

The ride into Indio was short. The family waited with Jean until the big Greyhound bus arrived from Yuma. After kisses all around Jean boarded the bus. She found a seat near a window where she could look out and wave to all of them as the bus pulled away.

"Hey dad," Michael said to his father, "can I stay in town and catch a movie? Billy Underwood is going. He can drive me home after the show."

"May I," his mother corrected.

"Sure," his father nodded. "See you later."

Charles drove the rest of the family back home. Arrived at the ranch house Mrs. Mulvehill went upstairs with Lynn to work on the girl's cheer leader costume.

"Good night, Cookie," he called to his sister. He kissed his mother.

"Dad is going to sit out on the porch so he can smoke his pipe. I'll just keep him company."

His mother turned out the dining room light and the two men sat down on the porch in the half light cast by the glow from the upstairs window. The older man settled in the large rocking chair, pulled out his tobacco pouch, tamped the tobacco in the bowl of his pipe and struck a match. He puffed contentedly.

Charles sat on the porch swing and faced his father.

"Coming home from the war," he told the older man, "I was sure I was going to pitch in and help you at the packing shed. I had no idea how restless I was going to be. And you had some idea about the bad dreams I was having."

His father simply nodded.

"I think it will be stimulating to work on this project. Hecht and Bergson," Mulvehill went on, "are remarkable men. And their goal, to get the British out of Palestine and establish a home for the Jewish people on the very land where Abraham and Jacob and the other patriarchs lived…gosh, dad…the idea, kind of takes my breath away." His father turned to look at him.

"It won't work," he said.

Charles was puzzled. "What do you mean, it won't work? Don't you believe those poor harassed people are entitled to a land of their own? Everybody else has a homeland. Look at us Irish. We're Americans. Sure. But we never forgot the old sod. Isn't that so? And you know how much blood was spilled before Eire was finally established as the Irish Free State."

The older man puffed on his pipe. "It's not the same thing, Charles."

Mulvehill felt his Irish rising. "Not the same thing? Why not?" Was his father, whom he knew to be the kindest and gentlest of men, anti-Semitic?

His father drew on his pipe and then set it down on the porch rail.

"Remember the prophet Samuel?" he asked his son.

"You mean the man in the Old Testament? No, dad, I don't," Mulvehill answered. He leaned forward on the swing.

"The prophet Samuel," his father began, putting his hand on Charles' knee, "and I'm sure you will remember once I get into the story, had two sons. Samuel was a judge in Israel and well respected by the people.

"When he grew old," the elder Mulvehill continued, "Samuel appointed his sons as judges over Israel. But they were not the man their father was. They took bribes, chased after money in other ways and perverted justice. The people were unhappy at this turn of events. They came to Samuel. 'You are old,' they said, 'and your sons do not walk in your ways. Make us a king to judge us like all the nations.'"

Charles waited but his father said nothing.

"Well?" he prodded.

His father looked at him. "Samuel did not like that. What did the people mean; 'give us a king so we can be like the other nations'. Didn't they know that they were Hebrews, selected by God for a special mission? They were not supposed to be like other people. So Samuel entreated the Lord…and God replied…'Listen to them. They haven't rejected you. They have rejected me. So give them a king. But warn them what it is going to mean to be governed by an earthly king.'"

Mulvehill looked at his father with new respect. There were depths to his father he had not suspected.

"You mean, dad, that the Jews are really not like other people? If they have a land of their own they'll screw up. Is that what you're saying?"

"I'm only saying," his father replied mildly, "that if your friends are successful in creating a Hebrew homeland for the Jewish people, I'm not sure they are going to be happy with what they get."

His father shrugged. "I don't know. I'm not a prophet." He smiled. "Remember what Mark Twain said about the Jews?"

Mulvehill shook his head. "No, what?"

The older man smiled. "He said, 'the Jews are like everybody else, only more so'."

He picked up his pipe, looked into the bowl, satisfied himself that the embers had died out and knocked the tobacco out on the porch railing. He swept the debris off the rail.

"Millions of Jews were killed by the Germans and their henchmen in the past five years," he went on. "Yet, with all those Jewish dead, anti-Semitism is still alive and kicking.

"You know, Charles, when I run into a problem at the shed, or when I just feel that I've got to clear my head of business matters, I'll drive into Indio. I like to go into Pedro's bar, over behind the railroad station. It's dim, not usually crowded during the day, so I find it restful. I'll take a seat at the far end of the bar. Ernie knows me already. He'll bring up the bottle of Harvey's Bristol Cream and pour me a glass.

"I'll sit there, sipping my drink, relaxing. Usually there are apt to be one or two or three locals there. I'll listen in on their conversations. Sooner or later one of them will cuss out the Jews. Like as not," the elder Mulvehill said, "the man hasn't known four Jews in his lifetime. But he's an expert on the Jews. He knows what's wrong with them and what to do about it. Kill 'em all. That's his simple minded, black-hearted solution."

He looked searchingly at his son. "I heard that talk before the war. And now, with maybe as many as six million Jewish dead, the talk hasn't changed one bit."

Charles breathed deeply.

"What does that all mean?"

His father looked at him silently for a long moment.

"There was a Nazi in Germany," he finally said, "who saw what was about to happen. He was an intimate of Hitler but, when he saw the senseless violence that the regime was launching, it was too much for him. He fled. First to Paris and then to London. He'd had enough.

"Writing from London, at the height of the nightly bombing of that embattled island, he wrote that the evil of the time, which had led to so much carnage and bloodshed, was an expression of a deep-seated, abiding evil. The evil was anti-Semitism. And it was not confined to Germany alone, he saw. He thought of it as a sort of sounding for the depth of the nihilist revolution in each country."

Mulvehill sat back on the swing. He listened intently. He had always treasured his father as a thoughtful man, and a loving man, but had never heard any expression of such profound observations.

"There is more to anti-Semitism than the political and social factors that are usually given as reasons why people don't like Jews." He looked at Charles. "You know what I mean? The claim that Jews are greedy, or

236

socially undesirable, or Communists, or Internationalist. There is much more to it than that. There is a metaphysical root. That is why anti-Semitism appears in all countries." He gave a short bitter laugh. "Don't be surprised if you find it cropping up in China, or Japan.

"No, Charles. I think if we want to understand what makes people dislike the Jews enough to want to destroy them, we have to look deeper. We have to look, not at the Jew, but at the one who hates the Jew. What is it in him that makes him hate Jews? I don't. You don't. Mother doesn't. And when Michael came home from school one day and made a crude remark about Jews we wanted to find out who he heard it from. It took me three days of investigation…but I found out. It was a kid name Touhey. He had heard it at home. I visited his home. His father was out of work, fired because the plumbing supply distributor he worked for had caught him stealing brass parts and selling them to a competitor. His mother was an alcoholic who was known to be sleeping around. It is in unhappy, broken homes where anti-Semitism is spawned. That's where the hatred starts and festers."

He rubbed his knuckles.

"So that's part of it, Charles. But there's even more to it than that. Rauschning, the ex-Nazi I'm talking about, looked around him and saw a nation of people where that hatred was festering. We can't just turn from it in contempt, shrugging it off as rudeness and barbarism. If we want to overcome anti-Semitism we must recognize the awful greatness and perversion of the temptation to give in to hatred of the Jews, and then overcome it."

He looked off into the night.

"I don't think that a Jewish State is the answer. "Rauschning saw that. He finally came to understand that anti-Semitism was not a fringe problem of Nazi thinking. Its importance in Germany was expressed by the fact that it was at the very center of Hitler's lunacy.

"The Nazis, with their diabolical instinct for the inarticulate feelings and stirrings of the collective unconscious, satisfied the human craving for personification by making the Jew the embodiment of the evil in man. For the Germans," Mulvehill's father hesitated, as if searching for the right words to express the idea he was pursuing, "the Jew satisfied the need for a visible embodiment of evil.

"And not only in Germany. Even as we fought German arms there were people in this country who felt that the Germans were right...that it was a Jewish war. So, in addition to making the Jew the scapegoat for everything bad and misshapen in the past the anti-Semite accused him of being the cause of the most brutal, most murderous war in modern history... conveniently forgetting that it was Japan, a country without Jews, which got us into the war by bombing a sleeping Pearl Harbor."

He excused himself to go to the toilet, leaving Mulvehill sitting and staring into the darkness and thinking about the Jews from Palestine, whom he thought to be as decent and courageous as any men he had ever known. When his father returned the older man refilled his pipe and lit it. He looked at Charles.

"Is this too much of a lecture?" he smiled.

"No dad. Please go on. Maybe it will help me understand Ben Hecht and his Palestinian friends better."

"Hating the Jew," his father picked up the thread of his discourse, "served a practical purpose for the Nazis. The function of anti-Semitism as mass propaganda served as a tool to unify almost all Germans around a simple theme: hate the Jews, who betrayed Germany in World War One.

"That was one side of German anti-Semitism. But behind that racial idea, that the Jews were defiling the pure German race, lurked another idea, the one that makes hatred of the Jews a universal phenomenon. And that is hatred for the children of Israel, the chosen people on whom the revelation of God was bestowed."

Mulvehill senior puffed on his pipe. The light upstairs had gone out. Mrs. Mulvehill and Cookie had gone to bed.

"The hatred of the Jew is an elemental craving, something perpetual. Anti-Semitism is as old as Western civilization...and even older. Anything alien can always be incarnated as the myth of Evil. Naive hatred of strangers is latent in all primitive peoples. But anti-Semitism is more than plain xenophobia. Hatred of the Jews is more like a subconscious reaction against the author of the Tables of the Law, in which good is distinguished from evil, and the distinction is based on divine will.

"Small men, Charles, men of little ability and, lacking achievement, don't really like civilization. They are uncomfortable with the restraints it imposes. They are subject to a grinding dissatisfaction, sloth, worldly melancholy. That's why anti-Semitism rises to fever pitch in times of spiritual crisis, of human uncertainty—not because 'distractions' are needed at such times, but because people grow weary of the burden of a higher life."

Once again Mulvehill's father lit his pipe. In the glow from the embers, as Charles looked at him, his father seemed to be seeing something in the darkness. Or perhaps immersed in a vision that he saw.

"Charles, strange as it may seem to us today, a Jew was once Foreign Minister of Germany. That was back in 1919, soon after the Armistice that ended the First World War. His name was Walter Rathenau. His father had founded the General Electric Company of Germany. The family was very wealthy and, maybe, their wealth was instrumental in young Walter being named Foreign Minister.

"In a letter to a Jewish friend, that year, Rathenau wrote something that ought to be inscribed on the walls of every school."

In the gloom the elder Mulvehill looked at Charles. His eyes gleamed even in the darkness in which they sat.

"'Do you know why we were born into the world?' Rathenau wrote. 'To summon every human countenance to Sinai. You won't go? If I don't call you, Marx will call you; if Marx doesn't call you, Spinoza will call you. If Spinoza doesn't call you, Christ will call you.'"

The two men sat there in the darkness of that June night. The heat of the day had dissipated and a light cool breeze blew across the valley floor. Mulvehill shivered, but he was sure it was not because of the coolness. After a long silence the elder Mulvehill again spoke.

"Marx calls us no longer, and even the voice of Spinoza has grown faint. But we are still summoned to Sinai today as always, and this, Charles, is precisely the metaphysical basis of anti-Semitism. It is our hidden, unconscious, hatred for the author of this summons. We think we can put down the irksome and ridiculous distinction between good and evil along with its herald."

His father rose, walked softly across the porch, reached inside the door and flicked a switch. The yellow porch light illuminated the area where they sat and some of the lawn beyond. The older man resumed his seat. Charles moved from the swing to sit on the porch rail facing his father.

"Anti-Semitism," the older man said softly, "is a temptation to look for evil, not in oneself but in some other, exterior quarter. It is a flight from an intellectual and moral demand upon oneself...a refuge sought in a material claim upon another, whom one can make responsible for one's own weakness and unhappiness. And, even more significantly, anti-Semitism offers an opportunity to substitute diffused activity for spiritual self- transformation. The evil that we are unwilling, or unable, to recognize in our own natures we combat in the shape of a plausible personification. We do it when we are no longer strong enough, as human beings, to struggle with it directly."

He paused and Mulvehill looked at his father, whose face seemed to glow with an inner light. The younger man sat quietly, fearful even to breathe, as his father looked off into the darkness. Again, in a muted voice, the older man spoke.

"Many elements unite in anti-Semitism," he said. "There is the hatred for an intellectually superior group that is felt to be alien, and that has managed to acquire exceptional influence owing to this superiority and to intellectual agility. There is the fear and envy that 'some day' the country will fall into Jewish hands like ripe fruit, to say nothing of all the primitive emotions of economic envy, social resentment and obtuse nationalist hatred of foreigners."

Mulvehill wanted to ask his father if he thought of Jews as foreigners, but did not want to interrupt.

"But none of these factors," his father continued, "is the key to modern anti-Semitism. The Jewish mind has played an outstanding part in the liberation of the human spirit. It has done its share to turn the process of liberation into an alliance between progress and barbarism that absolutely staggered Siegmund Freud. Because of its historical vocation the Jewish mind led the memorable struggle of the nineteenth and twentieth centuries for the deflation of all values. The Jewish mind, which in order to attain equal civil rights had torn itself loose from the strongest of bonds, from the old, venerable authority that governed every aspect of life…and became the model and example of what utter absence of authority man might dare aspire to. In an age when people were consciously seeking restraints and authority, there were also bound to be honest motives for combating the most prominent representative of the struggle for emancipation, at the same time that one fought against dissolution and for a new authority.

"When the movement of ideological deflation reached its logical conclusion and reversed itself," his father went on, "once again Jews were the leaders who called most audibly for a return from freedom to a new absolutism. Thomas Mann, the famous German author who is now living in exile here in California, wrote… 'It is not liberation and development of the ego that are the secret and the commandment of the age. What it needs, what it demands, what it will get—is terrorism.'"

"I remember that, dad. That's Naphta, Mann's hero in *The Magic Mountain*, speaking. We just read that last semester."

His father nodded. "Of course. Mann, with the acute sensitivity to changes in the human mind that this great artist always displays, knew exactly what he was doing when he has Naphta express that opinion in the days preceding the First World War. Remember, Charles, how Naphta says…'It is an uncharitable misunderstanding of the younger generation to suppose they find their enjoyment in freedom. Their deepest delight is in obedience.'

"Don't you think it exceptional that it was a German writer who could best see, and express, the German trait of obedience to authority, Charles?"

His son nodded. "Of course. No wonder Mann fled from Germany when the Nazis took control of the government."

"Exactly," his father said. "He accurately predicted what was coming. And he did it years before the Nazis came to power. He saw that it was the acute dialectic intelligence of the Jew that had helped create the situation. Here the liberty to which he owed his political and social equality reversed itself, becoming thralldom and terrorism. The paradox is that the Jew himself helped drown out 'the summons to Sinai'."

Out on the dirt road that led to their driveway, two pinpoints of light bobbed along. The men seated on the porch watched the car as it turned into the driveway.

"That will be Bobby Underwood bringing Michael home," the elder Mulvehill said. He looked at his watch and smiled. "Eleven forty five," he said to Charles. "Michael will be expecting me to bawl him out."

The car pulled up and Michael jumped out. On the driver's side Bobby Underwood came out and stood beside the car. "It's my fault, Mr. Mulvehill. We got talking and both of us forgot what time it was."

"That's all right," Michael's father said. "You just run along, Bobby." As Michael ascended the porch steps his father said, "Scoot upstairs, Michael. Charles and I are having a discussion."

Michael was relieved. "Okay, dad." He quickly entered the house. They heard him climbing the stairs two at a time.

The elder Mulvehill settled back in his rocking chair. He picked up the interrupted thread of the conversation.

"The whole domain of anti-Semitism is paradoxical. It isn't just a phenomenon of political and social life, or of a special historical situation like the rise of Naziism." He shook his head. "No, its real roots are imbedded in the transcendental level. Even the special rubber stamps that the Nazis used on the passports of Jews in Germany are a token of the metaphysical fact that the children of Israel are being persecuted as God's chosen people. It's not just the civil war of a majority against a minority." He knocked on the porch rail next to where Charles was sitting for emphasis. "It's not just a national calamity, as the German historian Mommsen put it.

"No. If we look at it realistically we see anti-Semitism for what it is. It is the attempt to deny what the Jews really stand for. The Jew's intellectual vocation is to stand on the side of law, conservation and tradition. Judaism is the strongest of the conservative forces. It is the oldest root of our Western tradition. In fact Judaism, along with Hellenic civilization and Christianity, is the imperishable substance of our Christian Occident, the eternal 'summons to Sinai,' against which man is forever rebelling."

He looked down at the floor, rubbed his hands together and looked intently at Charles.

"This tragic confusion places upon the Jew the burden of a never-ending battle. It is the perpetual conflict between revolution and tradition, between liberation and bondage. Because the Jew, of all men, suffers the most from this conflict, he is in danger of being made responsible for it."

He sighed.

"The impossible task of being human is what crude men rebel against through anti-Semitism."

Charles waited, but his father sat there silently, his hands clasped between his knees. Mulvehill could not think of any meaningful statement he could make in response to his father's lengthy discourse. He sat silently. At last his father looked at him.

"I apologize, Charles. I kept you imprisoned here while I relieved myself of a mental burden that has preoccupied me for years." He sighed. "But who could I talk to about these ideas that have been germinating for a long time."

"Gosh, dad, please don't apologize. I think what you've said has cleared up a number of things for me. But everything you've said tonight convinces me more than ever that Hecht and his friends from Palestine are right. Only when the Jews have their own land will they be free."

His father shook his head sadly.

"I'm afraid not. Even if the Irgun is able to drive the British out of Palestine, do you think all of the Jews of the world will move there? I don't think so. I think that anti-Semitism will disappear only when all men see why they should cherish the Jew instead of hating him."

He reached over and put his hand on Charles' knee.

"Maybe you're right. I hope so. Do what you believe is the right thing to do. If Hecht wants you to work with them and you believe in their cause, do it. That's what your mother and I have always wanted for our children…that they grow up and live their lives in such a way that you and your brother and your sisters will always follow your own convictions."

He rose from his rocking chair, placed his hands on his back and stretched.

"Goodness, Charles, your father is really becoming an old man."

Mulvehill got up from his perch on the railing. He put his arms around his father.

"Gosh, dad, I don't think I've done that since I was a kid in knee pants. I've got to admit that I'm astonished at the depth of your knowledge."

His father grinned. "You know, your mother is kind of attracted to the church. She likes to go with Consuelo and make a novena now and then. I think it's pure nonsense but, we all have our little individual insanities, don't you think? I'm sure she would not be as patient with me as you've been. And who else is there to talk to?"

He put his hand on his son's shoulder. They walked into the house.

15.

Mulvehill spent an obligatory week in Thermal. He expected Magda to be reproachful at his long absence but she was so happy to have him back that she limited her remonstrance to the command…"Into the shower with you, me bucko." She loved to be lathered and caressed by him and then lie naked on the cool sheets as her lust mounted and she finally grabbed for him.

It was a few evenings later that the phone rang.

"Charles? Hullo. This is Ben. Ben Hecht. Can you meet me at Linny's for breakfast tomorrow? I've turned in the script. We've had the usual tedious script conferences so the producer can 'lick the script'." He laughed. "I always take two sleeping pills in advance when a script conference has been called.

"Anyway, Charles, I've collected my check and will be heading back to Nyack but I want to see you first."

"Sure Ben. It will be nice to see you again. Is Linny's that delicatessen on Beverly Drive? O.K. What time? Eight-thirty? That's fine. I'll be there."

Magda had been rubbing his back while he talked. She unbuttoned his shirt and drew it down over his shoulders, as far as it would go while he was holding the phone with one hand. As he was finishing the conversation she started nibbling his right ear. He laughed and turned. She was right there with her mouth open and delicately slipped her tongue into his mouth as they kissed.

"What's this meeting about, sweetie?" she asked. "I hope it's nothing that will take you away from me."

He shook his head.

"No. Hecht has said he would like me to go to work for the American League For A Free Palestine. He and Senator Guy Gillette of Iowa are co-chairmen. I'm just going to listen to his proposal. Whatever it is I'm sure it will be local. But I'll tell you all about it after I meet with him."

They moved into the dining room. Magda had papers to correct.

"Keep me company, sweetheart." She ran her hand along the side of his cheek. Her eyes were molten. "I'm so happy when you're around darling. Don't ever leave me."

He kissed her. She settled down to work and Mulvehill picked up a book that Bergson had sent him from New York, *The Redemption of Democracy*, by Hermann Rauschning. As he read he came across some of the thoughts that his father had expressed in his discourse on anti-Semitism.

The radio played softly as they sat near each other. The music stopped for a short news brief. The government was planning a series of tests of more powerful atomic bombs on a lonely atoll in the South Pacific. And in Washington, one of the scientists who had worked on the original atom bomb was urging the government to approve, and fund, research to develop a still more powerful bomb, a hydrogen bomb.

He set the book down. He laced his hands behind his head and looked thoughtfully at Magda. Her head was bent down to her papers. He looked at the part in her hair and noticed that where the hair joined her scalp it was grey at the roots. He smiled. So that was what the dyeing of her hair was all about. As if it would make a difference to him. And then he remembered that her pubic hair was red. He smiled to himself. He would have to take a closer look.

She looked up as though divining that he was looking at her.

"What's that all about, Charles?"

"It's all about love, Mag," he said, and was astonished to see tears coming to her eyes. He got up, walked over and kissed her. She gripped his hand, wiped her eyes and went back to grading her students' papers.

They fell asleep that night locked in each other's arms.

He had driven his motorcycle up from Thermal and, in the morning, rode it over to Linny's. He wheeled it around into the alley and found a place to park behind the restaurant. Then he walked around to the street entrance. Beyond the first row of booths he saw a large booth in the back. Hecht was seated there. To his surprise he saw that Peter Bergson was there too. Then there were two women. Both looked to be in their middle to late thirties.

Ben and Peter rose from their seats as he approached. Each shook his hand warmly.

"Charles, sit down. I want you to meet our two formidable cohorts for the West Coast." Hecht put his hand on the shoulder of the woman closest to him. "Ethel Longstreet and," he nodded toward the other woman…"Frankie Spitz."

Mulvehill shook hands with each and sat down at one end of the curved bench, facing Bergson.

A waitress came over and passed menus around the table. Mulvehill looked at his menu only briefly. He knew what he wanted. Bacon and eggs. Canadian bacon if they had it. He put down the menu and looked at the other four people around the table. He felt, unaccountably, a slight thrill of excitement.

He sat there, his hands in his lap, waiting for the others to make their decisions. The waitress stood by, her pencil poised over her pad. She looked at Mulvehill and smiled. He decided to defer to the others. The Longstreet woman was the first to look up.

"Can I get the cook to prepare a plate of cheese blintzes for me…and how long will it take?"

The waitress looked at her.

"Absolutely. We have them made up in advance and keep them in the refrigerator. How do you like the 'bletlach'*—hard or soft?"

Ethel Longstreet smiled. "Not hard, not soft. O.K?"

The orders were given, one by one. It was Mulvehill's turn.

"Do you have Canadian bacon?"

---

* The soft crepes which hold the pot cheese fillings together

The waitress shook her head back and forth. He looked at her more closely. She was short, portly, and with heavy arms. He now guessed she could be in her sixties.

"For you, dollink, absolutely. Canadian bacon. And the eggs. How you like them?"

He was taken in by her motherly act and got into the spirit of things. He rubbed his hands together.

"Scrambled. But not too hard and not too soft."

They all laughed.

The waitress left.

Hecht turned to Mulvehill. "Charles, I'm returning to the East tomorrow with Peter. He has been out here for a week and we've had some discussion about you and the important role you could play—if you want to."

Bergson looked at Hecht. The writer nodded.

"Charles," Bergson began, "Germany has managed to deal the Jews a blow on a scale that surpasses anything we have endured in the past. If we had imagined that the defeat of Germany on the battlefield would put an end to anti-Semitism we were certainly indulging in self delusion. Hatred of the Jews continues to exist—in Rumania, Holland, France, England— even in the United States. 'Kill the Jews' remains the slogan for the anti-Semites, even after Auschwitz and Treblinka."

He paused. The restaurant had filled with people. Mulvehill looked around. There were animated faces, quiet faces, kindly faces and some distinctly Jewish looking faces. Now, after his father's long dissertation about anti-Semitism and, especially, after reading

Rauschning's book he no longer had to ask himself 'why?'

Bergson's voice interrupted his reverie.

"Our main focus now is on Palestine. There we have a young nation, active and alive, living on its own soil. Yet because of the British administration, our people there do not have the ability to exercise self-determination. They are not free."

Ethel Longstreet broke in.

"That's why we're here this morning. Ben and Peter have told me about you and we think you can be a very great help to us..."

"How?" Charles asked.

At this moment the waitress arrived and Mulvehill smiled to himself. It was two years now that he had been hearing that he could be of help to these people whom he had learned to admire, and to like.

As the dishes were set before the five at the table each picked up a fork and began to eat. But Hecht took a moment to say, "Charles, until now we have felt... Peter and I...that you were a gift from heaven." Mulvehill raised a hand in demurral.

"No," Hecht went on, "no false modesty. Eat your eggs and then we'll get down to brass tacks." He lifted his bagel, generously piled with lox and cream cheese, and bit into it.

They finished their meal in silence. When the dishes had been taken away Hecht took out a pipe and filled it with tobacco. Bergson lit a cigarette. Frankie Spitz, who had yet to say a word, took out an enameled cigarette holder, removed a cigarette and tapped the end on the case. She fished in her bag and brought out a slender gold cigarette lighter. Mulvehill looked at her. She was elegantly dressed, wore a beige turban over pulled back honey colored hair and had long fingernails painted a bright red. She lit her cigarette, inhaled, blew out a streamer of smoke, looked at Mulvehill and winked. He smiled back.

Bergson leaned forward.

"Charles," he went on, "our goal today is to win recognition for the existing Hebrew nation among the nations of the world, to achieve the right of self-determination for all the Hebrews in Europe, wherever they may be, whether still living in a German displaced persons camp or in the liberated territories, even though they may now be prevented, by the British, from reaching their homeland.

"The time has come to make clear, both for the survival of the Hebrews of Europe, and in the best interests of Jewish people everywhere, the fundamental difference that exists between the terms 'Hebrew' and 'Jew,' in the light of political realities of the world."

"I never knew there was a difference," Mulvehill said, "so I'll be happy to hear your explanation."

Hecht smiled from behind the smoke of his pipe but said nothing.

Bergson nodded.

"It is the difference between a nationality and a religion." Bergson tapped cigarette ash into his coffee cup. "You're an American. And perhaps you are also a Catholic." Mulvehill shook his head, but Bergson continued on. "One is a nationality, the other is a religion."

"Well, how is that different for Jews?" Mulvehill wanted to know. "Ben is an American and a Jew…"

Bergson smiled and looked at Hecht. Hecht laughed.

"We've got an interesting story about that," Hecht said. "My first project for our Palestinian friends was to put on a large meeting here to raise money for the Committee For A Jewish Army of Stateless and Palestinian Jews. I was to invite all the Jewish moguls I knew in Hollywood, and even some who were not Jews, to attend a meeting where Peter and I, Senator Pepper of Florida, Colonel Patterson of the Jewish Legion and a few others would talk about the cause. This was in May of 1941 as I recall. Britain was holding the fort against Germany. We were not yet in the war.

"I knew myself well enough," Hecht said, "to know that my name alone would only attract maybe a few of my card-playing cronies. We needed an important Hollywood Jewish name as a drawing card.

"I called on David Selznick. He was prominent, he was well liked and he was a Jew. I wanted him to co-sign a telegram of invitation. Selznick balked. 'I don't want anything to do with your cause,' David said, 'for the simple reason that it's a Jewish political cause. And I am not interested in Jewish political problems. I'm an American and not a Jew. I'm interested in this war as an American. It would be silly of me to pretend suddenly that I'm a Jew, with some sort of full-blown Jewish psychology.'"

Thinking back to that day, Hecht grinned. Both Peter Bergson and Ethel Longstreet had also been part of that meeting. They looked at Hecht with a bemused look.

"I looked at Selznick," Hecht continued. "I said to him…If I can prove that you are a Jew, David, will you sign the telegram as co-sponsor with me?

"'How are you going to prove it?' he asked.

"I'll call up any three people you name, I said, and ask them the following question—What would you call David O. Selznick, an American or a Jew? If any of the three answers that he'd call you an American, you win. Otherwise, you sign the telegram.

"David agreed to the test and picked out three names. I called them with David eavesdropping on an extension. Martin Quigley, who publishes the Motion Picture Exhibitors' Herald, answered my question promptly.

"'I'd say David Selznick was a Jew,' he said."

Mulvehill laughed. "One down and two to go."

Hecht grinned.

"My next call was to Nunnally Johnson, the well-known writer and director. He hemmed and hawed for a few moments but finally came up with the same reply. I then called Leland Hayward, my agent. Leland didn't hesitate a minute and, although it was I, not Selznick who was asking the question, broke out indignantly, 'For God's sake, what's the matter with David? He's a Jew and he knows it!'"

Hecht put down his pipe.

"David, honorably, admitted defeat," Hecht said. "Apparently, in everybody's eyes but his own, he was a Jew. He signed the telegram." Hecht picked up his pipe, sat back, and puffed contentedly.

Peter took over.

"Whether he wanted to admit it or not," Bergson said, "Mr. David O. Selznick is both an American and a Jew. So is Ben. But I'm not. I'm a Hebrew. According to my passport I'm a Palestinian. But when we have compelled the British to leave Palestine and we set up our Hebrew Commonwealth, by whatever name we collectively agree to call it I, and every other inhabitant of that land who is of the Jewish faith, will be Hebrew. So you can see, Charles, the difference between a nationality and a religion.

"There are seven hundred thousand Hebrews already living in Palestine. Hundreds of thousands of the surviving Jews of Europe are also Hebrews; they are those Jews who are not in Palestine today only because they have been physically prevented from going there. They are the stateless Jews of Europe. If they have not already lost their German, Hungarian, Rumanian or other citizenship they are ready to immediately give it up, if only they will be permitted to enter the Hebrew homeland."

"Okay," Mulvehill said, "I understand. But how are you going to compel the British to pull down their tents and leave Palestine?"

Bergson became animated. He placed his hands flat on the table.

"From New York, once I get back there," he said quickly, "I am leaving for Paris. There our Irgun men in France have an office of the Hebrew Committee of National Liberation. We will announce that we are a Hebrew Government in Exile, formed to tell the United Nations that Great Britain has failed to live up to its promise to the League of Nations to build a homeland for the Jewish people in Palestine and that they should, therefore, abandon the Mandate and get out."

"You don't really believe they will do that," Mulvehill asked, "do you?"

Bergson smiled a tight smile.

"Of course not. We will have to fight for our independence from Great Britain," he said, "just as your father's generation did in Ireland and as your American ancestors did in this country. And we of the Irgun are prepared to fight. Our men in Palestine are already engaged in military operations. And that, Charles, takes money."

Mulvehill grinned. "And that's what you want me to do?"

Bergson nodded.

Mulvehill frowned. "Maybe I can do that. I don't know. But what about the Arabs living in Palestine? What about their rights?"

Bergson nodded again. "Very good. Our mentor, Vladimir Jabotinsky, answered that question in the House of Lords, in 1937. He spoke for an hour and a half to the Royal Commission. He said that since Great Britain had accepted the Mandate they should live up to their commitment as expressed in the Balfour Declaration. He believed there was room in Palestine for a Jewish majority and for the Arabs there too. He pleaded with the men of the Commission.

"'Tell the Arabs the truth,' he said. 'You will see the Arab is reasonable, the Arab is clever, the Arab is just. The Arab can realize that since there are three, or four, or five wholly Arab states, then it is a thing of justice which Great Britain is doing if Palestine is transformed into a Jewish state. Then there will be a change of mind among the Arabs, then there will be room for compromise, and there will be peace.'"

Hecht shook his head. "Maybe in 1937 Peter. No longer. There has been too much shedding of Jewish blood by the Arabs, with the Arabs crying out *'Il Dula Ma'ana'*, the Government is with us."

Bergson shrugged. "Perhaps so, but it is really academic." He turned back to Mulvehill. "I see no reason why the Arabs who are now in Palestine cannot continue to live there without abrogation of their rights, but first things first. First we must establish a Hebrew Commonwealth in Palestine, on both sides of the Jordan, in all the land that was included in the original Mandate."

Mulvehill leaned back against the leather. "How can I raise money for the Irgun?"

Ethel Longstreet and Frankie Spitz leaned forward over the table and, almost with one voice, said, "We'll show you how." They looked at each other and laughed.

Ethel continued. "Charles, if you honestly believe that the Jews have a right to have a land of their own, a right no one has ever denied to any people, whether the Swiss, or the Irish, or the Sudanese or the people of Liechtenstein…if you believe that…then we will arrange for you to tell our story to Jewish audiences. I know you can help us win their support and I believe they will open their pockets to you."

Frankie took up the cue. "Alex Hadani, whose real name is Rafaeli, and who I understand you met in New York a couple of years ago, is out of the Army. He will be out here tomorrow. We have arranged for him to speak to the members of the North Hollywood Women's Club. Our friend Laura Gribin is their program director. When you listen to Alex speak to the women there you can take notes. He will be presenting the basic theme of the Irgun approach to driving the British out of Palestine and for establishing the Hebrew Commonwealth."

Ethel nodded. "Do you drive? How do you get around town?"

"I have a motor bike," he told them. "It's parked behind Linny's, in the alley."

Frankie smiled. "We've got better transportation for you because sometimes you will have to have a passenger. Perhaps one of our women members." She reached across and put her hand on his wrist. "The League has bought a surplus Army jeep. We want to place it at your disposal."

Hecht grinned. "It's parked behind the Beverly Wilshire Hotel. If you will meet us there Ethel will give you the keys."

"And I'll give you Laura Gribin's address," Frankie added. "You're to pick her up at her house at seven-thirty tomorrow evening."

Mulvehill looked around the table. None of them were smiling now. They looked at him expectantly. He clasped his hands together between his knees.

"You all seem to be pretty sure I would accept your proposal," he said. "Suppose I had turned you down?"

"When we came out here on the train, Charles," Hecht said, "I felt that your basic integrity and the sense of honor that caused you to enlist in the American army would impel you to want to help the Irgun's cause...as I am sure you would support any political or military effort that was honorable, that was reasonable, and that was just." He tapped out the cold ashes from his pipe and put the brier back in his pocket. "I always thought I was a pretty good judge of character. Was I wrong about you, or right?"

They looked at him. He nodded to Hecht. "You were right."

The five of them rose from the table.

16.

He looked at the Jeep and put his hand on the thin leather seat. The vehicle had been designed by the army for durability, not comfort. He thought back to the many miles he had ridden in just such a Jeep, first in Northern Ireland, then North Africa, and for a very brief time in Italy.

The tank was full and two extra five gallon tins of gasoline sat on the floor behind the driver's seat. Bergson helped Mulvehill strap his motorbike on to the back of the Jeep. He shook hands all around. Frankie Spitz handed him an envelope. "Here's your ownership certificate. And a few extra bucks if you should run out of gas."

He stuck it in his pocket and got into the driver's seat. Ethel Longstreet handed him the keys. "See you tomorrow," she said.

"See you tomorrow," he answered. He turned the ignition and the motor caught. He waved as he backed out into the street. They waved back. Hecht smiled.

"Break a leg," he called out.

Mulvehill laughed, let out the clutch and sped away.

He looked at his watch. It was eleven-thirty. He thought Mag would probably be teaching a class at that hour. Lisa was seldom home now and often spent days together with Mother Scarlatti. The old woman had a fine sense of discretion and gave Mag and Mulvehill all the leeway they needed to be alone for their lovemaking.

He left a note for Mag on the kitchen table, telling her he would be spending the night with his folks in Thermal but would be back tomorrow.

Driving the Jeep was refreshing, the wind whipping through his hair. He made Thermal in just under four hours. His folks were at the packing plant, Cookie was in school and Michael was back East at West Point. Mrs. Johnson greeted him warmly. He went to his room and packed some more clothing. He had an idea he might not be getting back down to Thermal for some time.

At dinner he told his folks of his decision to work with the people of the League. His father nodded, giving no hint of whether he thought Charles' decision was wise or foolish.

He slept soundly. The VA doctor had been right. It had been months since his sleep had been disturbed by any dreams, good or bad. On awakening he smiled languidly. Magda was the only soporific he needed. They slept well together. Only occasionally was he awakened in the night by her hand on his genitals and her warm breath in his ear.

Mrs. Johnson packed two sandwiches for him. After breakfast he kissed his mother, shook hands with his father, got into the Jeep and headed north.

He was back at Magda's house by early afternoon. He spent the afternoon reading a pamphlet Bergson had handed him as they left Linny's. Titled 'Palestine: A Jewish State or a Hebrew Commonwealth', it had been written by Bergson and clearly set forth his views on the country as a homeland for all those who wanted to be Hebrew nationals.

He was still reading when Magda arrived.

Instead of the warm greeting he anticipated he found her listless. He took her hand.

"What's wrong, sweetheart?"

Her shoulders drooped. She sat down on his lap and rested her head on his shoulder.

"I woke up with a belly ache," she told him. "I've had it all day. It just won't go away." She smiled wanly. "Maybe now that you're back, it will."

They went to bed early. Mulvehill handed her two aspirin tablets and a glass of water.

"Maybe you're coming down with stomach flu," he suggested. She took the pills, kissed him and turned to the wall.

She felt no better in the morning. Mulvehill suggested that she skip her classes and plan to see a doctor.

"We've got a nurse practitioner at school who is very good. I'll see her first," Mag promised.

At ten-thirty the phone rang. It was Hadani. He had arrived in Los Angeles that morning. Could

Mulvehill meet him for lunch? They could meet at the Coffee Shop in the Beverly Wilshire.

Hadani was waiting when Mulvehill arrived.

"Hey, you're looking very fit," Mulvehill greeted him. "Army life must have agreed with you."

Hadani nodded. "I've had some interesting experiences." The waitress arrived and they ordered. While they waited to be served Alex briefly recounted his experiences in the army. He was very excited to serve in the U.S. Army and, because of his fluency in German, was assigned to the 216th CIC Detachment, the key counter-intelligence unit of the 16th Corps. As they moved into Germany his unit began to encounter informers who wanted to get in good with the U.S. Army now that it was becoming obvious that Germany had as good as lost the war.

"I had not met any Germans since my graduation from Heidelberg," Hadani said.

"Now I encountered them again, first as prisoners-of-war in England, and now in their own homeland. These people were cowards..." He stopped momentarily as the waitress arrived and set the plates down before them.

"...they were mostly officers who approached me and claimed they were not really Germans," he continued. "Every one had a different story. 'My mother was Polish,' or 'My father was a Frenchman,' or 'My grandfather was really a Jew.'" Hadani could not conceal his disgust.

Mulvehill laughed. "Forget it, Alex," he said, "or you won't be able to enjoy your breakfast and these home fries are delicious."

Hadani finally grinned and began to eat.

"Well, I've joined your gang," Mulvehill said. "I think I'm actually on the payroll and I haven't even been told how much I'm going to be paid. But I've already got a Jeep and some money for gas."

They both ate silently for a few minutes. Hadani wiped up egg yolk from his plate with the white bread he had asked for. He wiped his mouth with a pink napkin, reached into the inside pocket of his jacket, took out an envelope and placed it on the table in front of Mulvehill.

"For you, Charles."

Mulvehill opened the envelope and drew out a check. It was made out to him, for forty-five dollars, and was dated six days ago, September tenth. He looked at it in puzzlement.

"This was made out last week. I didn't agree to go to work for the League until yesterday. How could they know?"

Hadani smiled.

"Peter called Zelinsky in New York and asked him to have a check made out so that I could bring it out with me. Peter and Ben Hecht conferred. They concluded that you were a good Joe and would throw in your lot with us." He folded his arms, leaned back and looked at Mulvehill. "Ben thinks he's a pretty good psychologist," Hadani smiled. "How about it?"

"Well, I don't know that I like being taken for granted," Mulvehill said, "but he was right." He fingered the check. "How much time does this cover?"

"A week," Hadani said. "Is that all right?" Without waiting for a reply he went on. "I talked with Ethel Longstreet earlier this morning. She has a talk lined up for me for this evening. You're to come along and take notes."

Mulvehill nodded. He reached in his pocket and took out the slip of paper on which Frankie Spitz had written an address. "I'm to pick up a woman named Laura Gribin. She'll tell me how to get out to the North Hollywood Women's Club."

Hadani rose and held out his hand to Mulvehill.

"Well then. I'll see you tonight. I can't tell you how pleased I am that you will be working with us," he said. "Everyone has a good feeling about you."

Mulvehill rose. "Until tonight." He reached for the check but Hadani was ahead of him. "I'll get this one."

They left the restaurant. Hadani walked north toward Santa Monica Boulevard. Mulvehill had parked the Jeep a block away, on Wilshire. They each went their separate ways.

It was after three when Mulvehill got back to Magda's house. She was not there. He was a little surprised because her last class was at one. He read Bergson's pamphlet again. When, at four o'clock, Magda had not yet shown up he called Mrs. Scarlatti.

"No," the older woman told him. "She's not here. She came by at two-thirty and took Lisa with her. I thought she'd be home by now."

Mulvehill was puzzled. Maybe Mag was feeling better and had decided to take Lisa to a matinee. At six she had still not arrived. He opened a can of soup, heated it and ate. He then studied a city street map to see how to get to Laura Gribin's house. He was there by seven o'clock.

He liked Mrs. Gribin at once. She was a widow, probably, Mulvehill guessed, in her mid-fifties and had a cheerful, earthy manner. She shook his hand vigorously.

"Ethel told me about you. She says you're going to be a great help to us." She gripped his hand again.

"An Irishman who wants to help the Jews. Wonderful."

Mulvehill grinned. "Well, you know, Mrs. Gribin, I'm an American. I was born in Thermal, down in the Coachella Valley."

"Yes," she smiled broadly. "But still, an Irishman." She chuckled and shook her head with a pleased look on her face.

They went out to the street and Mulvehill led her over to the Jeep. She looked at it. "How exciting, I'm going to ride in an army Jeep. But, you know," she hesitated, "it still gets chilly here in the evening. You wait here just a minute, sonny, I'll go get a coat."

They drove north through the Cahuenga Pass and arrived at an auditorium where the Women's Club met. A few women stood in front of the building, chatting. They seemed to know Mrs. Gribin and waved at her.

The seats inside were more than half filled. Hadani was seated at a table at the far end, just to the left of a lectern. Ethel Longstreet and Frankie Spitz were seated at either side of him. He was studying some notes that lay on the table in front of him.

Mulvehill turned to Laura Gribin. "I'll just take a seat here in the back," he said softly. "My only purpose here is to listen to what Alex says, and take notes."

She nodded, "Of course. And, by the way. I won't need a ride home. One of the women here will give me a lift."

She walked over to a group of women seated nearby. Mulvehill took an empty seat in the back row.

At eight o'clock the auditorium was nearly filled. Ethel Longstreet rose. She made a few introductory remarks about Alex Hadani, the fact that he had a doctorate from Heidelberg, his joining the Irgun in Palestine, and his service in the U.S. Army. There was polite applause. She sat down.

Alex rose and walked to the lectern. He stood silent for a long moment, looking over the audience. He then lifted several sheets of paper and slowly tore them in half, and then in half again.

"When one speaks from the heart, from conviction and from experience, one does not really need notes. True?"

He smiled warmly.

The women applauded. He had won them over.

"Please forgive me," he said, "if I take but a few minutes to review a bit of history with which you are all surely familiar."

He paused.

"But I am afraid that, this evening, I am going to say a few unkind things about one whom you all regard as a very great man, Dr. Chaim Weizmann, president of the World Zionist Organization."

The women looked at each other in some consternation. There was a low murmur of voices.

By a bit of shrewd manipulation he now had their undivided attention. First he won their admiration and then he stirred up a bit of controversy. They would hear him out.

"The idea of a Jewish State," Hadani reminded his audience, "in modern times, was first voiced by Theodor Herzl and discussed at the First Zionist Congress, in Basel, in 1897. But it had to wait twenty years until Arthur James Balfour, in 1917, wrote that famous letter, known as the Balfour Declaration, in which he expressed the opinion that 'His Majesty views with favor the establishment, in Palestine, of a national home for the Jewish people'.

"It is widely accepted that the Balfour Declaration was England's way of showing its appreciation to Chaim Weizmann for his discovery of acetone, an important ingredient in the manufacture of smokeless gunpowder.

"Or maybe it was a bit of shrewd British manipulation of Jewish sentiment," Hadani continued, "whose support England needed in World War I. Whatever it was it became quite obvious that Great Britain had little serious intention of fulfilling the terms of the Declaration because, no sooner had Great Britain been granted a Mandate to carry out that obligation than Winston Churchill, secretary of state for the colonies in 1922, split off all the land of Palestine east of the Jordan River, called it the Kingdom of Transjordan and brought in a Hashemite prince, Abdullah, and made him king. Now His Majesty's government had only to deal with less than eight thousand square miles as the site for a Jewish homeland, instead of the former forty-five thousand square miles."

"Are you blaming Mr. Weizmann for that?" one of the women wanted to know.

Hadani smiled.

"Of course not. We do not hold Mr. Weizmann responsible for what Great Britain does," Hadani said, "only for what Mr. Weizmann does. So now let us move forward another twenty years, to 1937. The crisis was approaching.

"Hitler was in the saddle in Germany and the danger to every Jew in Europe was becoming ever greater. The door to Palestine was still slightly ajar but England was getting ready to shut that door. It was that very year when Jabotinsky stood before the members of the Royal Commission in the House of Lords, pleading for greater access to the Holy Land. England turned a deaf ear. Jabotinsky took to stumping Europe, speaking to any Jew who would listen.

"'Get out, however you can, get out. Liquidate the Diaspora,' Jabotinsky urged, 'before the Diaspora liquidates you.'"

Hadani stopped to drink from a water glass that had been thoughtfully placed on the lectern.

"In that same year," he continued, "Mr. Weizmann also spoke to the Jews of Europe. He addressed four hundred and eighty Zionist delegates at their convention in London. He said, 'I told the British Royal Commission that the hopes of Europe's six million Jews were centered on emigration. I was asked, 'Can you bring six million Jews to Palestine?' I replied, 'No. ...The old ones will pass. They will bear their fate or they will not. They were dust, economic and moral dust in a cruel world. ...Only a branch will survive. ...They had to accept it. ...If they feel and suffer they will find the way—*beachareth hajamin*—in the fullness of time. ...I pray that we may preserve our national unity, for it is all we have.'"

A gasp, like a vagrant breeze, wafted through the audience.

One woman, in a quavering voice, asked, "Is this a matter of public record?"

"It was reported thus in the New York Times of the day," Hadani replied.

Another woman said she did not understand the Hebrew phrase that had been used by Weizmann. Hadani repeated it..."*beachareth hajamin*...When the Messiah comes all the dead will be revived."

He had scored a point. These ladies were not much given to the idea of a Messiah coming to revive the dead who had been slaughtered by the Germans.

"By 1939," Hadani went on, "the situation had become critical. We of the Irgun began to arm in preparation for our war against England. Of course," he shrugged, "that was all set aside when Germany attacked Poland. With the war on, we of the Irgun high command, under David Raziel, decided that Germany was a greater threat to the Jews than England. Many members of the Irgun volunteered to serve in the British army.

"Some of us," he continued, "came to the United States where we hoped to raise money and support in an effort to rescue as many Jews from Europe as we might possibly be able to get out. The first of the group to come was John Henry Patterson, the British army colonel who had commanded the Jewish Legion in World War I, and Robert Briscoe, the Dublin Jew who later became Lord Mayor of Dublin. That was the beginning of the Emergency Committee to Save the Jews of Europe."

Most of the women were now leaning forward in their seats. Hadani continued to relate the activities of the Irgun and its program; to get the surviving Jews out of Europe and to build a base of popular support among the Jews of the Yishuv…the Jewish community in Palestine. He went on to bring the audience up to date on the intensified war of the Irgun against England now that the war with Germany had been won.

"It had been a practice of the British in Palestine," he told them, "to publicly whip Irgun soldiers whom they had captured. But now the Irgun had a new commander, Menachem Begin.

"One day," Hadani said, slowly and dramatically, "an Irgun detachment surrounded two British officers in a square in Tel Aviv. Their shirts were torn off and they were publicly flogged by Irgun soldiers before the startled gaze of a Jewish crowd.

"From that day forward," Hadani reported, "there has been no whipping of Jews in Palestine."

. Mulvehill had taken out a pad and pencil he had brought with him and was taking notes.

"Similar draconian measures were carried out against Arab terrorists. An Irgun notice was posted publicly. For every Jew who is killed...two Arabs will be killed."

The audience of women seemed to be in shock.

Hadani continued.

"Ladies, the Irgun has accomplished something in Palestine that Jews have not known in nearly two thousand years. For the first time since the imperishable stand of Bar Kochba we have won the respect of our enemies."

He went on to cite other activities of the Irgun.

"For this we have been castigated by Ben-Gurion and by Chaim Weizmann as 'terrorists'...and they are right. Our objective is to terrorize both Arab insurgents and British soldiers alike...until we have established a Hebrew Government for our people in Eretz Israel... the land of Israel..."

One of the women applauded loudly and others took it up. Hadani waited until the clapping had subsided. He apologized for having talked for more than half an hour.

"There is much more to tell," he apologized, "but you probably want to get back home. Still, I cannot end," he said, "without paying homage to the brave men who fought for the freedom of Eretz Israel and paid with their lives on the British gallows…Shlomo Ben-Yosef, Eliahu Bet Tzuri, Eliahu Hakim, Meyer Nakar, Jacob Weiss, Absalom Habib and Dov Gruner, now under sentence of death in Acre Fortress.”

Mulvehill wrote the names down hurriedly. He would have to find out more about who those men were. He thought of young Kevin Barry hanging from a British gallows in Ireland.

The women sat in silence. Hadani said softly, “I will be happy to answer any questions.”

Ethel Longstreet rose. “Some of you may have children at home waiting. But before you leave I wish to remind you that Mr. Hadani came here from New York to raise funds that will buy food, clothing, medical supplies for the men and women of the Irgun and…” she turned to Hadani…“do I dare say it…arms and ammunition?”

Alex smiled.

Frankie Spitz walked through the audience with a basket, collecting dollar bills as she went. When she had completed making the rounds of the audience she went to the head table and called out…“Ladies, if our take is a little light tonight please be sure that if you want to write a check tomorrow at home Laura will be happy to come around and take it from you.”

A few of the women came forward to ask questions or make comments to Hadani. Finally all but one woman had left. She introduced herself.

“This is my first night at a meeting of the Women’s Club.” She nodded in Laura’s direction. “I came at

Laura's invitation. My name is Lily Oshan and I have an idea."

Ethel interrupted. "We're going out for some coffee and cake. Why don't you join us?" She turned to Mulvehill. "Charles, I've got a two-door car. Would you mind taking Laura and Lily? Laura will tell you how to get to Bob's Big Boy. We'll meet there."

Mulvehill nodded. The two women walked with him out to his jeep. The night air had grown chill and the Oshan woman was wearing a light dress. He took off his jacket and draped it over her shoulders. They climbed in.

On the short ride to the restaurant Mrs. Oshan said, "I'd like to have Mr. Hadani meet my husband. He owns an advertising agency. Maybe he can help publicize your program."

At the restaurant they found Ethel, Frankie and Hadani at a large booth in the back. They squeezed in. Lily Oshan turned to Hadani.

"I was very impressed with what you had to say. Most American Jews are so timid they don't have audacity enough to sass a waiter."

They laughed.

"I mean it," she said vehemently. "I would be so proud of the men you were talking about. I'd like to get my husband involved." She turned to Hadani. "Will you meet with him?"

"I would like to very much," he replied. "Unfortunately I must return to New York tomorrow. But I think that Mr. Mulvehill will be happy to meet with him."

He turned to Mulvehill. "This might be a good start for you, Charles. What do you think?"

Mulvehill nodded. "I'm game. I've been taking notes on your talk tonight. With that, and some guidance from Frankie and Ethel maybe I can handle it."

Lily turned to Hadani again.

"When and how did you first get involved?"

"My family is from Latvia," Hadani said. "I grew up in Riga. Our family name there was Rafaelovitch. In Palestine we changed it to Rafaeli. As an Irgunist I use the name Hadani...*man from Hadan.*" He smiled. "It's my *nom de guerre.* I received my doctorate from Heidelberg in 1933," he continued, "possibly the last Jew to be graduated in Germany. In the last few months there we heard of a Jewish suicide almost every day.

"I sailed for Jaffa, arriving there in October. Soon after I was invited to join the Irgun. It was then that I became acquainted with David Raziel, the remarkable commander of the Irgun, who was a true 'Talmud chochem'* who put on the tefillin every morning but who nevertheless spent much of his time writing manuals for weapons training and military operations.

"One of my early assignments," he told her, "was to go to Liege, in Belgium, to talk with Yiddish miners working in the coal mines there. My next trip was to Paris, where I met and discussed strategy with Jabotinsky. When I returned to Palestine, because of my training in the use of light weapons, I was assigned to a defense post in the Beit Israel quarter of Jerusalem.

* A wise student of the Talmud

"By 1937 it had become clear that we could not expect to have any cooperation from the men of the Haganah because they were controlled by the Socialist *Histadrut Federation* and their policy was 'Havlagah' or self-restraint." Hadani smiled. "We were more inclined to think of it as a policy of 'hang your head and bend your knee to the British'."

He sat quietly for a few minutes as the waitress refilled coffee cups and took an order for a sandwich from Laura.

"This was still two years before the German army invaded Poland," he continued. "Our program was three-fold; response to Arab terror attacks, expulsion of the British, and establishment of a Hebrew Commonwealth...on both sides of the Jordan. Our flag featured a hand holding a rifle and the legend *'Rak kach'*—Only thus!

"The Polish government at that time assisted us in our military training and even provided some rifles for our use. I continued my assignment in Jerusalem until 1940, when I was asked by Raziel to go to Europe to be the voice of the Irgun in the Galut.* Raziel impressed upon me that it was essential to acquire money and weapons. I spoke both Yiddish and German so it was felt I was best qualified for that task. When I sent the first money to Palestine from Europe," Hadani smiled, "Raziel wrote to say I had 'saved the situation' because the Irgun, then as now, was always short of those important commodities." He then went to Milan in Italy, Hadani told her, and called on the embassies there for visas to permit him to travel to Stockholm and

* The Jewish communities outside of Palestine

Helsinki. "In Finland we were able to buy revolvers and sub-machine guns. The quantities were small and we were able," he smiled, "to smuggle them into Palestine as musical instruments."

"Fascinating," Lily Oshan said. She looked at her watch. "It's getting late and my husband will wonder what's keeping me." She turned to Mulvehill. "Will you drive me back to my car? I left it about a block from the auditorium."

They rose. Mulvehill stifled a yawn.

It was nearly one o'clock by the time he got back to Magda's house.

17.

He knew as soon as he swung the Jeep into the driveway that something was terribly wrong. Every light in the house was lit and the front door was wide open. The garage door was up and Magda's little Hillman was parked in it.

Mulvehill turned off the engine and got out of the car. He walked toward the house, listening for any untoward noises. The house was quiet. He saw the policeman as soon as he entered the living room. The man was young, probably no more than twenty—a rookie cop. He was sitting in the chair that Mulvehill usually occupied, and stood up quickly as soon as Mulvehill entered the room.

"What is it?" Mulvehill asked. "Where's Mrs. Scarlatti?"

The policeman did not answer him, instead asking…"And you are?"

Mulvehill looked at him. "I'm Charles Mulvehill, Mrs. Scarlatti's friend." He was not yet prepared to offer any information beyond that.

The policeman looked at him. He beckoned. "Come with me," and led the way into the bedroom.

The bed was empty, the covers still intact. Mulvehill saw the impression of a body in the coverlet. On the bedside table there were two small medicine bottles, on their side, and an empty water glass .

There was a note on the table. The policeman picked it up and handed it to Mulvehill.

"It's a suicide note," he said. "Please read it and tell me if it is for you."

Mulvehill took the note from him and walked to the chintz covered chair in the corner. He sat down, looking at the impression on the bed. The thought went through his mind, 'That's Mag. That's the last I'll ever see of her.' He finally looked away, and unfolded the note. The policeman stood near the bed, looking at him.

Looking down at the note, Mulvehill saw that his hand was trembling. He drew a deep breath and began to read.

'My dearest darling,

I know I'm a coward. I can't stand pain. After being seen by the nurse this morning she arranged for me to see a doctor. The man examined me, asked a number of questions and told me I have cancer of the pancreas.

I didn't believe him, Charles. I couldn't believe him. I've always been in good health but that damned belly ache was something bad. I knew it. I told him I wanted to see another doctor. He said he understood and made a call for me. I saw the second doctor within an hour. After he had examined me he said the first doctor was right.

How could that be?

I asked about the disease. They say it is almost always fatal.

I immediately drove over to Mother Scarlatti's. I told her I wanted to take Lisa out for the afternoon. Lisa was happy to see me again. I drove out to the beach. I sat on the sand and watched Lisa play in the water along the shoreline.

After awhile, I don't know how long, I took her back to Mother Scarlatti. I came home and looked in the medicine chest. I found two bottles of sleeping pills. I figured that should be enough.

Charles, my darling, some of the happiest hours of my life were spent here with you.

The pain is getting worse. I feel it is better this way. You know, my dear, I always knew there was no future for me with you. I am even older than I told you. So you see, dear, on top of everything else I'm a liar.

I have taken all the pills. I am getting sleepy. I am sorry. I love you. Please take care of Lisa.'

The last part of the letter was written laboriously. The words were more widely spaced. He looked at the note. He folded it and put it into his pocket. The policeman stepped forward and put out his hand.

"I'll have to have that sir. We'll go downtown together."

He spoke kindly.

"The note pretty much tells the story, but they'll want to take a statement from you. It's just a formality, sir."

He waited.

Mulvehill rose, looked around, and went from room to room, turning off the lights. The policeman followed him around. When they finally got to the front door Mulvehill turned.

"Where is she? Where's the body?"

"They've taken her down to the morgue. Then that note was for you, right?"

Mulvehill nodded. "We were living together."

The policeman took him by the arm. "Can we drive downtown in your car or would you rather wait until I call for a squad car? I was supposed to go off duty at ten. My partner left. I waited for the men from the coroner's office and then I waited for you. I'm truly sorry, sir."

Mulvehill nodded. "Sure. I've got a Jeep. If you don't mind riding in that."

At police headquarters he was brought into a small room that contained a table and two chairs. Two plainclothes detectives came in. One sat down in the chair opposite Mulvehill. He introduced himself and his partner, who leaned against the wall.

The seated detective looked at him seriously.

"Suicide, technically," he said, "is murder, in which the victim and the murderer are one and the same. It is a case," he smiled, "in which the murderer always gets away. But," he said, "we must always be sure that it is suicide before we close the book. Sergeant Riley and I have read the suicide note. Is there anything more you can tell us?"

Mulvehill sighed.

"We've been living together for about six months," he told the detectives. "I had been her student. It was a convenient arrangement for both of us." A thought struck him. "She has a daughter, a little girl nearly three. She spends a lot of time with Mrs. Scarlatti's mother-in-law."

"We know," the detective who leaned against the wall said. "We found the old lady's name in the personal telephone book in the night table drawer. We've talked to her."

Mulvehill was concerned. "How did she take it?"

"Pretty good," the seated detective said. "She told us about her son being killed in the war. She likes you," he added.

Mulvehill sighed. "Gosh, she's had a lot of trouble. I'll have to decide what to do about the little girl."

The two detectives looked at each other and nodded. The seated one said, "We have nothing further to ask you. We'll write out our report." He stood up. "We're sorry we had to keep you waiting for more than an hour. We had a robbery investigation to complete."

Mulvehill nodded. "I understand. Then I'm free to go?"

"Sure, but just one more thing. We'd like you to identify the body for us."

Mulvehill shivered. He had seen his share of corpses, but this one was going to be different. He followed them out of the room and down to the morgue. The attendant on duty pulled out the drawer containing Magda's body. He drew back the sheet covering her face.

Mulvehill looked down at Magda's face. She looked peaceful. He did not notice that both detectives were observing him closely. One of her hands hung over the side of the tray. He picked it up absentmindedly and held it for a minute. Then he placed it back under the sheet. One of the detectives nodded to the attendant, who slid it back into the bank of receptacles holding the bodies.

Mulvehill turned to go. One of the detectives opened the door for him.

Mulvehill said, "Now?"

Both men answered in unison. "Of course." One of them asked, "Are you OK? Would you like one of us to drive you home?"

Mulvehill shook his head. "Thank you. I'm OK."

Mulvehill drove the Jeep back to the house. He unlocked the door, entered, closed the door, and stood in the darkness with his back against the wall.

He allowed himself one heartfelt curse. "Shit."

Light filtered into the room from a street lamp outside. He looked around. There was where she had sat at the table marking her students' papers. There was the chair he had sat in looking at her. He walked slowly into the bedroom. He did not want to turn the light on. It was bad enough looking at the bed in the dim light from the window. They had enjoyed many sexual pleasures there together. Sometimes tender and gentle. Sometimes almost violent. But always with mutual pleasure.

Now she was gone.

He turned on the bathroom light. He looked at his watch. It was almost four o'clock. He went into the bathroom, brushed his teeth and then washed his face. He turned out the light and walked back into the living room, drawing off his shirt. He lay down on the couch. He would sleep for an hour or so, then shower, dress and drive over to Mother Scarlatti's house, which was only five minutes away. He hoped she was able to sleep. He didn't think it would be a good idea to go over now.

When he awoke a bright sun was streaming in through the windows. He looked at his watch and was surprised to see that it was a few minutes past eight. After showering he made a cup of instant coffee, drank it hurriedly and drove over to Mother Scarlatti's house. She answered the door as soon as he knocked. They put their arms around each other.

Lisa, who had been standing in the doorway to the kitchen, came over and put her arms around his legs. He reached down and picked her up.

"Where's mommy?" she asked.

Mother Scarlatti answered. "She had to go away for awhile, darling."

Lisa put her hand on Mulvehill's face. "Mommy took me to the beach yesterday. Will you take me to the beach?"

He cocked his head, screwed up his mouth and looked sideways at her.

"Well," he said, "I was thinking about something different. Have you ever been down to the desert?"

She shook her head. Her golden curls swung back and forth.

"No," she said. "What's it like?"

He looked at her judiciously. "I think you would like it. That's where my folks live. And I've got a sister who is fourteen. I bet she'd like to play with you. There are sand dunes, and palm trees, and once a year we have a parade with camels.

"And Mother Scarlatti would come along." He looked at her.

She put her hand on Lisa's head. "Of course, darling. I think we would all like it."

Mulvehill put Lisa down. To Mother Scarlatti he said, "I'll call my folks and tell them to expect us."

He sat down and dialed. When the phone was answered at the other end he said, "Hi. Mrs. Johnson. Is my mother at the shed with dad?" He nodded. "OK. I'm coming down. I'm bringing company. Mrs. Scarlatti and a little girl. We'll be staying for a few days. And, oh, Mrs. Johnson, when my folks come home for lunch would you tell them I'd like my dad to call Mr. McLaughlin and ask him to meet us at the house after dinner. OK. Thanks."

To Mother Scarlatti he said, "Mr. McLaughlin is the family's attorney. We're going to have to make arrangements." He tilted his head toward Lisa.

The girl ran to her room. "I'll bring my doll with me."

They both looked at her. Mother Scarlatti said, "I came to America as a young girl, alone. I was fifteen. Since then I have lost a husband, a son, and now a daughter-in-law. I think I'm ready to go back to the

Old Country. There I still have some people in my home town of Livorno."

Mulvehill put his hand on her arm. "I hope you will stay with us for awhile. My folks will be most hospitable. And, if you have never been to the desert I think you will find it restful. Pack enough clothes for yourself and Lisa for a few days. Then, when you decide what we are going to do about Lisa I can come back and bring as much clothing as is necessary. We'll drive down in Magda's Hillman. It's too long a drive for an open Jeep."

"How long will it take us to get there?" the older woman asked.

"It's about a three hour drive. If the ride tires you we can stop along the way. And we'll stop whenever any of us need to go to a rest room."

Mother Scarlatti nodded. "I'll pack now."

Mulvehill looked around. It was the first time he had been inside Mag's mother-in- law's house. It was a small house not far from Sepulveda and National, but on a quiet side street. How sad for her, he thought. Her only son had married Magda. After he was killed in action against the Japanese in the South Pacific her daughter-in-law, whom she had genuinely liked, he knew, is made pregnant by a rich university kid. His father pays for the childbirth and then sends monthly payments to Mag to enable her to meet her mortgage payments and also some money for Lisa's support.

The father, apparently, had no interest in seeing his son's offspring and must have ordered his errant son to stay away.

Mulvehill did not know who the father was and did not want to know. What a tangled ball of twine. He'd let McLaughlin handle the details.

Lisa trotted out of the room where she slept with Mother Scarlatti. The old woman had found a toy suitcase that she had filled with a few of Lisa's things. For herself and Lisa she had packed two suitcases.

The three of them rode the Jeep back to Magda's house where they transferred the bags to the trunk of Mag's Hillman. Mulvehill locked the doors of Mag's house. They all got into Mag's car and Mulvehill headed for Santa Monica Blvd., which would take them to Highway 101 and then the long drive down to Thermal.

The ride was uneventful. Mulvehill stopped only once, in Riverside, where he bought an ice cream cone for Lisa and Cokes for Mother Scarlatti and himself. Soon after finishing her ice cream cone Lisa fell asleep. Mother Scarlatti wiped the stains off the girl's face with a handkerchief moistened with her saliva.

It was not quite three o'clock when he pulled into the driveway. Mrs. Johnson came out of the house and walked down to the car. She looked into the back seat where Lisa was sleeping. She crossed her hands near her throat and murmured, "Oh what a lovely child. May I carry her into the house? I'll put her on Cookie's bed."

Mulvehill introduced Mrs. Scarlatti. "Why don't you go along with Mrs. Johnson. I'll bring the bags in."

They all went up to the bedrooms. He showed Mother Scarlatti to Jean's room. "You'll be staying here.

It was my eldest sister's room but she's married and living in Chicago. I think you'll be comfortable here."

Soon afterwards there was a clatter of Cookie's bicycle and she came bounding into the house. The strange car out in the driveway had excited her curiosity. When she saw Mulvehill she flung her books aside, leaped up and threw her arms around his neck, almost knocking him over.

He laughed. "Hey little girl. Don't forget I've got a bum leg. But come with me. I want to show you something." He took her by the hand and led her up to her bedroom where she could see Lisa, asleep on her bed. She almost squealed but clapped her hand to her mouth and then, whispering, asked, "Who is she?"

Mulvehill was not quite prepared for how to handle the situation but Mother Scarlatti saved the day by walking in at that moment, saying, "She's my granddaughter." Mulvehill hastily introduced Mag's mother-in-law.

Cookie wanted to know, "Are you both going to be staying with us? For how long?"

Mulvehill laughed. "One question at a time, Cookie. Mrs. Scarlatti is the mother- in-law of my former math teacher at UCLA. Maybe you remember meeting her at my graduation."

Cookie shrugged, "There were so many people there."

"Well, anyway, Cookie, Mrs. Scarlatti and Lisa will be our guests here for awhile."

"She's beautiful," Cookie said. She turned to Mrs. Scarlatti. "Is it alright if I just sit here until she wakes up?"

"Of course," Mrs. Scarlatti said. She and Mulvehill walked downstairs. He led her out onto the porch. She looked around and out to the purple haze of the mountains far across the valley. She sighed. "It feels so tranquil here. I think I'd just like to sit here on that rocking chair until Lisa wakes up."

Mulvehill smiled. "Of course. Just relax. I'm going to drive up to Indio. I've got to talk to my father. It's a little complicated you know. But he'll know how to handle it with my mother." He sat down on the porch rail as the older woman settled into the rocking chair. "Mother Scarlatti, you'll find my folks are the most sympathetic of people. You'll be welcome to stay here as long as you like. But I've got to talk to my dad first, so he'll be prepared to meet you."

She nodded. "However you wish, Charles."

He went back into the house and told Mrs. Johnson he would be driving up to the packing plant. He went out back to the garage and wheeled the motorcycle out. To avoid waking Lisa with the roar of the cut-out he silently wheeled the bike down the path until he was well away from the house.

At the plant he drew his father away from the packing line. "Dad, can you ask Alberto to take over? I'd like you to come with me to Pedro's. I've got to talk with you." They got into his father's Buick and drove into Indio and around behind the old railroad station where's Pedro's saloon was located.

Pedro, whose real name was Ernie Halversen, was delighted to see Mulvehill. He reached across the bar and energetically pumped Charles' hand. Mulvehill followed his father to the end of the bar, where the two of them straddled the stools placed there.

Just as Mulvehill's father had said, the bartender reached under the bar and brought up a bottle of Harvey's Bristol Cream. He poured for Mulvehill's father and then looked at Mulvehill. "What are we drinking these days, feller?"

Mulvehill thought hard. Finally he asked, "Can you fix me a rusty nail?"

Halversen cackled. "Hey, we don't get many calls for that here, so this one's on the house." He placed a bottle of Old Rarity Scotch on the bar, felt around among the bottles under the bar and brought up the B & B. He mixed the two and handed the drink to Mulvehill. He waited until Mulvehill had tasted the drink. "Well?"

Mulvehill grinned. "Just like down town."

He got down from the stool, inclined his head toward a table in the dim corner and looked toward his father. The older man nodded his head in assent. The two of them walked toward the table, Halversen calling after them. "Mr. Mulvehill, yours is on the house too. It's good to see the lad back."

Once seated, Mulvehill sipped from his drink again, set the glass down, clasped his hands, leaned forward, and said, "Dad, I've been living in what the preachers used to call sin."

His father lifted his glass. "Here's to sin. You brought me out here to tell me about it so shoot."

He leaned back in his chair and made himself comfortable.

Mulvehill went through the whole story, from his first meeting with Magda when he was a student and she was still Miss Holm, to their recent, ongoing, affair and ended with her suicide. He included Mother Scarlatti's role in the story. His father listened without interruption. When Mulvehill had finished his recitation he sat quietly for a lengthy moment, drank from his glass and then pulled at his lower lip.

"Seems to me," he finally said, "that the first matter needs to be settled is the child." "That's what I felt, dad," Mulvehill replied. "I called Mrs. Johnson from Los Angeles and asked her to tell you that I'd like John McLaughlin to meet us at the house after dinner. Did she get through to you?"

His father nodded. "I figured this might be something you rather mother did not sit in on. I suggested to her that this might be a good night for her to take Consuelo to the Bingo game at St. Ambrose."

Mulvehill looked at his father in amazement. He put his hand on his father's forearm. "I'm one lucky guy, dad."

His father grinned. "Let's not get carried away." He tapped the table. "That's too good a drink to waste so drink up. I've got to get back to work."

Lisa was awake when Mulvehill got back to the house. Mother Scarlatti sat contentedly in the rocking chair on the porch as Cookie pushed Lisa on the tire swing that had been hanging from the limb of a gnarled Joshua tree on the front lawn since Jean had been a little girl. When Mulvehill drove up on his motorbike Cookie ran toward him excitedly.

She grabbed the handlebars. "Charles," she said breathlessly, "I gave Lisa a ride on the handlebars of my bike. She loved it. Will you give us a ride on the motorbike?" Without waiting for his answer she ran on, "Oh, Lisa and I are going to have so much fun together. It's almost like having a little sister. I asked Mrs. Scarlatti how long she and Lisa were going to stay. She said I'd have to ask you."

She took her hands off his handlebars and stood there arms akimbo.

"Well?"

He laughed. "We're going to decide tonight. So you'd really like to have Lisa stay for awhile?"

She punched him. "Are you kidding?" She turned serious. "Mrs. Scarlatti said that Lisa's mother has died. Oh that's so sad. Charles." She looked at him searchingly. "Do you think we might adopt her? Huh?"

He got off his motorbike and tousled her hair.

"Tonight, Cookie, we'll decide tonight."

18.

Mulvehill's check from the League, for a week in which he had done absolutely nothing, had been sent to the League's office in Beverly Hills and Ethel Longstreet forwarded it to Charles in Thermal.

The following day, feeling slightly guilty, he drove the Hillman back to Los Angeles. Mother Scarlatti relished the Mulvehills' easy hospitality and Lisa, pampered by Cookie, by both Mrs. Mulvehill and Mrs. Johnson, after a few queries about her mother, seemed to accommodate herself to the new surroundings.

Mother Scarlatti gave John McLaughlin the keys to her house and to Magda's house. He was going to send a law clerk up to Los Angeles the following week to carefully go through the papers in both dwellings and bring back essential documents to be reviewed preparatory to selling the properties, Mag's car, and to unravel Lisa's legal status.

Driving up to Los Angeles he thought over his conversation with Ethel Longstreet. She and Frankie Spitz had scheduled a meeting at an orthodox Jewish synagogue, Beit Hamidrash, pending Mulvehill's return. It was to be Mulvehill's maiden address as a fundraiser for the League. "Don't worry about a thing," Ethel had reassured him. "Orthodox Jews will fall all over themselves to be friendly. A 'goy' speaking on behalf of Palestinian Jews who were actually fighting the British so that the holy cities of Jerusalem, Hebron and the newer city of Safad in the Galilee will belong to the Jews! They will absolutely 'kvell'," she assured him.

"What's that?" Mulvehill wanted to know.

"'To beam with pride and pleasure'," Ethel interpreted. "It's what you do when your kid brings home a report card with all A's," she amplified. "Or when your son becomes a doctor. Then you can kvell as you introduce 'My son the doctor!'."

Mulvehill laughed.

"It's the high-falutin' reform Jews and the wealthy conservative congregations," she continued, "who tut-tut at the idea of Jews fighting the English. That's just beneath their dignity. But see if you can meet us at the office before five o'clock," she urged. "Up to five o'clock my body belongs to the League but after that my heart belongs to daddy."

'Daddy' was Steve Longstreet, a successful novelist and screenwriter who had first made a name for himself writing the book for the musical *High Button Shoes* followed by several novels. He was also an illustrator of note whose drawings could be found in the Fogg Museum at Harvard University.

Mulvehill arrived in Los Angeles by mid-afternoon. He drove the Hillman back to Magda's house, changed to his Jeep and, by four o'clock, showed up at the League office on Doheny Drive. Ethel was in her office, along with the redoubtable Frankie Spitz. They spent the next hour cueing an outline for Mulvehill's speech and provided him with an armload of literature on matters Jewish, British and political. He had all of the following day to prepare.

"What hotel do you recommend I stay at while I'm living in Los Angeles?" he asked the two of them.

Ethel scowled. "Hotel indeed," she said scornfully. "You're living with Steve and me. Our son is away at school. We'll fix his room up for you. And incidentally, Charles, we think we have the best cook in town. She's a mistress of 'haute cuisine'."

Mulvehill grinned. "How can I refuse?"

Ethel looked at the clock on the wall. "Time to lock up." She rose. "Frankie will meet us at the synagogue tomorrow night at eight. Where did you park?" she asked. "OK. Let me draw you a map for how to get to our house."

Steve Longstreet saved most of his words for his books but was cordial and attentive at dinner. He asked Mulvehill a few well chosen questions about Charles' war service, then sat back and let him talk.

They went into the den after dinner but Ethel excused herself to join the cook in the kitchen. Longstreet poured brandy into snifters for Mulvehill and himself, then sat down and lit his pipe. Mulvehill told of his meeting Marvin Zelinsky and Stacy Sheridan at The Brass Rail in New York. Longstreet nodded knowingly. "A great bar. One can always be assured of meeting interesting people. I've adapted more than a few for characters in my novels."

Mulvehill finished his drink. "I've got some studying to do, Mr. Longstreet," he said. "Is my room ready?" Longstreet rose. "No formalities, please. Call me Steve. I hope you will find it comfortable."

"I'm sure I will," Mulvehill said.

Longstreet led the way upstairs. "Ethel has already brought your study papers up and left them on the bedside table for you."

"Are you involved with the League, at all, Steve?" Mulvehill asked.

Longstreet grinned. They climbed to the top of the stairs and Longstreet led the way to his son's room. "Have you met Peter Bergson?" he asked.

Mulvehill nodded.

"Bergson stayed with us on his first visit to the Coast," Longstreet said. He sat down on the lone chair in the room so Mulvehill sat down on the bed. "That was in 1941 as I recall. Bergson had come out here with Ben Hecht to raise money for the Committee For An Army of Stateless and Palestinian Jews.

"Frankie Spitz, with her movie colony connections, managed to arrange for the use of the Twentieth Century-Fox commissary for a meeting of Hollywood big wigs. I came along to see how this would all turn out." Longstreet shook his head ruefully. "I had gained enormous respect for Bergson's intelligence, grasp of political realities, and exceptional tenacity. But I knew the Hollywood crowd and had my doubts about what kind of reception our Palestinian patriot would get. And Ben Hecht, I think," he said, "was probably more hopeful than optimistic."

"What happened?" Mulvehill asked.

Longstreet leaned back in the chair, straightened his legs and crossed them.

"It was a balmy night," he recalled. "Ben and Peter had gone out to the Lakeview Country Club to pick up Senator Claude Pepper of Florida, whom Peter had somehow bagged and induced to come to Hollywood as keynote speaker for the affair.

"To my surprise," Longstreet continued, "the commissary was crowded. Most of the people there were Jews, as we had expected. But Hedda Hopper was there, as well as Charlie Chaplin, which was unusual because this was, patently, a Jewish meeting and Chaplin had never before attended any Jewish affair lest his appearance would give credence to the persistent rumor that he was a Jew.

"I took a seat in the back to see what would transpire. Senator Pepper was the first speaker. His fine sonorous voice," Longstreet chuckled, "paid homage to the culture and virtues of the Jews. Some of the audience were carried away by the flattery of his saying anything at all, but the rest of us were puzzled. Were his foggy and vapid phrases all he had to offer when the invitation had sounded a bugle call for a Jewish army rising out of heaven knows where?"

"Then what happened?" Mulvehill asked. He plumped up the pillows and settled back.

Longstreet smiled. "The next speaker was Col. John H. Patterson, D.S.O., of the British army. Do you know anything about him?"

Mulvehill nodded. "Peter told me something about his leading the Jewish Legion in World War I."

"Yes," Longstreet agreed. "He was in command of the Jewish Legion under General Allenby when they beat the Turks back at Es Salt and helped take Palestine for the Allies. You have to remember, Charles, this was the Spring of 1941. We were not yet in the war and we admired brave little England, fighting with her back against the wall. The audience applauded. England was our hero that night and a former colonel of the British army, for all that he was really an Irishman, was a man for cheering."

Longstreet paused, thinking back to that night. Patterson was, in truth, a fine-looking man, tall, erect, with military bearing. He had been a famous lion-hunter in his youth and a book he had written, *Man-Eaters of Tsavo,* had a reputation as the lion-hunters' bible.

Now Longstreet laughed out loud, recalling that Col. Patterson's speech set his audience back on their heels.

"The colonel took off at once on what had moved him to side with the men of the Irgun late in his middle years; a precise and documented account of Britain's mistreatment of Jabotinsky's Jewish Legion.

"Here was a fine kettle of fish! Patterson spoke, not of the bravery of the British but of heroic Jews, of Joseph Trumpeldor, whom Patterson described as 'the bravest man I have ever seen'—and of instance after instance of British foul play and anti-Semitism against his beloved Jews. He told how the Jewish Legion, under his command, had driven the Turks back. The Jewish forces took eighty thousand prisoners and another ten thousand surrendered voluntarily.

"For this honor, Patterson said, every member of the Jewish battalions were cited for valor but, at the same time, degraded to the status of labor battalions. You should have seen how indignant Patterson was," Longstreet said, "when he described this insult to his beloved troops.

"The audience was stunned. They began to boo the colonel. Catcalls rang out and cries for him to be seated."

Longstreet shook his head.

Colonel Patterson looked at his audience coolly. He told of his personal experiences with British anti-Semitism and of Great Britain's betrayal of its promise to help the Jews create a homeland for their people in Palestine.

"People began walking out of the place."

Mulvehill broke in. "I take it the meeting was not a success."

Longstreet smiled. "Not entirely. The meeting went on. But the audience of Hollywood big shots, whom Ben Hecht and his cohorts had assembled with much difficulty in hopes of helping them put up the money to arm his champions—the young Stateless and Palestinian Jews who wanted to fight—had not only been outraged. Worse, they had been a little bored by the tale of British skulduggery in a distant desert for which they were in no mood. It was as if they had been asked to listen to the plot of an old silent movie starring Lewis Stone."

"What happened?" Mulvehill asked.

"Well, Burgess Meredith spoke in favor of the Jewish Army, and then Peter Bergson, and finally Ben Hecht.

"After Ben finished his speech there was a lot of talking among the members of the audience. The voice of Hedda Hopper, certainly the most famous of the Hollywood gossip columnists, sounded. 'We're here to contribute to a cause,' she said firmly. 'I'll start the contributions with a check for three hundred dollars.'"

Mulvehill held up his hand. "Wait a minute. I had friends at UCLA who knew her. She's not Jewish."

Longstreet laughed. "Neither is Patterson and neither is Burgess Meredith."

Mulvehill sat up on the edge of the bed. "This gets kind of confusing. Wasn't this supposed to be a Jewish audience gathered together to raise money for a Jewish cause?"

Longstreet grinned.

"Yes. And despite the shock of Col. Patterson's speech, and the confused objectives described by Pepper, Bergson and Hecht, a wave of largess swept the audience. One after another, people stood up to call out their contributions. These ranged from a hundred dollars to five thousand dollars. Those of us who knew the industry were chagrined to note that among the five thousand dollar donors were Gregory Ratoff, Sam Spiegel and a few others whose solvency at the time could be said to be in question."

Longstreet stood up. "A couple of weeks later Ben Hecht told me that, of a hundred and fifty thousand dollars that had been pledged that night, his field workers, consisting of Ethel Longstreet, Rose Hecht and a few others, finally managed to collect nine thousand dollars. Much of that money," Longstreet smiled, "was from Ben Hecht's friends."

Mulvehill stood up too. "What have I gotten myself into? It seems that the Jews are better at fighting themselves than anyone else."

Longstreet put his hand on Mulvehill's shoulder.

"Bergson explained it to me. 'It's the same old story,' he said. 'Jews must always battle Jews. It's the only politics open to a stateless people. The only victories they can hope to enjoy are victories over each other.'"

Longstreet looked at Mulvehill earnestly.

"That's why I think the fight of the men and women of the Irgun is so important," he said. "They are convinced that only when the Jews have a nation of their own, like every other nation, will Jews all over the world finally lose their ghetto complex, and win a sense of pride."

He put his other hand on Mulvehill's other shoulder and looked at him steadily.

"You see, Charles, that is why you are so important to the League. When you speak to Jews on behalf of a Jewish cause they will draw strength from your strength. 'If this young Gentile man is willing to speak up for us,' they will say, 'then we must have the strength to speak up for ourselves.'"

He dropped his hands. "Now I'll leave so you can study your notes for tomorrow's talk." He walked out the door.

Mulvehill sat down again on the edge of the bed. He thought for a moment, shook his head and then smiled.

If he was going to speak to an audience of elderly, pious, Jews maybe he ought to focus on their thoughts about the ancient land of Israel.

He looked through his notes and found what he wanted.

> *'Long before the name Palestinian was invented'*, he read, *'the Hebrew people, children of Abraham, Isaac, and Jacob, lived in Hebron. There Abraham purchased the Cave of Machpela, and there the Patriarchs and Matriarchs of the nation were buried. Hebron was the city given unto Caleb, the son of Jephune, for his faith in God. There David ruled as king for seven years before going to Jerusalem, and there Jews and Judaism were entwined for 3,500 years. In Hebron there lived some five hundred Jews, mostly Sephardic, many with roots going back hundreds of years. And there, in 1929, occurred a massacre that took more Jewish lives than Kishinev.'*

He turned the page.

> *'High in the beautiful Galilean hills stands Safad, the city of the Kabbalists. Its three thousand Jews had lived for generations with*

the Arabs. All spoke Arabic and the Sephardic Jews were hardly distinguishable from the Arabs in their dress. But on August 29, 1929, the 23rd of Av in the Jewish calendar, a mob of Arabs burst into the Jewish quarter, led by Fuad Hajazi, a young clerk of the local government health office...'

Mulvehill turned on the bedside lamp, undressed, got into bed and continued reading. It was well past midnight when he patted the paper notes into a neat pile, put them down on the night table, turned out the light and fell asleep.

He was awakened by a knock on the door. He opened his eyes. Bright sunshine streamed into the room. "Hullo," he called out sleepily.

The voice from the other side of the door was Ethel's. "It's a quarter past eight, Charles. Do you want to sleep some more or get up now and have breakfast with Steve and me?"

"If you give me ten minutes, Ethel," he called back, "I'll shower and join you for breakfast."

"We'll wait Charles. Don't hurry."

He sat up. During the night someone had entered and placed a bathrobe and towels on the chest that stood at the foot of the bed. He was in and out of the shower in eight minutes, dressed and appeared at the breakfast table in the ten minutes he had asked for.

Steve was reading the morning paper. He put it down and took off his glasses.

"How do you like your eggs, Charles?" Ethel asked.

"Over easy. Two eggs and one slice of toast is all I need," he answered.

"Did you hear that Emma?" Ethel called into the kitchen. The cook answered, "Ah heard."

Ethel poured coffee for Mulvehill.

Steve tapped the paper. "Palestine is in the news again. And so is the Irgun. They've blown a hole in the wall of Acre prison. Two hundred and fifty one prisoners have escaped. A hundred and thirty-one Arabs and a hundred and twenty Jews."

"This is the Irgun's retaliation for the hangings in Acre of Shlomo Ben-Yosef and other young men of the Irgun," Longstreet said. "And they are not through. Stories are leaking out of Irgun soldiers raiding British arsenals, blowing up railroad communications, theft of British motor cars and uniforms."

"Sounds like things are heating up in Palestine," Mulvehill responded.

"Do you want help in writing your talk for tonight's meeting?" Ethel asked.

Mulvehill shook his head. "No, I think I know the tack I'll take tonight. But I'm going to drive out to Santa Monica. I want to look at the water and think about what I'm doing."

Ethel reached over and patted his hand.

"All right. But try to get back for dinner at six. Frankie Spitz is joining us for dinner and then the three of us will drive over to the synagogue—Beit Hamidrash on West Adams Boulevard."

Mulvehill finished his coffee, wiped his mouth and rose from the table. "I'll be back in time." He turned to Steve. "You're not going?"

Steve grinned.

"I'm afraid not, Charles. I rarely go to meetings of any kind. But I'll be cheering for you."

They all left the table.

*　*　*

At dinner, Mulvehill ate lightly. Frankie noticed.

"Butterflies, Charles?"

He grinned. "A little."

Ethel patted his hand. "Don't worry. You're going to do just fine. Believe me. I know about these things."

Frankie drove. It was a warm night. She was driving her Mercury convertible and had the top down. Mulvehill sat next to her and Ethel sat in the back. As they drove east on Olympic and then south on La Cienega the manicured lawns and large houses of Beverly Hills gave way, first to smaller homes and two story duplexes and then, as they drove east on Adams, to a few industrial buildings, stores and poorer houses.

Frankie pulled up in front of the synagogue. It was early and there was plenty of parking space. Mulvehill remained seated in the car, looking up at the facade of the synagogue. The Star of David was engraved high up on the brick front, underneath a round stained glass window. Now that he was about to enter a Jewish synagogue, for the first time in his life, he was faced with a momentary hesitation.

Ethel, who was seated behind him, tapped his shoulder. "Out, Charles, it's just bricks and mortar." He turned around, looked at her and smiled. She smiled back, encouragingly. "Let me out, Charles, I'm cramped back here."

He opened the door and jumped out. He drew the front seat forward so that she could exit the car. He extended his hand and helped her out.

The three of them stood in front of the building. The front door, at the head of a flight of stone steps, stood open. A short rotund man, with a neatly trimmed beard, appeared in the doorway. "Ladies, I'm rabbi Kramer," he called down to them. "Please come up."

They ascended the steps. Ethel introduced herself and Frankie Spitz. She put her hand behind Mulvehill's elbow and drew him forward.

"This is Charles Mulvehill, rabbi. Your speaker for the evening."

The two men shook hands.

"Mr. Mulvehill," the rabbi said. "Please let me tell you how grateful I am, personally, for your help to the Irgun. Mrs. Longstreet has sent me some background on you so that I may make a proper introduction. Please come in."

Charles looked around. There was no baptismal font or statues of saints but, otherwise, the lobby could have been the entrance to any church. He followed the rabbi into the interior. The room was dimly lit. On either side of a central aisle curved wooden benches extended to either wall. There was a slight musty smell, as of old books. They walked forward down the aisle and Mulvehill followed the rabbi up to a raised platform. A few elderly people were already seated on the benches for the congregation. Ethel and Frankie took seats toward the rear.

The platform, which was entirely carpeted in rich purple tufting, extended almost across the width of the room and was reached by five short steps. High-backed, ornately carved, chairs with velvet seats were ranged across the back wall. Mulvehill looked up and saw a carving of two lions, rampant, facing each other across a representation of the tablets of the Ten Commandments.

A small bronze cup was suspended from the ceiling and in it a small lamp burned.

The rabbi followed Mulvehill's gaze.

"That is the representation of the lamp that was commanded by God to burn eternally in the tabernacle. It is no longer practical," he smiled, "to have an oil lamp so we settle for a low voltage electric lamp."

The rabbi gestured toward one of the chairs and Mulvehill sat down. The rabbi sat down next to him. "Our congregation president, Mr. Samuelson, will be along in a minute. He will join us up here. That is the tradition. And your audience will be along shortly."

He shrugged. "I am not sure what kind of turnout we will get, Mr. Mulvehill, but I assure you that those who come will be most interested in what you have to say."

The rabbi continued to make small talk, to help make him comfortable, Mulvehill reasoned, asking about how Mulvehill liked California, where he came from, etc.

While he was talking a slender man with a goatee, neatly dressed in a dark suit, mounted the steps. The rabbi rose. "Mr. Samuelson. How good to see you. Let me introduce Mr. Mulvehill."

They shook hands. Samuelson seemed surprised. "Mr. Mulvehill. That is an Irish name, is it not? You are here to speak on behalf of the Jews? How strange."

It was now almost eight o'clock and the room was filling rapidly. By eight the seats were filled and the rabbi rose and stepped forward to the lectern.

"My dear friends. A guten ovent.* I thank you all for coming. Our guest tonight is Mr. Charles Mulvehill, who is appearing tonight on behalf of the American League For A Free Palestine. That is the organization headed by Mr. Ben Hecht and Senator Guy Gillette of Iowa. The function of the organization is very simple. It is their purpose to raise money to help the men and women of Irgun Zvai Leumi[†] in Palestine in their struggle to oust the British from Palestine so that Eretz Israel will once again be the home for the Hebrew people, as promised in our Torah.

"Mr. Mulvehill is a genuine war hero. While fighting the Germans in Italy he was wounded. He was honored by being given the medal of the Order of the Purple Heart."

He smiled. "But you did not come here to hear me, so let me present Mr. Mulvehill."

* A good evening
† Organization. Military. National

There was applause but it was light and scattered. Orthodox Jews, Mulvehill had been informed in advance, are not accustomed to applauding people in the synagogue. Mulvehill walked forward to the lectern. His left leg throbbed unaccountably and caused him to limp more than was usual. He was embarrassed by the limp.

He took the notes he had made from his jacket pocket and placed them on the lectern in front of him.

He swallowed.

"I am an American," he began, "just as each of you is. I am of Irish descent. When I was in Ireland during the war I felt good about being in the land from which my father came, and where many of his generation fought the British for an Irish Free State. And they won.

"But if you were to go to Palestine today," he paused slightly to let the meaning of his words sink in, "you could not feel that you were in a free Eretz Israel." Some in the audience smiled at his pronunciation of the Hebrew words.

"You would know that you were in a land controlled and occupied by an alien oppressor. When you would see the uniforms of the British soldiers you would know that they were not there to help create a Jewish homeland, as their government had promised in 1917.

"There are many Jews living there who accept the British yoke. But there are some who do not. This minority, maybe just a few hundred, are the men and women of the Irgun. Perhaps I should say the boys and girls of the Irgun, because most of them are quite young. Four brave young men who were hung by the British in Acre Fortress for opposing the British were all under twenty."

As he warmed to his talk his discomfort left him. The pain in his leg subsided and a feeling of warmth and pleasure rose in him. He told of all the things he had learned from Ben Hecht, Alex Hadani, Peter Bergson and Samuel Merlin, and from the reading of the material that had been given to him.

He came to the climax of his talk.

"Those young men and women of the Irgun in Palestine, a mere handful, have fought the British for a free Hebrew Republic on both sides of the Jordan. Whether they will win or not we cannot yet know. But there is something that I know, and I would like to share this knowledge with you. The men and women of the Irgun have accomplished something that the Jewish people have not known since the heroic days of Bar Kochba. They have won the respect of their enemies."

Now there was no hesitation about applauding. The applause was thunderous and some cried out in happiness…"A shekoach."*

Mulvehill picked up his notes and turned from the lectern to return to his seat. He looked down at his watch and was astonished to find that he had talked for an hour and ten minutes. He looked out from his seat. Frankie and Ethel, in the back row, raised their clasped hands in the traditional boxer's sign of victory.

The rabbi and Mr. Samuelson came over and shook his hand warmly.

* To your strength and health

The rabbi stepped forward to the lectern and spoke to the audience in Yiddish. Mulvehill saw heads nodding here and there in agreement. Some of the women were dabbing their eyes with their handkerchiefs.

The rabbi concluded his talk and the audience rose. They sang the Hebrew song Hatikvah…'Hope'.

The rabbi walked back to Mulvehill. "A table has been laid in the basement with cookies and sponge cake. If you haven't tasted sponge cake," he smiled, "you must. It is the traditional Jewish cake for Bar Mitzvahs, weddings, and the Sabbath. We hope you will join us."

He led Mulvehill down from the Bimah* and out a door at the side of the platform which led down to the basement. There were no decorations there. Tables had been set at the back and sides draped with white tablecloths. Platters contained the cake that the rabbi had mentioned but there were also plates with herring and challah, the Jewish white bread. One of the men came over to Mulvehill and the rabbi, bearing two small glasses of whiskey. "Excuse me, rabbi," he said. "I only have two hands or I would bring a drink for you too." He held one of the glasses out to Mulvehill.

"I would consider it an honor to drink to your health and hope you will join me."

Mulvehill accepted the glass. The other touched the rim of his glass to Mulvehill's. They both drank. Mulvehill winced. "Wow. That's powerful stuff. What is it?"

The other grinned. "Irish whiskey."

* The raised platform that holds the lectern and at the back of which is the ark of the Torah

They laughed. The man introduced himself. "I'm Joe Fenstermacher. I'm a barber. You want a haircut? In my shop it's free. For life."

He reached into the pocket of his jacket and drew out an envelope, which he handed Mulvehill. "For the Irgun. And I wish it could be ten times as much."

Mulvehill thanked him.

A second man approached to shake his hand and also withdrew an envelope and handed it to him. "For the Irgun. And thank you for the kindness of your heart which makes you, a Gentile, want to help the Jewish people. May God grant you long life. Thank you. Thank you."

Mulvehill waved his hand deprecatingly.

Now the rest of the men and women came forward, shyly, to shake his hand, one at a time, and to slip him an envelope.

Frankie Spitz, standing at Mulvehill's side, began taking the envelopes from him and stuffing them into her capacious handbag.

The crowd thinned out. Mulvehill drank from a cup of tea that Ethel had brought over to him. It occurred to him that all this must have been orchestrated by either the rabbi or Mr. Samuelson else how would all these people already have money in an envelope to hand to him following his talk? Perhaps their feelings of appreciation were sincere, but still, the offerings were not spontaneous.

When the last of the congregation had come over to shake his hand and give him an envelope the rabbi walked over. Ethel thanked him for permitting them to tell the Irgun story to his congregation. They shook hands all around and left.

Back in the car, Ethel tapped Frankie on the shoulder. "Drive us over to Tiny Naylor's. I've got to have some stronger coffee than what was available here tonight."

At Tiny Naylor's they found a table in the back. There was but a small sprinkling of people in the restaurant and yet it was only a quarter to ten. Once again Mulvehill remarked to himself that Los Angeles was really still a small town where they pulled the sidewalks in at nine o'clock. He felt a vague yearning for the bright lights of Broadway and Times Square.

While they waited for the waiter and Frankie counted out the money in the envelopes Mulvehill leaned back on the padded leather bench, feeling both drained and exhilarated.

Frankie patted the bills into a neat pile.

"Six hundred and twenty eight dollars," she scowled. "Hundreds when we need thousands, and even hundreds of thousands."

Ethel shrugged. "But this is a rather poor congregation. We'll do better when Charles talks to more well-to-do groups. And Charles," she turned to him. "You were wonderful. You really were."

The waiter came and took their orders.

Frankie continued to shake her head. "No. No. We've got to do better. Charles is a wonderful asset. We mustn't waste him."

Mulvehill laughed. "I think you're overrating my value."

Ethel demurred. "No. Frankie is right. Steve told me what he had told you. We are very lucky that you care enough for Bergson and the other men from Palestine to agree to work with them."

Frankie put the money back into her purse and snapped the lock shut.

"Charles," she said. "I'm going to set up a meeting for you with Bill Bess. He's a producer at Republic Pictures and a really all right guy. I think you'll like him. He's not like some of the big shots at the major studios who look at you like you're crazy if you ask them to do anything for the Jews. Will you meet with him if he agrees to see you?"

Mulvehill shrugged. "Sure, why not? That's what I'm here for."

The waiter brought their coffee.

19.

The appointment Frankie had made for him at Republic Studios was for ten thirty. Mulvehill indulged himself by sleeping until eight. Both Ethel and Steve had left the house so he drove over to Googie's on Sunset Boulevard for breakfast. It was a beautiful sunny morning. When he went out to the Jeep in the parking lot he lowered the canvas top. Out on Cahuenga Pass the yucca plants were bright yellow.

He drove slowly, enjoying the look of the giant boulders that lined one side of the Pass. He thought ahead to his meeting. He was the least star-struck of human beings but the thought of visiting his first movie studio led to pleasant conjectures.

The guard at the gate asked his name and called the production office from his little gatehouse. He asked about Mulvehill, nodded and hung up. "Okay," he said, "you drive straight on this street to Stage C. Make a right turn there and you'll see a white, two-story building a little way ahead on your left. You can park alongside the building and go to the head of the stairs. The door at the top, on the left, says 'Bill Bess—Producer'. That's where you'll find him." He looked the

Jeep over and said, "I used to drive one of these when I was in the MPs. Third Army."

"Oh," Mulvehill said. He was carefully non-committal.

"Yeah," the guard replied. He stepped back. "Well, take it easy."

Mulvehill nodded and drove off.

He drove slowly, watching actors walking by. There were cowboys, Indians, troopers dressed in the blue uniforms of the Union Army and, in and amongst them, pretty girls in costumes of the Old West, side by side with script girls carrying three-ring binders. And, throughout, working men in overalls.

He had no trouble finding the office. Opening the door he was met by a strikingly good looking young woman. "Oh, Mr. Mulvehill," she exclaimed, "Mr. Bess was called out to a meeting. He'll try to get back as soon as possible and asked if you'll please be patient. He hopes you'll be able to stay and have lunch with him."

"That's perfectly all right," Mulvehill said. "I'm in no hurry."

"Would you like to watch an indoor shooting scene?" She pointed out the window. "They're setting up on Stage E. That's not far from here and if Mr. Bess gets back I can run over and get you."

"I've seen an awful lot of actors dressed as cowboys walking along," Mulvehill noted. "Do you just make Western movies here?"

"Just about," she nodded. "We're known as the studio for making 'oaters'," she giggled. "That's because we use lots of horses and horses eat lots of oats."

Mulvehill laughed. "Makes sense. Okay, I'll walk over there."

He made his way over to the Stage. There was a wide door, open to the outside. A ramp led up to the door and straw was scattered on the ground, both outside and within. He walked through. The inside was made up to look like an old Western bar room and dance hall, complete to the swinging doors through which, traditionally, both the bad guys and the good guys would enter the saloon. To one side there were several tables, upon which were trays with cookies, candies, sandwiches, and a large canister of what he took to be coffee. A few people stood nearby, munching. One of them looked up as Mulvehill approached.

"I'm a visitor...," he started to say to the young man, who was dressed in street clothes.

"No kidding," the other grinned. "Make yourself comfortable. They're just setting up the lights. You can sit in one of those chairs along the wall." He gestured toward the side of the building, and turned back to the food.

A man lifted a megaphone to his lips and bawled out, "Okay, let's have that door closed. We're going to test the lighting."

Although Mulvehill could not fathom to whom he was addressing the message, a young man materialized from outside the building and drew the large door shut.

Mulvehill noted that it rolled easily and quietly on its tracks.

The gloom was instantly dispelled by brilliant carbon arc lamps that blazed into light. He watched a large camera on a swinging boom move down toward floor level and saw that a cameraman was seated on the boom. Another man jumped up on the boom, alongside the first, and peered through a view finder. He called, "Okay, kill 'em," and the lights went dark. One of the actors was called to stand in front of the bar. A man with a tape measured the distance from the camera to the man in front of the bar.

Mulvehill heard a voice at his elbow.

"Mr. Bess is back in his office."

He turned and saw the secretary. She beckoned and he followed her through the gloom and out a side door.

"Did you find it interesting?" she asked as she led him back to the office building.

"I guess everybody is interested in seeing how movies are made." He smiled. "I'm no different."

He followed her up the stairs. She led him into a private office. The man behind the desk rose. The secretary made the introduction. "Mr. Bess, this is Mr. Mulvehill."

The two of them shook hands and the producer, who was a slight man of middle height, dressed in a plain white shirt and slacks, motioned Mulvehill to a seat. When Mulvehill was seated, the other reached across the desk and proffered a pack of cigarettes. Mulvehill shook his head. At that moment the phone rang. The producer picked it up and said "Bess." He looked at Mulvehill, nodded, and said into the phone, "Twenty minutes and I'll be there."

Mulvehill took the occasion to look around the room. It was plainly furnished. Framed pictures on the wall were apparently actors and actresses. He recognized two as prominent cowboy stars.

Bess lit his own cigarette, inhaled, blew out smoke and addressed Mulvehill. "I know very little about Palestine, but Ethel Longstreet, for whom I have a great deal of respect, says you want to raise money for an underground organization of Palestinian Jews. Is that correct?"

"It's quite simple," Mulvehill responded. "the situation was explained to me in New York by a man named Peter Bergson. He was born there. They call the native born Jews in Palestine *sabras* after the cactus that grows there. It's prickly on the outside and sweet on the inside."

The producer permitted himself a slight smile. "I've heard about the resemblance to the outside." He looked closely at Mulvehill. "You're not Jewish, are you?"

"No," Mulvehill agreed, "are you, Mr. Bess?"

The other laughed. "Call me Bill. Yes, I'm a Jew. But how did you get involved?"

"I think largely through Ben Hecht's influence," Mulvehill said. "We came out together on the train from Chicago."

"Ah, Ben Hecht," Bess said. "He's a hell of a screenwriter, maybe the best in the business. I've heard something about his involvement in a Jewish cause."

Mulvehill leaned forward. "I've had the situation explained to me this way. For the nationalist Jewish youth in Palestine the issue is clear. They see it as their home, both historically and morally. The Arabs in Palestine have no roots there. They are the residue of hundreds of years of transitory invasions, and the wanderings of tribal groups. The Irgun recognizes the Arab's right to live there in civil and religious freedom but only the descendants of the ancient Hebrews have a past—and a future—that is linked irrevocably with the land.

"In addition...," Mulvehill leaned back in his chair. He felt surprised, and pleased, that he was expressing the Irgun's position clearly. He felt comfortable. "The British, who were given a Mandate by the League of Nations," he went on, "to assist in creating a Jewish homeland in Palestine have abdicated that responsibility. Yet they linger on, giving comfort to the Arabs, and resistance to the Jews. Here is an interesting example," Mulvehill said, warming to his theme.

"If a Jew is caught carrying arms he may be punished by death or life imprisonment. There is also a law, Hecht told me," Mulvehill said, "that punishes an Arab for carrying a gun. The penalty in that case is a fine of five shillings."

"Doesn't sound quite fair," Bess said, "does it?"

"I cite it as just one instance of British prejudice against the Jews. The men and women of the Irgun," Mulvehill continued, "decided that the British must leave Palestine so that the Jews can form their own government. They have armed themselves and declared war against England. I'm on their side," Mulvehill said, "so I agreed to help them. There is an organization here in America raising money for the Irgun. It is called American League For A Free Palestine. I went to work for them. They pay me forty-five dollars a week."

Bess smiled. "A little less than we pay our writers."

Mulvehill shrugged. "The money doesn't matter. If I wanted more money I would go to work in my father's business. But I think the Jews are getting a raw deal." He smiled. "And you could say I've got a historical grudge against the British."

Bess raised his eyebrows. "Ah, you're of Irish descent."

Mulvehill grinned.

The producer reached into his desk and drew out a checkbook. He left it unopened on his desk.

He blew out some smoke and then stubbed his cigarette out in the ash tray. "Let me tell you something," he said. "Ben Hecht came out here before the war and tried to raise money for the same group of people, but operating then under a different name. He failed. It's important to understand what drives the Jews who own and operate the major studios. They believe they have some sort of responsibility to keep the product 'American'. That's why the respectability of the product is so important to them. They are personally favorable to the idea of a Jewish homeland but they are deathly afraid of being considered un-American."

"I think Ben understands that now," Mulvehill said.

"Okay." Bess scribbled in his checkbook and then swiftly wrote something on a pad on his desk. He tore out the check and handed both pieces of paper to Mulvehill.

Mulvehill looked first at the check. He whistled. It was made out for fifteen thousand dollars. He looked up quickly at the producer.

"Are you sure you can afford this?" he asked.

Bess smiled. "I crank out eight films a year. My budget is three hundred thousand dollars a film and I never go over budget. And we average three million dollars a film at the box office. Figure it out. Yes," he concluded. "I can afford it. I've got two stars who bring the audiences flocking to the theaters where my films play. Maybe you know them. Hoot Gibson and Ken Maynard."

"They're my favorites," Mulvehill said. He looked at the other piece of paper in his hand. It contained a list of names, none of which he recognized, and a list of film studios, all of which he recognized.

"These men will listen to you," Bess said. "They're good guys and they're all Jews. And not afraid to be known as Jews. If they believe that what you're doing makes sense, they will contribute. They will probably write it off," he grinned, "as script consulting work but the money will be good."

Mulvehill rose. He folded the check and put it in his pocket. "This is for a good cause, Bill," he said, "and it means a great deal to me that you are willing to trust me with a check made out in my name."

Bess waved his hand. "Ethel said you could be trusted and that was good enough for me. Just endorse it over to the League."

They shook hands and Mulvehill left.

He spent the next two weeks getting to meet the eight men whose names Bess had given him. A good part of that time was spent waiting in outer offices but, once he got inside, he came away with a check. Mostly he presented the platform outlined by Peter Bergson. It was described by Bergson in a letter described as "A Blueprint for Hebrew Freedom."

He saw the necessity, Mulvehill pointed out, of trying to repatriate to Palestine the approximately one and a half million Jews still alive in Europe. Those million and a half Jews, Mulvehill told the men he met with, would join the young Hebrew nation already living on its own soil in Palestine. The goal was to win recognition for that Hebrew nation, and to ensure that the British evacuate their troops so that the Hebrews could fulfill their own destiny.

The idea of a Hebrew nation in Palestine generally was well received by the men with whom Mulvehill met. They could see that the existence of a Hebrew nation on its own soil in Palestine would exert a beneficial effect on Jews in the Diaspora. It would make them proud to see a nation of Hebrews, whose identity in the eyes of the world as Jews, would be seen by the world as a nation, however small, but co-equal with other nations.

But it was now eighteen months after the end of the war, Mulvehill pointed out, and only a handful were getting into Palestine. The others, who arrived off the coast of Palestine in ships bought by the League, were being intercepted by British patrol boats and interned on the island of Cyprus. The enemy of the Jews were now the British.

When Mulvehill had met all the men he was scheduled to meet, and collected a substantial check from each, he headed back to the League office on Doheny Drive. Ethel Longstreet was in the office when he arrived. A young woman, who looked somehow familiar to him, was seated in the office with her.

Ethel made the introduction. "Charles, you remember Mrs. Oshan. She had been at Alex Hadani's talk before the North Hollywood Women's Club. She joined us for coffee after the meeting."

Mulvehill remembered.

Ethel handed him a business card. "This is Mrs. Oshan's husband's card. He has agreed to introduce you to people in Las Vegas who can help us."

Mulvehill looked down at the card, which read 'Richard Oshan, Advertising'.

Mrs. Oshan stood up. "Call Dick when you get a chance and then go downtown to meet with him." She held out a gloved hand. "And call me Lily." She left and Mulvehill handed Ethel the checks he had collected.

She grasped Mulvehill's hand. "Well done, Charles."

After dinner that evening Ethel brought a banana cream pie to the table. "I believe this is your favorite, Charles?"

He grinned. "Almost. Actually it's lemon meringue, but this will do just fine."

Steve excused himself to go to the den and work on a novel he was writing.

Ethel turned to Mulvehill. "Mrs. Oshan may turn out to be a lucky break for us. Her husband has two uncles on his mother's side who are in business in Las Vegas. They own hundreds of slot machines, which are popularly called 'one arm bandits' because you pull down a lever after inserting a coin. The pictures that appear in three windows determine if the gambler has won or lost. If three matching pictures appear, say three lemons, three cherries, etc., the machine releases a number of coins into the tray at the bottom. Or am I telling you something you already know?"

He shook his head. "No, I've never seen such machines."

"A lot of money floats around Las Vegas," Ethel continued, "every hotel, there are a number of them and several under construction at this time, has its own gambling casino and each vies with the next to see who can be more garish, brilliantly lit or flamboyant.

"Don't be surprised if your first visit to Las Vegas gives you the impression that it is sin town." She looked at him. "Because it is."

"Mr. Oshan's uncles," she continued, "place their slot machines in business establishments independent of the casinos and it seems," Ethel said, "that there is no business too small to be excluded from gambling. It is legal in the state of Nevada and the state government gets two percent of the gambling 'take' as its cut. Very lucrative."

Mulvehill nodded. "I'll call Mr. Oshan tomorrow."

They both rose from the table.

"There is a letter from your folks waiting for you, Charles," Ethel told him. "I've put it on your bedside table."

He took the steps two at a time. The letter was from his mother and several pages long. Lisa was happy to be with them. The child had not asked about her mother in days and they were delighted to have her with them. Cookie especially was thrilled with Lisa and took her with her wherever she went.

Michael was doing well at the military academy at West Point. His grades were good and he had successfully lived through the initial period of 'hazing' which Mrs. Mulvehill thought childish and degrading.

John McLaughlin had successfully concluded the legal work related to Magda's suicide and the elder Mrs. Scarlatti's move to Italy. Both houses had been sold. Mulvehill's mother and father had been named foster parents. Lisa would live with them, Mrs. Mulvehill artlessly noted, until, she hoped, Charles would marry and legally adopt the child.

Well, he thought, that was something to think about. Marriage, to him, now seemed to lie far in the future.

In bed that night he reflected on the work he was doing for the League and was buoyed by his recollection of what Alex Hadani had told him of Col. Patterson's devotion to the Irgun's fight for Hebrew independence. Patterson never wavered in his support of the League and what it sought to accomplish. He had been a valiant military man but, because of his outspoken defense of the Jews, he was penalized by the British military hierarchy and was never elevated to the rank of general.

That intransigence by Patterson and the subsequent snubbing by the British found a parallel, Mulvehill had learned, in the British military's treatment of Orde Wingate, another British army officer who fell into disfavor because, while stationed in Palestine he had trained Jews as night fighters against Arab incursions. He was considered by some to have been the founder of the Haganah. For his pains he was transferred, during World War II, from Palestine to Burma to head a group of Burmese irregulars, known as Chindits, to be air dropped behind the Japanese lines and harass them from the rear. In the course of one air drop Wingate was killed in the crash of his plane.

Thinking about the men on whose behalf he was now working, Mulvehill fell asleep.

Before heading downtown the next morning he called ahead to Mr. Oshan's office to set a time for a meeting and was asked to show up just before noon and he and Oshan could then go to lunch together.

He found Oshan to be an energetic, friendly man, a bustling advertising executive who listened to Mulvehill's presentation of the League's program as though he were making mental notes to develop an advertising campaign for the League.

"I'm going to write to both my uncles and tell them about your visit to Las Vegas. Here, in my social circle," he said, "there would not be much support for your group. They would consider your program to be divisive and possibly detrimental to the well-established Jews who are both my friends and my clients. I am not built for confrontations," he admitted, "so I'm not going to alienate them by telling them what I might think privately."

"But in Las Vegas," he laughed, "you won't find the Jews in the gambling business reticent about whatever they might think. They're in charge and they rule the roost. Wait 'til you meet them," he said. "You'll see."

"How do I get up there?" Mulvehill wanted to know.

"You can get a flight on Western Airlines from Mines Field," Oshan told him. "I'll take you to the airport. At McCarran Field in Las Vegas my uncles will be waiting to take you back into town. Wait until you hear from me. Then it will all be arranged."

He looked at Mulvehill quizzically. They were sitting in Berliner's Restaurant on Broadway and Oshan had prevailed upon Mulvehill to try a plate of cheese blintzes.

"Not bad," Mulvehill agreed, "but it takes a bit of getting used to."

"How did an Irishman get involved in a Jewish fracas?" Oshan asked. "You know, of course, that you are in the middle of an internecine conflict between opposing Jewish groups."

Mulvehill nodded.

"I had heard of the group you represent even before the war," Oshan told him. "I was then a student and read about one of your group, a Dr. Hadani, who had come out here to raise money and was ridiculed in the

B'nai B'rith Messenger, a local weekly paper, whose editorial writer called him a 'Baron Munchausen,' coming to Los Angeles to tell wild lies about the Jewish people."

Between bites Mulvehill assured Oshan that he knew he would not always be received in a friendly fashion and yet, Mulvehill said, he had so far been greeted very courteously.

"That's because," Oshan said, "you're a gentile, so most Jews are inclined to be skittish about offending you. But if you were a Jew," Oshan shook his head, "would you be set upon. Oy, vey."

Mulvehill laughed. They finished dinner and the two walked back to the building where Oshan had his advertising agency. "Come on up," Oshan invited. "I'd like to give you my own check."

20.

At eight thousand feet Las Vegas, from the air, was a sprinkling of buildings on the floor of a vast beige desert with a rim of mauve mountains in the background. It was ten o'clock in the morning and the turbo-jet was only about one-third filled. The stewardess came down the aisle, giving each passenger the conventional instruction. "Please put your seats back in the upright position and fasten your seat belts as we come in for the landing." He heard the thump as the wheels came down from the recessed well in the fuselage. The wheels bumped, lightly, only once and then they were rolling swiftly toward the terminal building.

The passenger across the aisle to Mulvehill's left made a circle of thumb and forefinger. "Nice landing," he said to Mulvehill. "You here for some fast action?" He made a fist of his right hand, palm side up, and simulated a throw of the dice.

Mulvehill smiled. "No, it's a business trip for me."

"Oh," the other said, "What business you in?"

Mulvehill looked at him levelly. "Collecting money."

The other looked uncomfortable. "Oh," he said, and subsided into silence.

Mulvehill stood up, brought his attaché case down from the overhead rack and walked down the aisle to stand behind other passengers waiting for clearance to disembark. The door opened and, swiftly, the passengers descended the aluminum ladder that had been wheeled toward the opened door.

Inside the terminal building two stout men in short-sleeved shirts looked expectantly at the arriving passengers. As Mulvehill walked into the building one of the two stepped forward. "Mr. Mulvehill?" Mulvehill nodded. "Hi," the first one said. "I'm Sol Birnbaum." He gestured to his companion. "This is my brother Irv." The three shook hands.

Exiting the terminal Sol led the way to the parking lot and stopped at a gray fishtail convertible Cadillac. He opened the door and Irv climbed into the back seat. "Give Irv your attaché case and sit up here with me," he told Mulvehill.

The air sweeping by as Sol tooled the car onto the highway leading into town was fresh, but warm. Sol reached into the glove compartment and brought out a flat leather case holding about five cigars. He held it out toward Mulvehill. "Smoke?" Mulvehill shook his head. The driver pulled out a cigar, stuck it into his mouth and pushed the lighter in the dashboard deeper into the receptacle. He handed the case to his brother in the back seat.

Mulvehill looked at the driver. His face was ruddy, neatly clean shaven. Although he had a paunch he looked solid and muscular. His forearms, under the short-sleeved shirt, were brawny. A small anchor was tattooed on his left arm, near the elbow. He appeared, to Mulvehill, to be about fifty. He looked at Mulvehill and followed his gaze. Mulvehill asked, "Navy?"

Sol nodded. "Both of us. We signed up in Chicago in 1936. You ever see the movie with Fred Astaire? *The Fleet's In*, I think it was called. They sang a song..." Sol cleared his throat. "We joined the navy to see the world," he sang, "...and what did we see...we saw the sea."

Mulvehill laughed. "As a matter of fact, I did. How long were you in for?"

From the back seat, Irv volunteered, "Four years. We shipped out only once, from San Francisco. To Cavite. That's a big navy base in the Philippines."

"I know," Mulvehill said.

"Well, once there," Sol picked up the story, "we didn't get to go any further. I was put in charge of the supply room. Made bosun's mate within a year."

"And I became a cook," Irv said. He patted his belly, somewhat bigger than his brother's and laughed.

"You know," the driver said, "we were pretty lucky. Our four years were up in 1940. We had saved our money by sending it home each month to our folks in Sioux City. Top o' that," he grinned. "we were both pretty good gamblers. I specialized in craps and Irv was ole' lightfingers himself with a deck of cards." He laughed. "We sent home enough money during those four years to set us up in business. And here we are."

"And we were pretty lucky in another way," Irv chimed in. "If we had re-enlisted we could've wound up with the poor footsloggers in the Bataan death march."

Sol nodded. He turned to look at Mulvehill. "Listen," he said. "My sister's boy, Dick, a good kid, told us why he wanted you to meet us. Smart move. Shit," he spat over the side of the car, "I hate to admit it but we didn't know what that cocksucker Hitler was doing to our people."

He scowled at Mulvehill. "It made us feel shitty when we saw the newsreels of dead Jews piled up like garbage in the concentration camps. And I tell you, I'm ashamed that we had to wait for an Irishman to come up here and tell us he wants our help in raising money for some fighting Hebes in Palestine to drive the miserable British bastards out."

He turned to Mulvehill. "You ever know any Limeys?"

"Yes," Mulvehill said evenly. "There were British units with us in North Africa. Their blood is just as red as yours and mine."

"Yeah, well OK. But those pricks are preventing even the few Jews that survived Hitler from coming into Palestine. Am I right?"

"You're right," Mulvehill agreed, "but I think it's important to keep objectives separate from emotion. The individual British Tommy in Palestine may be anti-Semitic or not, but he's not the one keeping your Jewish 'mishpoche' out of Palestine. It's the British government."

Sol laughed and slapped his thigh. He turned to his brother in the back seat. "You hear that?" He mimicked Mulvehill. "Mish-poka. Hey, you gotta say 'chuh' like you were going to spit out a wad."

He shook his head in admiration. "You're OK kid. We're gonna set you on the right track here. If you don't walk outta here with five hundred grand for your American League For A Free Palestine we'll eat one of our one-armed bandits."

"Hey," Irv tapped Mulvehill on the shoulder. "You know what a high roller is?"

Mulvehill turned to look at him. "No."

"Well, that's a guy who comes out here ready to blow a hundred grand at the craps table, on roulette, or at blackjack. The house treat him pretty good. He gets all the food he wants, all the drinks he wants..."

"And all the nooky he wants," Sol broke in. "I guess that's why Irv and I never married." He laughed. "Why buy a cow when milk is so cheap?"

"No," Irv said. "There's more to it than that. We don't want to dishonor our mother, 'olev shalom'*, by marrying one of the tramps that make a living up here. We want to marry nice Jewish girls. Until we find them we'll stay single."

He lapsed into silence.

Mulvehill pondered the deep tribal loyalty of many of the Jews he had met. These two men were coarse, vulgar, and earthy. But they revered their mother's memory and they were genuinely ashamed that they did not know of the brutal extermination of their kinsmen

* Rest in peace

in Europe, and now wanted to make up for that neglect.

As though he were reading Mulvehill's mind, Sol said. "You know, kid, when you live in Las Vegas you kind of lose touch with the outside world. This is a make believe world here. Wait until tonight and the town lights up. It's like a county carnival but ten times bigger and brighter. And the people who come here are suckers.

"Why should a guy who can afford to lose a hundred grand come here at all? What's he lookin' for, for Crissakes." He ruminated, tapped the ash from his cigar into the ash tray and said, "I tell you, there's something mystical about it. You know? It's like..." he sought for the words to express his thought. "It's like they want to escape reality."

"Or, to see if they can master fate," Irv said.

Sol nodded. "Yeah. That's good Irv. That's good. To see if they can master fate."

He stuck out his lower lip. "Makes sense. But doesn't make sense. 'Cause nobody can beat fate. And certainly not with a pair of dice."

He turned to look at Mulvehill. "We're going to stop at Vegas Village. We've told Bernie Seltzer about you and he wants to meet you. He's a pretty smart cookie. A lawyer. Came out here in the early days before gambling really got started here." They pulled into the parking lot. The hotel and casino were a sprawl of ranch style buildings. Mulvehill looked at the spread appreciatively. It looked like the old West of the movies.

He pulled the car up under the hotel's portico. The three of them got out. A youngster came around to the driver's side and addressed Sol. "Nice to see you again, Mr. Birnbaum." He accepted a folded bill from the driver, who nudged him. "No burning rubber, kid. Just drive nice."

Mulvehill followed the Birnbaums into the hotel.

It was not yet noon but, Mulvehill estimated, there might be half a dozen women seated at the 'one arm bandits' patiently feeding coins into the machines and stolidly pulling down the levers that set the internal machine into motion. The 'thump' 'thump' 'thump' of the machines sounded throughout the casino, muting the click of plastic chips that were tossed onto the crap tables and scooped in by the 'stick men' from those who lost on the toss of the dice.

They approached a well-dressed man who was watching the croupiers and dealers. Out of the side of one eye he saw the Birnbaums approach and held out a hand in greeting. "Hullo fellas, come to play?"

Sol laughed and punched him on the upper arm, a rapid tattoo.

"Hey, you know better than that. We're here to have lunch with Bernie. Would you call up to the office and let him know we're here?"

The man called to a passing waitress. "Polly. Call Mr. Seltzer and tell him the Birnbaums are here."

Irv took Mulvehill by the arm. "Let's walk around while we're waiting. This your first time in a casino?"

Mulvehill nodded. "Up to now I've only seen them in the movies."

"That guy we stopped to talk to," Sol said, "is the pit boss. He don't miss a trick. It's a tough job on the floor, whether you're a croupier, a dealer, the guy who spins the roulette wheel, or the pit boss. You're always on your feet." He shook his head. "Tough. And you've got to concentrate. Look at the croupier at that crap table." He pointed to a table where there were about a dozen gamblers clustered around the table. "The 'stick man' got to be right on top of the action. Ain't easy, I tell you."

Mulvehill looked around the casino. Waitresses walked around with trays, taking orders from the gamblers. The dice rolled, the gamblers called out their bets, the cards on the black jack tables flipped, the roulette wheels spun. To Mulvehill there was an air of unreality about it. Common sense had to tell you, he reasoned, that the house was always going to come out ahead. So why try?

He felt a hand on his shoulder.

"You the guy who came up here to take my money?"

Mulvehill turned to look at the speaker. He was tall, taller than Mulvehill. He had the typical paunch of the middle-aged man but gave the impression of being strong and light on his feet. Sol Birnbaum spoke. "This is Charles Mulvehill, Bernie. He was referred to me by my sister's boy in Los Angeles. I like what he's doing. But I'm going to let him tell you himself. Charles, shake hands with Mr. Seltzer." He waited until the two shook hands. "Shirley gonna join us for lunch?"

Seltzer grinned. "Try and keep her away." He led the way into the dining room.

When they were seated and the waitress had brought menus, Seltzer turned back to Mulvehill. "This your first time in a gambling hell, kid?" He looked at Mulvehill expectantly.

Mulvehill nodded.

"What do you think?" Seltzer prodded.

Mulvehill pursed his lips. "Funny thing, Mr. Seltzer. Nobody seems to be enjoying himself. Everybody seems to be tense." He looked around him. "And even here, they all seem to be dejected."

Seltzer laughed. "You're a good observer, kid. But if you come back tonight you'll see a different atmosphere. Every once in a while a crap table gets hot. And everyone seems to sense it. It draws people like a magnet. And then every one at that table seems to be having a good time.

"I don't try to be a psychologist. People come to Las Vegas to have a good time. It's not my business if they do or they don't. The games of chance are here. We also serve good food and I try to sign up good talent for our shows. Right now I got Shecky Greene. He's a good drawing card. When the show starts the gambling tables sort of empty themselves. Then the show is over and they're back at the tables, busier than before."

Seltzer looked up and then half stood up. A well-dressed woman arrived at the table. Seltzer kissed her lightly on the cheek. He settled back in his chair and the woman took the chair next to him.

"Shirl," he said, gesturing at Mulvehill, "this is our guest, Charles Mulvehill."

She nodded at him, friendly but not effusive. She looked like any well-to-do matron on her way to play mah-jong with her friends.

"The Birnbaum boys brought him over," Seltzer said.

She looked at Mulvehill. "This your first time in Las Vegas, son?"

He nodded. "First and maybe last."

"Oh," she said. "Why? Don't you like it here?"

"I'm a working man, ma'am, and I don't have time to play."

"What kind of work do you do?" she asked.

"I'm trying to save lives," he said.

She looked at him evenly. "How do you do that?"

He leaned forward. "Mrs. Seltzer, the Germans and their henchmen killed about six million Jews. We're trying to save the few who are left by getting them out of Europe and into Palestine."

She looked at him, searchingly. "You're not a Jew, are you?"

"No ma'am," he said. "I was born in California. But my dad is from Ireland."

"Then why do you want to save Jews?" She cocked her head and looked at him curiously.

Sol and Irv Birnbaum grinned. They wanted to hear how he was going to answer her.

"When Mr. Birnbaum and his brother brought me over here," Mulvehill said, "I noticed that you had a lifeguard at the pool. Did you instruct him to just save

344

guests who were gentiles? Or guests who were Jews? Or guests who were under five feet tall? Or even, if someone were drowning, to find out first if he was a guest?"

She smiled broadly and turned to Seltzer. "This kid's smart. He's got a Yiddishe Kupp."* She turned back to face Mulvehill, leaned over and pinched his cheek.

"All right, boychik,† tell me more about what you do."

Mulvehill pushed his plate away.

"More than twenty years ago," he said, "the League of Nations gave Great Britain a Mandate to help the Jews create a national homeland for their people in Palestine. To make sure the Jews would have a hard time doing that, Winston Churchill gave away all of Palestine east of the Jordan River and called it Trans-Jordania. He brought in a Hashemite prince of the Saudi royal family and named him Emir. That reduced the size of Palestine by more than eighty percent..."

"Are you talking about Winston Churchill who was Prime Minister?" she broke in.

"Yes. In 1922 he was British secretary of state for the colonies," Mulvehill said. "Then, to make it even tougher for the Jews to build their national home the British began to limit immigration and then, in 1939, stopped it altogether."

She shook her head. "Who do you work for? It must be some kind of organization. What's it called?"

* A Jewish head
† Little boy

"It's called American League For A Free Palestine," Mulvehill told her.

She shook her head. "I never heard of it." She looked at him shrewdly. "So if I give you money what are they going to do with it?"

"They buy ships to transport Jews to Palestine."

"Name one," she challenged him.

"It's called the S.S. Ben Hecht," Mulvehill said.

Her eyes opened wide. "Ben Hecht. Hey, it's beginning to come back to me. I think I read something about him trying to get $40 a head to get the Jews out of Rumania."

Mulvehill nodded. "That was a few years ago."

She turned to her husband. "What do you think, Bernie?"

He smiled at Mulvehill. "Shirl, I think the kid is pure gold. What do you say? Ten grand?"

She turned and patted Mulvehill's hand. "At least." She rose from the table. "Excuse me boys. I'm late for my mah-jong game."

Mulvehill smiled to himself.

She turned to her husband again. "And Bernie, send him over to see Jack Entratter at the Sands."

"I'm planning to do that and also I'm going to introduce him to Petey Horwitch."

She snapped her fingers. "Capital."

She got up, straightened her dress and took a step away from the table. She turned back. "Sol. Irv," she said to the Birnbaums. "Thanks." She walked away.

Seltzer looked at Mulvehill. "Anything more to eat? Another sandwich?"

Mulvehill shook his head. "No, that was fine."

Seltzer persisted. "A piece of lemon meringue pie? Our baker's the best."

"Well," Mulvehill yielded, "a small piece."

Seltzer beckoned to the waitress. "Trudy. Lemon meringue pie. All around."

He leaned toward Mulvehill. "I got an idea. We get lots of high-rollers. Guys with lots of money. They come out here from wherever they live, loaded for bear. Mostly they lose but, once in a while, one hits it big. If the guy's Jewish its only right he should give some of his winnings to a good cause. Like, say, the American League For a Free Palestine." He got up. "You guys stay here and enjoy the pie. And save my piece. I'll be right back."

The waitress brought the pie and served each one. She took away their coffee cups, brought fresh cups, and poured fresh coffee.

Mulvehill tasted the pie. He made a circle with his thumb and forefinger. "Just like downtown."

Irv Birnbaum leaned toward him and jabbed the air with a finger. "He's all right, huh?"

Mulvehill put down his fork. "I can't thank you both enough."

"Wait, wait," Sol said. "You heard Shirley say Bernie should introduce you to Petey Horwitch? That's a good idea."

"Who's Petey Horwitch?" Mulvehill asked.

"He's the publisher of the Las Vegas News. One of our two daily newspapers. Petey's tough. And, of course, he knows everybody in town. And he takes sides. For example, he took a dislike to Joe McCarthy, the senator from Wisconsin. So he calls him a fag, in print."

Mulvehill raised his eyebrows. "That's libelous, isn't it?"

Sol Birnbaum shrugged. "Well, so far we ain't heard that McCarthy sued Petey."

Seltzer returned. He took his seat, picked up a fork and demolished the pie with a few deft bites. He turned to Mulvehill. "We had a big winner a couple of hours ago. A manufacturer from Houston, name of Howard Teitelbaum. I arranged to have him brought up to my office in a little while. You'll be there." He nodded at both the Birnbaum brothers. "I want to thank you guys for bringing the kid over here. We can help him in the work he's doing. I've called Petey Horwitch. We've got an appointment over there at three o'clock." He looked at his watch. "Let's go."

The four of them rose from the table.

"Sol," Seltzer said, "leave Mulvehill with me. I'll see he gets back to where he's staying." He looked at Mulvehill. "Where are you staying? And how long you gonna be in town?"

Mulvehill looked from one to another. "I don't know. I thought one of you would recommend a hotel for me."

Seltzer touched Mulvehill's arm. "Okay. It's all set. You'll stay here at Vegas Village. If it was the weekend we'd be filled up. But tonight's no problem. Let's go."

The Birnbaums shook hands with Mulvehill and left.

Mulvehill followed Seltzer up the stairs to his office. Tastefully finished in dark grained woods it looked like the office of any successful executive or entrepreneur. The only touch indicative of whose office this was stood in the corner, a vintage slot machine. Seltzer motioned to Mulvehill to take one of two easy chairs facing the desk. He walked around behind the desk, plumped himself down in the comfortable leather chair there and took out a humidor. He lifted the cover and offered it to Mulvehill. Charles shook his head but thanked Seltzer for the offer.

"You don't smoke?" Seltzer asked.

"I used to," Mulvehill replied, "but I never smoked much and found it easy to give it up altogether. I don't have much opportunity to exercise these days and I'd rather save my wind for more important things."

Seltzer grinned. "Like Asiatic pushups?"

Mulvehill changed the direction the conversation was taking. "The Birnbaum brothers said you had been a lawyer in Minneapolis. How did you get involved with the gambling business?"

Seltzer peeled the cellophane from one of the cigars, passed it under his nose to sniff the aroma, then took out a platinum lighter and lit the cigar.

"One of my clients was a major developer there," Seltzer said, after puffing a few languid smoke rings. "A few of his friends and investors privately bought this hotel and casino. They offered me a small piece of the action. Shirley and I had had enough of Minneapolis weather." He grinned. "Nine months winter, three months cold. Las Vegas sounded like an interesting change. So here we are and we like it."

"Open," he called out loudly as there was a soft knocking on the door. One of the pit bosses entered, leading a portly, fleshy man with pink jowls.

Seltzer rose behind his desk and waited for the stranger to approach. The pit boss left and closed the door behind him.

"Mr. Teitelbaum," he said. "Pleased to meet you. Let me introduce Mr. Mulvehill. Have a seat. Please."

Mulvehill and Teitelbaum shook hands. The three of them lowered themselves into the chairs.

"Are you enjoying your stay in Las Vegas, Mr. Teitelbaum?" Seltzer asked jovially. The other nodded. "It's a nice place you have here and I enjoyed your show last night."

"Good, good," Seltzer nodded. "Mr. Mulvehill is also a guest here. But his purpose in coming to Las Vegas was different from yours. Mr. Mulvehill," he paused to make sure his words would sink in, "is an executive of the American League For A Free Palestine. Are you familiar with the organization?"

While Seltzer was talking to him Mulvehill took the occasion to slowly study the visitor. The man obviously enjoyed eating. A comfortable paunch extended beyond his opened jacket, which was well tailored. Mulvehill noted that the buttonholes were hand sewed. The man's hands were soft pads of flesh and a bright diamond ring sparkled on one finger of each hand.

"I'm this year's chairman of the United Palestine Appeal in Houston," Teitelbaum said. "It's interesting you should mention American League For A Free Palestine," he said. "I heard about their work of bringing Jews into Palestine. Illegally." He paused over the word. "Matter of fact," he went on, "I had a letter just last week from Henry Montor." He turned to Mulvehill. "He's the executive director of the United Palestine Appeal. What he said in his letter..." he turned from Mulvehill to Seltzer, "was that we had to be selective about bringing immigrants into Palestine. He claimed that many of the people brought into Palestine illegally by this young man's group were prostitutes and criminals. A great many of the passengers were old men and women, not fit for the hazardous journey."

Seltzer looked at Mulvehill. He laced his hands across his belly and sat back in his chair.

Mulvehill looked at Teitelbaum. "I've been told that about six million Jews were killed by the Germans during the war. To the best of my knowledge the Germans were just as adept at killing rich Jews as poor ones. I don't think they discriminated between honest merchants and doctors, between Jewish lawyers, artisans, dentists, prostitutes and criminals."

Teitelbaum moved around uncomfortably in his chair.

"I believe The League," Mulvehill looked at him steadily, "just wants to save Jews. They take the position, if I understand them correctly, that if the Germans didn't discriminate between killing rich Jews or poor Jews, or between honest Jews or crooked Jews, then the League was not going to discriminate about saving Jewish lives, regardless of what they did to survive the Nazi slaughter.

"No country seems to want the Jews. Including the United States," Mulvehill bore in. "The people I represent just want to get the surviving Jews into Palestine. The British don't want to let them in. So our people are getting them in...illegally. By strict observance of the law, as administered by the British in Palestine, I suppose," Mulvehill said, "we're criminals. How do you feel about that?"

Seltzer looked from Mulvehill to Teitelbaum. The casino owner's look was placid. He seemed to be enjoying himself.

Teitelbaum's face reddened. He looked down at his hands.

"I never thought I would find myself in a situation where I would listen to a gentile tell me what is right for me to do as a Jew." He looked up at Mulvehill. Charles thought he saw the beginning of moisture in the man's eyes.

"But you're right. I live a good life here while Jews live in misery trying to get into the Holy Land." He shook his head dolefully. "Sure I'd like to help. What can I do?"

Seltzer took advantage of the opportunity. "You've had a good day, Mr. Teitelbaum. A very lucky day I might say." He looked down at a note on his desk. "About thirty thousand, would you say?"

Teitelbaum nodded.

"Would you say," Seltzer persisted, "that maybe ten percent might not be too much to save some Jewish lives? Even if some of those Jews are riff-raff?"

The other sighed and withdrew a checkbook from his inner jacket pocket. He opened it on Seltzer's desk. "How do I make it out?" he asked.

"Just make it out to American League For A Free Palestine," Mulvehill said. "We'll see that it gets to the right people."

Teitelbaum wrote swiftly. He tore the check from the book and handed it to Mulvehill. All three men rose.

"Thank you," Mulvehill said softly.

The other nodded, muttered something, turned and left the room.

Seltzer beamed. He rubbed his hands together. "I like the way you work," he said, "Meanwhile..." he looked at his watch, "let me take you over to meet Petey Horwitch at the News. Then I've got to get back to work."

21.

The offices and printing plant of The News were in a modern, two-story, brick building, neither near the 'Strip' nor the downtown gambling area but further out in a developing area of the city. Seltzer pulled into the parking lot. Mulvehill followed him into the reception room. There was a counter where people wanting to place ads in the paper could submit their copy. A young woman seated at a desk behind the counter got up.

"Bernie Seltzer to see Mr. Horwitch," he told her. She nodded and went to the phone. She spoke into it then turned back to face Seltzer and Mulvehill. "Take the elevator there," she gestured. "Mr. Horwitch will meet you when you get off."

As the two got off the elevator a tall, slightly stoop-shouldered man was waiting. He held out his hand to Seltzer. "Good to see you Bernie. How's business?"

Seltzer laughed. "Always good." He turned to Mulvehill. "Shake hands with Petey Horwitch, the William Randolph Hearst of Nevada."

They both laughed.

Horwitch held Mulvehill's hand for an instant then dropped it to clap Mulvehill on the shoulder. "So you're working the West Coast for American League For A Free Palestine? Well, I'm glad to meet you." He turned back to Seltzer. "Got time for a drink, Bernie?" Seltzer shook his head. "No, thanks. When you're through with Mulvehill will you see to it that he gets over to the Sands? I'm setting up a meeting for him with Jack Entratter."

"Good as done," Horwitch said. They shook hands and Seltzer stepped back into the elevator. He gave a thumbs up sign to Mulvehill as the door was closing.

Mulvehill followed Horwitch into the publisher's office. It was sparsely furnished and the furniture looked worn. The top of his desk was covered with pages of newsprint. Horwitch went behind his desk, opened a bottom drawer and withdrew a bottle. He held it up. "Jack Daniels. Is it too early for you to have a drink?"

Mulvehill shook his head. "No. I'll be happy to join you."

Horwitch laughed. "Good." He took out two paper cups, filled each with the whiskey and handed one to Mulvehill. "First one today with this hand." He grinned and held up the cup. "*Erin ga bragh.*"

Mulvehill accepted the toast. "Up the rebels. Irish or Jewish." They drank.

Horwitch gestured to the easy chair in front of his desk. "Make yourself comfortable." They both sat down. Horwitch picked up the phone. "Hold my calls," he said, "unless it's a breaking story." He leaned back in his chair.

"I've been reading about the Irgun in Palestine," he said. "I've long been an admirer of Ben Hecht. A writer with guts. You don't meet them every day of the week. You know," he became ruminative. "Out here we're away from things. Las Vegas is mostly gambling and entertainment. We've got plenty of Jews here but hardly what you would call a Jewish community. But," he refilled his cup and held the bottle out to Mulvehill. The younger man held up a hand, palm facing Horwitch, and shook his head.

"Being in the newspaper business," Horwitch continued, "naturally I see all the wire stories, internationally, because I subscribe to both AP and UP as well as Reuters."

He quickly tossed his second drink down, shook his head and put the bottle away.

"All during the war I would see tiny items that would come across the newswire. They didn't tell much but if you added them all up you could see that my people in Europe were being systematically murdered by the Germans. And there didn't seem to be a goddam thing I could do," he swore. "Being too old to enlist I couldn't actively fight the Germans. So I take my hat off to you. I understand you fought and were wounded."

Mulvehill shrugged.

"When the war was finally won," Horwitch continued, "I was happy that our boys licked the Japs and the Germans. But there was little comfort for a Jew in this." He looked closely at Mulvehill. "Does it bother you if I talk this way? I know you're working for our people and I applaud you for it. But still, you're a gentile."

"I don't think justice wears a flag," Mulvehill noted. "What's right is right and what's wrong is wrong. I'm not happy about the fact that all during the war Eire accommodated a German embassy in Dublin."

"So you knew about that," Horwitch marveled.

"Okay, so you can understand that for me, as a Jew," he continued, "triumph was muted by bitterness."

Mulvehill nodded.

"I began to read a few items from the wire services," Horwitch went on. "An outfit in Palestine calling itself Irgun Zvai Leumi seemed to have declared war on Great Britain. At first it didn't amount to much. Some hotheads in Tel Aviv seemed to be taking potshots at friendly British officers out for a stroll, or stealing a few British motor cars, or holding up an honorable British bank.

"But a pattern was emerging," Horwitch said. "Now I read other stories under a Palestine date line. There were raids of British arsenals, blowing up of railroad communications and bridges and, wonder of wonders, a remarkable story of Irgun men breaking into Acre Fortress and freeing Jewish prisoners of the British."

Mulvehill permitted himself a smile.

"And I began to see ads appearing in American newspapers about your outfit, American League For A Free Palestine, raising money to get Jewish refugees who had somehow survived the slaughter in Europe, out of Europe and into Palestine.

"I began to connect the two. It was never the official Jewish organizations who were doing this but always the League. I began to make some inquiries. I wrote to Ben Hecht and I got an answer." Horwitch pulled open his desk drawer and withdrew a few sheets of paper. He looked up at Mulvehill, then down at the papers in his hand.

"I wanted to know what was going on." He held up the papers and Mulvehill saw that the hands of this hard-boiled newspaperman were shaking, just a little, but noticeable.

He began to read.

There are in the world many stories of Scots bagpipes and British drums and American 'yippees' rallying beaten men to victory; many stories of Frenchman, Magyar, Mexican, Turk, Bolivian and a hundred and one other sections of the human family raising a flag out of disaster and adding a radiance to the chronicles of man. The Irgun Zvai Leumi added such a Jewish tale to the sagas of the undefeatable.

The Jews who came out to battle the hundred thousand British soldiers encamped in Palestine consisted of two groups, the Irgun and an outfit called, sneeringly, 'The Stern Gang.' Jointly the two groups numbered less than three thousand men and women, almost as primitively armed as had been the Jews of the Warsaw ghetto.

If I discontinue reference here to the Sternists and write now only of the Irgun, it is not because there was anything less deserving about the Sternists. They were as valorous and nobly inspired a group of human beings as I have ever met in history.

But it is the Irgun I know. News of every gun it fired, every barrel of dynamite it exploded, of every arsenal it looted and railroad train it tipped over was brought to me in secret communiqués, some of them hidden in cigarette packages. I never read news with a more pounding heart. I had had no interest in Palestine ever becoming a homeland for Jews. Now I had, suddenly, interest in little else.

Here were Jews finally fighting for their own honor and not someone else's—usually their enemy's. You could ask for nothing more novel than that as a piece of Jewish news.

But the fact that they were willing to fight and die for the liberation of a land they called their own was not the great fact to me. Valor had not been missing in the long tale of the Jews. They had stood up often in alien parts of the earth and died memorably.

The great fact was that here were Jews with a new soul, or possibly, an old one returned. They did not dream of victory as a thing to be won by a tearful parade of their virtues. (Good God, how tired the goyim must have become of hearing how good the victims were!)

Horwitch looked up from the letter he was reading to look at Mulvehill. "That's from Hecht's letter," he said. Mulvehill smiled. Horwitch put back on the pair of half spectacles he had donned to read the letter. He continued.

Here were Jews who did not believe in the Jewish master plan of submitting always to injustice and then patiently removing it as one removes burrs from a dog's body. Here were Jews who had broken with the ancient wisdom of waiting piously and unprotestingly for the rage of their enemies to ebb. And I saw that these new qualities had been always in many of the Jews, but that without a land to fight for, they were like a great musical talent without an instrument for its playing.

But chiefly unwanted Jews had trained themselves for centuries in the business of dying carefully, of taking care never to protest too loudly against the villainy of their destroyer, for their descendants must live on among these same destroyers. Thus to give the destroyer a bad name was to make him look for vengeance against these descendants.

There was a heroism in this long-practiced careful dying of the Jews. But there was also a stupidity in it that kept ruining the Jews. The Jew managed, by his proud and pious silence, to give himself a bad name. He gave himself the name of Frightened Jew. This identity was almost a sufficient lure in itself for any group of Christians wanting to blow off steam in a pogrom.

Now here suddenly in the once miracle-haunted land of Palestine were all these new Jewish miracles. I looked at the finest of them with continued wonder—Jews ready to battle the anti-Semitism of their enemy rather than to bask, a little bruised, under his heel.

Horwitch took off his reading glasses and set them down on his desk. He looked away from Mulvehill, thinking thoughts, Mulvehill guessed, that would be alien to himself. He said nothing. The silence in the room became palpable. Somewhere within the building Mulvehill heard the thumping of the presses, banging out the daily newspaper. Off in the distance he heard the squeal of brakes and the blowing of an automobile horn.

He sat and waited for Horwitch to say something.

"I had been waiting," Horwitch finally said softly, for someone to come out here from the League and ask me for a contribution. In the meantime I would send checks to your office in New York. Fifty bucks, a hundred bucks, whatever I felt I could spare.

"So now," he grinned crookedly, "the League finally sends somebody out to Las Vegas, and what do I get? An Irishman."

"Col. John Patterson was also an Irishman," Mulvehill responded. "An Irishman in the British Army. He commanded the Zion Mule Corps at Gallipoli and the Jewish Legion in Palestine in World War I. And he never gave up trying to help the Jews," Mulvehill continued. "In 1940 he and Robert Briscoe, the Irish-Jewish one-time mayor of Dublin, set up an Emergency Committee to Save the Jews of Europe. I hope one day to meet him," Mulvehill concluded.

They sat and looked at each other. Horwitch opened his desk drawer and brought out the bottle. He held it out to Mulvehill. "Just one more?"

Mulvehill nodded. "OK."

Horwitch nodded approvingly. He brought out two fresh paper cups and poured a drink for Mulvehill. He waited for Mulvehill to take the cup, then poured one for himself.

He lifted his cup and held it out toward Mulvehill. "A shekoach."*

Mulvehill responded. "Whatever." They both drank.

Horwitch crumpled his paper cup and threw it in the wastebasket. He took Mulvehill's emptied cup and did the same. He put the bottle back in the drawer and pushed it closed with a gesture of finality. He leaned toward Mulvehill across the desk.

"The British in Palestine have begun to feel the heat. Your Irgun buddies have whipped two British officers in a public square in Tel Aviv." He laughed.

"That's Irgun justice. Retaliation for the British whipping of captured Irgun men. And after the British hung Dov Gruner for carrying illegal arms the Irgun hung two British sergeants in a forest in Netanya. I published that story in the News."

Horwitch stood up and paced the room. Mulvehill followed the tall man with his eyes.

"The British have asked the United Nations to settle the matter of Great Britain's Mandate in Palestine." He looked at Mulvehill with his eyes burning.

"They're licked. They want to pull out." The publisher approached Mulvehill.

"When England pulls out the Arabs will attack," he said. "Is there any doubt in your mind about that?" He stood near Mulvehill's chair, looking down at him.

Mulvehill looked up.

"I haven't paid much attention to the politics of the affair," he admitted. "I thought the British were

* To strength

betraying their own commitment to the League of Nations. I also thought they were pretty shabby about keeping the poor remnant of surviving European Jews out of Palestine." He stood up. "And I thought Ben-Gurion and his party were cowardly in failing to fight the British as the Irgun were doing. So I agreed to try to help. But all I was doing, really," he held out his hands, "was raising money so the League could use it as they saw best fit."

Horwitch put a hand on Mulvehill's shoulder.

"Maybe I shouldn't butt in," he said, "but I kind of feel that maybe you might like to do more."

Mulvehill furrowed his brow.

"What do you mean?"

The publisher walked back behind his desk and plumped himself down in his upholstered executive chair.

"Your group is buying a ship to carry arms...and men...to Palestine to fight the Arabs when the British pull out." He looked at Mulvehill. "Didn't you know that?"

"No," Mulvehill shook his head. "And how do you know?"

Horwitch looked at Mulvehill for a long moment in silence. He then opened his desk drawer and pulled out a sheaf of papers. He put on his half spectacles, peered over the tops at Mulvehill and asked, "In confidence?"

Mulvehill nodded. "In confidence."

Horwitch nodded approvingly.

"Okay, kid. Never mind who the writer of this letter is, or how it got to me. But take my word that it's on the level." He drew the papers close and began to read.

"...three of us met on a quiet, snowy afternoon. One was Abrasha Stavsky, whom I had first met many years ago. He was a big outgoing man with small squinting eyes, a warm laugh and a ready wit. He knew ships and shipping and was a hardheaded businessman when it came to leasing ships. And he was absolutely fearless when it came to the wellbeing of the Jews.

The other man, whom I had never met before, was probably in his fifties. He was of medium height, heavy set, with deeply lined hard prominent features. Like Abrasha he walked with a waddle and the two of them made me think of a vaudeville act.

Abrasha introduced his companion as 'Uncle Joe', a native of the Whitechapel section of London. He spoke a strange hybrid of Cockney slang with a Yiddish accent. Uncle Joe was a businessman, with many interests and even more friends, and was a special admirer of the Irgun."

"The upshot of that meeting," Horwitch said, "was that they began considering the purchase of a U.S. Navy surplus vessel. There were then dozens upon dozens of war surplus vessels tied up in the Hudson River near West Point.

"The letter writer," the publisher continued, "was an ex-G.I. who had been promised 'a break' by the Navy petty officer in charge of selling the vessels. The three 'agents' settled on an LST (Landing Ship, Tank) that had seen service in the South Pacific in a number of landing operations during the war. The craft seemed to be in good condition. It was a 1,820 deadweight tonner with twin General Motors diesels, and seemed to fit the bill for what our friends had in mind.

"After a few more trips of inspection our friends decided to make the purchase."

Horwitch looked at Mulvehill. "This is all news to you?"

Mulvehill nodded.

"The craft was bought for $75,000. The Navy CPO with whom our friends had negotiated the deal," Horwitch said, "turned out to be a good Joe. He threw in some spare parts and tools. The purchase order was signed by an officer of a newly formed shipping company, the 'Three Star Line'. It was estimated," Horwitch said, "that the ship could carry at least fifteen hundred men and vast stores of weapons."

Horwitch looked closely at Mulvehill. His eyes glinted with the spirit of adventure. He washed his hands conspiratorially.

"Gee, I would like to be aboard when that ship lands in Palestine. I can't, of course," he shrugged, "but there's a real news story in the making."

He leaned over and gripped Mulvehill's arm.

"You could go," he implored earnestly. "Ask the League for a leave of absence. I'll hire you as a news representative. I'm a member of the North American Newspaper Alliance. I'll give you a press card so that you can get a valid passport and visa. And I'll pay you a hundred bucks a week.

"The news credentials are important, Mulvehill," Horwitch said, "because it will make it possible for you to get back into the U.S. Otherwise, if you were to go abroad for the League you might be considered a foreign agent."

Mulvehill looked at him.

"Who said anything about going abroad? I'm employed by the American League For A Free Palestine. My assignment is to raise money for the political and public relations activities of the League." He smiled at Horwitch. "That's why I'm here. Remember? Aren't you going to open your checkbook?"

The publisher laughed.

"Okay." He took out his checkbook, wrote swiftly and handed the slip of paper to Mulvehill. The latter looked at the amount. "Seventy five hundred. Very handsome. That's already ten percent of the amount paid for the LST."

"Think about what I said," Horwitch urged. "You'll be a foreign correspondent. Doesn't that tickle your giblets?"

Mulvehill laughed. "It has a certain appeal," he acknowledged. "But first I'm going to raise as much money while I'm up here as I can. Then I'll think about your offer."

He rose and looked at his watch. "I'm supposed to meet with Jack Entratter at the Sands. How do I get over there?"

"My wife will drive you over." They shook hands. "But before you leave Las Vegas will you tell me if you'll give me an answer?"

Mulvehill said, "I promise."

That night Mulvehill placed a call to Ben Hecht in New York. He told the writer of Horwitch's amazing story, and his offer of a job and a press card.

Hecht listened in silence. "Where are you staying in Las Vegas?" he wanted to know. "O.K.," he said, "I'll look into it and call you back tomorrow."

When Mulvehill returned to the hotel after several successful meetings the following day, he found a telegram from Hecht waiting for him. 'All true', the message read. 'If you are interested call Bergson in New York and then decide what you want to do.'

Mulvehill finished his task in Las Vegas with three additional meetings. He gave the checks he had collected to Seltzer. The owner of Vegas Village whistled. "A hundred and fifty grand. Not bad for four days work."

"Can you convert these into a certified check and send it to the League in New York?" Mulvehill asked. He grinned to himself. With that money they could buy another LST. On the flight back to Los Angeles he leaned back in his seat and relaxed. He had done a fairly good job for the League, he thought. Now he thought about the news given to him by Horwitch in Las Vegas. And Hecht had confirmed it. Why hadn't anyone told him what was going on?

In Los Angeles he told his story to the Longstreets. Ethel confessed she knew about the ship purchase. Hadani and Bergson did not want Mulvehill to volunteer to sail with the ship for Palestine, as they were sure he would want to. The Palestinians had christened the LST the *Altalena* in honor of their teacher and inspiration; Vladimir Jabotinsky. The Jewish poet, soldier, patriot and writer had used that name as his *nom de plume* when writing as a young man in Italy.

"Our friends from Palestine are all going back," Ethel told Mulvehill as she, Steve and their young guest sat around the table having coffee, "in anticipation of the founding of their long dreamed of Hebrew Commonwealth. They are sure they will have to fight the Arabs, who have been armed by the British. And, who knows," she shrugged, "maybe even some Jewish followers of Ben-Gurion. The old SOB doesn't want competition from Begin, or anyone who might interfere with his assuming control of the emerging Hebrew State."

She looked at him sorrowfully. "Our friends don't like the idea of your being wounded," she said, "or maybe even killed, by either Arabs or Jews."

Mulvehill frowned. "Well, I've got some thinking to do. I volunteered to help. I'll go home for a few days and think it through." He stood up. "And I do want to thank you for your hospitality."

The Longstreets nodded. Mulvehill left the table and went up to his room.

22.

Mulvehill's mother and father listened as he explained his reasons for wanting to sail on the *Altalena* to Palestine. They were seated on the porch. Cookie, after dinner, had taken Lisa to the newly opened miniature golf course in town.

"Then your mind is made up?" Mulvehill's father asked.

"I've thrown in my lot with these people. I want to see it through," he replied. "The unexpected offer to go as a correspondent for *The News* is a real boon. All my expenses will be taken care of and I'll have a ringside seat to the creation of the first Hebrew Commonwealth in two thousand years."

"Maybe," his father said. "But remember, these are Jews we're talking about and it is said, even by Jews themselves, where there are two Jews there are three opinions."

Mulvehill laughed. His mother shifted uncomfortably in her chair.

"When do you leave, Charles?" she wanted to know.

He rose, walked over and kissed her. "Now that I've made up my mind," he said, "I may as well leave tomorrow, or as soon as I get my passport."

His mother crossed herself. "I'll be going with Consuelo tomorrow night and start making a novena." She rose and walked into the house.

Mulvehill's father winked.

The sun had set behind them and they looked out across the desert floor, watching the mountains change color in the distance.

"Charles, can you take Captain Hay's cane with you?" his father asked. "If Mr. Hay is in Palestine you ought to be able to find him. I'd be thrilled to learn he is alive and well."

Mulvehill nodded. "I'll try." He went up to his room and started to pack. The pay check for his week's work for the League had arrived. He voided it and addressed an envelope to mail it back to New York. And, he decided, he would endorse and send them the first check he would receive from Horwitch. He would call the publisher in the morning and tell him of his decision to accept the assignment.

In Los Angeles the next day he applied for a passport. Following a call from Horwitch to the State Department that Mulvehill was leaving for Europe on a roving commission for the paper the passport was granted swiftly.

A week later, in New York, he applied for British and French visas. He decided not to meet with anyone from the League, with one exception. He took a room for one night at the "Y" on West 34th Street. Then he called the League office and asked for Zelinsky. He hadn't seen the youth in three years and thought he would like to buy him a drink at The Brass Rail.

Zelinsky was thrilled to hear from him. "You're going on the *Altalena?*" he enthused. "Wow." He agreed to meet with Mulvehill at the Brass Rail at six the following evening.

Mulvehill thought about asking if Stacy was still working with the League but decided against it. Instead he said, "Don't mention this to anyone at the office, Marvin."

Zelinsky promised.

The youth was seated at a table near the window when Mulvehill arrived. They shook hands and Mulvehill was pleased with the firmness of the other's grip. Zelinsky was wearing a short-sleeved shirt. The pads of muscle in his shoulders were apparent under the shirt and his arms were muscular.

Mulvehill grinned. "Weight lifting?"

Zelinsky grinned in return. "I'm feeling good. Mulvehill," he said, "I'm not ashamed to be a Jew anymore. And I'm not afraid either."

A waitress interrupted. Zelinsky looked at Mulvehill. "Rob Roy?"

"You bet," Mulvehill responded. "Never give up on a winning combination. How's Iris?" he asked.

The waitress took their order and left.

Zelinsky leaned forward. "She's pregnant," he said. "We've been married almost two years. Gosh, Mulvehill, if not for that I'd be going on the *Altalena* too."

Mulvehill looked around the room. "This is where it all started, Marvin," he said. Suddenly he wanted to get away from there. When the drinks arrived he reached for his wallet. Zelinsky put his hand on Mulvehill's arm.

"No, Mulvehill, this one's on me," the younger man said.

"O.K.," Mulvehill agreed. "Well, here's one for the road." He quickly finished his drink and rose from the table.

Zelinsky rose too. They shook hands.

"When you get on the ship," Zelinsky said, "ask for Mike Ben-Ami. He's a real good guy, and tough. I'm sure you'll like him." Zelinsky finished his drink. "Ben-Ami was one of the first of the Palestinians to come over here. Now he's going home."

They parted.

Outside Mulvehill looked around. It was still light. The evening was warm. Without thinking about it consciously he found himself walking toward Seventy Third Street and the apartment where he had slept with Stacy. His steps slowed. 'What the hell is this?' he thought. 'I sure as hell don't have luck with women.' He turned around and walked back to Forty Fifth Street and entered the *Pink Elephant* lounge.

He found a seat at the bar and ordered Scotch, straight up. It was only seven o'clock. He had plenty of time to get back to the Y, pick up his barracks bag and take a taxi to the ship, which was moored at the foot of Joralemon Street.

The drink relaxed him and he had another.

Other than Hecht, Hadani, Zelinsky and Zelinsky's wife, he realized, he didn't know a soul in this whole huge city. A stranger next to him started a conversation and Mulvehill realized he didn't have the faintest idea of what the other was talking about. He looked at the change lying on the counter in front of him. The twenty dollar bill he had started with had dwindled down to a single and some change. He looked at his watch. 'Dammit. It's ten after ten.' He scooped up the change, threw some back for the bartender and weaved his way out the door. Now he had to find a taxi, get back to the Y for his bag and talk the cab driver into taking him to the pier. And, he realized, he didn't have the faintest idea how long that was going to take.

He kept falling asleep in the cab. The driver woke him when they got to the Y and waited while Mulvehill paid his bill and checked out. When he got out the driver was studying a street map under the light of a pencil flash.

"You know how to get there?" Mulvehill asked.

"Got it all figured out," the driver responded. "Hop in."

He lowered the windows on both sides of the cab. The wind blowing in revived him. It was a long ride and when the driver finally pulled up alongside the ship it was barely five minutes before twelve. He had planned to be there by eight. He paid the driver, hauled his barracks bag out of the cab and headed for the gangplank. A couple stood in the shadows thrown by the extended corrugated sheet metal at the roof line. Mulvehill did not look around. He made his way up the gangplank slowly, the weight of the bag slung over his shoulder, the weakness in his wounded leg and the remaining effect of the whiskey he had drunk combining to make walking difficult.

One of the crew at the head of the gangplank greeted him and sent him aft to his cabin. He briefly studied the man asleep in the other bunk, undressed and was asleep as soon as his head hit the pillow.

His cabin mate identified himself in the morning. Now there were at least two Charles aboard, Mulvehill and Duffy.

By the time the mid-morning orientation meeting was over the two were well acquainted. Most of the volunteers they learned, would join the ship in France. Mulvehill met the ship's captain, Monroe Fein and was, in turn introduced to Mike Ben-Ami. The latter was much as Zelinsky had described him.

Mulvehill presented his press card and was officially welcomed.

A week later, after picking up cargo at Cienfuegos, the *Altalena* sailed quietly east at a steady fourteen knots, the Diesel engines humming.

The morning the ship tied up at Marseille Fein invited Ben-Ami, Stavsky, Duffy and Mulvehill into the wheelhouse. He pointed across the harbor toward Port de Bouc. "That's where we'll load the weapons," he told the others. "French army trucks will bring the weapons there for loading on the ship."

As Mulvehill, Duffy and Ben-Ami left the wheel-house Mulvehill turned to the Palestinian. "Did

I hear correctly?" he questioned the older man. "The French Army is going to help load the ship?"

Ben-Ami laughed. "The French have their own list of grievances against the British. This is one way for them to get even."

The volunteers, more than a thousand of them, arrived the following day and the ship hummed with activity as food supplies were lifted aboard and packed away. Everyone waited impatiently for the French army supplies to arrive. They finally did and Algerian dockworkers started loading cases marked 'Agricultural Instruments'. One case was dropped accidentally, broke open and, when the Algerians saw the contents were rifles, went on strike. The volunteers replaced them, loading cases and equipment through the night. At one in the morning, Mulvehill and Duffy, who were helping with the loading, finally turned in.

The next morning, after breakfast, Ben-Ami sought them out.

"Follow me," he beckoned.

They climbed down into the hold. Several half-tracks, conventional, lightly armored army vehicles with wheels in front and tank treads in the rear, had already been loaded and locked into position. Against the bulkheads on either side, from the bottom to the deck, were hundreds upon hundreds of cases of weapons, ammunition and aerial bombs.

Ben-Ami was exuberant. "Do you know what this means? When we bring these arms, and the more than a thousand volunteers we already have on board, we'll be equipped to beat the Arabs."

At the captain's mess that evening Mulvehill saw that Sam Merlin, whom he had known only briefly in New York, was on board.

They sailed from Port-de-Bouc that evening. When Mulvehill awoke the next morning and looked out the porthole he saw that they had left the land behind and were sailing swiftly south.

After several days, as the ship approached the Palestinian coast, radio orders were received to proceed to a small settlement and watch for *Two Red lights. Vertical.* They were to unload at a place called Kfar Vitkin. Mulvehill and Duffy were both leaning against the railing when they felt the ship begin to swing.

Ben-Ami approached them at the rail. He pointed into the darkness. "There it is. Two vertical red lights."

Fein headed the ship in a straight line for the shore. At about nine o'clock it touched bottom. The gates designed to permit unloading of tanks opened and a small launch proceeded from the shore and pulled up alongside the *Altalena*. Excited voices on the ship called out, *"It's Begin! It's Menachem Begin!"*

The mystical underground leader of the *Irgun*, in hiding from the British for the past four years, now that the British had left Palestine, was out in the open and the hundreds of volunteers, gathered from a number of countries, were excited to see him.

The men began disembarking and weapons were unloaded and stacked on the shore. By shortly after midnight all of the men were off the ship except for the men of the Fifth Platoon, whom Duffy and Mulvehill had spent the last few days training in basic military tactics. Mulvehill had been pleased with the progress of the volunteers, many of whom were totally raw recruits. Now the unit waited on deck. When daylight came they would complete the unloading of the ship.

Suddenly shooting broke out on shore. Mulvehill and Duffy looked at each other.

Who was shooting? At whom? And why?

As the two looked at each other in consternation Stavsky came up to them. "It's a trap," he cried. "Ben-Gurion has set us up."

Mulvehill was stunned. "I thought there was a written agreement between the *Haganah* and the *Irgun*," he said, "eighty per cent of the arms to the Haganah and twenty per cent to the Irgun for the defense of Jerusalem."

Stavsky cursed and bounded up the steps to the wheel-house. They heard him angrily imploring Fein. "Close up the ship and pull out." Fein called back, "Pull out to where?"

Radio communications with the shore radio had broken down.

Mulvehill felt a hand on his arm. He turned around. Ben-Ami was standing at his side. "I'm going ashore. I've got to find out what's going on." He slipped over the gunwale and let himself down into the water. They could see him swimming toward the shore.

Begin in the meantime was standing on the deck surrounded by Fein, Stavsky and Sam Merlin. Mulvehill and Duffy joined them.

"Start your engines," Begin was telling Fein. "Move out quickly and sail to Tel Aviv."

They looked at each other.

"Do you think that's wise?" Mulvehill asked. "If you really have been betrayed by Ben-Gurion you'll be sailing right into his hands at Tel Aviv. From shore you'll be sitting ducks on this ship."

Begin waved his arm impatiently. "Excuse me, my young friend. You are wrong. Jews will not shoot at Jews."

Mulvehill raised his eyebrows. "No? Then who is shooting at who down there?" He pointed toward the shore in the darkness.

Begin shook his head impatiently. "Maybe just a few Haganah hot heads. Or, it could even, maybe, be some of our own boys, *God forbid!*"

Fein ran back up to the wheel-house. They heard the engines rapidly reversing and the ship moved slowly away from the shore. About a quarter mile out it turned and began to head south.

The following morning the *Altalena* sailed slowly into the waters off the shore at Tel Aviv. When the ship was close enough to the shore for Begin to use a loud speaker he implored people standing on the shore for their help in unloading the arms from the ship.

Mulvehill and Duffy stood at the rail, watching the people on shore. It was a curious spectacle. The crowds on shore might have come down to gape at a beached whale. Didn't they understand that there were weapons enough on board to help the Israelis beat back the Arab attack? He and Duffy looked at each other.

In the meantime some of the crew let a launch down into the water. Half a dozen of the men of the

Fifth Platoon unloaded crates of rifles and ammunition. The launch sped through the shallow waters and, beached on the shore, the cargo was quickly unloaded.

Begin was jubilant. "It will be all right," he cried.

The launch returned to the ship and was again loaded with weapons. Mulvehill watched. He saw soldiers on the beach moving into position. They set up a machine gun mount. Who were they? *Irgun* soldiers or *Zahal* men, the newly formed Israeli Defense Force?

He didn't have long to wait. When the launch was no more than twenty yards from the shore machine gun fire swept the beach and the launch. From his position at the rail Mulvehill could hear the launch pilot cry out. "I'm hit in the chest." He slumped over and the launch ran up on the beach. Irgun men scattered to take cover.

Machine gun fire continued to rake the waters and moved up onto the deck of the ship. The loudspeaker was blown off its mounting. Mulvehill dropped to the deck but, looking forward, he could see Stavsky had been hit. Mulvehill worked his way toward him. Stavsky was bleeding profusely. Within minutes he was dead.

It was time to get off the ship. If machine gun fire penetrated the hull it could set off the munitions below deck in a monstrous explosion. He looked around for Duffy and saw him emerging from the cabin. "Here, Duffy," Mulvehill called to him and Duffy darted forward. He was just a step away from the rail when a machine gun bullet hit him in the head. A surprised expression crossed his face, which then turned white, and he slowly slumped to the deck. Mulvehill reached him and saw that Duffy was dead. He cursed and swiftly headed for the rail. He started to climb over when he felt a stinging slap in his left calf. He looked down and saw blood oozing out from his trousers. Damn. Hit again, and in the same leg as at Cassino.

He let himself down in the water. He could see several of his companions from the *Altalena* floating dead in the water. Others, wounded, were swimming or crawling toward shore in the shallow water. Mulvehill decided the best course was to make a wide swing away from the ship and toward the beach. He made it and crawled up behind several large crates that littered the beach.

He turned over on his back and looked back toward the ship. Now it was being hit by cannon and mortar fire. A shell tore through the soft deck planking and exploded in the hold. Ammunition cases began detonating.

Mulvehill drew in a few deep breaths. Somehow he had better get off the beach. He had no idea of the extent of the carnage to the ship and its crew.

A shadow fell across him and he looked up to see a boy, maybe no more then ten or twelve, looking down at him. The boy crouched near his head.

*"Chaver?"** It was a question. Mulvehill did not understand. The boy tried again. *"Irgun?"* Mulvehill nodded.

"O.K. I help." The boy was surprisingly strong. With his help Mulvehill rose from his position and let the boy half-lead, half-support him. They made their way to a street leading away from the shore.

* Friend

Fortunately they had not gone more than a few hundred yards when the boy opened a door and led him through.

Mulvehill sank to the floor. He was in a simply furnished living room. The boy called out, *"Rivka, Rivka."*

A blond woman descended the stairs. She quickly took in Mulvehill's condition. She spoke to the boy in what Mulvehill assumed to be Hebrew or Arabic.

The woman, who was perhaps no more than twenty, Mulvehill guessed, tore away his trousers from where his leg was bleeding. The boy, who Mulvehill guessed was her brother, returned with a pan filled with water, a scissors and bandages.

Mulvehill looked at her as she studied his wound. Her hair was blond and piled on top of her head. She examined the wound and looked at him. In good English she said, "That bullet must come out. I don't have morphine. Can you take it?"

Mulvehill nodded. He looked at her. She smiled. Her eyes were bright green. "I'm a nurse," she said reassuringly. She spoke again to the boy and he returned with a bottle. Mulvehill looked at it. *"Old Rarity.* You've got good taste."

She smiled again and displayed remarkably even white teeth.

The boy uncapped the bottle and Mulvehill took a deep drink. As he spluttered, she cut quickly into the leg. He looked at a point where the walls and ceiling met.

She worked swiftly.

"It's out," she said, "but I'm afraid of infection. I'll have to go to the clinic where I work and bring some sulfanilamide powder." She smiled again. "I am with the *Irgun*. You are in a safe house."

Mulvehill looked at her. He thought he was going to faint. "Do you know what's going on out there?" he heard himself ask but heard no answer. He was out.

When he came to it was dark outside. A weak bulb burned in an unshielded lamp hanging from the ceiling.

The woman was sitting near him. His leg was bandaged. "Did you get the sulfa?" he asked.

She nodded. "Let's hope it works."

She looked at him. "I've made some soup." She laughed. "Chicken soup. In America they say it is good for you. *Emes?*"

"What does that mean?" he asked.

It means *True*.

"I don't know," he replied. "I think I've heard Jews say it is good if you have a cold."

"You are not a Jew?" she asked. He saw she was holding his passport and Press card.

"I went through your pockets," she said. "We must be careful."

"Oh, yes," he said. "We certainly must be careful."

"You are a reporter? Why were you on the *Altalena?*"

He felt too weary to answer. She called to her brother. "*Menashe*. Turn on the radio."

Her brother turned on the radio. It crackled and then, in Hebrew, a voice spoke.

Mulvehill watched the two of them. They listened intently for a few minutes. The woman said to her brother, "Turn it off!"

Mulvehill leaned up on an elbow. "What was that?"

"That was Ben-Gurion. He was boasting about the destruction of the *Altalena.* I will write for you what he said and then you can send it to your newspaper in America. The old bastard. He said…'Blessed be the gun which set the ship on fire—that gun will have its place in Israel's war museum.'"

The boy again spoke to his sister. She nodded. "We have our own radio. *The Voice of Fighting Israel.*" She turned to her brother. "Turn it on."

Now there was a different voice. Emotional. Choked up. A voice on the verge of tears.

"*Begin?*" Mulvehill guessed.

She nodded, and translated for him.

"*Irgun soldiers will not be a party to fratricidal warfare, but neither will they accept the discipline of Ben-Gurion's army any longer. Within the state area we shall continue our political activities. Our fighting strength we shall conserve for the enemy outside.*"

The voice broke. The radio went silent.

Mulvehill felt very tired. His head throbbed and felt hot. His mouth was dry. He felt himself drifting off.

Why did it seem he heard himself singing?

> *Those cool and limpid green eyes*
> *A pool wherein my love lies,*
> *so deep that…*

He was asleep.

23.

He opened his eyes. How long had he slept? A minute? An hour?

The blonde was still sitting at the side of the pallet where he lay. But something was different. He was no longer lying on a pallet but on a bed. And the woman was different. Her blond hair had been piled and coiled on top of her head. Now it hung loosely about her face. And the face was lovely. She had been wearing, he remembered, a flowered print dress. Now she wore a sort of nurse's uniform, of blue and white.

His calf still hurt but where were his pants? He looked down and saw that he was dressed in simple cotton pajamas.

In a corner of the room a heavy-set woman sat on a straight-backed chair. She was possibly, Mulvehill thought, in her sixties. Her hair was straight, and streaked with gray.

He began to sit up.

"How long?" he asked. He felt weak as a rag. The woman smiled at him tenderly.

Gently, she pushed him back so that he lay down.

"Three days," she said. "We put sulfa on the wound but it became infected anyway. Dr. Seroussi, from the clinic, visited and examined the wound. He said I had done well to remove the bullet." She patted his hand. "You had a high fever. We were very worried."

Mulvehill motioned to the woman in the corner. "Who's that?"

The blonde smiled. "That's Chana, the lemonade lady."

He was puzzled. "The lemonade lady?"

The blonde smiled. "Yes. She carries lemonade to the men in the Cabinet while they are in session. She has a photographic memory. It was hot the day when the *Altalena* appeared offshore. She was in the room where the fate of the *Altalena* was settled. I want you to hear what she has to say."

"Does she speak English?" Mulvehill asked.

The older woman rose from the chair and came over to Mulvehill's bedside. She began to speak in continuous staccato sentences, with much head waving and hand gestures.

"What language is she speaking?" Mulvehill wanted to know.

"Hebrew," the blonde woman replied. "I will translate for you."

At this moment the door opened and the boy who had helped him away from the shore entered. He smiled broadly. "Hello Yank. We know who you are."

Mulvehill nodded. "Yes. But I don't know who you are. Perhaps you saved my life."

The boy shook his head. "No, but you were not arrested."

Mulvehill looked from the boy to his sister.

"What does he mean?"

The blonde replied. "Ben-Gurion's men rounded up all the men from the *Altalena* who were Palestinians. Hillel Kook* is also in jail." She smoothed his pillow. "It is important that you know what happened."

"I know what happened," he said. "I was there."

"No," she said, "There is more to it." She turned to the older woman who again burst into a rapid-fire discussion. When she was finished, the blonde spoke. But Mulvehill put up his hand.

"I need to know," he said, "What's your name?"

The blonde moved over and sat on the side of the bed.

"My name is Rivka," she told him. "And my brother is Menashe. These are Hebrew names. In Austria, where we were born, we were Rebecca and Max."

"Are your folks here, too?" Mulvehill asked.

She shook her head. "I will tell you later." She looked from Mulvehill to the older woman. "There were nine in the Cabinet when the *Altalena* was sighted off the coast. Because the United Nations had ordered a cease fire, Ben-Gurion said he did not want to be held responsible for a shipload of arms arriving during the embargo."

She looked at Mulvehill. "Ben-Gurion is a liar. He had something else on his mind. Suppose the weapons were unloaded to the Irgun men in Tel Aviv. Maybe

*The real name of the man who, in the United States, called himself Peter Bergson.

they would use the arms to overthrow the new government. Ben-Gurion's government," she said bitterly. "He did not want the ship to land. The cabinet voted seven-to-two to stop the ship. By whatever methods necessary."

She paused. "Are you thirsty?" she asked Mulvehill. He nodded.

Menashe brought a carafe of water and Mulvehill drank. Rivka watched him.

"Ben-Gurion now had the title of defense minister. He phoned Yigal Allon…" she interrupted herself to explain that Allon was in charge of Zahal operations.

"Ben-Gurion told Allon not to fire on the ship unless Zahal men were fired on first."

She turned to look at the lemonade lady. "The men think she is stupid because all she does is bring lemonade. Chana is not stupid. She listened."

Rivka looked at the older woman affectionately.

"Chana heard Ben-Gurion talking to a few of his intimates, those who had voted with him. He wanted a showdown," she said bitterly. "Ben-Gurion was not going to let the ship unload. He knew that the Irgun, in Tel Aviv, was stronger than Zahal. Chana saw Ben-Gurion say something in a low voice to Yitzhak Rabin, deputy commander of the Palmach. Rabin went to his headquarters and began distributing hand grenades to his staff."

Mulvehill listened in amazement.

"So the whole show must have been rigged against the Irgun from the moment we sailed from Port-de-Bouc," he said.

He shook his head. "And I came over to help the Jews create their own state." He lay back and closed his eyes. He heard a door open and close. When he opened his eyes he saw that the boy and the older woman had left. Rivka had resumed her seat on the chair beside his bed.

She looked down at him sadly. He saw two large tears form in her eyes.

He took her hand. "I understand."

She shook her head and wiped her eyes. "Oh, I must bring you something to eat. You must regain your strength." She smiled. "I have prepared lamb stew, with humus and grape leaves." She looked at him in concern. "Perhaps you do not like lamb?"

He smiled. "I love it," he lied.

She left and came back swiftly with a dish on a tray. She puffed up the pillows and helped him sit up. She watched intently as he ate.

He ate a few spoonfuls and put the plate back on the tray.

"You do not like it? It is no good?" She looked worried.

"No, it's fine," he assured her. Again tears formed in her eyes.

He took her hand. "Really, it's all right. It's just that I'm not hungry right now."

She began to weep. He was confused. No one should make such a fuss over some food.

"You don't understand," she said. "I think I'm falling in love. And you're a *goy*."

He laughed in relief.

"Oh, then I'll just have to marry you."

She wiped her eyes. "Please do not joke."

To his astonishment he found himself saying, "No, Rivka, I mean it." And unaccountably found himself thinking that he did mean it. Perhaps it was the weakness induced by the infection and the fever. Time to think about that later. In the meantime…she was lovely.

They looked at each other in silence.

He sat up and reached his arms out to her. She sat down on the bed and rested her head on his chest. He lifted her chin and began to kiss her. First her lips, which were full and tender. Then her eyes and the rest of her face.

She laughed and cried alternately.

"You mean it? May I call you Charles?" She pronounced it *Sharl*.

He learned her story the following day.

Their name was Rossman. Her father had been a bookbinder in Vienna. By 1937 the strut of Nazi Brown Shirts evidenced their confidence. At that time Rebecca was nine and Max was four. Their mother was reluctant to leave but Rossman felt it was going to be dangerous to stay. Then word was passed around that it might be possible to travel on a barge down the Danube. A tramp steamer had been leased by Irgun men. The family got out on the ship, called the Sakarya. The ship managed to evade British patrol boats that were trying to intercept refugees trying to get into Palestine.

They came in under cover of night.

When she finished the story Charles closed his eyes. She kissed his forehead. "I am sure the fever is gone. But you need rest. Sleep." She left the room.

The next morning he felt his strength returning. When Rivka came in with breakfast on a tray he said, "I'd like to get up and walk around outside. Will you bring my clothes please?"

She left and he ate the food, which was mostly dairy foods, diced carrots, herring, humus, pita bread. And coffee, which was bitter and strong.

When she returned she brought his clothes, which had been laundered and pressed.

He sat up. I'll get dressed now. She sat looking at him and smiling. "Are you going to sit there while I dress?" he asked, "grinning like a Cheshire cat."

She frowned. "What is that? A Cheshire cat." He just looked at her and reached for his trousers. "I am a nurse," she said. "Remember? And I bathed you while you had the fever. You have a nice body," she concluded.

He sat up. "O.K. Have it your way." He dressed.

"If you feel strong enough," she said, "I would like you to come and meet another reporter. Arthur Koestler, of the Manchester Guardian."

"Koestler is here?" Charles was surprised.

"Yes," she told him. "You know him?"

"No, of course not, except by reputation. I read several of his books." Mulvehill looked at her. "He's quite famous, you know."

Koestler was staying at the Dan Hotel, on Hayarkon Street. They had lunch with him. Koestler had seen the entire *Altalena* incident from his balcony. He wanted to know if Mulvehill was there to report the war between Israel and the attacking Arab armies.

"That was the original idea," Mulvehill said. "But I feel differently about it now. I think I want to get back to America. I started out by trying to help the Jews rescue as many of the survivors as possible and get them into Palestine. Now the British have left, the Jews have their own State and start out by killing those who are trying to help them." He sighed. "I think it's time for me to get out." Rivka, who had been sitting quietly at his side, squeezed his hand.

He shook hands with the author and they left.

Rivka and Charles sat at a table outside a coffee shop on Dizengoff Street.

"I'll have no trouble getting back to the States because of my Press card," he said. "But the only way the U.S. State Department will let you in is as my wife." He took her hand. "So it's all settled."

She opened her mouth but he intercepted her thought.

"I think it best that Menashe finish school here," Mulvehill said. "Then we'll get him into the U.S." He took both her hands and kissed them. "How do you feel about leaving Israel?"

She sighed.

"There were eighteen men killed on the *Altalena*, and in the water," she said. "We'll never have the country I dreamed of, a strong, growing Hebrew Commonwealth on both sides of the Jordan."

She looked off into the distance. She stood up.

"Let's walk, Charles."

They walked slowly down to the shore.

She took his hand. "I've been reading the *Book of Ruth* again," she said. "*...for whither thou goest, I will go; and where thou lodgest, I will lodge: thy people shall be my people, and thy God my God...*"

She looked at him sadly.

"Does that mean I must become a Christian, Charles?"

He hugged her.

"I'm not a Christian, dear."

She looked puzzled.

"But you said you were not a Jew. And when I undressed you..." she blushed. "I mean..."

He laughed.

"I'm a free-thinker. Or a pagan. As you wish." He kissed her. "Darling, you can be whatever you want. It's all right with me."

She reached up and kissed him.

Each day he felt more of his strength returning. Rivka massaged his leg.

She would read him the reports of the fighting around Jerusalem. The deaths of Jews mounted but they were beating off the Arab armies.

Rivka worked double shifts at the hospital. Mulvehill marveled at the reserve he felt in his treatment of her. Was he somehow affected by his presence in this land, holy alike to Christian, Jew and Muslim? He felt sure she was a virgin and he had made up his mind that he would not take her to bed until they were married. To satisfy emigration requirements the official wedding ceremony was conducted by a Greek priest. No Israeli rabbi was going to sanction a marriage between a Jewish girl and an American gentile.

The day came when Rivka felt she could leave Israel.

Once again they walked down to the beach. The *Altalena* lay there in the water, a blackened, burnt out hulk.

"In two weeks we can be home," he said. "We'll be married again in my folks' house in California."

She leaned against him, her head resting on his shoulder.

"California," she said dreamily, and sighed.

Epilogue

Commencement Day at UCLA, that June of 1958, was warm and clear. The sky had been swept clear of smog by a brisk wind the night before. Now the sky was as brilliantly bright as the inside of a diamond.

Mulvehill looked around at the large graduating class, and at the smaller group of doctoral candidates, Rebecca among them. Once settled in the United States she had reverted back to her childhood name. Among her fellow students she was now 'Becca.

Lisa stood next to Mulvehill. She had been formally adopted by Charles and Rebecca after their marriage. She squeezed his hand. He looked down. At thirteen she was already a beauty. Her golden baby curls had turned to a dark, tawny mane. Long lashes shaded eyes as blue as the sky above. She had begun to show curves that suggested she would soon be as voluptuous as her mother had been. We're going to have to watch this girl carefully he thought.

Incredibly, Mulvehill thought, all the family were still together. His father was now more than half retired. Alberto was still foreman at the packing shed but it was the younger Rodriguez boy, Luis, who surprisingly showed real promise in the business. He now ran the show, was looking around for suitable acquisitions and planned to take the company public through a stock offering. The elder Mulvehill was agreeable and even encouraged Luis.

"Go ahead, hijo," he told him, "you're likely to make us all rich."

Menashe had been brought over on a student visa arranged by Petey Horwitch. The publisher felt that, with his connections, he should be able to arrange the necessary immigration papers. The boy, now called Manny by his friends, had grown several inches. He had carrot-colored hair, which contrasted with the black yarmulka that he wore conspicuously. He lived at Chabad House near the UCLA campus and followed the orthodox Jewish faith of his ancestors.

Mulvehill looked around contentedly. His mother and Consuelo Rodriguez stood arm in arm, two handsome matronly women, the one as dark as the other was fair.

All the Mulvehills, and the Rodriguez family, had driven up from the desert the night before in a convoy of three cars. Cookie was now a lovely young lady and had come to the ceremony with her boyfriend. Mike, already a captain in the Corps of Engineers, had managed to get a furlough to be there. Jean had flown out from Chicago but Dr. Hale had been unable to get away. He had sent a huge bouquet of roses for 'Becca.

Life could be good, Mulvehill thought. He was right to have brought Rivka back to the States with him. That first intuitive, and entirely spontaneous, response to her when he was being ministered by her after being wounded on the *Altalena* had been, he now knew, the real McCoy. His love for her had deepened with every passing day.

He picked her out from among the other doctoral candidates. Her golden hair shimmered where it showed under her mortarboard. She was as smart as she was lovely and was now to receive her Ph.D. in Political Science. They had talked often about it during the writing of her doctoral thesis. She had picked a highly controversial and little talked about subject. It revolved around the failed policy of the French in Indochina, now called Viet Nam, and centered on the defeat of the French Forces at Dien Bien Phu in 1954. Provocatively, and presciently, it was titled *After the French…U.S.?*

"Wait and see," 'Becca had told him. "The French will turn to America to pull their chestnuts out of the fire. And I'm afraid," she said sorrowfully, "that America will fall into the trap."

Mulvehill sincerely hoped not. He'd had quite enough of war. His interest in the fate of Israel had died when Duffy died. Strangely, Korea had not enlisted his sympathy. He thought MacArthur was an egomaniac, had sorrowed for the poor GIs suffering and dying at Porkchop Hill and other bitter engagements. Better to look to the future, he thought. 'Becca was his future. Now that her schooling was done he wanted to have children. Maybe a whole gang of kids, he thought, and grinned. There was plenty of room in the big old house down in Thermal. While

'Becca had completed her studies at UCLA he had gone back to the trading desk, but Mitchum Jones had been sold to Merrill Lynch and he then worked the trading desk at Sherwood Securities.

Time to go back home, he assured himself. Time to think later about what 'Becca was going to do. He himself might be ready to work with Luis in building the business. He caught his father's eye. The old man, still straight as a ramrod, winked at him.

Mulvehill smiled. The music started. *"Land of Hope and Glory."* The perennial graduation march still had the power to make his eyes mist slightly.

"America, America, God shed his grace on thee." With all its faults, the overweening ambition to wield the big stick in world politics, the corruption in high places, the clash of race, still, he assured himself, certainly this was the best country in the world. Here it was still possible to make as much of one's self as one had the talent for. And there was still more personal freedom here than in most countries.

He thought of the evils of the past and remembered the inscription over the entrance to the Hall of Archives in Washington…*What is Past is Prologue.*

The music soared. The audience applauded.

The End

Afterword
and
Acknowledgments

"As a teenager growing up in Brooklyn, New York, in the early 'thirties'," the author writes, "I was both alarmed and embarrassed to be identified as a Jew. Adolf Hitler was riding high in the saddle in Germany and his active cohorts in New York were defiantly strutting in the streets of the predominantly German enclave of Yorkville in Manhattan, wearing the Nazi's 'brownshirt' uniform with the hooked cross of the swastika emblazoned on their armbands.

"I was then an engineering student, a profession few Jews embarked upon in those days. My fellow students, almost to a man (no girls were permitted entry to a boys' school at that time), were youth of German, Norwegian or Swedish extraction, the protomodel that a writer of the day characterized as 'a big blond colossus with a cast iron crust'.

"Everything abruptly changed for me, but not quite, with the Japanese attack on Pearl Harbor. American Nazis quietly packed their uniforms away in mothballs for the duration, piously presenting themselves as American 'patriots'.

"I enlisted in the Army but, still uncomfortable as a Jew, identified myself at enlistment as a Unitarian and had a 'P' for Protestant stamped into my dog tags.

"The masquerade continued for my first three years in the Army until, one day, as a patient in an Army hospital, I came across Ben Hecht's seminal book on anti-Semitism; *A Guide For the Bedevilled*. I was barely a dozen pages into that monumental work when the Jew hiding under my skin began slowly to emerge.

"Returned home from the war in the Pacific I wrote to Ben Hecht to tell of my 'conversion'. A few days later I received the following letter from his wife, Rose:

Dear Mr. Gropman:

Your letter came to Ben Hecht in the hospital (where he had been in some danger with a gangrenous gall bladder) and I wish you could have seen the deep smile that came to his face when I read him the part of the letter where you became a Jew.

We have had many letters all through the war, where young Jews came to life with their fists suddenly before their minds came alive - but yours is the most remarkable - in its great truthfulness and insight.

I read the letter too to Ben's physician (a famous diagnostician who a few years ago thought that intermarriage and a mendacious document called The Jefferson Bible were the solution to 'The Jewish Problem') and he said the insight and strength in that letter were more of a success than a five year psychoanalysis.

May I suggest that you subscribe to our publication 'The Answer' and ask at the League about your further indoctrination.

Good luck and blessings from Ben Hecht.

Sincerely,

Rose C. Hecht

"I did as Mrs. Hecht had suggested and that led to my employment by the American League For A Free Palestine and association with the courageous men of the *Irgun Zvai Leumi,* an experience that I have always looked back upon as both halcyon and climactic, and which has led, fully fifty years later, to the writing of the book you have just read."

* * *

Permission to quote from Ben Hecht's own books was graciously granted by Ms. Diana Haskell of The Newberry Library in Chicago, which owns title to all of Mr. Hecht's literary output. The four lines from *Five Foot Two, Eyes of Blue,* appearing on page 25, are from the 1925 song by Ray Henderson, Sam M. Lewis and Joe Young. Title to that song is currently held by EMI Feist Catalog Co., Ray Henderson Company and Warock Corporation. The excerpt from Vladimir Jabotinsky's testimony before the Peel Commission in London, in February 1937, appearing on page 260 is from the official transcript. The telegram, in German, and the lengthy portion describing Rabbi Michael Dov Weissmandl's experiences with the virulent hatred of Jews expressed by the Papal Nuncio that begins on page 146 are from Weissmandl's book *Min Hametzir* and from an unpublished manuscript by Siegmund Forst. The elder Mulvehill's lengthy discourse on anti-Semitism, which begins on page 236, is taken from *The Redemption of Democracy* by Hermann Rauschning, copyright by Alliance Book Corporation, 1941. The reference to the history of Hebron appearing on page 306 is from *They Must Go*, by Rabbi Meir Kahane, published by Grosset & Dunlap, 1981, and used here by permission of Mrs. Libby Kahane. On page 278 Alex Hadani's (Dr. Alexander Rafaeli) reference to his family origin is from his autobiography *Dream and Action*, 1993. On page 365 the lines describing the finding of the LST, that was bought and renamed *Altalena*, are from Yitshaq Ben-Ami's memoir, *Years of Wrath, Days of Glory*, published by Shengold Publishers, 1983. The description of the sailing and ultimate destruction of the *Altalena* are adapted from J. Bowyer Bell's book about the Irgun, *Terror Out of Zion*, published by Avon Books. On page 385, "Aquellos Ojos Verdes", by Nilo Menendez, English lyric "Green Eyes", by E. Rivera and E. Woods, Copyright (c) 1929 by Peer International Corporation, Copyright Renewed, International Copyright Secured. Used by Permission.

* * *